THE SPELL

Alan Hollinghurst

THE SPELL

Chatto & Windus

LONDON

Published in 1998

2 4 6 8 10 9 7 5 3 1

First published in Great Britain in 1998 by
Chatto & Windus
Random House, 20 Vauxhall Bridge Road,
London SW1V 2SA

Random House Australia (Pty) Limited
20 Alfred Street, Milsons Point, Sydney,
New South Wales 2061, Australia

Random House New Zealand Limited
18 Poland Road, Glenfield,
Auckland 10, New Zealand

Random House South Africa (Pty) Limited
Endulini, 5A Jubilee Road, Parktown 2193, South Africa

Random House UK Limited Reg. No. 954009
A CIP catalogue record for this book
is available from the British Library

ISBN 0 7011 6519 7

Papers used by Random House UK Limited are natural,
recyclable products made from wood grown in sustainable forests.
The manufacturing processes conform to the environmental
regulations of the country of origin.

Printed and bound in Great Britain by
Mackays of Chatham PLC

for Eric Buchanan

I am very grateful for the hospitality of Yaddo, where part of this novel was written. – A. H.

Happy the heart that thinks of no removes!

Anon., 'Fine knacks for ladies'

1

He wondered if the boy had lost the way. They had started out on a driven track half-covered with small noisy stones; but it faded, was found again for half a mile, where it followed the rim of a dry wash, and then died away among the windswept contours and little dusty bushes of the desert. The pick-up roared on across long inclines of grey dirt. The boy kept his foot down and stared straight ahead, as if unable to consider the possibilities that lay to left and right. He was almost smiling – Robin couldn't decide if from nerves or from the pleasure a local person has in scaring and disorienting a stranger. An empty bottle rolled and clinked against the metal supports of the bench-seat. Robin sat with his forearm braced in the open window, and grunted involuntarily at each bump and drop: academic research had never been so wayward or so physical. He found that he was smiling too, and that he was not only shaken but happy.

They reached a low crest and there beneath them spread thirty or forty miles of silvery waste, crossed by the quick eclipses of windy sunlight; the wide plain was rifted with gulleys and dry riverbeds, and climbed distantly to mountains which were radiant towers in the west and unguessable obscurities in the blackly shadowed south. This was what he wanted to see: it was what had brought a rich man and his architect here half a century ago. It wasn't a terrain that could be ploughed or grazed or humbled by use: nothing could have altered unless by the gradual violence of winds and storm rains. The pick-up slowed, and Robin imagined that even his guide, who had surely seen nothing but this country all his life, was responding to its magic or its admonishment.

'What are those mountains called?' he shouted over the churning of the engine and the racket of stones and grit against the

1

bottom of the vehicle. The boy looked stoopingly across, and out beyond Robin at the morning-bright bluffs to the west. He nodded several times, perhaps he had only understood the word mountains, or was hesitating before so many mountains, with so many names.

Suddenly the cab was full of sand. The boy gave a wordless shout and the pick-up pitched sideways, the windscreen was dark with sliding sand, sand pumped through the open windows in a pelting rattle and in a moment was heavy in their laps and round their feet. Robin squeezed his eyes shut on the sting of it, and felt the boy's arm in his side, scrabbling for the gear-shift. He gulped a breath and was choking and spitting out sand, while the van stood still, or was it vaguely sliding. Then the engine rose to a scream, the sand came alive again, and they were lurching upwards and ahead in a panic of burning revs. Robin thought they wouldn't do it, weighed down by the element they were struggling with. He wondered if the sand was bottomless.

When they were free of it they shot forward across the slope, as if the racing machinery couldn't be reined in; or as if the invisible pit they had blundered into might follow after them, like a hungry and offended spirit of the place, clothed in a spiralling storm.

There wasn't much to see, and as Robin dawdled reverently around with his camera and his notebook he was unsure if the scare in the car had made the destination more preciously perilous or more evidently not worth the effort. Much of the house had been built of wood, marked grey and rose in Wright's insouciant sketches, or of canvas, which was useless against the freezing desert nights, and equally combustible. All that remained standing, at the end of a terrace of fissured concrete, was the rough bulk of the hearth and the chimney-stack, a little tower of boulders, the bluntly symbolic heart of the place. Robin knelt among ashes, paper rubbish, a half-burnt creosote-bush, and squinted up the open flue at the square of bright eggshell. People had been here, hundreds probably, scholars and students, and the unfriendly reflective men who lived in

2

the spell of the desert. He touched the blackened stones and thought of other lonely places – roofless cottages on Welsh mountains, pissed-in pillboxes squatting in the fields at home; and there was something of the outpost in this ruined site, of duty and homesickness. But then he straightened up and saw the view.

Away to the right, the boy was bailing sand out of the footwells of the car; he did it slowly, with an air of resentment at his own folly, and doubtless respect for the heat. Nothing was worth rushing – except driving itself, of course, unlicensed, off-road: that was the thrill for a teenage Indian with a father drunk and hostile at nine in the morning. Robin felt the constraints of the boy's silence drop away: the day was balanced between the upland cool in which it had started and the steeper heat to come. He took off his shirt, and felt deliciously both hot and cold at the same time. He clambered up and away from the site, among shaly hillocks, and chose a place to sit.

He had a copy of Wright's plans in his knapsack, and a single photo of the finished house, leached of detail by sunlight and reproduction – a copy of a copy of a copy. From here he could see the vestigial triangle of the layout, and, matching a distant mountain with a grey shadow in the picture, admire the defiant caprice of the project. He hoped he had shown a similar spirit in coming here.

He had never seen a desert before, nothing much emptier than the cropped Dorset heaths of his childhood, with clumps of pine, and the broom-pods popping like pistol-caps in the June heat; nothing much grander than Snowdon or Sca Fell. He liked it, the warm smell of the sagebrush, and the bitter-green herblike plants that grew sparsely under the rocks. The place was desolate but the air was benign, and had high flickers of birdsong in it – what were they, springing upwards from the shelter of bushes? Not larks. The word fieldfare came sheepishly to mind.

He was twenty-three, and it was his first time in America. He found the company of Americans made him stiff and formal, though these were qualities he was unaware of in himself before. His vocabulary felt embarrassingly large and accurate, though in conversation he had a recurrent sense of

3

inarticulacy. He was doing research for a doctoral thesis, but knew he was ignorant of the simplest things in the landscape he had come, in part, to see. Still, he anticipated discovery; as he sat frowning into the sun, with little breezes curling over his naked back, he felt he had Americas in him – he had never been so alert or so free.

A little way off from the concrete standing he scuffed over something white and squatted down to pick it out of the dust. It was a rough piece of sanitary porcelain, about three inches square, with the letters SEMPE on it, perhaps part of SEMPER, forever. He smiled at that, and because there was also an architect called Semper, so very different from Frank Lloyd Wright. With a quick suppression of ethical doubt, he opened his knapsack and dropped it in.

Back at the pick-up his driver sprawled behind the open passenger-door and smoked a cigarette. His blue T-shirt was dark with sweat, and his cheeks were red in his wide brown face. He raised his eyebrows as if to say 'All done?', and Robin said, 'Did you get it cleaned out?'

The boy flicked away the stub and stood up, shrugging his head from side to side and tugging up his belt. The open bed of the vehicle wouldn't have passed any very exacting inspection, but it was probably good enough for this dusty country. Robin assumed that no worse damage had been done. 'Go back,' said the boy, in a way that was both a question and its answer, but also held a hint of a rebuff. Robin was faintly hurt that, even after the fright they'd shared, his companion was so uncompanionable; he hardened himself against him, and protected his elation, which in some novel way sprang both from the visionary light of the place and from a thrilled muscular sense of himself. And a little bit, of course, from having walked a site that was sacred – at least to one of them. 'Yes, let's go,' he said airily, and turned for a last attempt at consuming the view. The distances had begun their delusory oscillations. He felt he wanted to store up the light inside him.

The black fabric of the seat was hot and Robin spread his shirt over it. The car crept off up the hillside: he thought the return journey might be more circumspect. For five minutes or so they trundled across what still seemed to him unmarked

4

territory, unrecognisable from the outward ride. The boy continued to stare narrowly ahead; then Robin realised he was looking at him – occasional glances, meant to be noticed. He half-turned in his seat, with a smile that was ready to absorb sarcasm, but could warm into friendship if that was allowed.

'So you big strong-guy.' His driver's social opener, impossible to have predicted. And was it mocking or admiring after all? Robin looked down at himself. In England, in Cambridge, his friends made jokes about his natural pleasure in pulling his clothes off – jokes that he saw as admissions of envy and covert excitement. But here in the desert maybe his unthinking health and handsomeness struck a vulgar touristic note?

He explained himself solemnly: 'I do a lot of rowing, actually. And I play rugby' – and then saw that neither term had the remotest meaning here. He mimed a couple of pulls on the oars, and then said, 'Rugby is like American football, of course. In a way.'

The pick-up rattled on, tilted on a long curving hillside so that he slid a little towards the boy. He was wondering how to salvage and further the conversation, and as he did so drifting his fingertips unconsciously over the plumped biceps of his other arm, angled in the open window. His mind ran on to the later part of the day – he needed lunch as if he was still in training, the carbohydrate boost; then a nap in the louvred half-light of the inn room, under the lulling sigh of the ceiling fan; then writing up his notes on the Ransom House. And an evening to follow, in a strange city; he knew there would be drink in it, and he wanted there to be sex, though he couldn't see how it would come about. Perhaps it was all that sport that had made him susceptible to the smell of sweat; the unwashed presence of the driver, the sharp warmth of his worked-in vest, blustered across him in the cab. He slid an unusually sly glance between the young man's legs, and was caught in a dreamlike few seconds of conjecture, the simultaneous narrative of sex that never happens. So that when the boy said, 'Hey, don't tell my pa', with his fullest and yet most anxious smile so far, Robin thought for a moment that the fantasy was shared, or that he must unknowingly have made a proposition. He found he was blushing. 'About sand-trap, man.'

5

Robin looked ahead and thought he saw the original trail again. By and large he had been well treated. 'Oh, no – of course not.' And really the idea was absurd – he had the itch as usual but he didn't fancy the boy, to whom such an activity, whatever activity it was, might well have been repugnant.

For a dollar more he drove him on, past the desolate Indian village and his father, scowling and stumbling by the road, and right into Phoenix. Robin asked no questions, though he registered the tense smoking of a second cigarette. To the boy it was a kind of escape, if only to the familiar limits of a further compound; while to Robin every store-front and hoarding and road-sign had the saturated glamour of America: so that they both felt pleasure, in separate and unshared ways. At first it seemed a little embarrassing to rumble into town in a battered old pick-up with a windscreen that was two arcs in a shield of dirt; but then Robin sprawled and embraced his situation. He wondered if he might be taken for someone local, but knew at once he was too bright with involuntary interest for that. The young people they passed outside a bar had long hair, and beards, silver jewellery and bright, tatty clothes; one of them was concentrating on a small recorder, whose failing notes gave Robin a twinge of loneliness.

They took an indirect route, he suspected, to his hotel; maybe the boy knew a short-cut, maybe he was conditioned to go a certain way that he had learnt in going somewhere else. It was midday, many of the streets were empty under the glare of the sun. I need a baseball-cap, Robin thought: then I'll fit in. There were breezes in the garden palms and shade trees of the sidewalk, but the heat, though longed for, was slightly shocking, like someone else's habitual luxury. They came almost to a halt at the end of one of the bleak cross-alleys that bisected the blocks – a central gutter, garbage cans, cables, the barred back-windows of stores and restaurants. The boy pointed and said,

'Good bar, Blue Coyote', and nodded several times.

'Oh . . . is it?' Robin squinted sceptically into the empty sun-struck defile. He thought it must belong to a member of the family. He hoped he wasn't suggesting they go there now.

'You like it.'

6

'Okay, thank you . . . I'll remember that', looking forward again, suddenly impatient for the hotel and the meal; but thinking, so rare were his guide's pronouncements, that he probably would remember it. And it turned out to be very close to where they finally stopped, by the shabby-romantic deco San Marcos, with its peeling pink lobby and display of grotesque old succulents.

Robin found himself waiting for change, then was ashamed at his meanness and raised his hand to stop the boy's unproductive gropings in a back pocket; he thought he probably didn't have change, and that he had gone just too far to save them both from embarrassment. The boy gave a dignified nod. Robin smiled his clean seducer's smile, though it was a mask to his confusion, his fleeting apprehension not of the honoured quaintness of being British, but of the class sense which tinted or tainted all his dealings with the world. He stuck out a hand. 'I'm Robin,' he said.

'Victor,' the driver replied, and gave the hand a lazy shake.

'Hi!' said Robin; and then got out of the car.

The Blue Coyote had no windows, and so saw nothing of the boulevard-raking sunset, or the gorgeous combustion westward over the mountains. When he found you had to ring a bell, he almost turned away, it was only a whim to have an early-evening drink there; but the door half-opened anyway and he was appraised by a stout young man who wore shades for the task and who stood aside with an accepting 'Yep'.

Any light in the room was husbanded and shielded – by the fake overhanging eaves of the bar and the hooded canopy above the pool table. Even before the door had shut behind him, Robin felt at a disadvantage. It was the gloomiest bar he'd ever been in and seemed designed to waken unease in the stumbling newcomer, eyed from the shadows by the dark-adapted regulars. A hush had fallen as he entered. He felt foolish to be so suggestible, so lightly carried here by his new sense of ease and possibility. Then 'Automatically Sunshine' sang out from the juke-box and as if startled from hypnosis the drinkers set down their glasses, the talkers resumed their

7

murmur, the pool-player blinked and stooped and potted his ball.

The barman poured the beer straight into the glass, so that the froth was at the brim in a second, and then over the brim; and stood the half-full bottle by it on the wet counter. 'So what part of England are you from?' he said, with a frown that might have meant distrust of England in general, or the suspicion that he might not know the part, once named. He was a large man in his fifties, with a black pencil moustache and an air of having borne indignities.

Robin said, 'Oh, sort of south-west. Dorset? Is where I grew up.'

'Dorset. Oh yeah, I heard of that,' said the barman, taking the dollar bill with a little twinkle of self-congratulation.

Robin turned and leant on the bar and scanned the room with a pretence of indifference. He watched a long-haired young man talking to an older businessman, who must just have come from work; making a point to him with hands jerked up and up in the air, and then, as the businessman laughed, smiling at him and bringing his hands to rest on his shoulders, the thumbs moving to a gentle caress behind his ears. Robin looked quickly away, and at the man on a barstool beside him, who he knew at once had been gazing at him with the same unsubtle fascination. He took in the glossy dark hair, the long humorous face, the legs apart in tight flared jeans. 'I guess I must have been in Dorset when I was down in Plymouth,' he said.

'You might have passed through Dorset,' said Robin punctiliously; 'though Plymouth itself is in Devonshire.'

The man smiled in a way that suggested he knew that. 'I'm Sylvan,' he said.

Robin accepted the information broad-mindedly. 'Robin, hi!' he said, and extended his callused rower's hand.

'Oh, okay . . .' Sylvan raising his hand from his knee and complying with the courtesy; and smiling rather insistently as if to press the stranger to a quick glowing acknowledgement of something as yet unsaid. Robin knew what it was and hid his indecision, and the snug sense of power it gave him, in an English innocence.

8

'What took you to Plymouth?'

Sylvan looked down. 'Oh, family. That kind of thing.' Then bright and intimate again: 'What brings you to the Valley of the Sun?'

It was never easy saying these things to strangers. 'Research, actually.' He slid the rest of the beer gently into the tilted glass. 'Yeah, I'm doing some stuff on Frank Lloyd Wright?' He saw he'd already got the habit of the interrogative statement. He glanced up at Sylvan.

'Okay, so you've been out to Taliesin West, you've seen the . . . stumps, those big pillars of the Pauson House, all that's left of them. What else?'

Robin smiled sportingly, and absorbed the fact that he was a tourist among many others. 'No, I've only just arrived.'

'First stop the Blue Coyote. A man who knows what he's after.' Sylvan slapped the bar lightly. 'I could do a lot of that kind of research. Same again please, Ronnie,' to the turning barman. 'And another beer?'

'I'm fine,' said Robin. 'No, I've been out to the ruins of the Ransom House today.'

Sylvan paused and nodded. 'Yeah. That's serious. I never saw that. You know, if you're in school here, you get to do all of that stuff. I remember the day he died, old Frankie Lloyd, and the teacher comes in for art class and tells us with a real catch in his voice, you know?, "ladies and gentlemen . . ." We were all pretty upset.' He looked at Robin with a wistful pout, as if he still needed consoling. 'So how the hell d'you get out there? You got four-wheel drive?'

'I got an Indian from the reservation to drive me,' said Robin, still proud of his initiative.

'Wo-ho! And you lived to tell the tale?'

'Just about, yes . . .' – and now he was uneasy about grudges and feuds, the hardened candour with which a local hopes to disabuse the naively fair-minded newcomer. He wouldn't tell him about the sand-trap. 'No, he was great. Just a kid.'

Sylvan looked at him with concern. 'Well you were lucky, man. Cos I'm telling you, they are the worst.'

It was true that Victor had been an unsettling driver. But he'd also been clairvoyant. In the moment or two that Robin

9

disliked Sylvan he saw how beautiful he was; and surely available to him, completely at his pleasure, if he said the word. He had to frown away the smile that rose to his lips on a kind of thermal of lust.

'It's the drink or it's the peyote,' Sylvan went on, fluttering a hand beside his head to suggest a crazy befuddlement.

'Oh . . .'

'You know peyote? Edible cactus. Gives you visions, man,' Sylvan swaying his head and making a little crooning sound. Then grinning and putting a reassuring hand on Robin's own, and leaving it there. 'No, it's part of their religion. Isn't that great? Big ceremony, eat peyote, trip out . . . Of course the kids here are into all that now, the hippies? They go out in the desert and they're out of their fuckin' heads for *days on end*.'

Robin wasn't sure if that was a good idea or not. He'd got a kind of trance off the desert as it was, he could breathe in and feel it again now, a partly physical elation; and something else, that perhaps was religious, or at least philosophical, the inhuman peace. He pictured that burnt-out folly, which was a lesson taught to a wealthy family who presumed they could make a home in such a place and lay a claim to it. Was it $10,000 they'd spent just on drilling for water? He was watching a very camp couple smoking and bawling with laughter. He thought how he wasn't that kind of person. He shifted his weight so that his leg pressed against Sylvan's knee. He realised he'd had a plan for the evening involving dinner and a phone-call; but the plan was meaningless in face of the unplanned. With a little freeing twist he withdrew his fingers and then slid them back between the other man's.

'So . . .' said Sylvan.

Robin looked into his long-lashed, untrustworthy eyes. 'Is there a phone here?' he said. 'I must just make a quick call.'

The phone was in the back by the Gents, in an area even bleaker and more functional than the bar. He dialled and stood gazing at the deadpan irony of an old enamel sign saying 'NO LOITERING'. He wasn't a loiterer. To him the words had only ever meant 'Get on with it!' When he made his infrequent visits to the lavs at Parker's Piece or in the Market Square, eyebrows raised as if at the exploits of someone else, he always seemed to find gratification at once, from a man who clearly was a loiterer, and had probably been loitering for hours. He was through to the operator, who sounded relaxed, almost sleepy, but a nice woman, who took pleasure in bringing sundered friends together. A man came past and nodded 'Hi!' to him, like an overworked colleague – Robin gave an abstracted smile and peered into the imagined middle-distance of the expectant caller. He was both keen to talk and keen to have the conversation over.

When Jane answered he was talking at once, and he felt it like a rebuke when the operator spoke over him to ask her if she would accept the call.

Then, 'Hello Janey, it's me,' he said, 'did I wake you up?' – and heard his words repeated, with a fractional delay, by the unsparing mimicry of the transatlantic echo.

'No, I was awake,' she said, as if it might be an emergency.

'It must be quite late.'

'It's twenty past one.'

'Anyway, you're all right?'

'Is everything all right?'

'Yes, it's amazing, I can't tell you.'

'Because if it is, I'm so glad you rang.'

'Oh thank you, darling,' murmured Robin, with a vague sense of undeserved success. 'I just wanted to hear your voice, and tell you I'm all in one piece' – and the echo gave him back his last words. When he spoke again, he found she was already talking.

'Actually I was asleep. I'd just got off, I'm extremely tired, but I'm so excited at the moment that it's quite difficult to go to sleep.'

Robin had left her only two days earlier and her words were at odds with his assumption that she must be missing him terribly. He was jealous of her excitement, but also reassured, in a way, that she could be excited without him; she seemed to license his own unmentioned freedoms. 'Has something happened?' he asked lightly and cautiously. He was surprised to hear a giggle, maybe just a sign of nerves.

'Something clearly has happened: in fact you probably remember it. More important, something's going to happen.'

11

He thought how you never really pictured a friend when you spoke to them on the phone: they had the shadowiness of memory, of something not looked at directly; you saw a presence in a half-remembered room or merely a floating image of their house or street. The phone Jane was a subtly stronger character – darker, more capricious and capable – than the Jane he lived with and loved. He said, 'Have you got another interview?'

'Oh really.' There was a pause in which he pondered why this was wrong. 'Robin, I'm pregnant. We're going to have a baby.'

It was the 'we' that disconcerted him. He thought for a moment she was referring to herself and some other man. And even when he saw, almost at once, that he must himself be the father, he retained an eerie sense that she had somehow done this without him.

'Oh Janey, that's fantastic.'

'Are you pleased?'

'Of course I am. Christ! When will it be? I mean it will change everything.'

'Oh . . .'

'Or a lot of things. Will we have to get married?'

'Well, we'll have to think about it, won't we? It's not till June.' She sounded mischievous, dawdling; and also to Robin indefinably larger. His blurred mental image of her had taken on already the pronounced jut of advanced pregnancy.

He dawdled himself when the call was over, with its awkwardly near-simultaneous 'Bye's and 'Love you's. His eyes ran abstractedly over the 'NO LOITERING' sign while the news moved slowly and spasmodically through him. In a play or on television the phrase 'I'm pregnant' was often a clincher, it solved things, or at least decided them. Robin gasped softly, and chewed his lip, and then smiled and nodded in a good-humoured acquiescence which there was no one there to see. It was still the first moment, but he saw himself in the sleepless moil of early parenthood, and felt a plunging anxiety, as if he had inadvertently ruined not only his own young life but someone else's too. But then nudging the worry came a reluctantly conceded pride, a nostalgia for his friends at the crew's

12

steak dinner and the 1st XV feast, who would have stood him drinks all night and shared in his achievement with foul-mouthed shock and envy.

He probably couldn't tell Sylvan. He would go back into the bar as if he hadn't just had a conversation that changed his life. He saw perhaps he could forget the conversation, and put off his new life till the morning. A beautiful man was waiting for him and Robin glowed in the urgency and the lovely complacency of their wanting each other. He wanted nothing in his mind, in his sight, in his hands but Sylvan. He span back into the bar almost in a panic for Sylvan.

13

2

Alex left the engine running, and walked hesitantly to the gate; he wasn't sure whether to open it and drive in, or to park outside in the lane. He saw the long roof of a cottage below, half-hidden by flowering trees, and a track of old bricks laid in the grass, where presumably a car could stand. To a town-dweller it seemed desirable to get a car in off the road; but perhaps a stronger sense of security would come from leaving it outside, ready for escape. He decided to back it up on to the verge, where it lay in long grass under a tall wild hedge. Climbing out and locking the door he brushed a hundred raindrops down across the canvas roof.

May had been wet and chilly this year, the spring evenings robbed of their softness and height, the mornings slow and dark. Alex woke each day to the early creak of the central heating, and still, after seven months alone, reached out in a little fumbled ritual to put a hand on the pillow where Justin's head should have been; or he shifted on to that side of the bed and lay there as if he was keeping himself company. The weather lent its grey weight to the suspicion that his life had been taken away from him. Then abruptly the summer came, and he was waking to the chinking of the blackbirds, and again after dream-muddled sleep to the footsteps and voices of the first leavers, and early-morning light that entered at a shy angle into rooms that were sunless all winter. There was a new sense of distance, of the drowsy rumble of a city stretching away in haze and blossom – a rumoured invitation, which took on a sudden unexpected reality when Justin himself rang up and invited him to Dorset. And then as he braked and spurted through the narrowing lanes of the Bride valley a short, rattling shower had come, like a warning and a reminder.

They hadn't seen each other since the dark October day

14

when Justin came back to clear his things out of Alex's house. Wet leaves blew across the windscreen as Alex drove him to Clapham with his little chaos of carrier-bags – the two of them silent, Alex out of grief and Justin out of guilty respect for his former lover's feelings. Justin's shoes and half-read novels and crumpled clothes, and the two or three pictures, the cushions, the dozen nearly empty cologne bottles and the brass travelling-clock that had been part of their home and were now on their way to become the unanticipated clutter of someone else's. It was months before Alex could bring himself to look at the thumbprint-covered polaroids of him, red-eyed and drunk; and he had no other mementoes – Justin had never been known to write a letter. He closed the garden gate noiselessly behind him and wondered what his old friend looked like.

The cottage was low and very pretty and Alex scanned it with an Englishman's nostalgia as well as a tall person's sense of imminent discomfort. It was almost too much, it was the ideal of a cottage tuned close to the point of parody, the walls of gold-brown rubble patched with bits of chalk and brick, the straw fantail pigeons on the crest of the roof and the real ones that sidled on the slope of the thatch below, the white clematis and yellow Mermaid rose trained tumblingly above the small dark windows, the air of stunned homeliness . . . And this was where Justin woke up now, and looked out, over the secretive garden, with its wallflowers and box hedges, old lead sundial and brick paths leading away through further hedges to glimpses of glass. He must have changed very greatly. Or if not, his new man must answer to needs in Justin that Alex himself had never guessed at. From one of the upstairs windows a bunched blue duvet was lolling out to air and gave the house a feel of heedless privacy, as if no guest were expected. At another stood a jar of flowers and a stack of sun-bleached books. Beyond them was the impenetrable indoor darkness of a bright summer day.

There was no answer to his knock, and he stood back on the flagstones in a muddle of emotions: relief, annoyance, real fright about the coming encounters, and an incongruous alert-ness and desire to please, like someone on a first date. After another, perhaps quieter knock, he walked round to the side

15

of the cottage and shaded his eyes to peer through a window. It was the kitchen, with something steaming on the Rayburn and a colander of chopped carrots on the table, which made him feel that he had in fact put them to some trouble. He turned the corner and saw the back garden, a lawn and a low wall, beyond which was an unmown meadow with a fast-running stream at the bottom. He wandered away from the house, still with the sense of being an intruder in an ordered but not invulnerable world; he thought he could call out, but part of him was clinging to the silence and secrecy. He felt slightly sick. It might still be possible, after all, to get back to the car and leave without being seen. Beyond a small orchard of apple-trees on the left there was a wooden shed with a tarred roof. He tried the door casually, then turned back towards the cottage.

At first he thought Justin was naked. He made a dip in the blue groundsheet, which spread in little hills and dales around him over the long, bent grass. Alex approached him warily, like a nature-watcher keeping downwind of some nervous creature – though the idea was doubly absurd for Justin, who was evidently asleep. Closer to, it turned out that he was wearing a kind of thong.

Alex loitered beside him for a minute, unable not to look, hot-faced and haggard above the sprawl of what he had lost. He wondered if it was a cruelly deliberate tease. His eyes took in the blond down on the calves darkened with sun-oil, and the slumbrous weight of the buttocks with the tongue of lycra buried between them, and the arms pointing backwards like flippers, and the head turned sideways; it was everything he remembered, but more than that too, correct in each unconscious detail, even in the changes, the new plumpness around the waist, the smooth fold under the chin.

He looked away, at the trees, the white glints and curls on the hurrying greeny-black surface of the stream. The air was drugged with the sharpness of flowering hawthorn and cow-parsley and the lushness of the grass in the heat after the shower. Wood-doves made their half-awake calls, and at the edge of hearing there was the trickle of the brook. He glanced at Justin again, who seemed very remote from him, lost in the

16

senseless countryside and the unsocial vacancy of sun-worship. Alex squatted down, and held his breath as he reached out a hand to wake him. Blue eyes opened wide, squeezed shut against the glare, then squinted upwards.

'You're outrageously early,' Justin said, with a further blink and a yawn.

'Hello, darling,' said Alex, and grinned to hide how wounded he was by Justin's tone. He watched him turn over and sit up.

'You're such an old pervert to be staring at me like that. How long have you been there? I'll probably have to report you to Police Constable Barton Burton.' He frowned, and Alex leant in awkwardly for a kiss.

'I've only just got here. Of course one didn't expect a welcome.'

Justin gave him a level, sparring look, and then smiled coyly. 'What do you think of my tanga?' he said.

'Is that what you call it? I think you've put on some weight,' said Alex.

'It's Robin, dear.' He stood up and turned round once: he was lightly tanned all over. 'He feeds me and feeds me. He also has a mania for getting one's kit off. He'll have you out of all that, darling.' At which Alex felt needlessly shy, as if warned at the beginning of a party of some worrying game to be played after tea. Justin put an arm through Alex's to lead him back to the cottage. 'You're looking very groomed, darling, for the country. This is the country.' He gestured weakly with his other hand. 'You can tell because of all the traffic, and the pubs are full of fascists. Apparently there's another homo moving into the village. We're terribly over-excited, as you can imagine.'

They were standing in the kitchen, in another kind of heat, fuelled and flavoured by cooking. Justin lifted the lid that half-covered the slow soup on the hob and peered in with pretended competence. Alex said, 'There's a wonderful smell.'

'That's the bread, dear. He pops it in before he goes for his run, and when he gets back it's the exact second to take it out again. He makes all sorts of different sorts of bread.'

Alex pictured his return. 'I don't think he ought to find us like this.'

Justin gave a smile and looked down at his sleek near-

17

nakedness. 'Perhaps you're right,' he said, reaching for an apron from the Rayburn's front rail, and sauntering out of the room in it like a French maid in an elderly work of pornography. Alex turned away from the sight.

He knew he'd been an idiot to come here. He stood where he was, fixed in the well-mannered paralysis of a guest who has been left alone, and humbled by the yeasty efficiency of this strange kitchen. He sensed the presence of the man who owned it, Robin Woodfield, with his capable country name, underlying or impregnating everything around him, and this was a bleaker challenge than he had anticipated. Justin had taken a clear, cowardly and sensible decision to swing along as if Alex and he were no more than good old friends. But Alex himself was petrified by the crackle of undead emotions. There was a squeak of floorboards above and the dulled coming and going across the ceiling of Justin's heavyish footsteps. Was their bedroom there then, with the warm chimney behind the bedstead, and baking smells rising through the floor? Alex gripped the back of the chair he was standing by, and then let it go, with doubting relief, like someone who thought for a moment he had seen a ghost.

And here Justin physically was, in crumpled linen shorts and trodden-down moccasins, which Alex remembered from earlier summers, and a baggy white T-shirt with the signature of Gianlorenzo Bernini, hugely magnified, disappearing round the sides. 'I see you're wearing Bernini,' Alex said.

Justin ignored him with a half-smile which hinted that he did indeed imagine Bernini to be a couturier. 'Do you want an aperitif? And then I'll show you round.' He plucked open the tall clinking door of the fridge and reached in for a jug of bloody Mary, from which he filled two virtually pint-size glasses. 'Come and see the house.' Alex followed him through a low, latched door, with an unannounced step down beyond, on which he jolted upright and hit his head on a beam. 'Watch out for the vernacular detail, dear,' said Justin.

Several tiny vernacular rooms had been knocked into one to form the cottage's main space, and floor-length windows opening on to the rear garden let in a modern requirement of light and air. It was sparely furnished with old oak and

18

hollowed-out sofas and a number of arts-and-crafts chairs like
conscientious objectors to the idea of comfort. At one end was
the empty grate of a big stone fireplace and at the other a wall
of books on architecture and gardening. Justin gestured at
the black-glazed vases on the deep window-sills. 'Those pots,
darling,' he said, 'were made by potters of the greatest probity.'

Alex walked about, watched by Justin, who seemed keen for
a favourable verdict. When the phone rang Justin left him to
look at the pictures. There were brown oils of Georgian
children, which might have been inherited, and a number of
just competent watercolours, signed 'RW', showing the cottage
itself. 'No, I'm sorry, Tony, he's not here,' Justin was saying.
'That's right, he's out. Yes, I'll get him to ring you . . . I'll ask
him to ring you . . . Yes, don't worry, I'll ask him to ring you.'
Robin's paintings made the place look impenetrably private, in
its circuit of trees and high old walls; leaves and petals in the
foreground half-obscured the lower windows of the house,
the rounded bulk of the thatch was shadowed by the bosomy
beeches above it.

On a side-table there was a framed black-and-white photo
of a young man in white shorts and a singlet, standing with
an upright oar, like a lance, on which he seemed to lean. When
Justin rang off Alex said at once, 'Who's this in the picture?'

His ex-lover wandered across with a little 'Mm?' of feigned
uncertainty and slipped an arm round his shoulder. 'That's
him,' he said – and Alex, who knew the whole repertoire of
Justin's tones, heard in the two quiet syllables a rare tremor
of pride and anxiety. It was a kind of introduction.

'He's very good-looking,' said Alex, in his own tone of dry
fair-mindedness. They stood, in their loose embrace, sipping at
their drinks, as if assessing this judgement on the big English
boy with his wavy hair and rower's shoulders and beautiful
long legs. The wide smile conveyed the certainty of success in
some imminent struggle, and so seemed to invite curiosity as
to how it had in fact turned out.

Justin gave Alex a couple of consoling pats as he drew away
from him. 'Well, you should see him now.'

'That was a long time ago,' said Alex, explaining the hair-
style, the whole look, to himself.

'Oh god darling. It's pre-war. I mean, it's Julia Margaret Cameron, that one.'

And that was a kind of comfort, along with the cold tomato-juice and its after-burn of strong spirits. All he'd known of his successor till that morning was his name, his profession, and his addresses in London and here. He had wanted as little as possible for his imagination to worry at. So it was something to learn that he hadn't been left, in his thirty-seventh year, for a kid on a sports scholarship.

Justin flushed and smirked like a braggart anticipating jeers. 'No, he's gorgeously old.'

(Even so, thought Alex, I hope I haven't lost him to a pensioner. And then dimly saw the powerless absurdity of such hopes – the muddled desire to have been replaced by someone better, which was crushing but evolutionary, and by someone inferior, which would show Justin's weakness of judgement, and prove to Alex that he was better off without him.)

They went up the narrow box staircase for a quick orientation of bathroom and sleeping arrangements – Alex only glanced over Justin's shoulder into the almost unfurnished main bedroom: he saw a huge bed with an oak headboard and footboard and invalidish stacks of pillows, and the little brass clock under the bedside lamp. His own room was next door, with only a plank wall, and a single bed under a flowered counterpane. He said he liked it, although he knew the bed would give him cramps like an adolescent, and he had a vague sense of being in a servant's room, despite the facetious collection of old brown books on the chest of drawers: *Queer Folk of the West Country, Who's Who in Surtees, Remarkable Sayings of Remarkable Queens.* Justin hung in the doorway. 'So are you seeing anyone?' he said.

The upstairs windows were set low in the walls, and though the midday sun made a dazzling lozenge on the window-sill the room was shadowy and cool under the thatch. The atmosphere was faintly illicit, as if they ought to have been tearing around outside but had sneaked back unnoticed into the open house.

'Not really.' Alex gave a little squashed smile. The truth was he had been too depressed, too shaken by his own failure, to believe that any other man would want him, or could ever fall

20

in love with him. He didn't often lie, and he was pained to hear himself say, 'There's someone who comes round; nothing serious.'

'Is he cute?'

'Yep.'

'Is he blond?'

'He is, actually.' Alex shrugged. 'He's very young.'

'He's another virgin blond like me, isn't he?' Justin made one of his experienced-barmaid faces. 'Of course I'm foully jealous.' And despite the big congratulatory smile that followed, Alex registered the truth in the customary hyperbole; and then saw that the congratulation itself was mildly demeaning.

'It really isn't anything,' he said.

They found Robin in running-gear and oven-gloves, knocking the loaves from their hot tins on to a wire rack. The latent smell of marjoram and garlic and rising dough had bloomed into the kitchen with its own stifling welcome. Justin scuffed through to the fridge and the jug of drink.

'Darling, this is Alex. Darling, this is Robin.'

'Just a minute.' Then, shaking off the padded pockets, Robin turned with a smile that Alex knew already, though he doubted if he would have recognised the rest of the big handsome boy in the big handsome man. Alex was in the first freeing ease of drink on an empty stomach, and came forward and shook his hand and grinned back; and then stood close by him for a second or two, feeling the damp heat of him. The sweat on his bare shoulders and in the channel of his chest under the loose tank-top, the sporting readiness of his manner, the glanced-at weight of his cock and balls in the silvery slip of his running-shorts, the tall cropped balding head with its lively but calculating grey eyes: Alex coloured at the mixture of challenge and seduction, then stepped back with a deflected compliment on the beauty of the house.

'It was a shell when he bought it,' said Justin, in a grim singsong that mocked Robin's evident pride in the place.

'Really?' said Alex, but still looking at Robin. 'I'm amazed. It feels so, um . . .'

21

'It was a big job,' said Robin lightly, sweeping the subject aside.

'There are fascinating before-and-after photographs,' Justin insisted; but Robin was already tugging his shirt from his waistband and saying he must shower.

Within a minute there were springy footsteps overhead, and the soft thump-thump of dropped shoes, and then the whine of the hot-water pipes.

Alex went to fetch his bag from the car, and walking up through the garden felt at once the pleasure of being alone; he realised it was too late to run away; he had a racing fuddled sense of surrender to the weekend and its rigours. It was like a training exercise, confusing and uncomfortable in itself, but possibly affording in the end some obscure feeling of achievement. In the bag he had a bottle of Scotch and another present for Justin, which he now knew was wrong, but when he got back to the sitting-room he handed it over, with a sprinting pulse.

Justin gave an 'Oh . . .' of tolerant surprise, and Alex watched in a painful clarity of recall as he frowned and blushed over the red wrapping-paper, rather brusquely got the book out of it, murmured its title, and with a little smirk turned and stuffed book and paper into the top drawer of the oak commode behind him. So he was still unable to say thank you, which was a perverse flaw in someone who lived so much by taking. Alex watched him knee the drawer shut on his gauche but extravagant token of forgiveness.

After lunch they were all so drunk that they had to lie down. They went upstairs with yawns and stumbles, as if it was the middle of the night. Alex pushed off his shoes and lay on his back with the door open, but Justin slammed their door perhaps harder than he meant to: the wooden latch clattered. Alex grunted and turned on his side, and hoped they weren't going to have audible sex. He woke dry-mouthed and horny in the still heat of the later afternoon.

Padding grumpily along to the bathroom, he passed the closed doors of other rooms not mentioned on the tour, and rubbed his eyes out of a dreamlike sense, in the half-dark, with only the spills of light under the doors, that the cottage must be far bigger inside than it was outside. At the end of the corridor hung the long ellipse of an old pier-glass, which only deepened the impression. He gave himself a friendly scowl.

It emerged that Robin had gone out while the other two were sleeping. Justin came down and found Alex drinking water in the kitchen. 'He's on a job,' he said.

'I didn't know architects worked at weekends.'

'I'm afraid they do if they're working for mad old queens. And mad old queens do seem to make up an awfully large proportion of Mr Woodfield's clients.' Justin sat down at the table, from which, Alex realised, the lunch things had all been magically cleared; the dishwasher must have groaned and fizzed through its cycle while he slept.

'Who's this particular one?'

'Oh, Tony Bowerchalke,' said Justin, with mocking fondness, as if they both knew him.

'Uh-huh . . .'

'Do you want a drink, darling?'

'Good god no.'

'Perhaps you're right. No, old Tony's quite sweet, but he worries a lot. Robin rang him up the other day and he said, "I'm just having a tomato sandwich", so he had to ring off and call him again later. His house is hideous.'

'You don't mean Robin built a hideous house.'

'No, it's a Victorian loony-bin.' Justin got up and moved indirectly towards the fridge. 'Robin doesn't actually build houses. He could be the Frank Lloyd Wright of the whole Bridport area, but mostly he just tarts up old queens' dados. It's called a country-house practice, darling. Of course, no one builds country houses any more unless they're neo-classical pastiche by Quinlan Terry, so it tends to be repairs and turning them into flats.'

'Dearest, you've never heard of neo-classical pastiche by Quinlan Terry.'

Justin raised an eyebrow. 'You'll find me changed in many respects from the old lezzy you used to know.' He prised open a bottle of beer.

23

Later they went for a walk up a rutted lane already mysterious in the early evening under thickly leaved hazels and oaks, and out on to the high seaward slopes above the village. It was an intermittent three-mile climb to the cliff-tops, which Justin said was too far, as a rule he would only go for a walk if it was, as the French say, in the car. But Alex suddenly felt the pull of the sea, a holiday freedom that had seemed impossible in the airless cottage. He sprang ahead on his long legs over the tussocky hillside.

'We're not in any hurry, are we?' said Justin, starting to breathe sharply and sweating enough for his face to give back an ethereal reflection of the light.

Alex turned and gazed at him and the improbable landscape in which they found themselves. He supposed that in the right kind of fantasy he might have appeared as a golden-haired drover or hay-harvester; but it would have been a fantasy. 'It's all so green,' he said, gesturing gratefully.

Justin came up and anchored him with an arm. 'Yes, it's the rain. I heard someone talking about it. Apparently it makes everything go green.'

They went on up, through gaps in hedges, past the low outbuildings of a farm with nettle-choked sheep-pens and a van full of straw, along the fenced perimeter of a silent pine plantation. They went on a dipping plank across a quick little stony stream, which Justin took as a place to stop and point out how it ran down and around and was the stream that raced past the cottage. Alex began to get an Alpine sense of distance and scale, though they were only a few hundred feet up. Beyond the stream there was a belt of young green bracken shooting out of the brown detritus of last year's growth, and high up in it they came to a shallow turfy scoop, the sofa of a stone-age giant, and sat down in it, looking back at other hills that climbed away more slowly northwards. In the huge open shelter of the valley the air was still and mothering, though Alex thought that up behind them there would be cooler breezes dropping about the cliffs.

The village of Litton Gambril lay below, and Justin pointed out its few features with a lazy imprecision which couldn't quite disguise his regard for the place, and for his own good

24

fortune in living there. 'That's the church, and that's the steeple, darling. Those are the houses of various old monsters. That house there, you can't really see it, is where the Halls live, who I must say are the most fabulous drunks. They're roaring drunk the whole time, except allegedly between about eight and nine a.m. We often go there, it's like a pub that never closes.' Alex peered at the church, which didn't have a steeple, but a tower whose ornate finials rose against green cornfields with an effect of unaccountable extravagance. There was a loose knot of old houses around it, and the high dark crest of a copper beech on the village green. Out to the right there were walkers on the stony track that led to the ruins of a castle – 'Ruined by the Roundheads, darling,' said Justin, to whom even the dustiest of *double entendres* deserved the experiment of an airing. The cottage itself was completely hidden in its cultivated hollow at the village's other end; but to Alex the whole place communicated a slow shock of domesticity and loss.

He thought of his own neighbourhood in Hammersmith, nothing so self-contained, just a block or two worn half-invisible by use, the place in the oblivious city where for him life slowed and gleamed and recovered. The newsagent and the butcher and the dry-cleaner still had the nicknames Justin had given them. For two years and a month Justin ambled through those streets, the buzzer doormat in the off-licence offered its alert reassurance, he walked to the same corner for a taxi heading into town.

It was amazing where love took you – and Alex thought it was the one thing you would go anywhere for. In their early days together Justin was his entrée to pleasure, to the routine of certain bars, the instant friendship of good-looking men, blowsy gay dinner-parties with their undertow of sex. Alex was with him, he was accepted with a lack of hesitation that was flattering if indiscriminate, his long pale face and glossy black hair became more beautiful, his rangy walk more touching and seductive. At just the moment he gave himself completely to Justin, other men suddenly started to want sex with him. He became a charged particle. And now here he was, lying on a hillside in a part of the country he had never seen before, still dimly magnetised. He put a hand on Justin's bare forearm, not quite unconsciously, and after a minute Justin, as usual at any place of natural or historic beauty, got up and went for a piss. Alex watched him standing a few yards off, playing the glittering arc over a patch of young bracken; in the level sunlight the curled-up fronds of the bracken twitched open here and there, giving the hillside an air of furtive animation.

'So what do you think of Robin?' said Justin when he had sat down again, his chin on his drawn-up knees.

It was kind of brutal. Alex looked away and then back and said, 'He's a good cook.' You couldn't say what you thought about people, not at the time. He remembered the things his friends had said about Justin, with funereal relish, after he had gone – how he was a cheat and a bore and a drunk and an ungrateful slut, and actually they'd always thought so. He'd been surprised, he'd never acknowledged their hinted hostility, and was still obscurely resistant to what they said, in spite of the wounding evidence that they were right. He said, 'I hope you're being good to him', which showed oblique generosity as well as suspicion.

Justin pouted and peered out at the village, his head rocking slightly, as if unable to decide between a nod and a shake. 'Try not being good down here,' he said. 'Anyway, what about your bloke? You've been pretty quiet about him.'

Alex smiled with complex regret. 'Actually there isn't anyone. I was just teasing you.'

'Oh darling . . .' said Justin, with a comparably subtle pretence of concern.

On their way down the hill, Alex slipped his arm through Justin's, in a decorous way, or as if one of them at least was quite old, and when Justin's smooth-soled shoes slid on the turf he caught at his wrist, they were almost hand-in-hand again for a second, then tumbled down together. They weren't hurt, of course, but a moment of recovery seemed legitimate, and they lay there, arms under each other, Alex's knee between his old boyfriend's thighs, their trousers tugged up tight, as if the stone-age giant had lifted them by their belts from behind and flung them down. Alex was gazing at the sky, the depth of blue just beginning to silver and crumble. He turned his

26

head slowly and with a little grimace which seemed to mock the wish that was making the pulse pluck in his neck; but Justin looked past him, as if meditating on something else. Alex half-lifted himself and kissed him unplayfully on the mouth; then struggled apart from him and stepped away with a breezy 'Come on, let's go.' He saw the lane that ran along the valley and climbed out towards London. He saw himself squealing through the villages on his way down here, in his optimistic old sports car. He glanced at Justin on the grass, still oddly expressionless, extending a hand so as to be helped up.

The sun had left the garden by the time they came back, the birds were silent, but the flowers and bushes glowed with a brief intensity of colour against the neutral light. The time of day touched an old anxiety and loneliness in Alex, but Justin, who had been oppressively thoughtful on the downward walk, and seemed half-aggrieved, half-gratified by the intensity of the kiss, brightened up at the sight of the lit kitchen windows. He led Alex in from a back gate, past the greenhouse and an open shed where pale-ended logs were stacked. 'That's where we stack the wood,' he said. 'When we've been wooding.' They came round the back of the cottage, where a relay of *Tosca* swirled out from the kitchen doorway and mingled for a moment with the colder music of the stream. Alex hung back outside the bright oblong and saw Robin, with a long whittled knife in his hand, stride towards Justin, who somehow slipped by, so that the kiss barely touched his cheekbone.

Alex lay in the bath with his hair sleeked back and his knees sticking out of the water. Justin had been in first, and the floor was wet, and there were arcs of scattered talcum-powder across it. There hadn't been time for the tank to reheat properly, and Alex played with himself listlessly, and more for warmth than excitement. His thoughts ran back and forth between this evening and last year, with a choking sense of mystery, of some missed briefing, an explanation he had failed to understand and which would never be repeated. He knew he'd been told, but he couldn't remember for the life of him why Justin wasn't still his boyfriend. He looked across heavy-heartedly at the

27

mingled soaps and cosmetics crowded round the basin, the muddle of crimson bath-towels, Robin's running-shorts and vest kicked into a thoughtless ruck with Justin's cast-off shorts, as if acting out their owners' lusts without them. Above his rising and falling navel his sponge grounded itself and floated free, grounded and floated. He pulled himself up and reached out to the shelf for Justin's favourite cologne, the squat decanter of Bulgari, and sprayed it upwards. When he leant into the costly mist it was instantly two years ago; and when he opened his eyes, his hopeless uncorrected feelings seemed to tingle around him in the scented air.

Justin was sleeping, or perhaps just sulking, in their room; Alex took his time dressing and perfecting himself, stupidly afraid of being alone with his host; he knew already that Robin cooked with a concentration that made talk artificial and discontinuous. He stooped downstairs, and wandered towards the kitchen and the noise of the opera, which he thought would be a cover for his discomfort; perhaps they could just drink and listen to it, and it would block out the roughly jealous appetite-killing sexual imaginings which the cottage seemed to force on him. Then amongst the music he heard a voice speaking, rapid and casual, not Robin's cultured baritone, which interrupted it with the stately answer 'Salmon', but a young man's classless indifferent tenor. 'I need a bath,' he said.

Alex paused before the presence of a further guest, a further fact which no one had thought worth mentioning to him: it rattled him, though a moment later he welcomed the idea of a fourth person who might ease the insoluble tensions of the other three. He heard his name with a start. 'Alex is in there, I think,' Robin said.

'Oh, right . . . Who's that?'

'Justin's ex.'

A hesitation. 'Is he cute?'

'Well . . . Quite.'

'Do you think he wants his back scrubbed?'

The noise of Robin scraping something quickly from a bowl with a fork or spoon. 'I'm sure he's longing for it. Though I'm

28

not sure it's you he wants to do it. No . . . no . . . he's perfectly all right. About nine feet tall. He's rather like a ghost – '

At which point Alex ducked into the room with a dim generalised exclamation of pleasure – the bath, the smell of food, the prospect of a drink, simply being there.

Across the kitchen, and framed this time by the thickening dusk beyond the back door, the two figures were standing, Robin with his right hand on the neck of the young man, in what Alex thought of as a gesture of special admiring tenderness. It wasn't what he'd expected; and Robin at once dropped his arm, while the stranger looked at Alex with raised eyebrows, as if also awaiting an explanation. Robin should have said something, but he let the social pause deepen, while Alex stepped forward, glancing at the newcomer, who seemed so at ease here, himself an ex perhaps, who shared with Robin certain unforgotten habits and tones; young though, twenty-two or three, with a cropped fuzz, and a pointed blond tuft under his lower lip and a black T-shirt tight on his lean figure. His mouth was plump, down-turned, sleepy, vaguely disdainful; but a smile woke up in it and you changed your mind. He moved towards Alex and squeezed his upper arm with a sweet spivvish suddenness of friendship. 'I'm Dan,' he said, tipping his head oddly towards Robin. 'He's my dad.'

Alex looked at him again, to confirm and explore this undreamt-of fact.

3

When Simon was very ill they had stopped making love, though much that passed between them seemed to carry the promise or the memory of sex. Robin had lain for night after night beside his friend, and fallen asleep with a hand laid lightly on his shoulder or thigh, in a gesture both distant and reassuring. He changed the sheets, and supervised the medication, and did everything for Simon, often complaining about the trouble and disturbance, as if he thought this was only a temporary problem. He treated him with the practical obtuseness of the healthy.

Simon was happiest in Dorset, he enjoyed the sheltered, sun-struck days in the cottage garden, and if there was a threatening breeze would sit in the greenhouse, with its sunken tank and humid unseasonal warmth, and read and doze like some doddery old expat. He liked the thick country darkness, which to Robin seemed newly sepulchral after the leaking glare and animation of London nights. Robin watched him slip over a threshold, into the tapering perspectives of fatal illness, in which all but the mildest pleasures lay in the past. In a terrifying dream he was himself the dying man, a mere consciousness gazing out from the eyes of a paralysed body, unable to call to the friends who hurried past the open doorway, on their way to tennis and dinner and sex. Occasionally a figure would stop and look in, with the resolve of someone testing their own capacity for suffering.

Robin was working that spring on a Queen Anne villa at Kew, and for much of the week he made his office in the little flat at Clapham, driving out each morning to watch the rotten beams come down, the riverward portico made safe, and then back at tea-time to Simon and rooms which seemed for the first few minutes peculiarly white and narrow. It was the sort of job he loved, the rescue of a house from near ruin, with a formal garden that could still be guessed at behind high red walls; the roof was made good, the cellar dried and sealed, a rainy week transformed by ancient colours scraped up bright on wood and stucco. But as the months went on, and the documents and photographs accumulated, he felt the countervailing force of the other record, the dipping graph of Simon's strength, with its comfortless statistics. It was the darker half-hidden face of the ambiguous April days, success threaded in all the way with defeat.

For his last week Simon was in hospital, it was that stage already, when help and reassurance were most necessary and most futile. Robin shared the evening visits, or vigils, with Simon's father and sister; then found his days troubled by a horrible anxious liveliness. He came back to the flat at lunch-time, so as to be on the move, then went out to run on the Common and exercised under the trees with his hand-weights. The horse-chestnuts were already leafing, the bushes bright green on black; there was a spring mood, casual but purposeful, and Robin envied the relief in the faces of other solitary joggers and unhurried couples.

One mild cloudy day he was turning home along the Common's edge and went into a newsagent's to buy a drink. He had to wait at the counter with a queue of punters handing in lottery slips, and found himself looking with unconscious intimacy at the man in front of him, who was half in profile to him, superstitiously checking the fifteen boards he had marked. It was like the impersonal closeness of a crowded tube train, which none the less fosters secret desires and lurches of excitement. Still warm and impatient from running, but slowed and held by the inertia of the crammed little shop, with its lurid video posters, its insulting birthday-cards, its amazingly compendious top shelf of thickly overlapping pornography, Robin had closed his fastidious inner eye, his architect's eye; and now it opened again, in the unexpected presence of some-thing beautiful among so much unregulated vulgarity.

In those queer, lulled seconds he looked more and more intently at the younger man's glossy blond hair and full lips parted in vaguely unintelligent concentration. There was some-

31

thing sleek and unreliable about him. Robin felt a kind of kinship with him, as with his own self of fifteen years or so before, habituated to sex and admiration. He wanted to hear him speak, to see if the generally public-school impression was accurate, but he handed over his chits and his foolish £15 without a word. Robin got himself beside him at the counter, almost as if they were together, and waited for him to receive his tickets, holding up his chilled bottle eagerly.

Out in the street whim thickened into necessity, goaded by the younger man's complete unawareness of him, as if he had become a wraith like his dying lover, when he wasn't, he was forty-six and big and fit and handsomely unshaven. He followed him back the way he had come, taking in, with a hushed involuntary groan, the heavily elegant backside, in tight and frayed old jeans, with one of the pockets half ripped off, as if by the failed flying tackle of an admirer. He felt his energies more and more focused and absorbed, and he saw that of course it was a long-obscured need of his own that was clarifying itself in the solid sauntering figure twenty yards ahead.

They went on, across the flat open Common, Robin remembering to look about him as if unconcerned with the lottery addict and trailing him by pure coincidence. They passed knots of schoolboys, a trampled goalmouth. He saw their course across a plan or map. An expert follower would have moved from tree to tree, or taken tangential paths that still kept his object inescapably in view. But Robin didn't care, in fact he wanted to be seen. They approached and passed a high graffiti-blitzed bandstand, beyond which was a low wooden building, like a broken-down cricket-pavilion, with a boarded-up stall that still advertised Teas and Ice Cream. The blond was briefly out of view behind it, and when Robin came round the corner he was nowhere to be seen.

He saw angled wicker fences that screened the entry to public toilets, the Ladies' was closed up with barbed wire, but from the Men's, by some benign perseverance or dreamlike oversight, the hiss of the flush was heard, and the metal door swung open to the bright protesting arpeggio of an old spring.

Twelve minutes later, jogging back past walkers who knew nothing of what he had just done, boys' shouts and football whistles on the breeze, an oblivious bounce in his stride, as if powered by some forbidden drug, the thrill of a secret transgression warming him to a blush that the innocent would put down to the wholesome effort of running . . . Of course someone saying couldn't he have waited? But there was no choice, just as there was no excuse. And the thrilling squalor of it, the blond's expressionless hunger, swallowing and swallowing on Robin's slippery, kicking cock, then crouched forward over the filthy bowl, hands clasped round the downpipe, the unlockable door swinging open behind them.

Robin should have showered, but he made do with a cold squirt of Escape under each arm, pulled on his jeans over his damp jockstrap and drove to Kew with aggressive speed, half guilty, half exultant. All afternoon, among the reliable old builders and the masked and overalled death-watch-beetle men, he had the smell of the stranger's moist arse and sweet talc fading on his beard and fingertips. By the time he drew in to the hospital car-park it had gone.

Simon made a few widely spaced and incoherent remarks, and smiled with an apparent bitterness that was perhaps only an effect of his gauntness and the recurrence of half-suppressed pain. Robin dreaded any irony about his own good health; he was glad that Simon was dying 'well', that is to say under sufficient sedation for the horrors of the grave to have masked their faces.

The following lunch-time he went straight to the pavilion, and did his exercises alongside the schoolboys' soccer pitch, almost as if he was waiting to go on. He kept the screened entrance casually in view. He liked the building's reminiscence of his own teens and their successes – smells of linseed and creosote and changing-room staleness. He had a long wait, running off and back on an improvised course between invisible markers, but the hour raced forwards for him, lost in the image of the nameless man. Robin loved the dull glow and the fleshiness of him, which seemed in some barely acceptable way a recompense for what had happened to Simon. It was only lust, of course – he must remember that; he hadn't even heard

33

the man speak, beyond a grunted disdainful 'Yeah' when he swiped a hand down his neck and whispered 'Okay?' before he left. But it was electric lust, nothing sane or resistible. The shadowed ground among the trees was brightened by his floating image, like the dazzle inadvertently thrown off by a moving windscreen or an opened window. A wide pale shoulder, the grey-gold dusk of hair between his legs, unrelenting blue eyes, glimpses and gleams in the air of a spring day. When the man at last appeared Robin saw him with a shock of recognition – he had been remembering someone so different.

That night Simon said to him, 'You look well', and took his hand with a confused stare, proud and doubting. To Robin there seemed something clairvoyant about him; Simon knew him best of all, it was absurd to suppose that he wouldn't know everything he had done. Robin felt he had been left to decide, by some punishing honesty system, whether he had been accused or absolved. He said, 'I love you', which he had never done before in the presence of the younger sister and the admittedly deaf father. In the early hours of the morning Simon died.

Robin took it calmly, he acknowledged the facts with a stoicism that was part of his natural pride, and was also a Woodfield thing: he knew he had been given an occasion to behave well, as well as Simon had died. And there was a certain resilience too that came from his still unnegotiated standing with the family. In the event neither he nor the father seemed to know which of them had lost more, and which deserved the keener, the more unconditional, condolences.

By late morning an almost physical discomfort had set in – faint nausea, a distracted clumsiness, panicky breathlessness. The stoically observed sequence in the hospital, the emphatic last breath and the following silence, the subtle relaxation and emptying of the face, the timid but steady squeaking of the nurse's shoes on the linoleum, and the dark confirming descent of the Indian doctor, came back to him with the clarity of something belatedly understood. He barged around the flat, picking things up and throwing them down, appalled by their irrelevance or their crude pathos. His thoughts were

34

unpleasantly sexual, he pictured Simon as he had been ten years ago, with his fat Jewish cock always thickening up and needing work; there was something suspect in thinking of his cock as Jewish, as if it was a little person; he imagined it now, cold and bloodless between the wasted thighs.

He went into the bedroom, got undressed, and then pulled on his singlet and running-shorts with tense excitement. He remembered the day twenty years before when his grandmother had died at her flat in the Boltons and he had gone out as if in a trance to one of the Earl's Court pubs and picked up a man in a leather cap and fucked him all afternoon.

When he hit the street he found a fine clinging rain was in the air. It was comforting, and intimate, like some barely palpable form of therapy; it seemed to define his warm agitated body within its weightless cool. He saw the trees of the Common at the end of the street, and ran without slowing across two streams of edging and accelerating traffic to reach them. He wasn't jogging exactly, it was faster than that. When the wooden shack came into view, with its boarded-up windows and offers of Refreshments, there was already something habitual about it, that filled Robin with relief and shame. He ran straight into the Gents, which was empty, and stood panting against the wall, silvered with drizzle.

But by three o'clock no one had come in, except a blind man with a stick and a dog, like a figure in a comic sketch, and some noisy kids in football studs who glanced back at him apprehensively as he withdrew into the cubicle. He leant against the door to keep it shut and cried silent tears of grief and humiliation.

The next time he saw the blond was a week later, in the West End, among the crowding shoppers in Long Acre. He was thinking of him, and there was a blurred half-second of adjustment as the remembered features dissolved into the real ones: the shock of his presence was sweetly subdued by Robin's sense that he had been there, on the floating gauze of his imagination, all along. He had the discernible aura of an idea made flesh. The clothes were different, he seemed somehow in disguise, but Robin smiled, to show he knew his secret, as the blond passed by, with a quick unrecognising stare.

35

He could hardly believe that the moment had come already, and gone; and after a few seconds of bumping into people he turned back. It was the stare that wounded and provoked him, he would have hated it in anyone else, and was already making peculiar allowances for it: the man was terribly short-sighted, or was himself perhaps lost in grief; or it was just an unamusing game. He stood alongside him at the window of an expensive men's shop, where the stare was directed with more affectionate concern at the mixture of oddly cut suits and sporty clubwear in black, orange and lime-green. The shadows of the two men who had twice had fierce speechless sex together fell vaguely across the stilted little tableau of clothes and accessories, the pinned baize, the bodiless folds of trouser-legs and shirt-sleeves. There was a faint reflection in the wall of glass, too pale and inconstant to let them see each other steadily. Robin's eyes milled over the baffling price-tickets. He started to feel that like an agent making contact he should produce a pre-arranged phrase, something gnomic but commonplace. He had never felt so constrained. He found he was gripping the other man's shoulder and saying quite loudly, 'I've got to see you again.'

They started meeting in the afternoons at Robin's flat. Justin lived with a boyfriend in Hammersmith, and arrived about 2.30 by taxi. The boyfriend worked for the pensions fund of a government department – Robin thought one day Justin said the Home Office, another the Foreign Office. Various facts came out in the conversations after sex, when Robin made strong coffee for himself and a precocious gin and tonic for his visitor: Justin had sometimes worked as an actor; he was thirty-four; he had an unusually old father, in his nineties, who was a manufacturer; he had been with his boyfriend for a year and a half, he loved him but was bored with him physically. Robin felt no guilt or hostility towards this other man, just a distant curiosity. He said nothing about having once been married, and having a grown-up son; but after a shamed little unseen pantomime of hiding Simon's photo in a drawer he left it on the bedside table, and Justin seemed gratified by its presence. Robin got the feeling that duplicity was a constant part of Justin's life.

He found him charming and funny, with a line in absurdity

that he hadn't expected. By the time of his third visit and his second gin and tonic they were grinning at one of his stories and holding each other's gaze above a sudden deepening of intimacy which seemed to Robin both dangerous and possible. When Justin strolled and sprawled around the flat, naked or in his boxer shorts, he created a half-pleasant mood of lazy confinement. Robin watched him with a new alertness to his own four small white rooms, as if given a fresh chance to judge their effect. But Justin noticed nothing, and so made all the considered details and improvements seem rather negligible – Robin wondered if Simon himself had ever really appreciated them.

At moments the sense of sacrilege was very strong – but then the point perhaps was that the stranger knew nothing of the man whose place he was taking: he had no obligation towards him. Robin sobbed when he told him of his death, but the loose hug that followed, the wiping of a cheek with a rough thumb, moved in ten seconds into sex – Robin heard his own tearful breaths modulate helplessly into gasps as Justin's flickering mouth got to work. He stroked and clutched at his thick golden hair – and how it all came back, the life of love and excitement he had once thought of as his right and his inevitable future.

In theory the afternoon arrangement was ideal for him, since it left the mornings free for visits to the site and he could work on through the lunch hour, while the builders sat out under the portico, with their sandwiches and cigarettes, and their incurious air of owning the place. Then he could be home in twenty minutes, and after his two or three hours with Justin the early evening opened out with its usual patterns of exercise, and unusual invitations from old friends who were clearly still making him a priority. Robin quickly saw that his preoccupied manner and sad lack of interest in other men were indistinguishable from the symptoms of contained English mourning. At times he wondered why he wasn't mourning more.

But after a couple of weeks the romantic secrecy and restriction were themselves becoming painful. The purposeful mornings were thrown askew by the intensity of looking

37

forward to the afternoons. He had to be told things twice, he was in a daze which again might be put down to grief, he got behind with his work while he watched the clock like a schoolboy. It was as if he saw through the plans he was studying to something uncontrolled and turbulent beneath. Justin crowded his thoughts, aroused him and slightly irritated him by having so complete and monotonous a hold on his imagination: he appeared to him both as a devouringly passive lover and as a kind of cock-teaser, a grown-up school tart, with his refusal to be touched, even to be seen, before 2.30 in the afternoon. Robin wore out his most intimate images of him by turning them over so persistently in his mind.

And then the whole movement of withdrawal, around five o'clock, the friendly but businesslike silence in which they got dressed, the new note of anxiety when Justin checked his watch . . . and the first seconds of being alone again after the door had shut, Robin wandering sightlessly from bed to desk to sink with the weak smile, tender, rueful and shocked, of a feeling suddenly deprived of its object. The dusks grew longer and lonelier day by day as his feeling deepened. He walked out again to the gym and in the softening light, the slowly precipitating pinks and blues of a lover's evening, he saw he was in a trap. The fact of having Justin was undermined by the fact of not having him; he needed nights with him, not hours. The old self that Justin had reawakened couldn't be satisfied by the arrangement he had imposed.

Robin had always been, in his well-mannered way, an initiator. He didn't have the predatory disregard for the other person that some of his friends had, but he was used to creating a mood and exploiting a possibility. He thought he had never been resisted by anyone worth having. If he had felt trapped before, in the years of his marriage, and in the early restless days with Simon, he had shown a proud instinct for survival and escape. He found he was thought of as slightly dangerous, the handsome, athletic young architect, whose father was Sheriff of the county, who had a son at a good prep-school, but who was also known to a more secret élite in the underground clubs of early-eighties London. So it was a new experience, like the troubling physical changes of middle age –

the sudden hair-loss, the slowing sex-drive, the half-doubted dulling of his hearing – to find himself in the submissive position of a mistress, the yearning but unacknowledgeable creature of the afternoons.

Worst of all were the weekends, the three whole days from Friday lunch-time to Monday lunch-time, the enforced or at least accepted silence . . . It was a silence with an irresistible sense of crisis to it, as if everything must be over between two lovers who left each other alone for so long. Robin went down to Litton Gambril, where the early summer was pushing on senselessly without him, and where he could invent useful jobs for himself, get the Rayburn going and cook an elaborate meal out of the garden and eat it with the sorry haste of the newly widowed. The cottage was solid and stubborn and as he had left it; it wouldn't come to life. He had a feeling he had made a mistake, and was acting with a parody of purpose. He lay on his customary side of the huge old farmhouse bed and swept out an arm over the cool double vacancy. He felt for everything he'd lost in Simon, and everything he needed in Justin, snivelling and exciting himself at the same time, till he felt quite freakish with pitiful and possessive emotions, and brought himself off so as to be able to sleep.

One Saturday lunch-time he drank a bottle of Gilbey's with the Halls and rang Justin's number when he got back, in a mood of truculent reasonableness. 'Let's cut the crap,' he said, as he span the phone-dial through the eleven laborious numbers, which seemed in their old-fashioned way to be giving him time to think twice about the call. After a couple of rings a pleasant unfamiliar voice recited the last seven digits back to him, ending on a little interrogative rise. It was a tone of such easy and unsuspecting efficiency that Robin hesitated, and when after a few seconds Alex said 'Hello', the tone hardening but still tolerant, he hung up. He sat hunched forward on the sofa in the stillness of the country afternoon. Up in London a young man he had never seen would be putting down the receiver with a shrug and speaking innocently to the man they shared; Robin knew he was house-proud, and pictured him in an apron. He found a note of reproach in that happy mechanical answering of the phone, in the enviable pleasant boredom of their affair. Then he got to his feet with a sullen longing to break it up, which he drunkenly allowed to become a plan.

Back in town he was in a mood of fatalistic excitement that was new to him. He thought he must at least see his rival and drove over early on the Monday morning to the quiet Victorian street where the two of them were living. He slipped into a space almost opposite the house, and sat looking at it, professionally adjudicating the commonplace glazing and pointless panels of terracotta tiles so as to subdue his sense of its special aura and of the bulging secret it sheltered. He saw an upstairs curtain pulled open by a shirt-sleeved arm, and then tugged half-back again, as if after a wincing protest. It was an ordinary redbrick terrace house, made remotely pretentious by arts-and-crafts details. Once it would have had a maid and children in it. Robin wondered how Alex and Justin lived in it, what they had done with it.

His view of the front door was interrupted by a battered yellow Escort dawdling past in search of a parking-space. The driver was a flat-faced young black with a gold cross ear-ring which glinted as he craned round. Seeing Robin in his car he mouthed a question as to whether he was about to leave, and when Robin shook his head gave him an incoherent grin, which seemed to have some kind of sex-sympathy in it. He stopped a short way ahead, in the middle of the road, and waited. It was the half-hour of going to work and to school. All along the street goodbyes were being shouted down hallways or front doors double-locked for the silent daytime. Robin started to feel conspicuous as children were hurried past. He looked carelessly at the black driver, who he thought might be an electrician or painter, and saw him angle the rear-view mirror so as to check his hair in it, and ogle his own eyes and teeth as if for crumbs of sleep or breakfast. He saw him squirt a little aerosol into his mouth. He missed the opening of the door opposite, but turned at the knock of its shutting and the rattle of the letter-flap. A pale young man in a grey suit came out on to the road; he was so tall that he seemed almost to trip over the flimsy front gate. Robin thought there was something rather 1890s in the long profile and the almost black swept-back hair; he was more beautiful than Justin had led

40

him to expect. At the same time he thought brutishly of the sex-life he had with Justin and couldn't imagine how this man could ever have satisfied him. He saw him stoop to unlock a vulnerable old soft-top Mercedes, and as he drove off, with a look as if surprised and embarrassed by the competitive noise he was producing, the driver of the Escort backed up alertly and into the space he had left.

So that was it. He had seen his lover's partner in the barely thinking routine of his workday morning; and it was better to see and to know than to be haunted by imaginings. He felt it had been worth it. And it was really only then that it occurred to him that he might see Justin now himself: he could be late at Kew and have a fierce half-hour with him first, in the musty marital bed, or over the kitchen table, shaking the breakfast things on to the floor. At the moment he loved the idea of sex that smashed things up. Even so, he waited. He was frightened of Justin.

A minute later he heard the remote trilling of a phone, and glancing across the road saw the black guy nodding into a mobile and then poking its little aerial back in before getting out of the car, reaching in for a knapsack, slamming the door shut. He was broad and muscular, with curvy legs in ripped old jeans; he strolled confidently round the car, through Justin and Alex's flimsy front gate, and in at the door, which opened already as he approached. Robin saw a flash of white bath-robe on a welcoming arm before the door closed. He sat with his mouth open, his lips hard and curled, as if about to be sick. Upstairs in the bedroom's bay-window the half-open curtain was tugged carelessly shut.

4

'Alex gets nicer and nicer when he's drunk,' said Justin. 'Don't you, darling?'

Alex gave a slow frowning nod of agreement and when Danny laughed slid a smile at him and held his eye for a second. 'Some of us do,' he said.

Justin noticed the contact and then took in Robin's steady gaze across the table, the turned-down smile that said that he usually indulged him but tonight might side with the others. 'I'm an angel when I'm drunk,' said Justin.

It was the end of a long rich dinner, Danny clearing the dishes in the rational way of a trained waiter, leaving Justin with his spoiled helping of now cold pudding, which he eyed with baffled alarm, like an emblem of a life he couldn't recall ordering. 'You can take my spotted dick, darling,' he said; at which Alex alone laughed, out of a remembered habit.

'Anyone for coffee?' said Robin loudly. 'Or homegrown borage tea . . .?'

'Come and sit on my knee,' said Justin, pawing vaguely at Danny's passing leg.

'I'm a bit busy at the moment, Justin. Doing the clearing up.'

Justin mulled this over for a moment. 'Well it's awfully good of you to do that,' he said.

Alex reached across to top up people's water-glasses. 'Have you got Justin to do any housework or things like that yet?' he asked Robin.

'Oh no,' said Robin hastily. 'I sometimes wonder if he'd like to. He watches *me* doing housework with what seems to be genuine interest, but I think without any real confidence that he could ever learn to do it himself.'

Justin smiled past them forgivingly. He didn't know at the

time why he had invited Alex down, except out of restlessness and a loose desire for trouble. But it was satisfactory to bring the two main men in his life together, and watch them politely squaring up and backing off, Alex with his Scottish dryness and hot hurt feelings, Robin with his well-bred charm and hints of sexual ruthlessness. He liked the power he had in knowing these two men as he did, the faces under their faces that were only visible in the light of their desire for him. There was a surplus of power, with its delicious tendency to corrupt. He looked at Danny, stooping to stack the dishwasher, the loose singlet hanging off his lean young shoulders.

'Hey-ho,' he said, lifting up his glass. 'Country life.'

'Country life,' said Robin, taking it defiantly as a toast; while Alex looked on with the old anxiety at Justin's menacing changes of tack and private ironies.

'There's the most marvellous pig in the village,' Justin said to him. 'I must take you to see it. It's probably the most interesting thing *in* the village. It's an enormous great big . . . pig.'

'Really.'

'Of course. You've seen it, haven't you, Danny?'

'I'm too busy for that sort of thing' remained Danny's line, and Justin saw him glow when it drew a mild laugh. Well of course the other two were going to look after the boy.

'We could go and see it now, but it's probably got its pyjamas on,' Justin said, as if dealing with a very young person indeed.

'Let's just stay here,' said Robin quietly.

But Justin got up anyway, and wandered out through the open back door to have a pee under the remote supervision of the stars.

It was a night blacker and more brilliant than any you ever got in London, even up on the Heath; and there there were warmer, moving shadows. Justin shivered, in the faint chill of nearly midnight. He longed for crowds and the purposeful confusion of the city; he wanted shops where you could get what you wanted, and deafening bars so full of men seeking pleasure and oblivion that you could hardly move through them. It was deadly still here, apart from the dark chattering of the stream. A bat or something flickered overhead. He

43

thought there were the great high times, the moments of initiation, new men, new excitements; and then there was all the rest. He turned back towards the lighted door. Only candle-light, but a subtle glare across grass and path. He thought resentfully of how this wasn't his house; it had been patched and roofed and furnished to please or tame another partner.

His new thing of fancying Danny was rather the revelation of this evening, and he had let his imagination run all over him while his two lovers trailed through their protracted routine of shared sarcasms about himself. He still found it uncomfortable that his boyfriend had a son, as though it showed a weakness of character in him. Justin hated weakness of character. He needed his lovers to be as steady in the world as they were in their devotion to him. He found himself apologising that Robin was not a more famous or original architect. And Danny himself was rudderless, doing bits of work here and there, sharing a house that smelt of smoke and semen with various other young pill-poppers and no-hopers; and yet always giving off an irritating sense that he knew where he was going. But tonight the freshness of him was abruptly arousing, the blue-veined upper arms, the fat sulky mouth with its challenge to make it smile and the little blond imperial under it, and the crotch thing, of course, the packet, which was the first and final arbiter with Justin, and qualified and overrode all other feelings and judgements. 'Like father, like son,' he said, with evident if uncertain meaning, as he thumped back into his seat.

'Now who wants to play Scrabble?' said Robin. He swept the crumbs from the table in front of him and smiled irresponsibly.

Alex looked ready to play, but ready too for Justin to say, 'You lot have a game. I'm far too dyslexic tonight.' In fact he could read and write perfectly well, even though certain words were liable to slippage: shopfitter, for instance, he always saw as shoplifter, and topics as optics, and betrothal as brothel. Last week, in a glance at one of Robin's plans, he had seen the words MASTER BOREDOM.

'I'm not playing,' said Danny, with anxious firmness, and wiped the draining-board and plugged in the kettle.

Justin said, 'Why don't we play Alex's Encyclopaedia game? Alex invented it, it's marvellous.'

'Okay,' said Robin, in a tone of fair-mindedness tinged with pique that his own game had not been preferred. 'What is it?'

Justin bowed his head to Alex, who gave a tentative explanation of the rules. 'It's based on the idea of a multi-volume dictionary, like the *OED* or something. You have to make up the names of the volumes, like "Aardvark to Bagel", that sort of thing. Except that they have to describe the other people you're playing with. Then they're all read out, and you have to guess who they are. It's not a game anyone can win, it's just a bit of fun.'

'I'm not sure about that,' Justin said, and watched Robin's rapid competitive assessment of the idea.

'You could get two points if you guess right,' Robin said, 'and one point if you wrote the definition.'

'I suppose so,' said Alex.

'Actually it's not fair on Alex,' Danny said, 'as he only really knows Justin.'

Justin said, 'It doesn't matter, because he'll be nice about everybody.'

Robin went to a drawer for scrap paper and a handful of chewed pencils and biros, and picked up a fine Rotring pen for himself. Alex said, 'Okay, so you can only go two letters ahead. You can have "Awkward to Cuddle", say, but not . . .'

'But not "Back to Front",' said Justin. 'Or "Bad to Worse".'

'Oh, I get . . .' said Danny.

Robin looked round at them all. 'Presumably one also does oneself?' And then smiled secretively.

Justin watched them as they pondered and scribbled and crossed things out. Occasionally one of them would catch the eye of another. Alex coloured slightly when Danny caught him looking at him; but Robin held Danny's gaze for several seconds and then looked away impassively – it was the bridge training that made even a game of Scrabble so steely, and filled Justin with an urge to cheat or deliberately misunderstand the rules. Danny frowned touchingly over his piece of paper, and when he had written something down looked at it sideways to judge the effect. Robin was already tearing his paper into separate strips, while Alex sighed and smiled weakly, and wrote

45

nothing down at all, as if stumped by politeness and anxious responsibility for the game.

When they were all ready they put their efforts into a bowl, and Robin drew a grid to record the marks according to his own system. Justin felt confident of winning, and knew the mixture of vanity and acuity required. He wasn't sure how the Woodfields would play; as it happened the first two entries read out, 'Devoted to Drink' and 'Architect to Aristos', were by Danny, and showed a rather bald approach. Justin took a chance on 'Homage to Industry' being a gibe at himself, and had no doubts about 'Beautiful to Behold', since he had written it, though Alex incautiously said he thought it referred to Danny. Overall Alex's contributions were embarrassingly candid: 'Irresistible to Justin' (Robin), 'Slow to Understand' (himself) and 'Hard to Improve (on)', which sweetly turned out to allude to Justin; 'Born to Disco' presumably encapsulated the one thing he had yet found out for sure about Danny. He looked a little crestfallen at Danny's tepid compliment, 'Interesting to Know', and thought that 'Far to Go' must be about himself (it was Danny's lonely self-description); it chimed somehow with Robin's blandly distant attempt at Alex, 'Ready to Travel'.

The mischief was short-lived but left them all feeling tender and stupid. They sat for a while picking through the discarded papers, wondering what Justin had been getting at with his palm-reader's 'Prelude to Romance' (for Danny) and his inscrutable 'Made to Measure' (for Alex). Robin did a recount of the scores, because Justin had won by such a large margin, while he had tied annoyingly with Alex. 'I thought my "Pillar to Post" was rather good,' he said. He doodled heavily over the grid, until it looked like the plan of a herb-garden.

'That's enough games,' said Danny, and stood up to do something.

'Have you got a boyfriend at the moment, darling?' asked Justin.

Danny turned and looked at him, with hands on hips. 'I've got quite enough trouble with my dad's boyfriend, without getting one of my own, thanks very much,' he said; though as he came past he leant over Justin and gave him a squeeze, hand into shirt-front – and Justin thought he had a nice cosy way with him after all, with his unplanned, almost meaningless little clinches. He reached up to him as he slipped away, and again caught something more than mere noticing on Alex's face, an involuntary interest, a protesting glance. He said,

'Alex would make you a super boyfriend.'

'I'm sure he would,' said Danny, breezily but not impolitely.

'You're like me, darling, you need someone older to look after you. I know Alex is rather shy and sensitive, but he's got plenty of money and a comfortable house and a sports car – and in bed . . . well – '

'Please!' murmured Alex.

'It's the leverage he gets with those long legs . . .'

There was a knock at the door-frame. 'Am I interrupting?' A broad-faced young man with slicked-back dark hair came hesitantly out of the night. He wore painter's dungarees over a blue T-shirt, with the bib unbuttoned on one side, and scruffy old gym-shoes. The effect was authentic, but you felt he was exploiting it. 'I'm just on my way to my mum's,' he said, with the distinctive vowels of the place.

'Come in, Terry,' said Robin; and Danny ambled over to him and squeezed his arm.

'Have a drink, Terry,' said Justin gruffly. And so a chair was found for him and a glass, and the bottles were lifted to the light and tilted to see if any wine was left.

'I'm surprised you're not busy on a Saturday night,' said Robin, in what seemed to Justin an equivocal way. Terry was a local factotum and Romeo, with a family interest in the Broad Down caravan park, a famous eyesore on the other side of Bridport, as well as a vaguer association with the pretentious Bride Mill Hotel.

'I've been doing some work for Bernie Barton,' said Terry. 'Papering his back room.'

'Do you mean PC Barton Burton?' Justin enquired.

Terry was uneasy with Justin's humour, and said merely, 'Whatever you say', and grinned at the others for solidarity.

'Been over to the Mill lately?' asked Robin, in a tone that irritated Justin. 'How are the prices doing? Still £3.5 for fish and chips?'

'Something like that,' said Terry. 'Cheers' – taking a cautious drink and then laughing retrospectively. 'Or it may have gone up.'

What was annoying was the slightly roguish joviality, the way Robin's own vowels became ambiguous, half-rusticated, a sort of verbal slouch as if to disclaim their differences in age and class. He should be what he is, thought Justin, who was not too drunk to know that his annoyance was sharpened by guilt. The present impromptu occasion was a test for Terry as much as himself. He didn't know how practised Terry would be at deceit, and it was perhaps his own snobbery to assume that a Londoner would do better at concealing a transaction like theirs. He was far cheaper than the London boys too, and Justin believed in general that what you paid more for must be better. He should have given him a larger tip. Glancing at him now, with his forearms and broad brow already pinky-brown from the sun, Justin felt the sweet bite of his addictive nature, and looked forward to other mornings when Robin had gone to Tytherbury and left him in the waking surge of hangover lust.

'This is Alex, by the way,' said Danny.

'How do you do?' said Terry, half getting up to shake his hand across the table.

'Do you live near by?' said Alex feebly.

'Very near by,' said Terry, with a genial laugh at his ignorance. 'No, my mum lives up here, in the back lane.' He tipped his head backwards. 'I can slip in through the back gate.'

Justin wondered how artless all this talk of back bedrooms and back lanes was. He said, 'Mrs Doggett grows marvellous delphinia.'

Terry frowned at this, in the suspicion that it was another joke. 'She's won some prizes,' he said. 'It's Badgett.'

Justin himself was slow on the uptake – it was a genuine confusion, arising perhaps from Doggett's Coat and Badge, a pub on Blackfriars Bridge where he had lost several evenings with a randy young sub from the *Sunday Express*. He thought there was no point in apologising.

'You don't need any jobs doing?' Terry asked with a vague head-shake.

Justin said, 'Robin's famous for doing all his jobs himself.'

There was a little pause. 'Are you running the disco this year?' said Robin, as though it was an event he especially looked forward to.

'Yeah, I expect so, come the holidays, come July,' said Terry quietly, and continued to nod at the difficulty of the task and his readiness to perform it. Justin could see his blue briefs through the side-pocket of the dungarees. Nothing else underneath then.

'We'll have some great music for my party,' said Danny, leaning forward from the other side and resting a hand on Terry's thigh in a split-second enactment of Justin's own fantasy. 'You're all invited,' he went on, apparently making it up on the spot. 'Two weeks' time, right here. That's cool, isn't it, Dad?'

Robin shrugged and spread his hands: 'Sure . . .' Justin saw it at once as a plan dense with potential opportunities and embarrassments. Alex obviously wouldn't be there, though he was already accepting with a show of flattered surprise; and maybe Robin too, as a parent, would see fit to pass the evening with the Halls . . . He supposed there would be drugs, which always made him uneasy, and seemed to make their users amorous but incapable.

'How old will you be, darling?' he said.

'Twenty-three,' said Danny, with a grimace at the ghastliness of it; then muttered histrionically, 'What have I *done* with my life?' At which everyone but Terry harumphed and refilled their glasses with a despairing leer.

'Well, Alex has done very well in his chosen profession, of pensions,' said Justin, and smiled to see his former lover unable to sift the compliment from the mockery. 'Robin perhaps hasn't quite fulfilled the promise of his early work on The House in the Landscape and the Landscape in the House, have you sweetie?'

'You haven't exactly broken every known fucking box-office record as an actor,' said Robin, in what was probably a parody of annoyance. Justin looked at Danny and Terry side by side, uncertain which to enlist.

'I was *in* a play,' he said.

49

Soon the party broke up, Terry called back 'Cheers' from the door, and Danny went out with him, talking quietly. Justin saw Alex start to wander after them, as if sleepily attracted, or simply from an instinct to escape; then stand in the doorway with a pretence of stretching and yawning. Upstairs in the bathroom Justin switched off the light and squatted on the low window-sill, letting his eyes adjust to the night outside: the unsuspecting trees, crowded dim moons of cow-parsley, and slowly more and more starlight on the slope of the greenhouse, on the motionless roses, and the immensity of the hill beyond. He couldn't see the boys, though occasionally he heard a louder phrase or both of them laughing, and then for a minute or more only the brook. He wanted to turn the brook off. He thought Danny would walk Terry home, through the gate in the wall and fifty yards up the shadowed lane; but there were their voices again, close by, the words indistinct, with the idling rhythms and inscrutable pauses of the overheard. Well, if Terry wanted to tell Danny what had happened, he would do so. They had woken a bird up and it gave out a series of disoriented chuckles.

5

Robin decided to go to Tytherbury on Sunday as a break from
Alex's apologetic presence and the unnecessary tensions of the
weekend. But then Tony Bowerchalke said to bring over
the whole party, not for lunch but for a drink before lunch.
Getting them into the Saab had not been easy. Alex, who had
started out unconvincingly in shorts, rushed upstairs to change
and hit his head quite hard on a beam. Then both Alex and
Justin seemed to want to sit in the back with Danny, though
Danny himself said he wanted to sit in the front. Justin won
by arguing that Alex had the longest legs, and then drove
Danny mad by playing 'round and round the garden' on his
bare forearm. Danny was clearly in a sulk after Robin's
frowning and in fact rather frightened encounter with a naked
Terry Badgett in the bathroom at 3 a.m. Perhaps after all Alex
was the best person to have in the passenger seat, with his
responsible pleasure in the villages and the riot of flowering
chestnuts and may.

As they turned in between the tall brick gate-piers Robin felt
the fresh awareness that went with showing a familiar place to
newcomers – he seemed to share their curiosity and vague
social apprehension as the pitted half-mile of the drive
unwound between dense banks of rhododendrons, fields
planted up close to the road as in wartime, eerie poplar plan-
tations with pheasant-runs in their straight alleys, through to
the horrible shock of the house itself. The kids, as Robin found
himself thinking of them, slipped reluctantly out of the car, as
though they had just been brought back to boarding-school.

Tony was standing around on the rough daisy-crowded lawn
to the left; he was evidently waiting for them with his usual
nerviness and fear of accidents, though he pretended not
to have seen them until the car-doors were arrhythmically

51

clunking shut. He hurried across, tugging down his pullover and smoothing back his flat oiled hair. Introductions were made, Tony holding the hands of Alex and Danny for a second or two to help him memorise their names. They stood in an uncertain group, loosely focused on the central feature of the gravelled circle, a bare stone plinth on which some welcoming deity or tall, nasturtium-spilling urn might once have stood, but which now presented them with nothing but a short rusty spike.

'You'd like a drink, I expect,' Tony said quickly, and after a glance at his watch led them off around, rather than through, the house. Robin let the group straggle ahead, Alex talking to their host, whom he heard say, in a tone of mild hysteria, 'Not everybody likes this style of architecture.' Robin remembered trying to convince him of its virtues as an example of 'rogue Gothic', but Tony, who had been a juvenile star at Bletchley during the war, had quickly decoded the professional euphemism.

They sat on the terrace with their backs to the house. There were a couple of old deck-chairs and two straight-backed dining-chairs, their ball-and-claw feet wispy with damp grass-cuttings; Danny, in his lively disposable way, perched slightly apart from them on the low wall. Tony peered at him gratefully and said, 'Would you all like a Campari?', as if it was their favourite; and they all pretended they would.

They looked out, frowning into the sun, at what was left of a High Victorian garden, a wide round pond with a disused fountain of crumbling tritons, like angry, pock-marked babies, at its centre; the water had dropped to show the weed-covered pipe that fed it. The surrounding parterres had all been put to grass ten years before, when help had become a hopeless problem; though here and there a curved seat or a sundial or an unkillable old rose made a puzzled allusion to the plan it had once been part of. Beyond this there was a rising avenue of chestnuts which framed the brick chimney of a successful light-industrial unit.

Tony came back out through the tall french windows ushering and encouraging Mrs Bunce, who carried the sloping drinks tray. Robin knew she would not be introduced and so called out, 'Hello, Mrs Bunce'; and she looked flattered if flustered by the attention. She was a widow whose age was disguised and somehow emphasised by her defiantly dyed hair and cardinal lipstick and remote resemblance to the Duchess of Windsor. She would have taken off her housecoat and straightened herself up before coming outside, where she played an ambiguous role as a silent hostess. Indoors she cooked and cleaned and managed the shrunken latter-day life of the huge house. Robin offered her his chair.

Soon Tony was admitting to the worry of the place, though no one had exactly asked him about it. Bits of the estate had been sold off in the sixties to meet beastly Labour taxes, the small farm was let on a long lease to a company which used allergy-causing crop-sprays. Now he was having two self-contained flats made in a part of the house that was no longer used, with a view to attracting well-heeled childless tenants from London. And then the Victorian Society had started to make a fuss about his great-grandfather's mausoleum, a vandalised curiosity in what he called the park. It was in the last two matters that Robin's practice (if you could call it that) was involved, and Tony raised his glass towards him.

'I love the house!' said Danny, grinning over their heads and up and up at the bastions of unageing red and white brick. 'It's amazing.' And more quietly, over his glass, 'It's a trip!' Tony looked pleased, but no nearer a solution to his problem.

Alex said ambiguously, 'It's stunning'; whilst Justin pulled his sunglasses from his shirt pocket and masked himself in them. On ordinary social occasions he would often be shy and ungiving.

'Did you ever think of selling the whole place?' asked Danny, as if he had a potential buyer in mind, or even wanted it himself.

'Well of course I've thought of it,' said Tony. 'They could turn it into a training college or a merchant seaman's orphanage and put up prefabs on the lawn. I don't think I could let it go – you know my mother was very happy here. I couldn't, could I . . .?'

Robin had heard him use this reasoning once or twice before and thought it must reflect a code of honour and sentiment so rarefied that Tony himself was perhaps its last surviving adherent. But Danny, whose relations with his mother were intense, seemed to take it in his stride; and Mrs Bunce said, 'So you always say, Tony.'

'It will all be fine,' said Robin, who found his function here was as much therapeutic as architectural.

Tony smiled at Danny, and said, 'I once met your grand-father. We didn't really see eye to eye. General Woodfield,' he explained to Mrs Bunce, in a tone of inseparable ridicule and respect, 'was said to be the handsomest man in Wessex. His wife, Lady Astrid, was the daughter of the Earl of Hexham.'

Mrs Bunce patted her hair apprehensively, as if about to be introduced to this magnificent couple.

Robin said, 'I'm just going to look at that plaster.' And he stepped into the house, with a surprising and childish sense of relief.

He went through the high dark drawing-room and into the hall. Most of the rooms at Tytherbury were conventional, with severe classical fireplaces and sash-windows that ran up square behind the pointed Gothic openings; though some had gloomy half-panelling and Tudor doorways. The hall was different, it was a showpiece, with a dark brick-vaulted entrance like a traitor's gate, giving on to a hair-raising staircase, with joining and dividing flights, which ran up through a great bleak shaft the height of the house. Sunlight through the crudely coloured stained glass dappled the vigorous and unattractive woodwork. For all its fantasy, it shared with the rest of the house a stripped-down, semi-furnished appearance, as if it had already been sold to one of the institutions that Tony was holding at bay. A row of hooks still projected high up, though apparently the mythological tapestries that once hung from them now lent a murkily classic air to the ballroom of a Beverly Hills mansion. Pictures, furniture and armour had been disposed of in irregular bursts over the past fifty years. Robin never knew if he found the effect haunting or depressing. He climbed to the first floor two at a time, as though it were any old staircase, and entered one of the oddly inconsequential corridors that opened off it.

The flats had been contrived in the service wing. When Tony Bowerchalke's great-grandfather had dreamt up the house, an ambitious local architect undertook the plans for him, differentiating the various offices and quarters of the male and female servants, the sculleries and pantries, the plate safe and the fuel stores. At the end of the wing was something described as 'Odd Room', provision having outrun the most ingenious requirement. Tony claimed that he and his sister had played a private version of fives in it when they were children.

Robin wasn't happy, and he didn't want to show it. He wasn't in control. Justin had insisted on sex at eight this morning and moaned and yelped like someone dubbing a porn film. They heard Alex shifting in his bed next door, and when the excitement was over Robin couldn't help imagining the effect of their grunts and laughter, and felt humiliated to have behaved so cruelly. The absence of any allusion to it in Alex's face and conversation over breakfast was a clear sign of how upset he must have been. It seemed he had made a pass at Justin yesterday, he was obviously still in love with him and having a ghastly time. Robin felt sorry for him, but in a theoretical way: his loss was Robin's gain, it would be awful to lose Justin, but Robin himself had never been left.

He stood in the Odd Room, where the new plaster had quickly dried in the hot weather from rosy chocolate to the sand-pink of a powder compact. The arcs of the workmen's floats could be faintly seen in the surface, which was marble-smooth and yet left a chalky dust on the fingertips. The room held the pleasing smell of plaster and fresh sawdust. His footsteps reverberated. He liked this clean practical phase of the project, when nothing was compromised by use.

Back outside, Mrs Bunce was collecting the glasses, and told him the rest of the party had set off to see the mausoleum, a word she produced with a lightly mocking grandeur. 'Your young man wanted to see it,' she said, by which he supposed she meant Danny. Justin would only have wanted to see it if everybody else didn't.

He saw them from the top of the field, just too far away to shout to without sounding silly. Danny and Alex were on either side of Tony, Alex stooping attentively and looking quickly about like a royal duke being shown something enterprising. Away to the left Justin wandered, swiping at grasses, unsocial, fuelled by nothing more than a weak aperitif. Robin climbed the fence and jogged down towards them; all he could think of was claiming Justin, jumping him or tackling him into the long grass.

Tytherbury had been built a little inland, out of sight of the sea, and the estate reached to the shore only at one point, a mysterious sunless combe or chine, raggedly wooded with yews and rhododendrons and overspreading cedars. A small, almost hidden stream ran down through it and under a fence and cut a wandering channel across the beach. The wood had an unusual abundance of lichens and epiphytes, which gave it the look of a dwarf rain-forest, and Tony sometimes sent obstructive letters to ecologists who wanted to study it. He had learnt his lesson with Sir Nikolaus Pevsner, whom he had entertained to dinner and given the run of his archive, and who had repaid him, in the Dorset volume of *The Buildings of England*, with a merciless sentence about the house: 'An extreme example of a justly neglected type.'

Pevsner didn't record his impressions of the chine, or of the discomforting structure perched above it, in a clearing among storm-wrecked Douglas firs: 'In the grounds, MAUSOLEUM of Thomas Light Bowerchalke. A pyramid.' After several inspections Robin found it still had its monumental effect, the steep planes of finely mortared purple brick confused the visitor's sense of scale: was it thirty feet high? Forty? Fifty? It gave a squeeze to the heart and called for a mild bravery in those who approached it. It was completely smooth, until at the very top of each face a glazed oculus let light into the unimaginable interior.

Tony hurried forward, like a put-upon sacristan, searching through his keys. The door of the pyramid was below ground level, and he seemed to step down into the earth as he entered the long ramp that led to it. Robin followed him, and Danny, and Alex and Justin with their different hesitations. Robin glanced round and saw that Justin had turned his back to have a piss. Tony was saying something about the mask over the door – an impassively staring Roman face that had been vandalised into noseless Egyptian flatness; Robin at least was never sure if it was a man or a woman. Above it there was an inscription in Greek, which no one was quite clear about, but which Tony said meant, 'He is going to his long home.' A padlocked grille covered the door, which had oxidised bronze fittings and scraped open heavily across the floor.

Inside, the first surprise was the still cold after the breezy heat of the day, and the before-dawn dimness on sun-narrowed eyes. Justin came in last with his shades on and groped his way round the happily shivering Danny. Alex was gazing at the crossing brick trusses overhead and stumbled backwards into the sarcophagus, on which he found himself demurely sitting down for a moment – a single polished slab of brown marble, quarried at Purbeck twenty miles to the east.

Robin was still puzzled by the structure of the building. Where other such pyramids he had seen, in landscaped parks and manorial churchyards across the country, contained a domed chamber, which looked almost as if quarried from the heart of a solid mass, the Tytherbury one was an open space from the sunken burial chamber to the apex. It was like being inside a church steeple, or an oast-house, except that the joists were not made of timber but of brick, and seemed to hang in narrow intersecting arcs one above the other. The effect, in the grey gleam from the weather-limed skylights, was both mysterious and claustrophobic. Tony claimed that the mosque at Córdoba had been its inspiration. It was the buckling of one of these brick strainer arches that Robin was expected to remedy. A shallow dip half-way up on the lichenous north face had alerted them to the danger. Robin explained it rather cryptically to the others, as if expecting, or even hoping, not to be understood, pointing to a spot high up that none of them could honestly see. 'How can you work on that without what's above it falling down?' asked Alex.

'I don't know', said Robin.

There were frills of damp between the courses of brick just beside them. He didn't like this building, and had a clear image, a tiny loop of film, in which it fell in on him. He found its lack of religious assurances surprisingly bleak. It was over a year since they'd buried Simon, but he was chilled and troubled by literal-minded imaginings, standing within a few feet of a dead body that must be withered and grinning after more than a century of unbelieving rest. Alex gave him a rueful smile, perhaps about the repair job, though it seemed to have some subtler intuition in it. He said, 'I never know how you know, how people ever know what will stand up.'

'Well . . .' said Robin broadly, as if it was, actually, within the competence of any intelligent adult. He thought, he'll start on stresses and strains in a minute.

'It's the whole thing of stresses and strains, isn't it?' – Alex looking away to where Justin was speaking quietly to Danny, Danny tracing a line with his toe in the gritty dust on the stone floor. 'And we certainly know something about them . . .'

And that was what Robin disliked, the spurious intimacy that Alex was ready to suggest between them, as though to bring him down to his own level of failure and niceness. Robin had what he thought of as an upper-class mistrust of niceness.

He turned away on a pretence of looking for something, to show he wasn't here merely for pleasure; he unclipped the metal tape-measure which he carried like a carpenter on his belt, and measured the low doorway, to see what might or might not be brought in. When he turned back the other four were smiling about something, standing close together just beyond the sarcophagus. He was embarrassed to hear Danny saying something about opium. Tony had once confided in him, as if it were still a problem, that his great-grandfather had been an addict; and Robin had mentioned to Danny his theory that the pyramid, and perhaps the house itself, was an attempt to realise the architectural phantasmagoria of an opium dream. He heard Tony making some hasty rejoinder, and Danny saying, 'That's so cool.'

Outside in the sunlight, hearing the door dragged to, the grille padlocked, a brief silence of readjustment among the group – his son, his lover, his guest, their sweet expectant old host – Robin wondered at his own paranoia, and made a characteristic effort to banish it: a deep breath, squaring of the shoulders, an irritable frown and then a wide handsome smile at the others. Justin was a flirt and it meant nothing, he liked to be a nuisance; when drunk he would sit on the laps of virtual strangers who had come to dinner or push himself against old friends of Robin's in little faux-fucks, like a dog. He said it was just a sign of his shyness.

Justin went ahead on the walk back, chatting to Tony in a casual suggestive way, as if to a man of his own age and experience; perhaps he was hoping to secure another drink. It made Robin feel he had been too formal with him. He watched them walking, shoulder to shoulder. The sight of Justin from behind could still startle a little noise from him, half grunt, half gasp, of lust and admiration. It was love's clear thrilled focus on its object in a blurred irrelevant field. Alex was talking to him but Robin looked only ahead, with a fixated half-smile. When he did turn, to show a form of courtesy, he saw that they had both been staring at the same thing.

In the car going home there was a mood of idle resentment among the others, as if they had behaved well for very little reward. Robin said, 'Bowerchalke's a nice old boy, isn't he,' but it was only Alex who bothered to say yes, whatever he might really have felt. Robin saw how you could play tricks on someone so self-repressing and ready to agree. 'Of course he's a silly old fool,' he said; but Alex merely gazed out of the window with a wincing smile at the sunlight from a high cloud's edge.

Justin said, in a tone both loud and confidential, 'I gather you were a very naughty boy last night, Danny.'

'Not particularly,' said Danny.

There was a little pause. 'Well, that's not what your father says, Danny.' Justin spoke like a mother who has landed the task of conveying a sad parental disappointment. 'Up till all hours hobnobbing with Terry Blodgett; and what-have-you. And you know your father's feelings about rough trade.'

'Oh do I,' said Danny.

'And don't be cheeky.'

'Terry may be rough trade to you,' said Danny, in a light bored voice, 'but he's an old friend of mine.'

'Mm, old friend maybe. But you hadn't . . . you know . . . before, had you.'

Danny made it clear that while the whole discussion was a

joke it was also beneath him. 'Only half a dozen times,' he said; which got him a scream and a slap from Justin.

'The young today. It's enough to break a mother's heart.'

'Fortunately I have a very tough-hearted mother.' Danny buzzed his window half-open, and let in a refreshing draught across the back of the car.

Robin allowed this nonsense to go on behind him, because he felt he had already said enough, and Danny was right, even though he himself was not wrong. The parental instincts that Justin was lampooning were awkwardly strong sometimes. Even though the marriage had broken up eighteen years ago, Danny's visits still left Robin with an aftertaste of disappointment, of adulterated sweetness; sometimes they had been anxious charades of the life they might have led together, but played out with an eye on the clock and a mawkishness which shifted from one to the other. The weekends, the half-vacations, were planned as treats, but for Robin were always reminders of his failure as a husband. The failure remained, however much he reinvented it as a triumph of instinct. He avoided meeting Jane, and could be severe with Danny, as if to refute some imagined accusation of negligence. He ran a good house. He wanted to know who was sleeping under his roof. He didn't want his boy turning into a slut. But Danny had come back from California last summer in a perversely independent mood, which Robin blamed feebly on Jane, a Distinguished Professor now, who wrote acclaimed books in an idiolect Robin couldn't understand.

He looked in the mirror and felt a tug of futile envy for Danny's freshness and freedoms – even a smothered mood of rivalry, having watched Terry Badgett grow up over the years and turn from one kind of trouble-maker into another. It was exciting as well as distasteful in the small hours to find Terry frowning naked into the bathroom mirror, still glowing from sex, the cast-off condom unflushed in the bowl. It was the first unignorable evidence he had seen of Danny's sex-life, and his anger surprised him, as did the lingering sense of protest.

Alex was smiling tensely at the backseat badinage. Then Danny said, with mischievous brightness, 'Justin, why don't you tell us the story of how you met Dad?' – and didn't see the full triangulation of his blunder for a moment or two, when the others started speaking simultaneously on unrelated subjects.

As they came into Litton Gambril Alex said, 'Can I buy us all lunch at the Crooked Billet?' and looked round forgivingly at his friends. There was a brief silence, the mildly raised eyebrows of hesitant acceptance, and Robin said,

'I'll get lunch at home. I mean, thank you. But we can't actually go to the Billet any more.'

'Oh,' said Alex, as if wounded by his own craving to give; the pub, with its long thatched eaves and hanging baskets, was coming up on the right. Two round-faced men, looking rakish in riding-boots, came out with sleek pint glasses in careful hands, and perched on the low wall. The odd bottle-glass panes in the window of the public winked impenetrably. The Saab went past without a wave.

'We'd been going there for years, of course,' said Robin. 'It's a nice old pub. Hardy mentions it in *Tess* as a well-known stopping-place on the old road from Bridport to Weymouth. Tess was looked after by the landlord. Unfortunately, relations with the present landlord are rather less cordial since Justin got very fresh with him, which didn't go down well, and then relieved himself in the back porch. So lunch there really isn't a possibility.'

'Does Hardy also have a bit about the lavs being the smelliest in Wessex?' said Justin.

'It's a marvellously unreconstructed pub,' Robin said.

'Like the views of most of the people in it . . .'

'Still,' Alex said, 'I'm surprised at you falling out with a publican.'

Justin sighed. 'Thank god for the Halls. Though even he turns nasty after a couple of bottles of Famous Grouse.'

Robin said, 'We do have drink in the cottage', and then, just as they were approaching the gate, braked, put the car through a bad-tempered three-point turn, and raced off. He knew he had antagonised each of the others in some fashion today, and felt a collective tension in the car; it was quite enjoyable and immediately made him feel better.

61

'My god, we're being kidnapped,' said Justin languidly. 'No doubt we shall be chained together.'

'I just realised we haven't shown Alex the cliffs,' Robin said. 'He can't go back to London without seeing the cliffs.'

'The cliffs will still be there after lunch,' said Danny, in words a father might more naturally have used to a child.

'We can have lunch in a pub in Bridport, where Justin is still unknown.'

'Well I'm paying,' said Alex. Justin reached round the head-rest and slapped him lightly on the ear.

Robin drove fast out of the village and then, instead of taking the main road along the valley, turned abruptly into a narrow lane that climbed and levelled and climbed again. He felt half-smothered in a whiteness that brushed and lurched at the car, the ragged may tumbling into banks of cow-parsley, horse-chestnuts with their balconies of dropping candles, the dazzle of sunlight through leaves flowing up over the wind-screen. There were even daisies growing in the green crown of the road. As he climbed towards blind corners he gave two or three jabs on the horn and pressed on with a gambler's instinct that there would be no contest. When he braked it was a long second after his passengers had done so.

Alex had to get out and open the gate, and Robin thought for a moment how funny it would be to leave him there and to watch him determinedly taking it as a joke when he later caught up with them. Then they powered up a wide open hillside, sending off the nearby sheep in stupid curving runs. Robin found some remembered pleasure in this off-road driving, days spent outdoors with handsome unsuspecting schoolfriends whose fathers were farmers, the boys already allowed to drive the Land-Rover, roaring and bouncing through the fields, learning handbrake turns on a disused airstrip. Once they had revved and revved and charged at a ditch, and through the fence beyond, a line of barbed wire and a rotten post flying into the air. Road driving seemed rule-bound and processional when he began with it a year later.

The cliffs along here rose to regular arched heights, with sweeping grassy shoulders between them. They were the crumb-ling cross-section of the line of hills that sheltered the inland

62

villages, and as the car trundled up the incline, with the higher gorsy crowns swelling grandly on either side, the sea-wind began to bluster around it, and in at the half-open windows. The sea was close but still invisible: Robin felt his pulse quicken at its nearness, an old excitement that was swallowed up in the dangerous acceleration of his mood. Justin started talking, with deliberate irrelevance, or as if he thought it polite to ignore the roughness and inconvenience of the journey, about a restaurant in Battersea. 'Do you know it, darling, it's a gay restaurant. It's called the Limp Ritz. It was the first restaurant in England to serve openly gay food.' Robin thought with undiminished annoyance of his aunt who, set down in front of Chartres Cathedral, went on about something she'd had to take back to Marks & Spencer's. He kept his foot down and drove straight towards the cliff edge, the sea suddenly lifting into view beyond it in a vast unconscious arc of silver green.

There were only a few seconds of fun, of calculated trouble, Danny shouting 'Dad, for god's sake!' and Justin sort of whining with fear disguised as irritation, whilst Alex stuck out a hand in front of him and was about to make a fatal grab at the wheel. Of course Robin turned in time, it was a trick, though he was shocked to find how clenched he was, and how much nearer to the edge than he intended: as the car swerved back through 180 degrees a spray of loose stones and scorched-out divots hurtled out. Justin and Danny were not wearing belts, and Danny was thrown on top of Justin, whose head smacked the window and left a feathered smear of blood on it.

6

Alex left for lunch a little early, and trotted out down the resonant staircase and through the vaulted vestibules which formed so misleading an introduction to his small, net-curtained office. In the street he unclipped his security pass, and slipped it into his suit pocket; a coach was slowly releasing a team of garish old holiday-makers, with their own badges saying 'Warren' and 'Mary-Jo' in large schoolroom script. He felt for a moment both anonymous and at home. The sunshine flashed off moving cars and vans, and gleamed in the polished visors and swords of the motionless horse-guards, but there was a lively breeze too that flapped at his jacket and span the dust around as he crossed the Horseguards Parade. He was trying not to hurry, but misjudged the traffic in the Mall, and had to hang back and then sprint to get across.

In the courtyard of the Royal Academy, under the blank windows of the various learned societies, he felt a familiar awkwardness, as though being watched, though he knew the only watcher was himself. At the top of the stairs he showed his Friend's ticket and signed his name. He sensed the grand continuity of the galleries with the building in which he worked, the pillars and architraves, the high commanding forms, and the dark-suited figures who moved among them, old or prematurely ageing, their talk, when you overheard it, both imperious and discreet. There was an astounding exhibition of sculpture from a great private collection, but the objects, which ranged from primitive grave-goods to rococo saints, from Iceland to Oceania, were commented on with the same mixture of diplomatic wariness and faintly hostile amusement as the affairs and crises of foreign countries were in Alex's place of work.

He swooped and rambled quite quickly through the first

couple of rooms, and when he saw what he was looking for in the third room he approached it obliquely, and with a pretence of donnish absorption in some other items. He inspected the chin, mouth, nose and right eye of a young man, eloquent, polished features with the slight crystalline sheen of marble, and saw them dissolve as he passed by; from behind, the fragment looked like a rough missile, or a meteorite. He came round it again and saw the splinter of face reassert itself. Then he let his gaze float to the head beyond it, a different but perceptible sheen in the crest of blond fuzz and the unweathered smoothness of the skin. The young had a bloom, it was true – despite the hooded, hung-over stare directed half-accusingly into the middle distance. Alex came forward with a grin already going and an odd third-person sense of himself as a figure unexpectedly descending. He watched closely, and with a kind of fascinated relief, as Danny's disgruntled mouth opened into a wide smile.

'Hello, Alex!'

'Hi, Danny . . .'

They shook hands, looking keenly into each other's eyes, Alex's other hand lightly gripping Danny's upper arm, feeling his quick uncertain attempt to harden up the biceps, then letting go with an admiring fingering of the stiffish grey-blue serge of his uniform. Danny shrugged his shoulders round inside the jacket and shuffled to attention. With his epaulettes and his big patch pockets and his No 3 crop he looked like a bolshy wartime recruit to the RAF, though the triangular tuft beneath the lower lip was a mid-nineties detail. The walkie-talkie in his left hand crackled, he listened to the incomprehensible message and said 'Yeah' with a little sneer of tedium for Alex's benefit.

'So how's it going?' said Alex, in an idiom that was slightly unnatural to him.

'He's a wanker, that one,' said Danny, shaking his head at the receiver in his hand. 'He's been on my back all day because I was five minutes late – if that.'

Alex smiled, sympathising, but knowing instinctively that it had been nearer half an hour. 'Don't you go mad with boredom?' he asked.

Danny gaped and slumped as if at the grossness of the understatement, but then said with a smile, 'No, it's not too bad. It's a lot better than supermarkets. There you get chatted up by housewives, here you're cruised to bits by men. This is more responsible, of course.' He stepped back to keep his eye on a woman apparently mesmerised by a sleek stone Buddha. 'They hurl their phone-numbers at you,' he said. 'I've had twelve this week.'

'Really,' said Alex, already resenting these other suitors, and confused to find he wasn't alone in thinking Danny beautiful. 'And how many have you — '

But Danny was moving warily away, as another security-man, a bald, scowling Indian who looked unlikely to receive such advances, came marching slowly through from the next gallery; with a delicate regard for Danny's position Alex sidled off to see something else, wondering at the same time if Danny really wanted to talk at all. He had worked their friendship up so much in his mind, and followed it through the coming months with such tender imagination, that it was a shock to discover he still had all the work to do. He found himself in front of a sixteenth-century Spanish Saint Sebastian made of brightly glazed pottery. Holes had been left all over it for the arrows, so that it looked like a huge anthropomorphic strainer. He imagined it being pulled from a pond and water jetting out of it for a few seconds, then slackening and dwindling to a drip.

There was no sign of Danny now, and he walked round discreetly searching for him among the thickening lunch-time crowds. He wondered, with his usual instinct for the bleakest view, if he was just another old queen hoping for the young man's favour, pressing his number on him like a supplicant bringing his absurd request to a shrine. He looked around at the detritus of old religions, vessels of exhausted magic. In front of him was a mask of blistered bronze, paper-brittle and azure with age. For a moment he remembered the broken-nosed mask on Tony Bowerchalke's pyramid. Perhaps he was wrong, but he thought something had passed between him and Danny as they groped round that unsettling building.

'Don't breathe on the objects please sir.' Danny was beside him, and slid an arm quickly round his waist.

'Are you okay?'

'Yeah, fine.' His demanding mouth twisted into a grimace. 'It's so great to see you,' he said.

'You too,' said Alex. 'I suddenly realised on my way here you might be on duty.'

'You mean you didn't come just to see me?'

'Of course I did really,' Alex said, glad that the little pleasantry was also the truth.

'I was going to give you a ring actually.'

'Oh . . .'

'See if you wanted to go out one night.'

This was exactly what Alex wanted to do, and he said, 'That would be gorgeous.'

'I felt so sorry for you last weekend,' Danny said, perhaps revealing that his motives were mainly charitable. 'What *is* the matter with my dad at the moment? Justin not giving him his Weetabix, maybe.'

'I don't think that can be it,' said Alex quietly, with a sick second of recall of the sound of the two of them at it. 'It was probably stupid of me to come.'

'No, I'm glad you did. It made it much more bearable for me, you know. I was getting such a heavy number about Terry staying over.'

'Ah yes . . .'

Danny looked around to see if they could be overheard. 'Dad's not all that together about me liking blokes.'

'Oh! . . . Well . . .'

'That stunt in the car!' Danny frowned and slowly shook his head. 'What the fuck was all that about . . .?'

Alex gave a curt unamused laugh; then said, 'He was very upset afterwards.'

'Must be the time of life . . .' Danny said, sagely or cynically, Alex couldn't tell.

A couple of young men drifted past, one of them in sunglasses as if the art might hurt his eyes, the other talking and swivelling his arm from the elbow, perhaps to explain it to his friend, but eyeing Danny lazily up and down – then gasping and stretching back to him, flicking his fingers as if he had been asked a difficult question. Eventually he said, 'Sean!'

67

Danny nodded tolerantly. 'It's Dan,' he said.

'Dan! I nearly walked right past you, in all that butch clobber. This is Hector by the way.'

Hector winced in acknowledgement.

'This is my friend Alex.'

'Pleased to meet you Alex. I'm Aubrey.' He gazed at Danny and clutched his hands to his chest in almost tearful amazement at the encounter.

'Well!' he said. 'Haven't seen you out for ages.'

'I was in the country last weekend – we both were,' said Danny, signalling Alex and giving a surprising suggestion of closeness. Aubrey looked unimpressed by this.

'Ooh, not settling down, I hope.'

'How about you?'

'I don't know . . .' He gestured in turn to the speechless, perhaps non-anglophone, Hector, and gave him an irritable sluttish stare. 'What you doing this weekend?'

'Not quite sure,' said Danny. 'May be at the Ministry tomorrow night.'

'Oh . . .' Alex murmured, wondering which Ministry, and picturing some familiar function, Danny in uniform checking bags and coats.

'It's a bit straight, isn't it? Though what's it matter when everyone's off their face anyway?' Aubrey smiled wearily. 'Can you get us on the guest-list?' Alex thought that would be pretty unlikely, unless it was somewhere very socially compromised, like Ag and Fish.

'Look, I'm not supposed to talk to people when I'm on duty,' Danny said, and pointed to the tab on his shoulder, on which the word ALERT was embroidered.

Aubrey took it well. 'All right, doll, well maybe see you' – giving him a kiss on the cheek, which was obviously also not allowed. Hector smiled and shook hands firmly, as if after an invigorating exchange of views.

'Shagged them both,' said Danny, when the couple had turned the corner; 'though Aubrey doesn't know that.' He glanced around naughtily. 'Hector is' – and he merely mouthed the word 'huge', with a comic mime of staring incredulity. He walked off, in his squashy, slightly squeaky Doc Martens, but turned, in front of a long Greek lion. 'I'll ring you tonight . . . but Saturday, okay. Keep it free.' And he gave him the smile again, which to Alex seemed more than ever private and unpredictable, like something you might normally only discover with more intimate knowledge of a person, like Hector's hugeness, but which to him was far more exciting than anything like that.

On the way back to the office he realised he'd forgotten to have lunch, and ate a sandwich on a bench in St James's Square. The plane-trees, in their grandly reluctant way, were only just coming into leaf. Alex felt the beautiful unwise emotions of something starting up, and grinned to himself between bites, as if his sandwich was unaccountably delicious; though what he was savouring was the longed-for surprise of being wanted. He looked up, with a sense of being still in the exhibition, at the statue of William of Orange on its tall plinth. The king was heroically bare-chested, and reined his horse back with a glare into the future he was destined to command. The horse's high bronze foreleg was frozen in the air – and Alex pictured it plunging forward, along the paths and away under the trees.

Danny lived just off Ladbroke Grove in a tall terrace house which until last Christmas had been a private hotel. Beside the front door the words HOT AND COLD and APPROVED could still faintly be seen through a covering of whitewash. Alex arrived early and walked on past; he wasn't sure how keen he should appear to be, though he had been thinking ravenously about Danny for the past two days. He had forgotten the mood of a new affair, the compulsive mix of risk and reassurance. He had spent an hour that morning in Sloane Street having his hair made fractionally shorter; and more than an hour walking about the house in different clothes and glancing soulfully but self-critically into mirrors. He never put on weight and at thirty-six could still wear everything he owned. He found himself zipping up jeans and laboriously unbuttoning shirts he hadn't touched since long before he met Justin; some of them were probably fashionable again, though others, he was pretty sure, were merely evidence of a styleless past. He finally left home in blue jeans, a white T-shirt and a short black leather jacket, an anonymously classic effect which belied the carnival of uncertainty that had produced it.

So this was Danny's neighbourhood. Alex wondered if he ever used that gloomy, velvet-curtained pub, the Chepstow Castle – though of course gay men nowadays were meant to use bars, where there was nowhere to sit down and the drinks cost twice as much. There was a launderette, a caged West Indian off-licence, and an Italian restaurant which looked attractively mysterious from outside, though photos in the window showed the interior as a hell of crowded tables, sadistic gypsy fiddlers and dangling Chianti bottles. He thought of the evening he'd been meant to spend, *Traviata* and then dinner with his old friend Hugh, and Hugh's swiftly hidden envy when he learned why he'd been chucked.

He came back and searched the tall panel of bells. A housing trust now ran the place and seemed to have welcomed in an extraordinary number of people. The bell marked 'Woodfield' was near the bottom, and seeing the name again, with its trilling resonance of sexual power, Alex felt the incongruity of chasing after Robin's son. He wasn't sure if he was taking a devious revenge on Robin for stealing Justin, or if he was helplessly joining Justin under the spell of the family. But then Danny himself was jumping at him with a kiss on the cheek and a tight hug that was almost aggressive.

He led him through to a tall room at the back of the house, with a window open above the garden. It still had the built-in cupboards and corner washbasin of its hotel days and an overwhelming wallpaper of bunched pink roses on a pale yellow ground. There were various house-plants, some thrusting and barbed, others droopy and sprawling, like conflicting moods. 'I've just got to get ready,' Danny said, half-unbuttoning his shirt and pulling it over his head like a kid rushing for games. Alex smiled at him, and tried to look casually at his lean hairless torso, the surprisingly fleshy brown nipples. He immediately loved the ordinariness of him as well as the oddity. When Danny turned and stooped to splash water from the basin on his face and neck Alex saw the small blue knot, like something from a scouting manual, tattooed on his

70

left shoulder-blade. He felt abashed that Danny had already marked himself for life; he turned away and slouched about the room in such a relaxed fashion that he looked as if he might fall over.

He took in the jumble on the mantelpiece, but didn't study the curling snapshots too closely for fear of cutting himself on the grins and glints of Danny's world. He had an impression of life as a party, as a parade of flash-lit hugs and kisses, in a magic zone where everyone was young and found to be beautiful. He drifted over to the bed, which was wide and low, with a red cotton bedspread neatly pulled up. Danny's phrase about 'shagging' Aubrey and Hector came back to him.

'Now what shall I wear?' Danny said, towelling his head and coming over to Alex with half a smile and the peculiar promise he seemed to give off that there was going to be fun.

'I'm not the person to ask,' Alex said, uncertain whether to admit to his own dress anxieties, his desire to fit in while still somehow being himself. He saw that since Justin had gone he was in tatters as a social being; he didn't know what effect to make, or how to make it.

'You look great,' said Danny, with an emphasis on each word, as if contradicting someone else. He crouched to undo his shoes, then stood and unbuttoned his trousers and wiggled his hips to make them fall down. Alex felt a bit breathless.

'Oh yes,' he said inside his head, with a split-second glance at the leftward tumble in Danny's black boxer-shorts. He wondered if he was meant to make a move on him now, and if he would always regret not doing so, but Danny turned and opened the big cupboard, in which clothes were hung or folded in a way which suggested discipline and self-respect. And in a couple of minutes he was dressed, in green and beige gingham bags that might have been made from the curtains of a holiday caravan, and a loose pink tank-top and a white sleeveless shirt left open and hanging out; he sat on the bed to pull on black trainers with soles suggestive of a specialised orthopaedic need.

'Do you want some white wine?'

Alex said yes, and Danny went out to the kitchen, leaving

the door open – he could hear him talking to someone. He went to the window, so as to be somewhere when Danny returned, and gazed out at the tangled garden and at other figures getting dressed and undressed and pouring themselves drinks in the tall back windows of the next terrace. That brief routine, the stripping, the picking out of different clothes, had moved Alex and confused him. He saw how long it was since he had shared such unselfconscious moments with another man, or even allowed himself to think in terms of his own happiness. He had a sense of the danger of it, like the neglected reminder of an old injury, as well as an amazed absorption in Danny; he found himself forgetting that Danny was fourteen years younger – or half-forgetting: the clothes he had finally chosen were a cheery signal of the distance between them.

Danny came back in still talking unencouragingly to the man from the kitchen, who had a black pony-tail and bare feet and looked as if he had just got up. 'Yeah . . . great . . . okay . . . I'll let you know . . .'

'I'm Dobbin,' said the man, leaning in the doorway and scratching himself.

'Hi,' said Alex cautiously. 'Alex.'

'Alex. Nice one.' Dobbin winced. 'That was some fierce gear,' he went on, as if Alex knew what he was talking about. They both looked vaguely at Danny's trousers.

'We've got some stuff to do,' said Danny. 'I'll catch you later.'

'Okay, man.' Dobbin winked a gummy eye and wandered away, maybe hoping to be reminded where he was or what he was supposed to be doing.

'Dobbin's had a little bit of a heavy night on Special K,' said Danny, in the tolerant sotto voce of a well-paid nurse.

'Oh . . .' said Alex, who had a sympathetic regard for bowel troubles. 'He probably needed something stronger.'

Danny smiled at him narrowly and Alex felt he had missed an allusion. And then how could Dobbin's night be finishing at 8.30 p.m.? They raised their glasses and began to drink.

By the time they left the house they were both a little hectic

72

from the wine, though Alex began talking responsibly about dinner. There was a harmless tension between them as to who was in charge. Alex kept glancing over his shoulder for a taxi, and gave amusing descriptions of various expensive restaurants that he liked, in each of which he had already pictured the two of them dining in old-world gloom or unsparing post-modern glamour. Danny bounced along the pavement saying 'Yeah' and 'Sounds great' with indiscriminate enthusiasm. One or two of the places Alex listed had strong associations with Justin and with nights of memorable happiness or misery, and in either case seemed to offer the furtive prospect of an exorcism. Alex longed to reinhabit the disused wings of his life. He felt the tingle of benign power in having someone to pay for again.

In the taxi his hand lay on the seat in the early dusk between them; when he glanced forward he saw the wild pink aftermath of the sunset reflected in the wing-mirrors. The cab rattled along the length of the Park, with the windows down and a cool draught that took away the need to say anything much. At the lights they felt the brief proximity of roller-bladers under the trees, and the evening's ordinary flux of pent-up energy and fatigue. When Alex looked quickly at Danny he saw something mischievous and self-absorbed in him that he hadn't noticed in Dorset; the half-bottle of wine had freed him up surprisingly and in the running shadow and glare his face seemed coloured by suppressed or anticipated amusement.

They got out in Soho, where the cab was immediately taken by someone else and whisked off, leaving Alex with an odd subliminal feeling of no return. He'd forgotten how crowded the streets were, and wondered if in fact they had been quite so busy in the old days. Danny's mobile phone rang, and he turned away to laugh and jabber into it, while Alex stood and was bumped into. There was something festive about the streams of people; but he felt he hadn't yet entered the fun. He thought of his usual Saturday nights in Hammersmith, with only the noise of dinner-parties breaking up, and then the distant rumble of the Great West Road; and the weekend, once a month or so, with his parents near Chelmsford – the firm sympathetic grip they had on him since Justin had left.

'Come on,' said Danny. 'Day-dreaming.'

73

'Where are we going?'

'I've got to try and find someone.' He took Alex's hand, but people barged between them and he let go. He followed on, caught up with him, then was suddenly alone when Danny stopped to hug and kiss someone. Which was how it continued. He began to think they would never get to the end of Old Compton Street. Danny knew every beautiful or interesting-looking person who came towards them, and those he didn't know were registered, with a raised eyebrow or turn of the head, for future investigation. A bar or café with its tables out on the street could take five minutes to get past while he squeezed in between the chairs, bestowed stooping embraces, sat briefly on people's laps and uttered bursts of mildly hilarious nonsense, underpinned by casual hand-holdings and caresses. Alex couldn't tell if he was a star or a mascot. 'This is my friend Alex,' he said punctiliously to everyone, and several of them found the time to say 'Hello', or at least 'Hi', and give him a cursory upward glance, before getting on with their chat, during which Alex stood about with a distant but forgiving expression. He felt somehow provincial, and afraid of showing his ignorance. Words like Trade, Miss Pamela and Guest-list were produced and received with the gratified ennui accorded to a well-established ritual. Anecdotes of excess got the most laughs, and Danny himself carried one or two that he heard to the next little group, in an easy pollination of gossip. When he moved on he waved impatiently as if it was Alex who was keeping him waiting. 'Come on,' he said. Alex knew already he would do whatever he said. He thought he was showing off by marking his place in this world so insistently, it was really quite childish. But then he saw his own childish longing to be known and greeted in a world other than a third-floor corridor in Whitehall.

In the restaurant Danny was rather quiet and ordered only one course, as if hoping to discharge a social obligation as quickly as possible, while Alex chose a soufflé with a twenty-minute handicap. They had a table in the window, and Danny sat breaking up bread and looking out past Alex's shoulder at the parade of pleasure-seekers outside. At first he said 'Yes . . . yes' with distracted regularity while Alex was telling him

74

sweetly self-deprecating stories about the office: he had never had any special arts of courtship, being very nice was his only technique. He watched Danny's cool grey eyes slide from right to left, passing briefly over the obstacle of himself. He said, 'I'm sorry, it's a bit dull in here', feeling the gloom and discretion of the restaurant as if they were expressions of his own character, or indictments of it. He seemed to have picked the one place among these gay blocks that was still a haven for heterosexuals. Then Danny smiled enormously, and reached across to touch Alex's arm. He leant forward, and re-angled his attention – it was a change of gear that thrilled Alex and slightly unnerved him, since he had seen Robin do just the same thing the previous weekend, in a physical convulsion of remembered manners; he had been glad of it and doubted it at the same time.

Danny said, 'I wonder what Dad and Justin are up to this weekend.'

Alex looked at his watch. 'Ten fifteen. I don't know about . . . your father, but Justin will be drunk.'

'Mm,' said Danny nostalgically, and pulled the bottle out of the ice. He was drinking quickly but not heavily – it was the acceleration of the evening, which Alex only resisted because he couldn't tell where it was going. 'Did he always drink that much?'

It was a hard and posthumous-sounding question, like something asked in court. Alex wasn't sure whether to protect Justin or expose him. 'It varied. He never really gets hangovers, I don't know why. It's never really been a problem. He drank a lot last year, after his father died. That was a bad time for us. The beginning of the end, I suppose.' Alex found himself looking into the shallow bowl of a camera obscura in which a country scene was projected, lawns and chestnut-trees, a saturation of green, the agonising stupor of a summer day, Justin in a dark suit walking steadily away from him. 'After the funeral things were never the same.'

'When was that?'

It really wasn't what Alex wanted to think about – it was everything he was trying at last to escape, and it gave him a sense of foreboding to have it conjured up by the beautiful

75

young man he hoped would be Justin's replacement. 'Exactly a year ago.'

Danny seemed to be working it out. 'So when did he meet Dad?'

'Actually, I'm not sure. Some time after that.'

Danny was already laughing. 'And we won't go into *how* they met.'

'No, quite,' said Alex plonkingly, to hide the fact that he didn't know and never wanted to. When at last the food arrived, the waiter drained the bottle into Danny's glass and accepted his enthusiastic nod at the suggestion of another one.

'He's quite a change from Simon,' Danny said, holding his knife and fork straight up as his eyes explored a plate of capriciously disguised cuts of guinea-fowl. And again he seemed to be smiling at a recollection he couldn't politely explain. 'Quite a change . . .'

There might have been some mockery of Justin in the air, and again Alex, who knew better than anyone what Justin's failings were, was surprised to find himself lightly wounded on his behalf. 'Why, what's Simon like?'

Danny waited till he'd finished chewing and then said, 'You'd have to ask in Golders Green cemetery', and laughed quietly and bleakly. 'No, he died last year.'

Alex raised his eyebrows and nodded, taking in the fact and with it a sense that he might have been unfair to Robin, whom he'd thought of up to now as a mere loose libido, a lordly saboteur of other people's happiness. 'AIDS?'

Danny paused and said, 'Yeah', as if it was unnecessary or even bad form to mention it.

'But . . . Robin's okay?'

'Oh yes.' And with a grin: 'My impression is he's always been a pitcher not a catcher.' Alex wasn't sure if they both saw the double meaning. He was oppressed again by his own dark inner loop, the melting fade into fade into fade of his memories of sex with Justin. 'This is delicious by the way.'

'Good – this is too,' Alex said, though even the fugitive demands of a soufflé were a little much for his amorously shrunken appetite.

'I mean he looks different, Simon was dark, I suppose they

both had rather gorgeous bums. Do you think people always go for the same type?'

Alex wondered this about himself; part of the point of Danny was that he wasn't like Justin. 'It can be very nice to have a change. Some people have to have a blond, or can only get it up with black guys, or only like short people.' He sounded stolidly expert.

'Yeah, what about you?'

'Well, almost everyone's short to me. Though I admit I never quite see the point of other tall people.'

'I like the way they go on and on,' Danny said impressionistically.

'Do you?' Alex gave a grateful smile.

'I do,' said Danny, acting sly.

Alex loved being with him, it went off like a rocket in his heart, the fierce ascent and all the soft explosions of descending stars. He wanted passers-by to stop and watch them leaning together in the candlelight and speculate enviously about them. He said, 'I suppose the thing is, with types, it's not so much the look as the psychological thing. Whether you're drawn to givers or takers.'

'Mm . . .'

'I've got a ruinous taste for takers.'

Danny was picking ferally at the last brown-mauve flesh on a white bone. 'That's just a typically modest way of saying you're a giver,' he said, smiling with grease on his lips. 'It's really sweet of you to take me out to dinner.'

'It's a pleasure, darling,' Alex murmured, obliterating, with the gentle pounce of his endearment, a momentary discontent – he hadn't yet said he was treating him, so Danny had robbed him of a moving gesture later in his synopsis for the evening. It was strangely as if Danny knew this when he said,

'I really want you to have a good time tonight. This is your night.'

'Is it? Thank you . . .' said Alex, though still with a feeling that he was being pitied or at least humoured, and that it was 'his' night in the exceptional way that a birthday was, or the annual visit to town of a terrified old relative. 'Well, I'm in your hands.'

Danny nodded his head with a firm, self-confident moue. 'I thought we could go to Château, it's pretty fantastic right now. If you'd like to.'

'Great,' said Alex. He'd seen the club's name fly-posted over derelict shops and on switch-boxes at traffic-lights, and would recognise its logo of an exploding castle. If it had truly been his night he would never have thought of going there. But he kept to his deepening sense that he must put his trust in Danny, who had been sent by the magic of coincidence to take care of him. And he loved dancing, even if he hadn't done it much in the past ten years; when he imagined bopping around it was to a song called 'Let's Hear It for the Boy', which he knew had been the big hit of summer 84. Sometimes he walked past the queue of a club after a dinner in the West End, saw people keyed-up in front of the ropes, and felt his own inhibitions like forces in the air, dark columns of crushing barometric pressure.

While they waited for coffee Danny went to the loo. Alex watched his swinging shirt-tail as he sauntered between the tables where suited older men and their glossily coiffed women were expensively stuffing themselves. He found there was something sexy after all in having come to this starchy place, where he and Danny struck a note of casual deviance. Then he watched him coming back, the unemphasised beauty of his strong young body in the bright baggy clothes, the mixture in his face of natural eagerness and moody self-possession. Alex thought to himself, 'This isn't going to happen', and at once offset the idea with a resolution that he would simply get what fun he could from it. The mechanism of disappointment in him was rapid and supple with use.

The coffee came, and Danny sat back, turning the little cup with outstretched fingers. 'Have you ever done E?' he said, and gave him an amiably calculating look.

Alex said, 'No', firmly and quietly, perhaps primly. 'No, I'm a narcotics virgin, really'; he might as well own up, and indeed he wasn't ashamed of this, though his choice of words seemed to hint at the need for a deflowering.

'Nothing?' said Danny, with kindly incredulity. 'Never?'

Alex pondered. 'Well, you had to smoke dope at school. But it never did much for me – I stopped when I grew up.'

78

'Ouch,' whispered Danny.

'You know what I mean.'

'Didn't you and Justin do drugs?'

'Justin has a horror of drugs – if you don't count alcohol, of course.' Alex paused, still unsure if he should talk about the foibles and phobias of someone he loved and who now stood in a nameless relation – uncle, stepmother – to Danny himself. 'He had a bad trip on acid once, when he was a student. He looked in a mirror and his face was all made of animals. He never took anything after that.'

'Very Arcimboldo', said Danny.

Alex was looking ahead, down an avenue of easy-going criminality, with busy shadows between the wide-spaced pools of light. He was pliant and emotional with drink, and said humbly, 'You'd have to look after me.'

Apparently Dave, a friend of Dobbin's, was the man they had to find. When they were out in the street, Danny recovered his air of bossiness and mystery, like a prefect in the school of pleasure. He conferred on the mobile for a minute, then led the way through a couple of alleys, with people pissing and snogging in them, and out into another busy street, bright with restaurants and cafés, and crowds of drunks threading among the stalled traffic. Alex looked up at the narrow strip of night sky, a pinkish grey, any stars smothered by the glare of the district. Then he found Danny had doubled back abruptly and darted in through the door of a shop; Alex followed him as the strings of the bead curtain swung into his face.

Dave sat among the shiny flesh-colours of shrink-wrapped pornography and rubber sex-aids like a big black deity in a garish little shrine. He had the jaw and the firm weight of a boxer, but his hair was dyed, like blond astrakhan, and his voice was jaded and high as he tried to hustle a punter into buying a video. 'Yeah, you'll like it. There's a bit of leather in it. It's got older guys. You don't like that? Well, it's got plenty of young guys too. It's got everything really . . .' He winked at Danny as the man, with a briefcase under his arm and perhaps a train to catch, squinted hotly at the TV screen on which an extract was playing. 'Can I help you?' he said to Alex, as if dealing with a notorious browser. Alex jumped and clung to Danny's arm.

'We're together!'

He felt compromised being here, he found pornography depressing, and the glimpse of the video, in which a man was rolling a condom on, was a flustering anticipation of what he hoped himself to be doing in a few hours' time. He stepped back and wandered round, insofar as wandering was possible, coming face to face with the raring phallus at every turn, like a surreal sequence in a fifties thriller: there was no escape from his depravity. He picked up a magazine called *Big Latin Dicks*, a title more blunt than exotic; *penes magni*, he thought, and for some reason found himself imagining the men who printed it, perhaps as equably as if it were *Homes and Gardens*, and the men who put it together ('What does your dad do, by the way?' 'He's the deputy editor of *Big Latin Dicks*. I thought everyone knew that.')

Now they were alone and Dave and Danny were talking coolly about doves, pyramids and bulldogs. Alex wasn't innocent to this of course, and found it had an anxious-making glamour. Dave stood about in the shop, in his tight pin-stripe jeans. 'I had Tony Betteridge MP in again tonight', he said.

'What was he after?'

'Oh the usual. I sold him this piss video, that's his thing, *We Aim to Please* it's called, great title. He said, "I've had this video before." I said, "I thought you were into recycling." '

Alex sort of got it, and actually that was one of Justin's preoccupations that he never went along with. He wondered if Robin was more obliging. 'I didn't know he was gay', he said.

'I ought to have photos of them outside, the MPs and that. What do you call it . . . "by appointment".'

'Testimonials,' said Danny.

'So what was it?' Dave asked, with a seller's confident return to the subject of mutual interest. Danny took Alex aside and muttered,

'Have you got sixty quid?'

Alex paused. 'I can get it.'

He slipped out of the shop and hurried up the street, already half-expecting to be jumped by the drug-squad, and possibly the vice boys too.

He paid off the taxi outside the club, and kept close to Danny as they strode past the hundreds of people queuing. At the crowd barrier Danny leant over and kissed the bomber-jacketed security guy on the lips, a few jeering fondnesses were exchanged, and that was all it took – the barrier was pushed back and they walked through, a ripple of nods and calls going over their heads from echelon to echelon of bouncers and greeters to signal their exemption and desirability. Inside the door a beautiful black woman as tall as Alex said 'Hello darling' in a chocolatey baritone.

They were moving at once in the element of music, the earth-tremor bass and penetrating shimmer of high metallic noise. Alex checked his jacket, and as he stepped down with Danny on to the edge of the immense dance-floor, swept by brilliant unpredictable stabs of light, a shiver of recognition ran up him from his heels to his scalp, where it lingered and then gently dropped downwards again through his shoulders and spine. On the wall behind him was a sign saying 'Dangerously Loud Music'. Alex was shocked and laughing at the sound. Crowds of men were moving in blurred inexhaustible unison with it. Others, in tiny shorts and lace-up boots, danced alone on platforms above the heads of the crowd, some strutting like strippers, others sprinting on the spot with a flickering sema-phore of the arms. And all around the floor, and trailing away into other unguessed spaces, there was an endless jostling parade of half-naked men, faces glowing with happiness and lust. Alex howled 'Do you want a drink?' into Danny's ear.

They took their Es at the bar. 'Get yer gear down yer neck,' Danny said, with a big rascally grin, pushing the tab between Alex's lips with his thumb to make sure it went home, but watching him carefully too as he swallowed and screwed up his face at the bitter admonitory taste.

'Anything that tastes that bad must be good for you,' Alex said, imagining the small grey pill tumbling down inside, dispersing its molecules of pleasure and risk. Danny knocked his back with a swig of Vittel.

'You're going to have a fabulous time,' he said. He pulled Alex's head down close to his and shouted confidentially, 'You tell me if you feel anything bad, if you're not well – tell me straight away.'

'I will darling.'

'You're going to have a fabulous time!' He was jiggling about and his smile seemed full of affection and something close to mockery as he watched Alex drifting towards his unimagined thrill. 'I'm really envious.'

'But you're doing it too.'

Danny shook his head. 'There's nothing like the first time.'

Even so, within a few minutes Alex saw him altering. They were out on the floor, in their own disputed little space among the thrashing dancers. Everyone was staring, but like people gripped by thought, without much knowing what they were looking at. Alex kept being jabbed by elbows and hands that milled to the beat like tick-tack or lightning kung-fu. The boys glistened and pawed at the ground. They looked like members of some dodgy brainwashing cult. Alex pursed his lips at so much willing slavery, and imagined it all going wrong for him, and the incomprehension of his family and colleagues as to why he had done it. He felt abruptly sober and self-conscious about his expressive, old-fashioned 1984 style of dancing. Danny flung an arm round his neck in his sweet way, and he was warm and excited, like a drunk who has lost his sense of the other person and asks a question because he wants to tell you something. 'How are you feeling?'

'Fine,' said Alex, with vague irritable pride, like someone immune to tickling or hypnosis. 'I mean, I don't feel anything.'

'God – I'm spinning!' Danny said, but drew away from him very slowly, his hand round his waist. Another little clinch. 'Tell me if you don't feel okay.'

'Yes, darling.' He saw it wasn't quite like drunkenness, Justin for one was never so trusting and attentive. Danny danced up against him, lovingly, but unaware how he was lurching into him.

After thirty minutes Alex acknowledged to himself that he

felt quite pleasant, but he could easily argue the feeling away as the elation of drink and dancing and the company of a thousand half-naked men. Though the men were beautiful, it was true, in the cascades and strafings of coloured light. Each of the men round him seemed somehow distinct and interesting, in a way he hadn't understood when he wandered in past the long line of cropped heads and top-heavy torsos. But of course people were unique, one tended to forget. He twirled round with a smile and saw Danny getting out of his short-sleeved shirt without stopping dancing. He thought he was lost in a world of his own, chewing and licking his lips, fumbling as he tucked the shirt through a belt-loop. Then both arms were round Alex's neck:

'Fuck, these are strong, I'm going to sit down for a bit.'

Alex hugged him loosely, with a slight queasy sense that in fact it was he who was going to have to look after his guide. Danny took his hand and they sidled through the crowd and flung themselves down on a wide raised step that ran along the wall. Others were there already, heads nodding, dancing in a way though they were sitting down. Alex still felt shocked at this wholesale surrender to the drug, but the abandon was beautiful too, he could see that. The music built and built in ways that were inevitable but still exceeded anything you could expect – arms were raised towards it in a thronging silhouette against jets of dry ice; and that was the last time Alex saw anything sinister or inhuman in it.

Danny said, as if unaware of a break in the conversation, 'Wow. How are you feeling, darling?'

'Fine. I don't feel anything much yet' – with an exaggerated desire not to exaggerate, to be sure of whatever happened when it did. He looked at his watch.

'How long?'

'Forty-five minutes.'

'Just sit back, breathe deeply, don't fight it, Alex!' – with a tiny spurt of annoyance, as if the novice was stubbornly defying the master.

He did as he was told, and found himself putting an arm round Danny, his fingers playing dreamily on his bare biceps,

83

his head against the wall rocking as the music climaxed and broke off in gorgeous piano chords.

'Mmm. The music's fabulous.'

'I know.'

'What do you call this music?'

'It's house.'

'So this is house. Why's it called that?'

'Not sure actually.'

'It's fabulous.'

'I know.' Danny smiled at him with what might already have been the tenderness of love when it is first revealed. 'Go with it . . . Think what you want. Say anything you want.'

He didn't know about that. He closed his eyes and snorted in air as if about to dive for something he'd lost. Now Danny's arm was looped over his knee, his hand fondly but abstractly stroking his shin, which had never seemed so sensitive a place. The music pounded and dazzled but had its origin in somewhere subtly different, grand and cavernous; yet when Danny spoke again he didn't need to shout – it was as if they'd been granted a magical intimacy in the heart of a thunderstorm. What he said was, 'Fuck, this is good.' And then again, with what seemed an angelic concern, 'Tell me straight away if you don't feel all right.'

Alex felt a trace of shyness still because what he wanted to say was deeply to do with Danny. He closed his eyes and his mind sped ahead down the glittering tracks of sound. It wasn't a hallucination, but he saw his own happiness as wave on wave of lustrous darkness, each with a glimmering fringe of light. The words when they came were totally inadequate, but he knew at once that Danny would understand them and read his indescribable sensations back into the tawdry syllables. He said, 'I feel ravishingly happy. I've never felt so happy.'

Danny had his arm round Alex's shoulders, they half twisted towards each other and kissed, though the wonderful thing was the silky feel of Danny's neck and arms and the heat of him in the sweat-damp tank-top. Alex saw that what he most wanted was happening and groped marvellingly between the different kinds of happiness, the chemicals and the sex. It seemed that happening and happiness were the same, he must

84

remember that, to tell everyone. Danny sat behind him and hugged and stroked him. Wherever he touched him little shivers swept over his skin. Alex gripped and stroked the arms that were stroking him, and pulled Danny's feet round inside his legs. He wanted them to touch all over simultaneously. He could feel Danny's nipples as they rubbed against his tingling back.

They were dancing in the middle of the floor, in a loose group with some other friends of Danny's. Alex had never felt so agile or so energised. He pulled off his wet T-shirt, and knew what a shining streak of sinewy beauty he was from the way people looked at him and lightly touched him. His thick black hair was soaked, and fell forward and was flung back. He danced like everyone else now, but better, more remarkably. He found himself staring rapturously at the dancers around him – it was never deliberate, it was as if he woke up to find his gaze locked with a grinning stranger's. Or he was suddenly talking to someone, or taking a drink from their bottle. Everything was immediate, but seemed to have started, unnoticed, a few seconds before. The music possessed him, he lived it with his whole body, but his ear had become so spacious and analytic that he could hear quite distinctly the hubbub of everyone talking, like the booming whisper of tourists in a cathedral.

Danny left him in the bar with a friend of his, a muscly young Norwegian with silver blond hair. 'You look a bit like Justin,' Alex said to him, with a laugh at how little he cared about Justin or anything that had hurt him in the past.

'Do I now,' said the blond.

'Do you know Justin?'

'No, darling, but don't worry about it. This is your first time, right?'

Alex loved the Norwegian's accent, and his fluency in English. 'You're gorgeous,' he said, and they bumped their lips together in an unsentimental kiss.

'You're pretty cute yourself, as a matter of fact. You're feeling quite great, am I right?'

Alex just laughed and shook his head, and gripped his friend tighter. There were three of them now, Dave from the porn-shop had his arms around them both, and Alex kissed him on the cheek and kept squeezing the back of his neck in a state of almost unconscious oneness with him. He had never done more than shake hands with a black man, or tackle one perhaps in a school rugger game – he sighed at how black he was, and ran his fingers in slow arcs up and down the small of his back.

'Those pills were all right then . . .'

Alex was trying to formulate an amazing truth. He confided it first to Dave, as the purveyor of all this bliss, and then to the blond. 'I feel so happy I wouldn't care if I died.'

'Oh don't do that!' said the Norwegian, in his practical way. 'You can always get happy again.'

Alex kissed the two strangers and they stood and caressed him for minute after minute with the indulgent smiles of all-knowing, all-forgiving friends.

He was parched and drank a little bottle of Lucozade. He twisted his watch to the light and saw he'd been here nearly three hours. He knew he had to have a piss and roamed off from his guardians with a vague idea of where the lavs were. Walking was somehow harder than dancing, and he almost lost his footing on some stairs littered with empty plastic bottles. In the passageway a shirtless blond boy was dancing in front of him, beaming, pupils dilated, alight with drugs. He hugged him, and they started snogging – there was a tiny round bolt through his tongue, which lolled and probed and rattled against Alex's teeth whilst their hands gripped each other's backsides and they swung about with fierce hilarious grunts and gasps. Alex pushed him slowly away, with soft pecks on his nose and forehead, and when he looked back a few seconds later he could see that the boy had already forgotten him.

Waiting in the ringing brightness of the lavatory he felt a tinge of loneliness, and wondered where Danny was. Everyone was busy here, men in pairs queuing for the lock-ups, others in shorts or torn jeans nodding tightly to the music, caught in their accelerating inner worlds. A guy in fatigues half-turned and beckoned him over to share his stall – Alex leant on his shoulder and looked down at his big curved dick peeing in intermittent spurts. He unbuttoned and slid in his hand and for a moment couldn't find his own dick, he thought perhaps at some stage in the zipping forgotten hours he'd had a sex-change, but there it was, so shrivelled that he shielded it from his friend, who said, 'You're all right, you're off your face', and 'You can do it', and then, hungrily, 'Well, give us a look', while he stroked himself and stared and stared.

An hour or more later Alex was sprawled in a chill-out room with his arm round Danny, chewing gum, still rocking and tapping to the music in the vaster space beyond. There were fluorescent hangings that absorbed him for long periods. The blue was transcendent, infinitely beautiful, all-sufficient. And then the *red* . . . People drifted past, or sat down touching them as if they were old friends and said 'All right?' Sometimes they were friends of Danny's, and they hunkered down peaceably for five minutes and said nothing much, though everything they did say was charming and inexplicably to the point. The giddy excitement of earlier had subsided into a perfect calm without boundaries, across which figures moved with something of their vivid drug presence still about them. Once a boy called Barry something, whom Alex sometimes passed in the corridor at work, loomed up in front of him open-mouthed and doubting, and after a moment's thought said, 'No, you look like Alex, but you're not Alex', and went on his way.

Danny shifted round so that they were face to face, their legs hooked round each other as though they were talking in bed. 'All right?' he said.

'Yes, darling. I know why it's called house music, by the way.'

A humorous pause. 'Why's that?'

'It's because you just want to live in it.'

Danny pushed his hand through Alex's hair and kissed him. 'Do you want your other E?'

He was interested to find that he didn't. 'I wouldn't mind just lying here for ever.'

But Danny was a little moody and restless. 'Yeah, I've really come down now.'

'Well, do you want another?' The idea seemed grossly greedy, like eating dinner straight after lunch; though he'd read about how people did four, or six, or twelve. He couldn't imagine anything better than what he was still going through.

87

'Nah . . .' Danny was struggling to his feet, and looking down to help Alex up, as though he were pregnant and delicate with his own happiness. 'Let's go home,' he said.

Justin listened to the bang of the front door, the brisk and wounded footsteps up the path, the remoter thump of the car door, the noise of the car starting up and then swiftly receding. When Robin worked at home Justin seemed naturally to sleep on, but now that he had the cottage to himself he felt relieved and alert. He rolled over on to Robin's side of the bed. They had been keeping to their own sides all week, and he snuffled up his lover's smells from the sheet and pillowcase with a fetishistic pleasure that was keener at the moment than his feelings about him in person. To wake up to the smell of Robin after a night of sex and before another mumbling half-conscious morning bout was the firmest promise of happiness that Justin could expect; but he refused to wheedle him out of his sulks, and admired his own connoisseurial way of enjoying him in his absence.

Nothing had been quite right since the weekend with Alex. Justin opened the door in his fantasy of that Sunday morning and had Alex join them in bed for a rivalrous threesome. Alex never sulked and never refused him. He had to admit that the shock of seeing him again had brought a hidden trail of quiet after-shocks. He didn't know at the time why he'd asked him down, but now it appeared like a covert reckoning, a need to compare, a weighing-in as if the fight hadn't long been over; he wanted to be sure he hadn't made a mistake. In the week that followed he had thought about Alex, especially his innocence and – what was it? – his lack of ego, with more and more puzzled fondness and with illicit whoofs of lust.

He dozed, and woke to the noise of horses' hooves in the lane, and remembered someone he used to see who lived in Gloucester Place, and the clatter of the troop of horse that went through on Sundays, at six in the morning, on their way to exercise in the Park. Robin had gone up to London for the day, and Justin was jealous of that, although he'd refused to go with him. He pulled on a pair of Robin's dirty shorts and wandered downstairs to fill the kettle. In the kitchen his breakfast had been laid and a slow imponderable soup on the Rayburn was already flavouring the air with lunch. There was a brown envelope for him franked from his late father's stockbrokers – he couldn't quite deal with that yet; and the *Independent* covering all but the black-letter masthead of the *West Dorset Herald*. He opened the back door and stood looking accusingly at the long grass, the cow-parsley, the brook.

Really he shouldn't be left alone like this. He'd had years of it now, the awful neglect of lovers who had jobs. And he saw, with the sharpness of something remembered for the first time, the little leaded window-panes of Alex's bedroom, and the view of similar windows across the road on all those days that he was left there, with nothing to do but play with himself and watch *Neighbours* and get drunk. Here you had the noise of cuckoos and sheep and tractors; there it was the workmen's drills in the street, or a car-alarm, with its merciless re-startings, or the clink of shirt-buttons against the glass door of the drier. Loading the drier was a thing he could do. Alex suggested early on that he try housework, but the washing-machine broke the first time he used it, and anything to do with cooking was beyond him, though he looked forward to food. He found washing up depressing. He did once hoover, the thing pulling behind him like a recalcitrant dog that had smelt a bitch in the opposite direction, its lead tangling and jamming around doors and chair-legs. He remembered even Alex could be a bit snappy when hot from hoovering.

One simple possibility for today was to give Terry a ring, but he rejected it with a clear sense of tactics. He mustn't give Robin any new occasion for his old grievances, and Terry's discretion was still untested. He took a mug of tea through to the sitting-room and then remembered that there were some photographs of Danny in the little commode. He kept forgetting that he fancied him now as well. He squatted down to pull open the drawer and there on top of the albums and the Scrabble and the boxes of candied fruits was something half-

90

wrapped in shiny red paper, it looked like a book, and it was only after he'd read the title that it all came back to him. He never thanked Alex for it properly, but Alex knew he couldn't say thank you, it was his one unconquerable inhibition. And then a *book* ... After all, there had been bleakish passages back then, those evenings with the opera CDs, squashed up side by side to follow the tiny libretto, Alex turning the page surprisingly soon, while Justin was still trying to square what he was hearing with the words of the previous aria, never quite sure which was Aroldo and which Enrico, even with the help of the waxen pomaded costume portraits in the booklet. Actually Alex was a frightful stick-in-the-mud. Dame Kiri te Kanawa sings Rodgers and Hammerstein was the risqué thing he sometimes put on after dinner when people came round ('So good to hear it done by someone who can really sing').

Justin got out the photo album that Robin had once shown him, a big optimistic-looking thing designed to house a whole family's sentimental history, but reverting, after the first few cheerful episodes, to thirty or forty pages of charcoal vacancy. There was baby Danny in the bath, which didn't give one much to go on, and dancing up and down in a sling hung in a doorway to make him walk. There was Robin, a mere soft-faced boy himself, in his tight flared corduroys, bending sexily over his little son; and Danny's mother, ample, exhausted, maybe a bit stoned, smiling out from under five years' growth of thick dark hair. There were Robin's handsome parents, in their changeless county couture, admiring the baby but clearly glad that they wouldn't have to hold it for long; and proudly unaware, like Edwardian gentry, of the upheavals ahead. In one of the pictures the young Woodfields were joined on the lawn by the hunky little Marcus whom Robin was probably already seeing on the side. There was a seventies mood of sexual conspiracy about them, as if they had all just been in bed together; though clearly that was far from the case – Jane had been blind to her husband's dammed-up queerness.

Tucked in loose at the end of the album, roughly where it would have been if the sequence hadn't been broken, was another photo of the boy and his mother, taken last year on the beach at La Jolla, Danny lean and sunned in long baggy

91

drawers, Jane fierce and fit in a one-piece black swimsuit, hair cropped, something fanatical in the way she gripped her son round the shoulder and pulled him off-balance, though they were both laughing and doubtless acting up to the photographer. Danny had such big nipples; they must come from his mother, like his big soft lips. He wondered if he shared Robin's thing of looking as if he was about to be sick just before he came. Though he never acknowledged it, Justin was longsighted, and he had to hold the picture away to study it in detail. You really couldn't tell if that curve of shadow was a crease in the shorts or a hugely lolling half-erection. Or maybe it was caused by something heavy in the pocket. Justin found the uncertainty undermined the fantasy, oddly enough; and the presence of the mother was chastening too. After a minute he put the photos away.

He bathed through to elevenses, and waiting again for the kettle to mark the next stage of his virtuous pre-drinks morning, leafed through the local paper. There was an eye-catching headline about Bridport boys dicing with death, though it turned out their way of doing it was to dive into the harbour beside the ferries and pleasure-boats. Apparently they did it for dares. An editorial said local people must make sure they knew where their kids were. And that in itself set him thinking. There were pages and pages of property, for locals and strangers alike, everything from cowmen's prefabs to fortified manor-houses; and the thriving and abstruse classified pages, abstruse at least to someone used to the different codes of *Boyz* or *Gay Times*. Still, Justin looked through them with an irreducible tinge of hope, wondering brightly if the 'Mangles for Sale' were machines or vegetables; and there, in its own black-ruled box, as if placed by his personal tempter, was the question 'Need Something Doing, Now?' and the favoured solution, 'For All Those Odd Jobs – Terry', and what Justin well knew to be a mobile number. He smiled and folded the paper away. Well, he could hardly ring him, especially since Robin checked every entry in the itemised phone-bill; they'd already had a row about some £30 calls to a gay chat-line.

Justin had a glass of wine with his soup, and followed it with a couple more: a substantial Australian red of the kind

Robin often kept for special occasions. Staying with Australia he watched overlapping episodes of three soaps on different channels, thumbing between them to make sure he didn't miss any shirtless appearances of his favourite actors. After that he found he'd had a bit of a snooze, and had woken up to the still, heavy country afternoon in a state of delinquent horniness. He thought of the period, later on with Alex, when he went to the Common at this time of day; and his wild afternoons early on with Robin, who'd been quite mad then, and the most exciting sex he'd ever had. 'Dove sono,' he said out loud, which was an aria Alex used to try to sing. He thought he might at least toddle up to Mrs Bodgett's cottage and see if Terry was around.

He loitered admiringly through the garden, stopping to sniff the roses and wallflowers, as if he might be being spied on by his better conscience; and in the back lane, with its convenient gate and mood of secret access, he still had the air of someone merely out for a stroll. There was no sign of Terry's 'Love-mobile', his pale-blue A-reg soft-top Talbot Samba; but his mother was working in the garden, tying up bean-canes, and told him she was expecting him to look in soon.

'Something I want to ask his advice about,' said Justin.

'Oh . . .' said Mrs B., evidently impressed that her son should be required in a consultative capacity. 'I'll send him straight over.'

'Only if he gets in in the next hour or so,' Justin added cautiously.

'I'll tell him.'

'Thanks a lot.' He turned for home, and then called back, 'Tell him to come just as he is . . .' He had liked the thing last time of Terry shrugging off his overalls.

And now, really, with the appointment pretty well certain, he thought how outrageous it was of Robin to leave him locked up here, like a slave, a mistress with no life of her own. He walked on, past the back gate, along the lane to the main entrance, with its view towards the sea-obstructing hills; he despaired of the country, with its loathsome hedges and alarming animals and smelly little shops selling nothing but canned fruit and knicker elastic. No one he could talk to down here would know the meaning of anything he said. He began to wonder if they were even going to get the old queen who'd been promised as the next tenant of 'Ambages' – or 'Handbags' as Justin called it. He could walk up by the church and have a look, but he didn't want to miss Terry.

He thought about how he wanted to be found. It wasn't a sunbathing day, it was overcast and the air was full of idly circling insects, but it was hot enough to be about in nothing but his old linen shorts. He checked the effect in the wardrobe mirror, frowned down at his midriff, where sleekness was feebly holding out against slackness, and glancing up without moving his head caught sight of what could only be called a jowl. His mirror work was normally more carefully censored. What on earth did he look like in – well, three or four unflattering sexual positions came galloping to mind . . .? Thirty-five was youngish for jowls. He wondered, with a prickling of the scalp, quite what he was being fattened up for. But then a rap at the door sent all such worries out of his head.

Terry had come, charmingly enough, with his tool-box; and it took a minute or so of laborious *double entendres* to establish what sort of odd jobs needed to be done. Then there was some less charming banter about money. Apparently a couple of Hollywood location-scouts staying at Bride Mill had been astonished by Terry's modest tariff. 'They had one of them scratch limos,' he said. 'They taught me a thing or two, I must say.'

'One's never too young to learn,' said Justin.

'I gave as good as I got, mind,' Terry added cryptically.

'Let's go upstairs, darling. How old are you, by the way?'

'I'm twenty,' said Terry, following him with the tool-box, for verisimilitude. 'Well, nineteen, to be honest.'

Justin shook his head in wonder at a rent-boy who not only was honest, but pretended to be older than he was.

In the bedroom he got him out of his jeans and T-shirt and had him sit back on the rumpled sheets while he nosed round his pleasingly stained briefs – pale blue, which was so much his artless country colour. He could smell his cock through the tautening cotton and knew he'd already had sex today, he loved

94

the sense of the kid being inexhaustibly in use. 'That's it,' said Terry. 'Let him out, give him some air.'

Justin did as he said, and wondered if his pride would be hurt if he asked him not to talk.

'He's a nice one, isn't he?'

'Mmm,' Justin agreed, his mouth suddenly full.

Terry gasped. 'He likes that.' He spoke of his penis as if it were some rare and lively rodent that he'd raised himself and could show to selected other boys with justifiable pride. 'He's thick at the bottom,' he explained, 'and he's even thicker at the top. He's got a big broad snout to him.'

Justin sat back on his heels. 'Yes, you said that before.'

'Well, you know you like him, Justin. He's a nice one, all right.'

The fuck that followed ('That's it, show him the way home!') was disappointingly brief. Justin was about to upend into his favouritely abject position and found that Terry had already come. He brought himself off quickly, just to finish the thing, and wondered bleakly why he hadn't done so hours before.

After that Terry quite settled in, and lay there talking pointlessly. He really ought to have left, but Justin remembered he was sort of a friend of the family, and felt an odd delicacy about asking him to go. The afternoon had grown darker and darker and indoors it was doubly gloomy. From time to time faraway thunder was heard. It seemed to hurry the evening towards them, and the moment that was conjured up by the loose spin of the whisky-bottle cap, the wonderful renewal of booze.

'So when's Robin getting back?' Terry asked, looking about into the shadows with a certain satisfaction at having tenanted the master bedroom.

'It could be any time now actually . . .'

'He'd better not catch me again.'

'No. That's right.'

Terry sat up and the pale singlet-shape of his untanned chest had a vulnerable gleam. 'Everything okay between you two?' he asked, a little too sagaciously. And then, with oblique persistence and a further frowning survey of the room, 'It's a nice house, this.'

'Yes indeed. We love it.'

'I thought you might be getting a house of your own now.'

Justin lay back and stared at the rough oak beams above. 'Who or what gave you that idea?' He heard Terry shift, and the thump of his feet as he searched for his clothes.

'I thought you were a wealthy man,' Terry said after a bit. So was that what they said about him in the village? Or was it just Danny's pillow-talk?

'You didn't tell Dan about us, did you?' said Justin, severely, and with a hint of shame.

Terry tugged up his zip and said, 'I never tell nobody nothing'; which if you didn't construe it too strictly was a reassurance.

8

Danny asked his friend George to the party, and then rang him to suggest he might like to drive them both down to Dorset in his BMW the day before. George always raised objections, and sometimes ended up doing what Danny wanted. 'Won't you be working?' he said.

'No, I've quit.'

'I see. You've been fired.'

He sensed George's disapproval and hoped to deflect it with a joke. He paused and said, in a Brooklyn whine, 'So I was five minutes late . . .'

A year ago, on Danny's first night alone in London, he had met George in a bar and gone back with him to a richly over-furnished flat in Holland Park. He had almost no sense of himself as a stroke of luck to a man pushing forty, and in fact was relieved by George's wanting him, and comforted by the stuffy clutter of the rooms. It was as if the entire contents of a country house had been herded into one apartment by an aristocrat who couldn't bring himself to sell – though it turned out that everything was for sale, since George was a dealer in antiques, with a special line in baroque tapestries, indoor obelisks and highly varnished paintings of dead game. He gave Danny his first experience of cocaine, and they spent a couple of days in a languid binge of sex that was magically protracted and insulated by George's mastery of hangover deferral: a fat new line, the crack of a fresh Jack Daniels cap, at just the right moment.

After that George went to Paris for a week, and Danny couldn't stop thinking about his dark cynical face and the vague first knottings and stretchings of age in his wide flat body, which moved him and aroused him so unexpectedly. In the lamplight, with a lover's closeness, after a little silver pipe

97

of hash, he had touched the tiny creases around the eyes and mouth and seen how they changed his dully faceted handsomeness into beauty. Danny had never had such intense and prolonged excitement with another person, and knew at once that he couldn't go on without the certainty of more of it. George didn't return his messages, and when he finally went round to the house seemed surprised and slightly annoyed to hear him on the intercom. The minute's coolness in the hall, in the glow from a bronze torchère, and under the provoking gaze of a marble faun, was all it took. Danny knew he was in love.

George was a self-reliant bachelor unused to much genuine emotion, and wary of entanglement with a kid of twenty-one. He was moved by the poetry and artistry of things that he sold but had the low human expectations of a sexual predator. He was vain of his appearance and his largely uneducated instinct for *objets de vertu*. He could see how ripe Danny was to be hurt, which was why he decided not to see him again after the dream debauch of the first visit. But now here Danny was, with his boots off, and a drink in his fist, sitting up beside George in the deep Knole sofa and longing for a sign that it was okay, that he could touch him again, and more. George had been in analysis, and treated Danny to a confusing and grandiose half-hour tour of his psyche, which apparently had two poles: a delight in artifice and a mania for honesty. In fact his frankness could sometimes upset people. Danny listened and perused the carpet, only half understanding what George's point was, feeling the possible diplomatic chill of so much reasonable talk, and waiting only for the tone of voice that meant yes, whatever the words were. Then he found George was pushing him on to his back, and felt his heart thumping through the black roll-neck shirt, and his hard dick at least grinding out the longed-for syllable. He told him later that he had felt vulnerable to Danny's own vulnerability.

The affair that followed was doomed, Danny saw it now, and he sometimes wondered if he would rather have done without the difficult four months; the ending, certainly, was the worst thing in his life. But then George, perhaps out of a guilt that even he was not frank enough to acknowledge, had insisted on their staying friends. This was hard for Danny because they had never been friends, they were lovers from the start; but George had also been his guide, and that perhaps was what made it possible to meet again, like a bright pupil and the teacher whose affection he had won. George had given him fluent access to the many-roomed edifice of London gay life, from the cellars to the salons. People had envied him his good-looking young protégé, who would sometimes say, as they left a luncheon in Mayfair or an East End sex-club at five in the morning, how friendly the people were. George only explained it once: 'Dearest, anyone would be friendly to you.'

Now, a summer later, Danny was waiting on the front step of his rooming-house. He had a couple of cases of cheap white wine and a hold-all of tapes and various party clothes. When George drew up he felt the old shock at the sight of him, a moment or two's heavy-heartedness, as if the lessons and adjustments of the intervening months had never happened, and then at once a lightening, a mood of sentimental accept-ance. In the boot of the car there was a case of champagne, but he said nothing about it – he couldn't be sure it was intended for him. He got into the passenger seat and only then gave George a friendly kiss, and pictured, with a hum between his legs, what he would still do to him given the chance.

They got out of town just as the Friday rush, with its atmos-phere of suppressed panic, was beginning; and urban though they were there was a sense of release as they came clear of the outskirts. Danny looked through the CDs and pressed Schumann's 'Rhenish' Symphony into the player, not sure if he would recognise it, and then exhilarated by the horns at the outset, which seemed designed to be heard at eighty miles an hour on a long trajectory through the summer landscape.

'So who's going to be there?' said George, in his faintly despairing way. 'I hope there's someone I can talk to.'

'You can always talk to my hunky daddy.' And Danny laughed, as he did more and more, at the farce of sex, and the thought of novel pairings of people he knew.

'Of course, I want to meet him.'

'Then there'll be Jim and François, and Carlton, and Bob and Steve and Jerry and Heinrich . . .' He remembered he'd wildly asked a number of virtual strangers at Château, though with no idea if they had accepted, or would themselves remember.

'So you're bussing in a whole crowd of dizzy disco bunnies and letting them loose in the beautiful English countryside.'

'I know . . .' Danny murmured, with a fresh sense of the experiment of life.

'They may not be able to breathe country air. You'll need respirators of poppers and CK One.'

'I think they can be relied on to bring those with them.' Danny squeezed George's knee. 'I'm hoping you may be going to stimulate our central nervous systems, darling.' At which George merely raised an eyebrow. Danny added, 'Bob's always loaded with goodies', to offset the surfacing suggestion that George had only been asked for his coke and his car.

'So who are you going to set me up with?' George resumed, in a tone of voice that emphasised his appetite and a cheerfully heartless readiness to use his old lover in his turn.

'What are you like?' said Danny. And then, mischievously, 'There's young Terry, of course . . .' He made a pretence of conducting the music, with hammy head-shakings and no clear sense, so far from a drug and a DJ, of the rhythm of the thing. 'Local boy.'

George scanned the road ahead with narrowed eyes. 'You say young.'

'Twenty-two, like me, at least until midnight. Oh, professional age, twenty. If not nineteen.'

'I'm not paying, sweetie.' Though the idea had clearly taken root, since George said later, 'Any other members of the profession coming down?'

Danny was pretty sure that, even during their affair, George had sent out for sex, he had seen ringed numbers in the back of *Gay Times*; though now he made himself laugh at the image of those boys, buzzed into the building with their knapsacks of accoutrements, and witnessing their own performances in one of George's Empire mirrors. 'I've asked Gary – the black one with the broken nose? But he may not come, it being the weekend . . .'

'Any women coming?' asked George, as if he missed Danny's

meaning, and was suddenly concerned with the propriety of the gathering.

'I hope Janet will be there.'

'She must have turned into a faggot by now, just from natural adaptation.'

'She was the only woman at Colon last week.'

George gave a slow nod of concession to the other point of this sentence. 'Well, you're certainly managing to find your way around without me, darling. Even I don't go to Colon.' Though the odd thing was that since their clubbing days together, Danny had hardly ever seen George out; which made him think that either he had changed his habits, and entered a maturer phase, or that without having Danny to show off and show off to there were easier and quieter ways of getting what he wanted. Even in the old days, while Danny danced like a madman, George tended to loiter against the wall, where the boys were staring and fumbling with their wraps of speed.

'And who knows, my dad may be glad of some female company.'

'I see. He's still interested?'

Danny didn't want to overstate the case. He'd seen him sometimes watching a woman and felt there was something beneath the apparent impassivity and courtesy. 'It might be a bit of a relief . . . But no, I think he just got queerer, like Oscar Wilde or someone. Once he thought he could do everything, then it polarised towards the one thing.'

'It's pretty . . . cool, to have an out gay dad,' George said, supportively but humorously.

'Oh I quite agree,' said Danny, with a readiness that made him sound a bit straight himself. And there was a sort of anxiety, which he tended to blink away, that one of the figures at the edge of the dance-floor could perfectly well be his own father. There were still leather trousers and a studded thong in the wardrobe of the London flat.

Later George said, 'You'll have to tell me where to turn off.'

'Not for ages yet . . .' Danny was afraid the whole thing might pall on him as the necessary three hours unrolled. 'You have to wait for the Crewkerne turning. Then it's sort of . . . not as far as it was.'

101

'I take it you've got someone lined up for yourself, by the way. Total frankness, remember,' George went on; and Danny thought there was a tension in his voice, at the prospect of meeting a successor.

'Total frankness. Okay,' said Danny, confused to find how much he wanted to tell and how much he would have liked to keep the thing secret. Perhaps it wouldn't hurt him to set it out for someone else, though he knew from the awful stalled debates of their break-up that frankness wasn't in itself a solution. If you were truly frank you saw only what a muddle you were in, and how you felt three different things at the same time. He said, 'Well, I've sort of got a new boyfriend.'

'Right. How old is he?'

'Thirty-six.'

'Uh-huh. Name?'

'Alex. Alexander Nichols.'

'No, I don't know him. Good Scottish name,' said George, with an absurd air of expertise.

'I suppose so. He sounds completely English. Went to Bristol University, his father's a solicitor in Chelmsford. He told me loads about his family, but you know how it is when you're talking in bed, you get much more interested in their shoulder-blade or their armpit or something.'

'What's his dick like?'

'You waited such a long time to ask that.'

'One doesn't like to pry.'

'In fact it's a bit like him – longer and thinner than . . . the norm. He's six foot four.'

George mulled this over as if he didn't really find it satisfactory. 'Does he have a job?'

'He works in the Foreign Office. He's quite well off,' said Danny, with an evident sensible belief that this was an active element in someone's appeal. Then, rather shyly, stroking his throat, 'He's given me this gold pendant thing.'

George glanced across as he pulled it free of his shirt. 'I'll have to look at that,' he said. 'It could be valuable.'

'It is valuable,' said Danny.

They drove on in silence for a while, till George said, 'He

must be keen on you'; and with a sudden and lonely burst of charm, 'not that I find that hard to understand.'

'I think he's madly in love with me.'

'And you?' George asked.

'No, I like him, I think he's really sweet.' Danny couldn't explain his sense of bewilderment at being adored so unconditionally by Alex, or his wariness, since George, of allowing himself to feel anything strongly. The past six months had been a riotous escape from all that, compressed by hindsight into a continuous orgy of casual sex.

'I see. You haven't said where you met him.'

Danny chuckled. 'This is the funny thing. You're going to have to be really discreet about this, actually. He's Justin's ex, from before my dad. And of course, Justin doesn't know; and I don't want Dad to know either, not yet anyway. We met at where we're going, Hilton Gumboot as Justin calls it, two weeks ago. Alex came down and I could tell he was a bit keen; then I went out with him last weekend – and I've seen him a few times since.'

'Well, it certainly sounds like we're going to have fun,' George said sourly.

'I put him on his first E,' Danny went on with a slow smile. 'I thought he was never going to come.'

George paid this remark the homage of a knowing snicker due to any drug anecdote. 'But the sex is good?'

Danny wondered for a second how he'd ever got on with George's dreary sexual supremacism. 'Sex is fine. He's quite passionate.'

'You mean passion – but not genius. Technique? Technique can sometimes be mistaken for genius.'

'George, he's so innocent, and strange . . .' How was he going to explain him? 'He's thirty-six, he's only had one real affair in his life, with Justin, who I would have thought was totally inappropriate. Anyway it was a big deal for two years, until, of course, Justin broke his heart. The first night he told me he hadn't touched another man for a year. Then he talked and talked all next day. He was still very mellow from the night before. As I say, I couldn't take it all in, but . . . He's just different. He's not jaded. I sound like I'm a hundred years old

103

but it was so sweet to be out with someone who finds every-thing new and amazing. He's quite serious too. He kept analysing everything he felt. You should have seen him at Château.' Danny smiled. 'He kept saying, "Look at the men! I love men!" It was like he was coming out all over again.'

'I hope you took him upstairs at Château.'

'To be absolutely frank, I did leave him for a bit and go upstairs, because Gary wanted to . . . see me. I think upstairs can wait for later. Anyway, I wanted to keep him for myself.'

'He's a cultured sort of chap, is he?'

'Oh, yeah, he knows all about opera, and he's read masses.'

'It'll do you good to get some culture,' said George. Danny stored this remark away, and went on as if he hadn't heard,

'Though he clearly hasn't read *Vanity Fair* – I caught him out on that.'

George seemed to ponder the whole thing for a while, then said, 'So what is it you care for least about him?'

But Danny wasn't prepared to be negative. After they'd taken the Crewkerne turning, and certain features, an old T-junction sign, a pub, a row of trees, began to stir the subtle anxieties of arrival, he did briefly think about it, but only out of slightly decadent curiosity. There was something frustrating perhaps in a companion who had never heard of most of the new gay bars and had no conception of the pivotal importance of the DJ, who he clearly thought was just the bloke who played the records; at moments in the past week, as Danny showed Alex round what was after all his own town, he'd felt towards him as you do towards the duller schoolfriend you lend your notes to and end up almost teaching yourself.

9

'Is he a scholar?' was Hugh's first, rather off-beam question.

Alex said, 'Not at all.'

'God, you're lucky. I've got this kid after me who just won't let up with the scholarly references and talks non-stop in about ten different languages. He makes me feel as if I'm All Souls College and he's taking a fellowship exam to get into me. Actually, of course, the door's open and the kettle steaming on the hearth.'

'No,' said Alex, who hadn't come here to talk about Hugh's dimly prospective amours, 'Danny's extremely bright and adaptable but he doesn't really know anything. I mean, he's seen one opera, by Handel, and he can't remember which one. He seemed persuaded by each of the titles I suggested. He's got a degree in something called cultural studies, which apparently doesn't quite involve reading a book. I don't know why I'm being so catty. And of course he's terribly young. He does know all about dance-music.'

'*Coppélia* and stuff.'

'No, darling.'

'I didn't really think you meant that. How young is he?'

'He's twenty-three tomorrow.'

'Ouch,' said Hugh, turning away with an envious grimace and looking for the bottle.

Alex and Hugh had been together at university, though Hugh had gone on to Oxford to pursue a D Phil and then landed a job in Coins and Medals at the British Museum. He was a wonderfully sedentary person, who nowadays rarely left a shallow rectangle of streets between the Museum, an Italian restaurant in Dyott Street, and his dark disorderly flat above the Spiritualist Meeting Rooms in High Holborn. Alex sometimes dropped in there for a drink, since it was hard to get Hugh to

Hammersmith. Amazingly, they had been to Greece together, in 1980, though on an old-fashioned Hellenising trail rather than to the alarming possibilities of a modern gay resort. Hugh had been quite slim and attractive as he blustered self-consciously down the beach in his tight old swimming-trunks, but since then he had given way to the steady spread of luncher's middle and office bottom. 'Let's not' was his usual response to any suggestion of activity.

His friendship with Alex was intuitive, protected by their shared timidity and steeped in its own atmosphere of culture and fantasy. They talked on the phone, they listened to Haydn quartets together, they got drunk and ruminated obscenely about boys they had fancied, often long ago, looking out from Hugh's rooms towards the roofs of Bloomsbury like a pair of dirty-minded spinsters. Alex's occasional adventures were received by Hugh with curiosity and an oddly prudish pique; Hugh himself seemed not to have adventures, and his way of denying his needs was the recurrent fiction that someone was bothering him with their attentions, and he couldn't decide about them. The appropriation of the gardens next to the Museum as central London's liveliest cruising area gave him a new pretext for jokes and hinted misdemeanours. Alex felt that Hugh and Justin were the only two people who properly understood him; though, of course, when Justin came along – picked up, just like that, in the street – Hugh had retired wounded, as if somehow found wanting by his old friend. He was first with the condolences and candid analyses when Justin left. The announcement of a new affair was bound to be a little ticklish.

Alex told him how it had happened. 'I went down to this cottage in Dorset in love with Justin and came back in love with Danny. It was a completely magical thing.'

'Surely you weren't still in love with Betty Grable?' said Hugh.

It already seemed so long ago. 'I think, in spite of everything, if I could have woken up beside anyone in the world it would still have been him.'

Hugh shook his head in a distress of incredulity; but then saw the bright side. 'Anyway, it's now definitely over.'

Alex chose not to be tryingly truthful. 'The last two weeks have been extraordinary – I feel as if I'm under a beautiful spell.'

'The thing about spells,' said Hugh, 'is that you don't know at the time if they're good ones or bad ones. All black magicians learn how to sugar the pill.'

'Well I never had your mastery of the occult.'

'What's his dick like, by the way?'

Alex gestured implausibly with both hands. 'But you know I don't care about that sort of thing.'

'Of course,' said Hugh, smacking his forehead, 'I keep forgetting.' And then, 'It's like money, it's easy not to care when you've got it.'

'Talking of sugaring the pill,' Alex said, and went on to give what account he could of taking ecstasy. The urge to tell had been distracting him all week, it seemed nearly a necessity, like the born-again's compulsion to spread the word at bus-stops and street-corners. He thought it best not to confide in anyone at the office, though he guessed from overheard phone-calls that his sober-suited secretary was, technically, a raver; he met young Barry's curious, doubting look with the blandest 'Good morning'.

Every detail of his initiation was touched by the magic, though it was in the nature of the night – arriving drunk, the wild sprint of time once the drug took effect – that most of it was forgotten. He kept saying, 'It was fabulous, it was fantastic, I can't describe it.'

'Hmm,' said Hugh, poised somewhere between scepticism, envy and shock.

'It was the combination of the pill and Danny of course, feeling suddenly on the inside of life rather than the outside. It made me see how depressed I'd been, I think the depression was so insidious and all-pervasive that I only noticed it when it was gone.'

'It's only a drug, though, isn't it. It's not a real high.'

'I don't know, it's real enough when it's happening. I'm not a philosopher.'

'But what about the after-effects?'

'You just carry on feeling wonderful. I've been talking to

people all week. Danny's amazing like that – if he likes the look of someone he just starts talking to them, where I would normally wait ten years for an introduction in writing.'

'Wasn't everyone else about sixteen? – they are on television', Hugh said, and Alex looked at him, with his scruffy haircut and his dense brown habitat of books and folders, as if he had suddenly slipped a generation. He felt a vague affectionate dismay at Hugh's life of paper, the teetering research for the still unfinished thesis, the stacks of numismatic journals with a dirty cup on top or a half-dead Busy Lizzie, and doubtless, tucked away deep down, an issue or two of *Big Latin Dicks*. 'I didn't notice, darling.' The truth was he had no regrets, he longed to do it again, he loved his late start and was glad to think he hadn't exhausted these pleasures when he was Danny's age. Danny spoke already about mid-week glooms and short-term memory loss. Alex said, 'I feel somehow I've been set free.'

'Well, don't become a slave to your need for freedom, will you,' Hugh said, with a mixture of concern and self-satisfaction. 'I mean people do die.'

'I find I've overcome a lot of crusty old prejudices,' Alex summed up. 'Until last week, I was appalled by the idea of drugs, as you know I thought pop music was witless rubbish, I really couldn't be doing with the noise and trash of the gay scene, I hated chewing-gum and trainers and baseball caps with writing on, in fact any clothes with writing on the outside. And now I think they're all absolutely marvellous.'

'So you're going to be turning into a whatsaname, are you?' said Hugh.

'I don't know what I'm turning into,' Alex said. ' "We know what we are but not what we may be": Ophelia.'

'Well, look what happened to her,' said Hugh.

Hugh put on his jacket and they strolled down to Dyott Street for a quick bowl of pasta before Alex set off to Dorset. The staff were Sicilian, and a hand-coloured photograph of the 1928 eruption of Etna hung above the bar. Hugh knew them all well, and spoke to them in confident Italian. The waiters made a fuss of him, but were quick and business-like, and brought San Pellegrino and a plate of bruschetta without being asked, since that was what he always had. Perhaps just because of his speaking their language everything that was said by either side caused immediate amusement, and left behind a mood of wistful reassurance. Alex chatted and drifted, and nursed the plan that had just come to him, to take Danny away to Sicily at the end of the summer: the plan swallowed him up so that he couldn't do much more than prod and repeatedly re-coil his tagliatelle. He was dying for a drink, the glamour of any kind of stimulant was immense, but he knew that he had a long drive ahead, and held off. He sensed a continuity between the benign routines of the restaurant and the larger movements beyond it, flights, journeys, days and nights. It was the oneness he had felt on ecstasy, which came back now and then like an image from a dream that surfaces again in the absent-minded mid-morning. He had never been to Sicily, and said casually to the waiter who was clearing the plates, 'Does Etna still erupt from time to time?'

The waiter tucked in his chin and said, 'No, signore', with a warm smile, as if to discourage a harmful rumour; and then, seeing Alex's disappointment, said, 'Well, a little bit, signore. Yes, from time to time.'

Hugh walked with Alex to his Mercedes, and they stood for a while looking down at it in the odd hesitation before saying goodbye, with its trail of unnecessary recaps and puzzled attempts to remember something else that needed saying. Hugh was more cheerful and loving after a flask of Orvieto and the chance to absorb the impact of Alex's news. He kissed him on both cheeks, and said, 'That club sounds fantastic, actually. You must take me some time.'

'Of course, darling,' said Alex, slithering into the car, but thinking, as he drove off with an uncharacteristic toot, that if it came to it Hugh would certainly decide 'Let's not'. They had once been to Heaven together, twelve or thirteen years ago, and Alex still remembered Hugh's way of taking the floor, with hands on hips and his legs kicking out spasmodically as if in some distant holiday recollection of Greek folk-dancing.

He sped across town as the sun was setting. It was the Summer Solstice. Everywhere people were launching on their weekends, thronging into restaurants and bars. He wished them well, but he felt the town was largely pointless now Danny had left it; he and his friend must already have been at Litton Gambril for three or four hours, they'd have had drinks with Justin and Robin, and perhaps dinner, though the friend was staying at Bride Mill, so perhaps was dining there. Alex picked at the plans. The presence of Justin was going to be almost surreal, as was the agreement with Danny to keep their affair a secret. He wished they could have gone down together, but there wasn't room for everything in his two-seater, and he already had a case of champagne in the boot. In other respects, though, the car had come into its own; Justin had always shown a non-driver's inability to distinguish it from any other car, but Danny admired it from the start, and in the past week they had driven on a number of unnecessary diversions along Old Compton Street with the roof down, Danny waving like an over-eager starlet, and often shouting quite loudly to make sure he'd been seen by some dim disco acquaintance.

Alex switched on the radio, and it was one of Haydn's opus 76 string quartets that he had sometimes listened to with Hugh. It held him for a minute with its familiar novelties, and he tapped lightly on the wheel to demonstrate his involvement with it, but he couldn't resist a feeling that it would always be there, and found himself reaching into the glove-box for his latest purchase from Harlot Records, *Monster House Party Five*, a three-CD compilation of forty pounding dance tracks mixed by DJs Sparkx, Joe Puma and Queen Marie.

The thwacking bass at the opening of Joe Puma's set (if that was the word) made him grin and shiver. His drugged remark about wanting to live in house music had only shown up how unobservant he was: he had been living in it all along. Now he heard it everywhere, or something very like it to the novice's ear: in cafés, clothes shops, of course in gay bars with Danny, and thumping from a van in slow-moving traffic in Whitehall, so that he kept catching up with it as he walked away from work; idly channel-surfing on a night alone, he found it glittering like an open secret through programmes on fashion, holidays, local politics, and ads for drinks and cars. He almost envied the barmen and shop-assistants who lived with its promise of pleasure all week long. Maybe they wouldn't even wait for the weekend to go dancing and be off their faces again. Driving west into the last of the day with the music in his ears he saw the electric storm of the dance-floor, the racing languor of the chill-out room – it was literally heart-warming, he felt his pulse hurry and his face colour up. And then he remembered waking in Danny's room on the Sunday afternoon, their foreheads pressed together, the same tired lungful of air breathed back and forth between them, the muted sunshine through unlined curtains . . . Alex had rolled gently away and examined his happiness to the rhythm of the wallpaper, the clutches of pink roses like featureless putti floating hypnotically ceilingwards.

It was dark by the time he reached the Crewkerne turn-off, and he drove on in silence so as to concentrate on the signs and the bends. The road was unrecognisable from his first journey. He rolled down the window to smell the trees and fields and the cool air that had been warm all day. On corners his headlights swept past tree-trunks, a white cottage dark for the night, impassive horses in a field. He felt romantically alone. On a high open stretch of the road he saw the stars, which at first he thought were the upward reflections of the car's lit dials in the windscreen; later there was the glimmer of a town beyond the long black line of a hill. Moths, labouring through the dark on their own amorous callings, rushed to obliterate themselves on the beacon of the car.

Robin seemed surprised, even exasperated, to have Alex in the house again; it was one thing for Justin to invite him, but then for Danny to take pity on him too . . . Alex watched the Woodfield social reflex come into play, the sudden overcompensation of smiles and offers of drinks – that making the best of things that could seem faintly schizoid. Justin's welcome had been more muted but more genuine. He said, 'I didn't think you'd come back, darling', and held his hand in a way that asked for affection more than it offered it. It was midnight, of course, and he was a little maudlin. As for Danny, there was a tantalising distance, crossed only by touches and winks that felt almost negligent in their furtiveness. They hadn't worked

111

out their story properly, and acted as if they had barely met. The effect was that all three of them appeared to wonder why Alex was here. Alex felt that Danny's surely rather cold and watchful friend George was being treated with an easy fondness that he would have been glad of himself. Danny messed around nerve-jarringly with tapes of something called drum 'n' bass, which he said was 'massive' this summer; house, apparently, was all too commercial, you heard it everywhere now, you had to have been there four years ago, when it was at its underground zenith. 'Oh,' said Alex, unable to protest, and feeling obscurely betrayed by his own teacher. When they came to turn in, Robin took him up to a different room from last time, with a filing cabinet in it, and various large objects covered with a cotton bedspread. 'You shouldn't be too uncomfortable,' he said. Alex lay awake in a horrible turmoil as to whether he should have come; then woke with a start to a presence in the room, the muttered breaths of sleepy concentration, a cool hand patting the pillow, patting his shoulder, his elbow, then the warm weight of a man stretching gently, half-clumsily along him in the dark.

Robin was up early next morning, with a number of noisy jobs to do. Baking smells spread slowly through the house, and as soon as the dew was off the grass he was out with the mower. He was taking the party seriously, and there was to be enough food for more than the thirty people Danny thought might turn up. Alex came down to find him shirtless by the fridge, with a wisp of grass caught in his chest hair, drinking milk from the bottle, then brusquely wiping away the white moustache. He still gave off his air of challenging competence, although for Alex his threat had been nicely displaced: the rival had emerged as the potential father-in-law, whose approval he might one day hope to win.

Alex offered his help and it was agreed he would drive into Bridport to do some shopping and pick up some things on order. Danny was busy with more abstruse planning. He stood around in the sitting-room saying, 'Right, they'll come in *here* . . .' with great decisiveness, then pondering the matter again. He had a large flat notebook, a survival of his American student days, with pictures of rock stars taped to the cover, and a headline from the *National Enquirer*, 'DAN THE BEAST'; he was writing in this in a sunny spot of the garden as Alex went up to the car.

The secrecy was certainly a bore, and went against Alex's mood of expansion and freedom. In the car he kept telling his news to himself, though he couldn't get the wording right. 'I'm madly in love with him' gave the first quick spurt of release, and the cliché, as happened in love, seemed fresh after all. But it wasn't sufficient. 'I'm wildly in love with him', 'I'm utterly in love with him' – he couldn't find an adverb pungent and reckless enough.

He spent an hour in the town, with its broad Georgian streets called North, South, East and West, the compass of a region remote from London, and with its own procedures. In the cake-shop there was worried talk of a customer preparing to go up to the Smoke. When it was Alex's turn, the baker said, 'How are you today?' as if he knew of some ongoing health problem.

'Very well indeed, thanks,' said Alex. 'How are you?'

'Not too dusty,' said the baker, to which Alex could only murmur 'Ah', unsure from his tone if that meant pretty good or a bit off-colour. He asked for a large white cake in the window, which the man lifted out with pride. 'That's a lovely wedding-cake,' he said. 'You're not the lucky man?'

'I do feel quite lucky,' Alex said. He had the eerily restful country feeling that his homosexuality was completely invisible to these people.

Alex found that he'd contracted that occasional ailment of the late developer, an aversion to his own past. He had grown up in a country town, different from this one, duller probably, and more defiantly conformist; but his mood of ghostly familiarity deepened as he went from shop to shop. The poverty of the little supermarket, with its own-brand biscuits and jams; the high prices of the farm shop, with organic vegetables and free-range eggs crusted in authenticating dung; the brown old men who slapped down all their change on the newsagent's counter, not yet used to the decimal currency, or leaned wheezily at the urinal under the town clock with their leather shopping-bags; the old outfitters selling brown and mauve clothes, and the

113

charity thrift-shop indistinguishable from it, and the derelict boutiques with a spew of mail across the bare floor; the photos of fêtes and beauty contests and British Legion dinners in the window of the newspaper office, which might almost have been the window of a museum; the peeling front of the main hotel, with its promise of fire-doors and meal smells; the word MONUMENTAL on an undertaker's sunlit window thrown in sharp-etched shadow across a waiting tablet; the shyness of the country folk and the loudness of their jokes and greetings – he felt he knew it all, and was horrified by it, as though by some irremediable failing of his own. Then the cloud of the mood heaved slowly past and he drove out of town with a quivering sense of how his luck had swung round, like a weather-vane.

Something came back to him for the first time, it might have been waiting for its explanatory moment. It was the late summer of 89, the eve of his thirtieth birthday. He had left town on a Friday evening to drive out to his parents in Essex for the family celebrations. As always he felt he was leaving a scene of potential pleasure, even if only getting drunk with a straightish group of friends. He had a route through the lanes to the village where his parents had just bought the Old Rectory, with its acre of demanding garden. There was never any traffic, only local people heading to the pub in their Austin Maxis; but this time he ran into a line of cars, red tail-lights backed up in the twilight as far as he could see. After a while engines were switched off, and Alex watched the young men in the Dormobile ahead of him get out to stretch their legs and talk to the other drivers. He leant out himself and asked a boy standing on the verge what the trouble was. 'They're blocking us off,' he said. 'We're waiting for new directions.' A girl in leathers with a mobile phone came walking down the road, and the drivers, who were all young and excited, called out questions to her. The whole thing had the feel of a chaotic exercise by an oddly high-spirited rebel army. Pop music from different radio stations mingled in the still air. It turned out they were going to a rave.

Alex didn't see why he should pretend he was going to a rave, perhaps he panicked slightly, though the mood was not aggressive, just voluble and collective. He wasn't sure exactly

114

what happened at a rave. He knew it was a horrible inconvenience to the people who lived in the area. He started up his
engine, pulled out of the line and went up the just passable
other side of the road, with kids gesturing and shouting things
at him. Some of them clearly thought he was one of the wide-
boys who'd organised the thing. Now and then he had to
mount the low verge. Before long he came face to face with a
police motor-cyclist. He could see he was in the wrong, but he
explained where he was trying to get to, spoke vaguely of
having just come from the Foreign Office, and after the
policeman had spoken to colleagues up ahead, was told to
follow him, he'd get him through. Alex saw it all now, his
problematic progress through the lanes, up and down between
second and third gear, the flashing stanchion of the motorbike
revolving ahead of him. They went on past a mile and a half
of stalled vehicles, the cheerful faces at the open windows, the
thump of music and shimmer of petrol fumes in the scented
evening. He began to feel like a fool, who had missed what
was happening around him and asked to see out the last night
of his twenties under lonely safe conduct.

10

Robin and George both went to meet the 19.10 arrival at Crewkerne station. Eight guests were expected to be on it, all of them unknown to Robin, though George was confident of recognising several. Robin didn't warm to George and disliked his sarky intimacy with Danny; he hoped he wasn't being trailed as a new boyfriend. George had avoided the day's preparations by touring antique shops in Beaminster and Lyme. As they waited in the station car-park he praised one piece of furniture in the cottage, but only one.

When it came to it, there was no doubt who the party party were. Among the few Saturday commuters, local kids and dun-coloured hikers there was a swishing little posse of metropolitan muscle and glamour. In appearance the boys ranged from sexily interesting through very handsome to troublingly perfect. Robin watched them for a few droll seconds as they collected under the Gothic arch, looking careless but a little abashed by this alien place, a couple of them chewing gum and candidly eyeing Robin and George, so that when George called out 'Hey, guys!' and contact was made, something else was slyly acknowledged by their smiles. Robin had put on, almost unconsciously, his sexiest old button-fly jeans, and George was wearing leather trousers, which rather confused Robin with their hot attractive smell. He couldn't help thinking they must look like a pair of affluent queens who'd hired a whole chorus-line of hustlers for the weekend. Perhaps it had looked like this to local people when those aristocratic buggery scandals of forty years ago were taking place.

Robin wanted to know his son's friends, and had felt happy and punctilious all day at the prospect of welcoming them. George at once asserted a louche sort of claim to three of them, who went off with him in his BMW; Robin had to take four in the back of the Saab. They grumbled a bit, and made sluttish jokes about the tight squeeze. 'Ooh, what's that?' they kept saying. 'Whose is this?' Robin couldn't help thinking they were rather common; or perhaps it was just his concern about Danny, and his conviction that no one could be good enough for him. The standard of manners was certainly variable. 'Can we stop for some fags!' one of them called out, as if Robin were merely a taxi-driver. Up front he had a charming Norwegian called Lars, who reminded him of a trimmer, musclier Justin, and also, in the deliberate courtesy of his talk, of certain schoolfriends whom Danny used to bring home for weekend exeats. Though presumably he had been found, like the rest of them, in the new club scene where Danny was clearly so popular, and which Robin knew little about. He hadn't really been out since Subway was closed down in 1984.

When they got back to the cottage there were several cars in the lane and another half-dozen boys stretching their legs on the verge beside a rented minibus. Bright-coloured groups were strolling through the garden with what looked like glasses of champagne. A window was open to let out surprisingly nice music. There hadn't been a party here since the circumspect celebrations of Simon's last birthday, nearly two years ago. Robin felt a tiny proprietary shock at the take-over by strangers.

He came round the house to find the Halls standing together, looking irritably at some shrubs. They had only 'dropped in for a drink', as Robin had suggested, though on their lips the phrase had a worrying looseness, with no implied promise of their dropping out again. Like all awkward guests they had arrived early and would have to be introduced cold to some unsuitable stranger. They had brought a little present for Danny – 'It's only a bottle, I'm afraid' – and Robin was pleased they had come: they were among the few people in the village who remained friendly and hospitable after Simon's death. Not that they could be said to revel lubriciously in the reported details of gay life. On occasion they were merrily caustic. (It was Mike Hall who had said, when shown a volume called *The Cultivated Fruits of England*, 'Good god, a book about Woodfield and his chums.') They made a wonderfully inadvertent contrast to

117

the other guests, who were exploring the garden as if it was their first one – there were shrieks of laughter and worried gasps from the woodshed and the greenhouse. Margery was red-eyed and exhausted; the rape that was in flower in great garish blocks around the village gave her rashes and hay-fever. 'I'm not supposed to drink with these pills,' she said, taking the vast gin and tonic that Justin had made for her. Justin had an almost reverential fondness for the Halls, and ushered them indoors, perhaps relieved not to have to talk to what he called the Orchidaceae. There was something both evasive and host-like in this. Robin stood swaying in the wake of his beauty, and went off to struggle with the barbecue as if physically grappling with the malign mechanics of the situation, the enforced indifference. He had built the little sheltered griddle himself and was vexed by its frequent failure to draw.

When he came back to the kitchen, Danny was hectically opening bottles of champagne: it was that startling moment when you find that the party has taken off and is using up fuel. He was wearing black trousers and a crisp white collarless shirt, as though he'd been interrupted in dressing for some more formal event.

'Hi Dad!' he said. Then, 'Have you got a drink?'

Robin realised that he hadn't, and that it might be a good idea. 'Where did all this bubbly come from?' he said.

Danny looked confused – it was a look he'd had as a kid, on far earlier weekends, when Robin found him playing with expensive toys that were given him by Jane's new men-friends. Well, he still came for weekends, and he had chosen to be here for his birthday – it was something, but it wasn't nearly enough. 'George brought a whole case,' he said.

Robin gave a murmur. 'That's very generous of him.' Perhaps George hadn't yet got anywhere with him, and was giving him lifts and expensive drinks as an old-fashioned way to his heart; but it seemed out of character. He must have been frowning, because Danny said,

'Don't worry. There's nothing going on. Oh, by the way, Mum rang, to wish me happy birthday. She said to tell you hi.'

'Is that what she said . . .' said Robin.

118

They went out together with clutches of glasses. A dark Arabic-looking boy, with a shaved head and a goatee, sprang up to Danny so that he jogged the drinks, and kissed him on the mouth. 'See, I made it!' he said. He was holding a loosely wrapped present, and slipped it under Danny's arm. When his hands were free Danny opened it, and shook out a white T-shirt, with the disconcerting legend M$_A$DMA$_N$ on the front. 'Put it on,' said the boy. There were one or two whistles as Danny fiddled with his cuff-links, and someone said, 'He's off . . .' It was a tiny change in the climate, a casual tension, as if more than a young man's upper body had been briefly bared. He had a small pendant on a chain, and Robin wondered if that was one of George's gifts as well. Alex was standing close by with a protective but unpleasantly lustful look, and tucked in the label at the neck of the T-shirt when it was on. There was laughter and clapping, Robin said 'I don't get it', though Alex seemed to find it funny, or wanted to suggest that he understood. Robin hoped with curt benevolence that Alex would get off with some nice London boy tonight, and stop hanging round his fucking house.

He was relieved to find that the coals had reached a pinkish orange, and tied on his apron; soon there was the expected smoke and spatter, and the reek of seared meat was drifting among the fir-trees and over the field where cows themselves stood munching unrecognisingly.

Danny behaved with a sweet combination of shyness and bossiness appropriate to a birthday boy; and Robin was aware too of the restraint that his own presence imposed. Some of the boys didn't yet know who he was and said, 'Oh, you're the cook, are you – great food!' or 'How long have you known Danny?' as though he might be some secret sugar-daddy rather than his real inadequate father. He brought out candles in jam-jars as the dusk set in and listened to Danny talking about his exchange year at college in Vermont. He thought it must be then that he had started taking drugs, though Jane claimed omnisciently that he never touched a thing at that time.

'There was this guy who had really bad asthma,' Danny said. 'And he was always really speedy on some stuff he had, called Blocks Away ®?' – he drew the trade-mark sign with his finger.

'So we started trying it, and it was amazing, it made your heart race, but you were really concentrated as well – it had ephedrin in it.'

'Oh, right,' said one of the boys.

'It was great for working late at night. Though more recreational uses did . . . suggest themselves once exams were over. We used to go into this little pharmacy in town, wheezing and panting, and the old guy there would say, "Sure is a lot of asthma up at that college", and we'd say, "I know, sir, I reckon it's the pesticides they put on the fields up there – that's the one disadvantage of a college in a beautiful rural location like this, sir", though often we were pretty high already and probably overdid the explanations. What my English prof called "trowelling on the authenticating detail, Whitfield". And he never did get my name right . . .'

Robin smiled and got up to collect plates. He wondered how he could worry about Danny doing things he had done himself, or would have wanted to do. He'd never seen him like this, as an adult at the centre of a circle of friends. It was as if the revolve had brought a whole tableau of characters swiftly on stage, already drinking and laughing. Whether the detail was authentic he couldn't tell. He went towards the back door and the lights went out, and then a gleaming white oblong of candlelit cake seemed to levitate into the garden, and high above it, in its ghostly but lively light, Alex's pale captivated face.

Robin had worried from time to time about the Halls, but whenever he saw them they were caught up in serious talk with some new group of Orchidaceae. Margery was a quiet, stoical woman, with the spare weight and poor concentration of a reformed heavy smoker. Mike was the retired bursar of a military college, proud of his own intelligence, and always hungry for talk. His drunkenness had three phases: first an expansive open-mindedness and principled respect for ideas, then a rather moody period of stifled impatience with his interlocutors, whom it emerged he simply couldn't agree with, and third, launched with sudden sneering force, an hour or so of unbridled contempt and obscenity, ending with an abrupt collapse. As he came through the house, Robin heard Mike's voice in the front garden reaching a steady dogmatic yap, and thought it might be time to ease them homewards. He found him in an improbable group of young style-queens, whom he seemed to have roused to unexpected animation. 'You know nothing of war,' he was saying.

Lars said, 'Well, in Norway the military expenditure . . .'

'Look, what's your name, Mike,' another cut in.

'Who *is* this guy?' a third one said to no one in particular.

Margery saw Robin coming up, and said, 'I think we'd better go now. It's been lovely.' She looked around. 'I don't know about Mike.' Then Justin was there too, offering another gin and tonic, and put out to find she wanted to leave.

'Oh, Margerina!' he said, which he'd never called her to her face before, and carried on as though he hadn't said it, 'Well, at least let me walk you home'; and then snorted after all.

She said weakly, 'Mike'; and somehow she managed to catch his eye and pass him a wordless but familiar message. At that moment the music jumped into a new mode and volume, it was another of those meaningful shifts of level as the party moved nearer its instinctive goal; and the effect must have been alien and horrible to a couple in their late sixties.

'I'll walk our friends home,' said Justin.

'I'll come too,' Robin said. 'I might leave Danny to it for a bit.'

'It's okay,' said Justin, with a meaning look of his own.

Margery made a little cringing grimace and said, 'I don't think they want us old crocks around.'

The four of them went up the shadowy path, Mike turning, like someone dragged from a fight, to call out, 'You think about it', with a grim laugh.

'Now the fun's really going to begin,' said Margery, without a smile and with the remotest hint of nostalgia. 'Though I don't know who they're going to find to dance with.' Robin couldn't tell if she was being mischievous; and as it happened, when they reached the gate a goggling taxi-driver was setting down a pair of virtually naked girls, who, if you ignored their crew-cuts and tattoos, might just have fitted the bill.

121

They walked slowly along in the warm late twilight, Justin and Robin flanking their guests. Robin glanced about into uncurtained windows, the flicker of televisions. You could certainly hear the party from some way off, but he tried not to care. A yellow quarter-moon had appeared between the beautiful tall crocketed finials of the church tower. Margery said, 'I suppose it's all a sort of Midsummer Night's Dream.'

Mike wasn't having this. 'It is *not* a Midsummer Night's Dream,' he said. 'People are always getting this wrong. *Yesterday* was the longest day, the 21st. That's a fact, an astronomical fact. Midsummer *Day*, which is an ancient pagan festival, is on the 24th. Tomorrow, if you must, is Midsummer *Eve*.' He shook his head furiously. 'Today is nothing, absolutely nothing.'

'I suppose I meant . . .'

'It drives me *mad* when people get that wrong.'

They parted at the Halls' gate, though Robin glanced back to watch Mike muttering over the door-key. Margery must be very drunk too, of course, but she showed it only by her expressionless heaviness, and the occasional utterance of a harmless but incensing remark. There was a chink of light, and then the slam of the door.

Robin and Justin turned for home. Their shoulders touched lightly as they walked and Robin took Justin's hand for a few steps, till Justin pretended he had to blow his nose. He felt miserably in love, with an almost teenage pain brought on by the distant presence of the dance-music in the summer night, and an older person's bleaker ache at the shouts of his son's friends funnelling into pleasure. 'All right, darling?' he said.

'Fine,' said Justin, as if he'd been accused of something.

A few paces later Robin said, 'What do you make of this George character? I hope he hasn't got designs on Dan.' He peered into the heavy shadows under the copper beech on the green – its huge trunk was ringed by a seat where two of the boys from the party were sitting, you couldn't quite see but they were obviously snogging, and he wondered if that could ever have happened before in the tree's 300-year history. He thought it was the tree Hardy had in mind in his poem 'An Assignation – Old Style'.

Justin said, 'It's a bit late to worry about that, I'm afraid. He was bragging to me just now about how crazy Danny was for him, and how he'd had to choke him off. His phrase, not mine. While you and I were settling into rustic bliss in Little Gumdrops it seems young Danny was round in Holland Park servicing Arthur Negus.'

'You're not serious.'

'Well that's what he said.'

'So you mean Dan is clinging on?' It was more disturbing and unwelcome than he could rationally account for. He felt he should somehow have been there to screen and approve his son's lovers, it was another dereliction too subtly painful ever to have been expected. 'I mean, he's so . . . charmless, and self-satisfied.'

'He is quite sexy,' Justin said. 'You know boringness can be so arousing. One day I'll have to work out why that is.'

In a mood of obscure retaliation, Robin said, 'Your old boyfriend's becoming quite a fixture.'

'It was sweet of him to bring that champagne,' said Justin, in a tone of serene acceptance he would never have shown to Alex in person.

'No, George brought the champagne.'

'I think not.'

'Alex brought the cake, and George brought the champagne. Danny told me so.'

'Darling, I saw Alex get the fucking champagne out of his car and take it up to put it in Mrs Badger's fridge. You were far too busy strimming to notice.'

Robin stopped, less to argue than to enact his puzzlement. 'But why?'

Justin took a moment to answer, out of delicacy, Robin thought. He looked down at the coping of the low wall beside him, where snails had left tracks that shone in the moonlight like chalked hearts and girlfriends' names. 'He just wants to fit in, darling. He's terribly lonely – he obviously thinks you hate him. Alex is always giving people things, and often his presents are too extravagant, sometimes people are so embarrassed that they never speak to him again.'

'But I'm giving this party,' Robin said, with a childishness that he heard and couldn't help laughing ruefully at.

'You can hardly object to someone presenting you with a case of Bolly.'

'No, I suppose not. It's not Bolly, actually, it's Clicquot, but still.'

'It's unquestionably Bolly.'

'Oh what the fuck does it matter what it is?' Robin shouted quietly and stamped off for a few paces, then turned and almost ran at Justin, who looked slightly frightened. Since the absurd and shaming incident in the car, Justin had shown a physical mistrust of him, and still winced if he touched his face, even though the bruise had gone. Now the kiss was long and hard, Justin didn't resist, but there was something desolately stagey to it, as if it were very late in a run of one of the plays he no longer auditioned for. His tongue performed the usual explorations, Robin felt the awkward hardness of his trapped dick pressing against his own, that homosexual conundrum with its various witty solutions. But when it was over it was over, Robin saying, 'I love you', with tears of frustration in his eyes, and Justin, like a secretary briefly disarranged by an importunate boss, smoothing himself and murmuring, 'We'd better get back.'

During their absence a new arrival had parked at the top of the lane, a battered yellow Escort that half-blocked the gateway of their tight-lipped neighbours the Harland-Balls (subject of some of Justin's freest wordplay). Robin anticipated trouble and strode down through the garden with a new resolution to forget himself and think only of Danny. There were hours and hours of party to go, which seemed, from moment to moment, a torture and a blessing.

Little groups were standing or sprawling in the garden, some intimate around the steady candles, others more noisily out of control. He saw that they were weaving shelters out of their London lives around themselves, though maybe the magic of the country night still glinted in through the chinks. In the sitting-room, with the french windows open, dancing had begun; the relentless club atmosphere of the music seemed slightly comic in a setting of watercolours and Bernard Leach

124

pottery, and the first dancers were drunk but self-conscious, smiling a lot or staring at the floor. Robin thought he would move one or two things, and took a large vase through to the kitchen, where an intent little circle was gathered round the table. Danny had his back to him, and turned with a lazily criminal look, which he immediately guyed into a joke. 'You're not supposed to be in here!'

'A father's place is in the kitchen, dear,' Robin said, and heard how rare it was for him to be camp.

George was sitting chopping coke on the back of a dark shiny cookery-book. For a second, Robin worried more about the marks the razor would make on the cover than the sub- stance the razor was so finely fanning and gathering and trailing into lines. It was something he had once done in this kitchen himself, though not of course when Danny was there; and evidently it was a ritual Danny had some experience of too; but it wasn't an event that father and son had ever taken part in together, or that one had taught the other, and Robin felt embarrassed and a little compromised by the business. He saw the almost sexual expectancy of the ring of young men and the corrupt generosity of George, who had laid out so much money to impress them, and perhaps make them more malleable. He set down the vase that he was still clutching, and started putting plates in the dishwasher with censorious scrapings. George sniffed and pushed back his chair and was soon congratulating himself on the excellence of the stuff. Robin glanced across to see Alex being coached by Danny in how to snort a line, but when Danny's own turn came he went outside.

He picked up a nearly full glass that was balanced on the window-sill and knocked it back – it was the cheap wine Dan had brought from London, and its appearance marked a further phase in the party's downward career. He felt for a moment like a person who's not much good at parties, the sort you find by themselves plucking books from the bookcase as if perfectly happy. He looked at the stars above the still trees and wondered if he wanted to be rescued and swept away by someone charming. The scene in the lane with Justin made him flinch with wretchedness and anger at having been snubbed. He had never been in such a situation before, and had a dread of life

125

being different from now on, his powers steadily withdrawn, like cancelled memberships. He saw what they meant by the change of life. He stood hunched in a horrible new atmosphere of doubt, his mind crowded by Justin's sexual presence, hardly able to believe that something so banal was happening to him. The tall black man who came round the corner of the house seemed to emerge quite naturally from this painful ruck of thought, and struck Robin as at once unexpected and inevitable. He was chatting in a careless hilarious way to one of the boys Robin had brought from the station; he was differently dressed, in a black roll-neck shirt and beige pants with a low crotch like an American serviceman, but Robin knew his rolling muscular walk exactly, and the naive friendly effect of his broken nose, and the glint of the gold cross that hung from his ear-ring.

He followed them indecisively through the back door and watched them drawn into the charged field of the coke-tooters, whom Danny seemed to be calling forward or discouraging according to some inscrutable regime of his own. Then Justin was coming through from the sitting-room, raising his hands to screen the drug-takers from his sight in a slightly old-maidish charade of his genuine disapproval, and Robin caught the moment of unprepared contact, the black man saying, 'Oh, hello!', Justin touching his arm and saying merely, distantly, 'Hello darling' as he passed by, and the black man watching him go with a humorous, remembering look.

Justin put his hand on Robin's shoulder for a few seconds and Robin welcomed the gesture and the palpable guilt that prompted it. 'I knew it would come to this,' Justin said, with no awareness of the heart-stopping larger way in which his words could be taken; he meant simply the cocaine. And perhaps Robin's anxiety on both subjects gave the edge to his question:

'Who's that black guy you just spoke to?'

Justin turned with a heavy sigh; and clearly he was broadbrush and indiscriminate with drink. 'What, that one, darling? No idea. Never seen him before in my life.' It was the most unguarded lie that Robin was aware of having heard from him, and he saw he couldn't respond to it with the little sarcasms and chidings he used to sort out the minor evasions, some mystery in the phone-bill or a vanished bottle of wine. 'Why don't you ask Alex?' Justin went on. 'He appears to be an old friend.' And it was true that Alex had an arm round the man's shoulders, and in the middle of speaking to him suddenly plonked a kiss on his cheek. Robin thought, you poor fool.

He strolled over and interposed himself before the black guy could take the rolled-up banknote. 'Hi, I'm Robin. I'm Danny's father.'

'Oh. Hi – Gary,' said the man, half offering a long and beautiful hand, which Robin ignored, and assuming a look of insincere respect. Robin wondered if he knew he was gay, if Dan had talked about him, and for the first time in the evening hoped not.

'Is that your car, the yellow Escort?' He thought angrily of it trundling its way through all the months since he'd seen it before, and homing in at last by some mechanical instinct on this cottage a hundred miles away. He pictured it on the verge of the A303 at two in the morning, with the bonnet up and Gary jumping back from it flapping his elegant fingers. 'I'm afraid it's blocking our neighbours' drive. Can you move it?'

Justin had come up, and said with a nervousness only Robin would have traced, 'They're called the Hairy Bollocks, darling. You mustn't get in their way.'

Puzzled, smiling fairly good-naturedly, Gary followed Robin from the room, round the edge of the now almost unlit dance-floor, out of the house and up through the garden. Robin's heart was thumping, but he felt concentrated; he knew he had the involuntary prim smile of masked tension. When they got to the gate, he said, 'I'm sorry, I don't want you here, you're going to have to go.'

There couldn't have been any doubt about his tone, but Gary sniggered, and stopped in the near-darkness to try to read his face. 'Huh?'

'Please go.'

Gary shook his head, and the cross twinkled for a second. 'What's the problem?'

'It's not your fault,' Robin said reluctantly. 'I just don't want you in my house.' His unreasonableness made him sound more

127

bitter, as though to justify itself. He wished the guy wasn't black, and so obviously nice enough. He thought he had the characterless niceness you'd expect from someone who pleased strangers for a living.

Gary said, 'I just got here, man. I just drove three and a half hours, to see my mate Danny. It's his birthday.'

'I know that,' said Robin quietly. He knew he was being a monster, and in the thick of this clumsy little episode saw objectively for a second that this was the kind of thing he did now. 'You'll have to stay somewhere,' he said, in a feeble concession, and pulled out the crumpled notes from his back pocket and thrust them at the insulted guest without counting them. He thought it was £40 or so.

'I wouldn't touch your fucking money,' said Gary; though the offer clearly marked a point of no return. He backed away, and Robin was glad he couldn't see his expression. The boys who had been smooching under the copper beech were just coming home, and one of them greeted Gary, who was too angry and hurt to say more than 'Look out for that one, he's a wanker' as he got into his car. They all watched his squealing, snaking reverse down the lane. Then the boys slipped past Robin with an evasive murmur. He waited for a minute or two, thinking what he would say to Danny; then went slowly down the path with the sense that what he'd done might one day be forgiven but could never be explained. He came into the kitchen with a sure feeling that word of the event had preceded him; he took up a bottle brightly and offered it round but he knew he brought with him a mood of smothered crisis and a host's too evident desire that his guests should know nothing of it. Alex came up and put an arm round him, with a ridiculous new friendliness, and asked confidentially what had happened to Gary.

'He had to go,' Robin said, and remembering the half-dozen breakfast-times he'd seen him in Hammersmith, explained, 'he got a call on his mobile.'

'Oh,' said Alex sentimentally. 'He was rather sweet.'

Robin thought, You stupid cunt, day after day, within minutes of your going to work, that rather sweet man used to go into your house and fuck your boyfriend, in the bed you'd

128

just got out of, or perhaps over the kitchen table, or even on the hall floor, and you knew nothing about it. But to tell that story would be to picture himself waiting outside in the car. The anxiety and humiliation gripped him again for a moment. He went to the cupboard and poured himself an anaesthetising Scotch.

Somehow the incident was kept from Danny, and when he found Gary had gone he was too reckless with coke to concentrate on the story. Robin alternated between keeping an eye on him and wondering if there was any point. The party was becoming sweaty. One or two of the bigger boys had taken their shirts off, and though Robin himself was often shirtless in the house and loved muscle weight and tone he found the effect disconcerting, as if guests had come to dinner and stayed on to play strip poker. He saw Terry Badgett come through, in his party clothes, sharply pressed navy-blue trousers and a baggy white shirt, looking, to Robin's rusticated eye, far sexier than the city boys, who were so habituated to fashion and fun. He was wary of Robin, after the row of a fortnight ago, but Robin nodded at him genially and saw that he was Danny's by right. As for himself he would never have anything so young again; a thirty-five-year-old was trouble enough. And if he did fall prey to some doting nostalgia for the lustre and stamina of twenty-two, he could always ring Gary or one of his colleagues; maybe that was the sort of thing that lay in wait in this unwelcome new phase of his life. 'Hello Terry,' he said, and they shook hands.

'I'm going to be doing some work for a friend of yours,' Terry said; which made Robin wonder what friends he could be said to have. 'Over at Tytherbury, at the mansion. Mr Bowerchalke's got me in to do some decorating in his new rooms.'

'Oh, great,' said Robin, though he wasn't sure Terry was up to the kind of thing he intended for the Odd Room. Tony was evidently saving money again. On his last visit Robin had agreed to a second Campari, saying 'Really, just a drop', and watched Tony, with no obvious intention of offending him, decant exactly that, as carefully as a chemist in a lab. 'How did this come about?'

'Ah, my mum's an old friend of Mrs Bunce,' said Terry, with a narrow-eyed smile that suggested even larger networks of obligation at his command. It was something else remotely Italian about him, along with the dark, slicked-back hair, and the wide-hipped unclassical body that reminded Robin of a Vespa-driving boy he'd been distracted with lust for on an early art-trip holiday with Jane. Then Dan came up and hugged them both and took Terry away to dance, like an old-fashioned host at a different kind of party.

Robin was looking around in the relief and tolerance of new drunkenness when Lars came up to him. He was clearly a bit spacy from the coke, but retained his air of wanting nothing more than to talk to whomever he was with. This was charming in itself and in its rarity; he didn't have the feverish, alienated look of most of the others. And in fact he said, 'I was thinking it's quite like some gay club here, you don't mind?'

Robin shrugged, smiled and said, without working it out, 'I was going to gay clubs before you were born.'

'Oh . . .' said Lars, with amused surprise, though Robin couldn't tell what part of his remark had provoked it. He said, 'I agree it is a bit different in your own home,' and finished his Scotch. 'Actually, it's just what the village needs.' They laughed and Robin said, 'Do you want to smoke some hash?'

'Oh, sure,' said Lars, with the unintended tone of someone agreeing to do some light chore; but hesitated as Robin moved off, perhaps uncertain where they were supposed to do it. Robin turned to see where he was, and he came up and touched his elbow, and followed him out across the garden to the dark shape of the work-room. They both looked up at the moon, and even in the context of driving dance-music and half-naked men there was something miscreant about them. The Arab-looking boy ran into them, coming back from doing who knew what under the trees, and they spoke meaninglessly for a minute. Robin was glad Lars made no reference to their own little plan: his silence was a confirmation.

He felt for the key in the crack over the door, and let Lars in, reaching round him in the deep shadow to turn on the hooded brass desk-lamp. 'So this is your den, am I right?' Lars said, looking at the books, the pinned-up drawings, the white slope of the drawing-board; silently taking in the photos of Justin, and Danny at his graduation, and Simon, whose very existence had been unknown to him. On the desk was the chunk of white vitreous china with SEMPE on it; he seemed to find it amusing and weighed it in his hand while Robin opened a drawer and took out an old tobacco-tin and his little hash-pipe. In the tin, wrapped in foil, was the dense cube of stuff he'd brought back from London earlier in the week, and had hidden here, with a rare and trivial sense of keeping a secret from Justin; though now it seemed, with Lars smiling and humming, and swinging round to perch one big handsome buttock on the edge of the desk, to be part of a larger deception. He found it hard to keep the amused expectancy out of his face and voice. He said, 'Dan seems to be having fun.'

Lars smiled indulgently. 'Well, that's as usual.'

Robin picked up the lighter and said, 'You must know him quite well?' For a second he heard a distorted echo of another kind of chat, the pipe-smoking housemaster and the prefect he wants to trust; though Lars seemed to understand, and even to be waiting for some mild interrogation.

'I've known him for a long time,' he said. 'Five or six months.'

'Gosh,' said Robin, and sucked the flame down to the bowl and held the smoke in – it was a brief suspension of ordinary manners, he and Lars holding each other's eye with impersonal concentration, as if waiting to record an experiment. Then he breathed out slowly, and passed the pipe over. It was like a little silvery spanner you use to mend a bicycle; Lars had trouble getting anything through it, and Robin reached up with the lighter and covered his hand with his own. Again they stared at each other – though he knew the hit would take a minute to come. The boy looked down with a quiet laugh and idly fingered the china fragment.

'This must have a story connected, am I right?'

Robin said, 'My boyfriend Justin says it's just a bit of an old bog', with a sense that it would be honourable to mention him.

'Ah yes . . .' said Lars, perhaps uncertain of the slang. 'Yes, he's so funny.'

'He's a scream, isn't he.' Robin got up and came round the

131

desk and dropped sideways into the old armchair. 'It's special to me, anyway,' he said. Of course he hardly noticed it any more, it was a sort of paperweight; but there were times when he remembered its tenuous accidental story and the quivering light of the day he stole it, or picked it up, which was the day he learned he was to become a father. All he told Lars was, 'It's a bit of an old bog from a house in Arizona that I went to when I was a student. When I was Dan's age.'

'So what does SEMPE say?'

'It's trying to say SEMPER, which is thc Latin for always.'

'Ah,' said Lars wistfully. 'So it's almost always' – and then looked down at Robin with a coyness that dissolved to reveal something fiercer and less voluntary.

'Do you know everyone here?' Robin asked, aware of the bad continuity – it came from embarrassment and also perhaps from the muddling onset of the hash. He didn't often smoke and was surprised each time by the stealthy twist the drug gave to his thoughts and sense impressions.

'Oh, most of them,' said Lars, with a shrug, as if the distantly thumping party was a forgettable preamble to this scene in the hut. The room still held the old-fashioned warmth that had gathered in it all day – an odour of wood-stain and tar, like the shed at home where they had stored the tennis-net and the croquet box. Robin was sensitive to the smell and its sugges-tions. He shared with Justin an aroused openness to smells, which was why they both liked sex first thing on a summer morning, after sweaty sleep which was itself brought on, magi-cally quick and deep, by the abrupt exhaustion from sweaty sex before it. He saw his mind caught up in the blurred rhythm of remembered and expected sex, and glanced down dopily to see how noticeable his erection was; and then remembered further that he and Justin had barely touched each other for a fortnight. Of course the room had the illicit smell of hash now, though he could still pick up Lars's ambiguous cologne, he was just beside him after all, a beautiful lime-scented presence sitting side-saddle on the edge of his desk. For the moment it made him careless and ironic about Justin. 'Pass me the pipe again,' he said.

When they'd both had another hot pull on it, he watched

132

Lars get up and go across in front of him to shift some papers from the other chair and sit down. His movements were decisive but inaccurate, and Robin found that a comforting proof that they were getting out of it together. He had the feeling with this young man that he didn't need to pretend, that he could perfectly well tell him things about his life and how it wasn't one he'd ever planned on, things he hadn't yet told to anyone else. It was the feeling of unexpected arrival that marked out some friendships in their first hours, and left other chance encounters as memories of unexplored potential. Even so, he was forty-seven, and stoned and horny, and knew what he was allowing to happen.

'Wow,' said Lars, 'this is quite something', and shook his head and pushed both hands back through his shiny pale-blond hair. It was a three-legged Frank Lloyd Wright chair he was sitting on, with his thighs apart, following the suggestion of the triangular seat. Robin knew they weren't saying much, but wasn't sure if the boy did, or if they savoured the smiling silence in the same way – how many parts lust, how many mere stunned surrender to the drug.

'You probably had a lot of coke first,' Robin said, and they both found something a bit comic in his words; sometimes everything you said was funny, and waited for with a bottled-up laugh, as if the simple fact of enunciation were preposterous – as it had often seemed in the giggly tedium of adolescence.

'Whatsaname,' Lars said, 'Danny's lover is quite off his face, I think.'

The words hung for a while in Robin's mind before finding any clear referents in the outside world. He watched Lars undoing one, two, three shirt-buttons and sliding a hand in to stroke and comfort himself. The phrase 'Danny's lover', which Robin had never heard before, was coolly unambiguous, but he couldn't attach it to a particular person. He saw how lover had become a gay term; you didn't hear straight people talk about their lover, there was a new defiance in the bucolic old word. He thought Lars might mean George, and said, 'Well, he brought the stuff, didn't he? He's probably had much more than anyone else.'

Lars was smiling distantly at him, as though he hadn't heard

133

him. Then he said, 'No, you mean George. I mean his new lover.' He looked down, the matter seemed to be closed, but he added, 'I hate George.'

'Yes, he's an absolute shit,' said Robin, which they both found extremely funny.

'I've been with George,' Lars went on, 'and I can tell you – quite uncategorically – how he treated me, well . . . he treated me like shit.'

'He dumped you!' Robin said, with a broad new sense of metaphor. 'Baby, you were lucky.' He swung round with a grin to sit square in the chair, with his strong Blue's legs in their pale old denim stretched out in front of him. He let the matter of Danny's new lover slip away into the remote context of the party and the night outside. He wasn't going to do anything with Lars, but it was thrilling being with him. The reflection of the lamp in the window obliterated the view of the moonlit field they might otherwise have had. Robin felt a steady buzz between his legs, and a ringing in his ears, and surreally imagined them connected, like an impatiently thumbed doorbell. He laid a hand loosely across his lap, concealing and emphasising. It was a lovely mood, he felt his unrefusable sexual power again, with the certainty that it was what made his life worth living. Just the weight of his hand was electrifying. He saw the photos on the wall, and thought of Simon when he had first met him, and Marcus coming round in the afternoons while Jane was at the library; and Justin in the stinking Gents on Clapham Common – he dared himself to think of him, and found he could do so with a new complacency.

Lars was crouching by Robin's chair, with an arm across his knees to balance himself. His finger drew a little pattern again and again on Robin's right thigh, but he was looking up into his face, hardly aware of what he was doing. Robin found himself gasping quietly, as if he kept forgetting to breathe. Lars's features had taken on a marvellous intensity, they seemed to have been cleansed to their essential beauty in a solution of desire. Robin had never taken ecstasy, but he thought its effect might be something inexpressibly vivid like this. Lars was familiar, but he was compellingly strange too – Robin frowned and sneered as he ran his fingers over the young man's cheeks and nose and open lips. Lars butted his face repeatedly against his hands, licking and biting them, and muttering what Robin might have said, 'You're so beautiful.'

He slid up along Robin's sprawled body, and the warm squeezing weight of him was almost a torture of excitement. They were face to face when someone tried the door, and after a moment a slow loud voice said, 'I dunno, it's locked, there's a light on', and the handle was rattled again. 'Someone shagging in there already' – and a sullen laugh. Then the voices retreating, with a shouted afterthought, 'Give 'im one from me!' The two of them were still, their parched mouths inches apart, faces a flushed blur. Robin smelt the stale coke-breath that outlasted the sweet reek of the hash smoke; he tested it for its own perverse sweetness, since it was Lars's breath. And then there was the kiss, slow and luscious at first, and then choking and ferocious, as though each was trying to cram his head into the other's mouth. Something happened then for Robin, maybe it was the ghost presence of his lover's cold kiss beneath the passionate kiss of this virtual stranger, some oblique and painful reminder, the drug's jumped connections. He felt it sharpen and chill like the alarm that penetrates a dream before it wakes you. He held the boy's heavy head away from him – he kept pushing towards Robin's ear with the slurred whisper, 'I want you to fuck me . . .' Robin said, 'No . . . no . . .' firmly, regretfully, and made himself awkward against him, though he knew he was in no state to understand. He watched with guilty dismay as Lars struggled to his feet, pushing down his trousers and pants in a sort of sexual fury. Robin shut his eyes and heard the shout and felt the warm accusing strokes fall lightly across his face.

'Darling, have you heard, we're all going to Sicily,' said Justin, though the last word didn't come out quite right. He was leaning by the sink with his arms round two young men, who were chewing and grinning on and off as they remembered or forgot where they were; one was half-naked and had a faint stubble across a once-shaved chest. Each of them seemed to

135

support the others by some clever structural counterpoise. It was clear that Justin, who was merely very drunk, had happily synchronised with their different disarray. 'We're going to Sissy with Marge, and Curtains,' he said, shaking each of them in turn to win confirmation of this delightful new fact.

'Mark, and Curtis,' said one of the boys, with actually rather thin tolerance, and lifted an empty champagne bottle to his lips.

Robin looked at them from his own stoned distance. Standing alone by the stream for five minutes, ten minutes, his head ringing, his eyes twitching across the plains of stars, he had been gripped by a ghastly adolescent sense of helplessness – though he knew his thoughts had been wilfully fucked up or unblocked by the hash. He was still so randy that he shivered and swallowed as his mind groped round Justin, round one or two others at the party, and Lars of course, to whom he'd ended up feebly saying, 'I'm very sorry, please don't tell anyone'; as he'd watched him go off into the shadows he was picturing what he might have done with him if they'd met up fifteen years ago in some club – though Lars was only about nine then probably. Robin found himself laughing dully at the thought that he could have seen him as a schoolboy on his honeymoon trip northwards with Simon; their visit to the wooden palace at Trondheim came back to him with extraordinary clarity. That was another effect of the drug, a vividness of memory, almost as if under hypnosis, he could walk from room to room of a house he hadn't seen for twenty years, or feel the presence of a long-forgotten man with the stifling closeness of a figure summoned up by a medium.

'Where have you been darling?' said Justin, and the boys tittered because he had an amusing way of speaking – he could hint at a lurking joke in 'Pass the salt', which was why there was something so grim to his black moods, when his command of the saving funniness of things was shown to be a mere rhetorical trick.

'Have you missed me?' Robin asked, running his hand over the top of his head with a sudden horror that it might still be streaked with Lars's dried semen.

Justin paused to consider this opportunity for marital

pleasantness. Maybe he sensed Robin's unusual odour of guilt, maybe Lars had in fact blabbed about being led on by Danny's daddy in the garden shed. Justin said, 'I'm entertaining, darling. I can't think of everyone', at which Robin managed a pained smile and turned away to find a drink. He felt the usual loneliness of the party-giver heightened, a memory of something he didn't know had happened to him, the time when all the guests had gone and you went to bed alone.

A hawkishly handsome young man was standing by the fridge, watching the party's lurching rallies through the kitchen with a cool smile. Perhaps because he was wearing both a shirt and a jacket he gave the impression of being unpopular. Robin cracked himself a beer and nodded at him, and the boy said, 'Hullo there, you don't know me, my name's Gordon', as though he was trying to sell him double-glazing over the phone.

'I'm Robin . . . Danny's father.'

'Ah yes!' They shook hands, Gordon lowered his head and peeped up at him in a mock-modest way that seemed to carry some reproof. 'You're enjoying the party,' he said.

'Am I?' said Robin, wondering just how bombed and sweaty he looked.

'I mean, I hope you are.' Gordon laughed, and of course it was the slight Scottish colouring to his voice that gave him his critical leverage. He nodded sideways, at the boys, the music, the chaos. 'It might be quite a shock having all these youngsters in the house.'

'I was a youngster myself, you know, until . . . well, quite recently,' Robin said, with a powerful smile.

'I didn't mean to suggest you were *old*.' Gordon gestured at his own physiognomy, and then toiled in his error: 'Heavens, I'm thirty-four myself. It was my birthday last week, in fact. Born June the sixteenth 1962, in Perth's Memorial Infirmary.' Robin nodded and raised his can in salutation. 'Ah, there are a couple of seats free,' Gordon said, and ushered him towards them as if, whatever he might claim, he was venerable enough to need a sit-down.

'Um . . .'

'You may be asking yourself how I know Danny,' Gordon

137

was saying. 'We slept together a couple of times, not far apart, back in February. Once at his place, once at mine.'

'Ah,' said Robin, wondering if he'd missed the passage of some new freedom of information act. 'And just how far apart did you sleep?'

'Ha-ha,' said Gordon dryly. 'No, we've kept in touch. And I was very honoured to be asked to the party.' Robin supposed he could see what Danny had seen in the young man; the humourless twinkle was itself obscurely provocative. 'I don't really do this sort of thing any more.'

Robin hid his sympathy with that remark. 'You've not done any of this, for instance?' – nodding at a couple leering rivalrously over the busy razor.

'What, the charlie, the snow, the laughing powder?' said Gordon, with the weary sarcasm of a customs officer. 'No, I don't do that stuff. I don't drink, either,' he added, clarifying something else Robin found odd about him, the scary availability of his hands for exaggerated gestures; again there was the sense of salesmanship. 'No, no. I prefer the high of life.'

'Ah, that,' said Robin.

Gordon leant forward – they were knee to knee. 'I think the real excitement comes from embracing life as it is, not escaping from it into unsustainable fantasies.' He was smiling, but Robin thought there was some kind of challenge in his unconversational tone, and said easily and courteously,

'Don't you think sometimes the escape can be part of the embracing? I mean, altered mental states, or whatever, may all be experiences worth having.' Gordon was looking at him intently, and Robin recognised the attitude of someone who waits with apparent respect for a phrase they can attach their argument to. 'How do you go about embracing life as it is?' Robin asked. 'At any given moment?'

Gordon didn't answer this directly; he smiled thinly to suggest he'd spotted a trick question. Then he said, very quietly and confidentially, 'We have to be ready for change, when it comes.'

Robin said, 'Yes, quite. Though as an architect I have a certain taste for permanence . . .'

'I don't think we have any idea of the changes that are going to happen, very soon, as God's plan for the new universe is worked out.'

Robin snickered, out of irritable embarrassment at . . . *his* name being mentioned, and also at the contrast between this encounter and the previous one in the shed, which he saw in a vivid regretful flashback. Of course the boy was an evangelist, and an evangelist of change, which would make him all the more inflexible. He said, 'I don't know about that', and looked around. Gordon had rather cleverly got them trapped in these chairs behind the door and out of the rescuing flux of the party. Robin saw his own progress through the evening, a veering line through the margins of his son's event, a sequence of volatile encounters in the near-dark. But Gordon's next question seemed to let him off:

'Do you read much?'

'Not as much as I'd like,' said Robin. 'I've been reading a bit of Hardy lately; for local reasons.'

'Uh-huh?'

'Thomas Hardy? Celebrated Dorset novelist. And poet.'

'Right . . . You haven't read Arthur Conan Doyle.'

'Oh. Well, not since I was a boy. I suppose everyone reads him when they're young, don't they? Or used to, anyway.' Gordon nodded – that seemed to confirm something he'd heard. 'Do you just like the Holmes stories or do you like Brigadier Gerard as well?'

There was a pause while the question was assayed for relevance. 'I've spoken to him,' Gordon said.

'Brigadier Gerard, you mean, or – ?'

'I've spoken to Arthur.'

'Recently?'

'A friend of mine is in close and frequent contact with him.'

'I see,' said Robin. 'You mean your friend's a medium' – aware that he had thought of mediums only minutes before, which was in itself faintly spooky.

'Arthur is very much one of the higher spirits working for world change. A truly great spirit.'

Robin's eyes made a quick panicky search of the kitchen. Danny was just slipping out into the garden. He wondered if his son had heard all this from Gordon, or if they'd been too

139

busy having sex. He supposed he must have invited everyone in his address-book, perhaps from a fear that few would come so far – though the bores, of course, were always eager to travel.

'He has a very fine voice,' Gordon was saying. 'I may say a truly fine voice.'

Robin didn't know quite how to signal that for him the conversation was over. 'What did he say?' he asked, and took a scowling swig from his beer-can.

'I've got to wait. He told me I've got to wait; and when the time comes to move, then he'll let me know. With the Millennium, of course, there will be many and great changes. He said, "You're in the right place at the right time", which was truly wonderful. It's already been a great help to me with traffic problems, always getting a green light, avoiding the major tailbacks at road-works and so forth.'

'That must be useful.'

'Oh that's just a tiny example. It was Arthur who told me that I had been a sixteen-year-old fish-seller in the Holy Land at the time of Jesus Christ.'

'You'd never suspected?' Robin had an abnormal sense of himself as a fount of unnoticed irony.

'He also told me that I'm not really gay. I just happen to be attracted to certain men. It's a spiritual thing, in fact, a spiritual magnetism; usually we've known each other in another life. Arthur said what I really have to find is a wife, he was strict about that.' And here Gordon too looked round the room with a tinge of anxiety. 'It's the woman's destiny to support the man,' he said; which perhaps gave some idea of the nature of the new world order, when it came about in four years' time.

'I don't know about that,' said Robin, shaking his emptyish beer-can and beginning to nod goodbye.

Gordon had an almost cunning look. 'I understand you're now living as a gay man,' he said.

'Well I am a gay man,' said Robin. He stood up, and as he did so he saw Justin stepping cautiously out into the garden. 'Ah, there goes life,' he said. 'And now, if you'll excuse me, I must go and embrace it.'

11

Early in July, Danny got a new job, working nights in security at a City office-building. He knew Alex wouldn't be pleased, and mentioned the hours – eight till six – quite negligently, like a child vainly hoping to slip some new freedom past its parents. Alex looked aside with an instant bright flush, as though he'd been slapped, the corners of his mouth turned down. Danny saw that he hadn't chosen the moment all that well, the early-evening chat over Alex's kitchen table; the distinguished bottle of wine he'd persuaded him to open was a clumsy palliative – of course he wouldn't want to celebrate. 'I'm not working Saturdays,' Danny said.

All Alex said was, 'Oh darling.'

Danny felt the reproach, and said, 'I need the money, Alex.' And then, 'I know the hours aren't great for us, but the pay is really good.'

Alex was both hesitant and impatient as he took up his old theme: 'I've got masses of money . . .'

Danny sighed in acknowledgement, and said, 'I know that. But I can't live off you.' He wondered if he should bring in a gibe about not being a kept boy, but saw the confusion in Alex's face and took a shifty sip from his glass instead.

'I don't see why not.'

Danny said quietly, 'I'm not Justin', and then gave a little laugh at the idea, picturing him in this house. It was the careless mockery of a predecessor, with its tacit fraction of suspicion that the predecessor might still be a rival. 'You know I hate doing nothing.'

'I know, sweetie, but nights.' He could see Alex doing the calculations he had already done, as to how they could meet, and for how long; and keeping them to himself in case the correct answer was even worse than it seemed. It was wonderful to be loved so much by somebody, and Danny jumped up with a surge of cheerful fondness for Alex and went round behind his chair and hugged him loosely from above.

'We'll have fantastic weekends,' he said.

'Mm.'

He poked his long tongue into Alex's ear, and when he had him shivering and swallowing he played him the tune he knew he wanted to hear, though he did it like an urchin, not a tempter: 'I'll take you out and stuff you full of drugs.'

The effect wasn't immediate. It would have been rather hurtful if it was. Alex had to bend slowly and gracefully to the idea without suggesting that it erased his earlier doubts. 'But you could do that anyway,' he said. Danny saw the benefits of having kept him on such a short leash – he had yet to give him his second E, though Alex had begged him for it, and even sulkily pointed out that he'd paid for it. 'Well that would be lovely,' he said.

Danny slid round and sat across his lap for a short snog. 'Anyway,' he said, 'you know me: I'll probably resign within a week.'

He started a couple of days later and pretended to Alex that it was a terrible drag; he never tried to tell him quite how much he liked the job. He had always been a night creature, sometimes went to clubs that didn't even open till three or four in the morning, and found himself in a state of incredulous alertness whenever Alex wandered off at 11.30 or so to clean his teeth and clamber into bed; so there was nothing abnormal to him in sitting out the small hours in St Mary Axe except the silence and the sobriety. The expanse of time he had learnt to set aside for the long trajectory of an acid trip or a couple of Es was now spent keeping a casual eye on the blue eventless-ness of a bank of video monitors, or making hourly tours of the corridors in the fifteen floors above.

Three guards were on duty at any time, one of them a superior. They took it in turns to move about, and Danny was given a break at 1 a.m. when he went to the staff-room, made a new thermos of tea and read for an hour, or wrote in his notebook. The life of the building wasn't simple, there were several firms that worked there, some of which closed down

142

at six, while others straggled on till late, a couple of voices in an office, a single desk-lamp or computer-screen reflected in a window. The lifts were all switched off and waited with their doors open and mirrors gleaming, but he had a special key to operate them for the planners and dealers of the early hours. It was high summer, so the shift began in the refined late daylight and came to a close with the light strengthening again beyond the tinted plate-glass of the lobby. Around five their reflections began to dissolve and the narrow old street outside to redefine itself, remotely as though some trance-like stimulant were wearing off. The cleaners came in as he was hanging up his uniform, and he could leave for the early Tube with a beautiful sense of having seen something through that you never got from a banally visible day-job. Then there would be breakfast with Alex and if he didn't feel like sex he could tease him and deafly press for second and third helpings, heaping on praise for his cooking, until Alex simply had to get dressed and leave for work; and then a long uninvaded morning of sleep from which he would wake about three with a bizarre absence of hangover symptoms or other toxic after-effects. The successful discipline of it all gave a sparkle to his self-regard.

His first week he worked with the same people; the senior one, Martin, was a moustached fitness-freak of about fifty, with a barrel chest and upper arms that stretched the vented seams of his short-sleeved shirt. Danny imagined he was gay, though various discreet remarks based on this conjecture had been met with a distancing sarcasm. The other man was a morose heterosexual with a pudding-basin haircut and a copy of *Mayfair* in his locker. There was a mood of stifled sexuality about the place through all those vacant hours, and Danny assumed that the other two were also caught up in private worlds, and imagining quite different scenes as they gazed at the steeply angled views of the lobbies, the goods entrance and the underground car-park.

One night at the beginning of his break Danny went up to the fifth floor to have a wank in the Gents; it seemed too obvious to use the staff toilet, and the choice of floor was subliminally tipped by the attractive young banker who often worked late up there and might be glimpsed or smiled at or even run into in the mirrored seclusion of the Gents. After five days of soft-soled patrols Danny was alert as an Indian guide to the faintest tremor of sex. A superficial search of desk-drawers had confirmed his suspicions about two or three of the brokers and re-insurers. He grinned at their shared secret, and then at the image of himself in the windows, trapped above the dark City like a lonely volunteer for an experiment in deprivation: he noted he was grinding his teeth from sexual frustration; already he was masturbating up to three times a shift.

He sprang his dick admiringly from his uniform, and was just getting going when he heard the door of the gents open and swing shut and then a voice call out a tentative hello. He said nothing, and after a moment the newcomer went into a further cubicle and bolted the door. Danny couldn't check on him, as the partitions came prudishly down to the floor – there was no opening for the quick bold contacts you could have in American rest-rooms. Still, he heard the knock of the seat-lid being closed, and just made out the rustle of paper and the hurried chopping noise of a plastic card on the china cistern; then a pause and a couple of sniffs; and then the chopping and sniffing repeated. Danny smiled – from amusement, and an unclear sense of power, as a kind of proxy-policeman, zipping himself stealthily back into his navy serge; and from reckless fellow-feeling, the pounce of hunger for a line or two – no, a whole night – of cocaine.

There was the sound of a flush, for authenticity, followed at once by Danny's – he pictured the suspect's alarm, and saw it too, in the man's guilty search of the mirror as he stood vigorously washing his hands. Danny came up behind him and his mood was an oddly sexual mixture of strength and need, though it wasn't the pretty banker standing there, it was an unlikely user, with glasses and a wedding-ring glinting through the slather of suds he was unconsciously working up – Danny saw the strains of the job and the marriage and the funny confidence of the coke being tested against them. He turned a tap on too, and smiled at the man in the mirror – he thought there was a certain friendly menace in his own bearing, with the blue epaulettes on his white shirt, but the tie left off, two

144

buttons open. He made up a joke that had a nasty blandness of euphemism to it: 'Who'd have expected snow on a night like this?'

The man covered his uncertainty with a deprecating frown – he clearly wasn't much of a fighter, hiding out in the office after midnight on the pretext of a crucial phone-call or a report to write; he hoped to slip out of the door without saying a word. He was at the paper towel dispenser when Danny added innocently, 'Though I love snow myself. I sometimes feel I can't get enough of it.' At which the man said,

'Ah. I see. Well . . .' – and they started their improbable transaction. Danny imagined the man would give him some, but saw in a second how that friendly idea was also a kind of blackmail. He had the narrow envelope of his first week's pay in his back pocket, and he was suddenly ready to spend sixty or seventy quid from it; he thought with slovenly affection of Alex's longing to pay for him, his readiness to make up any shortfall. He put his money on the tiled surround. The little banker had taken out his wallet and fiddled a tiny oblong packet from an inner crease. Danny unfolded it and dipped in a finger to taste it, and rub a few grains on his gums. He looked into the mirror, as if it might enhance his connoisseurship, and saw his own white-shirted figure shockingly replicated, as though by another mirror in the shadows behind him – replicated and distorted. Martin was even more noiseless than he was.

Danny tidied everything away, with a rare deep blush, and a sense that they'd all agreed this was a bad idea. He put his money back in his pocket and did up one of his shirt-buttons. Martin went to the door and held it open. He said, 'You've got five minutes to be changed and out of the building.' The muscles of his raised arm did their own impressive police work. Danny was silent and didn't want to plead or make terms in front of the other man. 'And you, sir, I would advise to be very careful.' Then Martin was gone.

'I was being careful,' said the man to the closing door, as annoyance quickly replaced fright.

Danny gave him a perhaps unallowed half-smile. 'It was my fault,' he said. He did feel very foolish, and looked back on

145

his thuggish little 'snow' jokes with a cringing reluctance to think he had made them. 'Well, I'd better get going.'

The little banker in his suit, with his huge expendable income, and his worries quickly dissolving, said, 'Look, I'm sorry about this.' Danny shrugged, half annoyed by his genial tone. The guy must be feeling really good, as the two huge lines of coke kicked in.

'My fault,' he said again; but as he turned away the man touched his arm and said,

'Why don't you have this, if you'd like it. It might help, tonight at least. Really, I'm trying to stop it – this must be some sort of sign. Besides, I've got loads more,' he added incoherently. He laughed and offered Danny the doll's-house letter again. 'It's tip-top stuff.'

So, with a halting eagerness, as though such an offer could only be a trick, he palmed the thing.

'All the best,' said the man, quite sentimentally, when they were in the corridor. He swung away towards his office, a hand across his mouth for the moment to hide the irrepressible smile.

It was 1.30 when Danny got out into the deserted street. He walked for a few yards and then turned and gave a jeer of defeat at the dark glass building with its random high-up squares of light. It was surprisingly chilly. In Leadenhall Street a lit taxi came sailing magically towards him, and he got into it, and saw he had to make a plan. It was too late, or too early, to go to Alex, and anyway he wasn't in the mood for explanations. If he went home he would fidget morosely and feel sorry for himself. The decision hardly needed to be made, and he told the driver to go to Charing Cross Road. As they raced out through the plastic chicanes which constituted the 'Ring of Steel' around the City he wished he could give the place some symbolic insult, like Becky Sharp throwing her Dictionary out of the carriage window. It had been an expulsion, but his mind would soon be working to turn it into a triumph, or at least into a providential moment of change. It was what Gordon had said to him, between, or even during, their bouts of excessively conversational sex: you had to embrace change. He saw Gordon bouncing up and down as though Danny were an exercise machine, and burbling on about God's plan for the universe to show that he wasn't out of breath. Poor Gordon! That was an affair that had never been likely to work, even if they had been lovers in Galilee in the first century AD. He chuckled noiselessly to himself at the thought of his real life, with its multiple choices and general freedom from censure, and saw that he felt better already. He would have a night of excess, and then the whole episode could be forgotten.

The Drop was packed when he arrived and he pushed his way through to the bar and ordered a large brandy and coke. It was important to be served by Heinrich, whom he'd had a brief intense fling with, and who always gave him back in change the whole amount he had just handed over in payment. As the coins slipped from hand to hand it was clear that neither of them could remember why they weren't still together. Danny swung about a bit with his drink on the edge of the dance-floor, and leaned in at the little gate of the DJ's desk to give him a kiss between the wires of his headphones. He exchanged nods and smiles with a few regulars, the older men he was sometimes so drawn to, and let his eyes run over what he called the usual strangers, young tourists who jammed these low brick cellars all summer long, and gave off such a heady mood of temporary trashiness. Then he went into the Gents and chopped some coke up crudely with a phone-card and snorted the biggest line he'd ever had, since it was free and he felt he'd earned it. He waited there for a moment or two, wondering impatiently how Martin had got on to him, what he hadn't noticed. He thought he might have followed him for some sexual thing; maybe he should have offered himself to Martin. He pictured the scene, and gripped himself between the legs as the coke opened up his mind and sent its amusing surge of energy through his limbs. It was tip-top stuff. A bit speedy, maybe. He was going up more sharply than he'd expected – he was olympian, but alight. He wondered if he'd ever been randier. He burst out into the club with something between a laugh and a snarl.

Even so, he danced for a while, just because of the power in his legs and the spreading hilarity he felt. Someone he vaguely knew came up and hugged him and he told him he'd been fired – he raised his hands as he danced and shook the thing away,

147

the veil of shame and self-accusation. The boy laughed too, since Danny was happy, and said, 'Congratulations!' Danny was so relieved to find that everything was all right.

He didn't think this guy was hot enough to have sex with. He had a look in the Ladies, which was always very busy on a Friday or Saturday night, when ladies themselves were not allowed in the club. The main space was sometimes taken up by a slowly mutating body of men, a couple maybe having sex in the middle while ten or twelve others pressed around them, staring and saying 'Yeah' and 'Fuck him', jacking off and getting caught up with each other in turn. But at the moment nothing much was happening, though rapid jolting noises from one of the cubicles showed that someone had got the right idea.

There was a mysterious dim passageway which started outside the lavs and went round two corners before ending up by the front door and the cold draught down the stairs from the street above; Danny had sometimes emerged from the corridor blinking as if from an improbable erotic dream. He swaggered along it now, past heavily groping couples, and at the first corner he met Luis, a big Brazilian boy in boots and falling-down jeans and a leather waistcoat, muscly but a bit plump too; his back was long in proportion to his legs and he had a big head of curly dark hair. He looked like a giant dwarf, Danny thought, as Luis frowned at him, and then gave him a smile with some gold in it, and put his arms round his neck and his tongue in his mouth. Danny pushed him against the wall, with one hand in the cool sweat at the top of his bum, and the other, after a moment's polite hesitation, working roughly at his loose crotch.

They agreed to go back to Danny's place – this was too good to squander in five minutes in the toilet. It turned out Luis had a friend in the club, another Carioca, whom they went to say goodbye to, a thin, poetic-looking boy all in black. After a minute of impenetrable muttering, perhaps an argument about keys and plans for the morning, Danny placed a hand on both their necks, apprehending them from the utopian height of his mood, and said to Luis, 'Why doesn't Edgar come with us?'

*

148

He rang Alex at 7.30. 'Hi darling,' he said, in an airy, somehow miserable way.

'Hello, sweetheart. I hope you're hungry!'

Danny let out a little groan. 'I'm not really. Actually, I'm at home.'

'Oh darling. Are you okay?'

He paused in the face of Alex's innocent whole-heartedness, the maternally prompt note of worry. 'Yeah, I'll be fine. I just felt a bit strange in the night. I don't know . . .'

'I'll come over. I've made the pancake mixture, but that doesn't matter. Let me see, can I bring you anything? Have you got some Disprin?'

'No, don't. There's no point,' Danny said, with an edgy jump of volume that he regretted. 'Really, Alex, I just need to sleep for a few hours. I've been up all night, remember . . . Okay . . . I'll ring you later, darling . . . I'll ring you later . . . okay . . . bye . . . bye', and he squeezed the End Call button with a vivid, not wholly serious image of prising someone's fingers from a life-raft.

He pulled on his boxer shorts and went to the kitchen to make a cup of tea. Dobbin was sitting at the table, with a haggard but sentimental look. 'Dan, my man,' he said. 'That was some wild shit last night.'

'You look like you had a good time,' said Danny.

Dobbin cast around the room for help in conveying what he had been through. 'I was stuck down this fucking K-hole for like, forever,' he said. 'And they're all saying, "Come on, man, let's get out of here", and I'm like, "I can't move, guys! Don't leave me, guys!"'

'You're always getting stuck down a K-hole,' said Danny. 'I don't know why you keep doing that stuff.'

'Am I . . .? Yeah . . .' Dobbin pursed his lips and nodded slowly to suggest that Danny was right, he'd have to get a rein on this thing. 'What about you man?' he said.

But Danny didn't feel like accounting for his night with Luis and Edgar. When the kettle boiled he said with a yawn, 'I think I'm going to give up this job. It's too boring, being stuck there all night, with nothing happening.' He'd never had ketamine,

149

with its notorious hour-long 'holes' of dissociation, but he said, 'I might as well be in a K-hole.'

'Right,' said Dobbin, with a slow laugh. 'Except of course you get paid for it.'

Danny took his mug of tea to his room, closed the door and then set about stripping the bed. The rucked bottom sheet was damp with sweat and blotted with drying semen. Dark pubic hairs jumped up from it as he pulled it tight. He searched the duvet and the bedspread, which had been thrown aside at the beginning, and pulled the pillows out of their cases. He ran his hands over the roughness of the carpet under the edge of the bed. He looked for a second or third time in impossible pockets. But the truth was unavoidable: he had lost the chain.

He tried to think how or when it might have happened. The night was rather a blur. They'd all had their hands in each other's pants in the taxi, and from the moment they reached the house it went – wild: Danny was no better than Dobbin at expressing where he'd been. They had wolfed up all the tip-top charlie, which even the Latin Americans were impressed by, and drunk a whole bottle of brandy that the Halls had given him for his birthday. They had been through every reasonable sexual permutation that three men could manage, and given up on one or two others with baffled laughter. They just didn't stop. Edgar was what Alex quaintly called Danny: a demon. Though what that made Luis . . . The time shot by. And then the boys were getting dressed, talking quietly to each other in Portuguese, with odd nervy gestures in his direction. There was something weird about it, a sudden professional distance, as if his time was up. It was true there was no more drink or coke. They hid in their language, they couldn't explain why they were going. Luis left a number on the mantelpiece, and said 'Call me'; he and his friend, in their jeans and boots and sweat-shirts, each gave the naked Danny a friendly but formal embrace. Then they left. And then Danny, puzzled, drifting round the room unable to decide if it was accusing him or congratulating him, raised his hand to his throat and the shiver of a suddenly noticed loss. He dialled the number now, and was told by the pleasant unanswerable woman in the machine that it was not available.

The chain couldn't have slipped off, whatever they were doing; it was too tight, and the pale stone mounted in the little pendant hung high on his chest. The reddish gold could simply have snapped, but it seemed unlikely, old and fine though it was. Looking at the night in which he had lost both his job and his lover's antique gift he had a sense of himself as a person in a fable, caught up in a sequence of symbolic actions. He remembered inconclusively a story in which a fish swallowed a wedding-ring. And then he knew that that was what had happened. Luis had bitten through the chain, and swallowed it. All the kissing and biting of Danny's neck had been a preparation for the theft, he could have made a dozen unsuspected attempts at it. Danny saw the glimpses of gold through saliva when he smiled, and recalled one odd po-faced stare when perhaps he already had it in his mouth and didn't know if his action had been noticed. It made Danny shiver again, and then wonder if it could possibly be true.

12

The phone rang. 'Alex, it's Robin here.'

Alex was at work, and for a moment he thought it must be someone in the building. 'Oh . . .'

'Robin Woodfield . . .'

'Oh, *Robin*. I'm so sorry. Yes!' And he heard himself coming vocally to attention to meet the challenge of Robin and sustain himself at the right pitch of pretended friendliness.

'I hope it's all right ringing you at the office. I can't get through on Dan's mobile.'

'Of course. I probably won't be able to talk for long,' said Alex, proud and embarrassed at the same time to be coupled with Danny by his father.

'I'll keep it short. It's simply that we've got to spend the next two weeks or so in town, and we wondered if you and Dan would like to use the cottage for some of that time – all of it, even. I don't know what your holiday arrangements are.'

'Gosh.' He hadn't heard that smoothly unanimous 'we' before, and felt the force of it like the buffeting air of a passing limousine. He said, with a critical kind of modesty, 'Well, I can't speak for Danny. But it sounds a lovely idea.' He glanced at his secretary – it was the first time he'd mentioned his new boyfriend in the office – but she seemed unshaken by it; though she must have noticed, he certainly hoped she'd noticed, his general rejuvenation and hip new taste for life. 'I'll ask him later. And one or other of us will give you a ring.'

'Fine.' There was a pause, in which Alex flicked through various pointless possible topics. All he said was,

'It's very kind of you,' with a certain suggestion that he didn't expect kindness. But Robin was saying,

'And again, I'm very sorry about what I said at the party. I wasn't in my right mind, I'm afraid.'

'Well, none of us were.'

'No . . . You must have thought I was mad. I think I am going a bit mad,' said Robin, with such candour that Alex felt it must be an act.

'I'm sure you're not,' he said firmly; he did think Robin's behaviour worryingly erratic, every time he saw him he did something you might call mad, but he didn't want to give him that excuse. 'Don't worry, I can hardly remember it myself.' What Robin had said was, 'Christ, Dan, you can't be serious.'

Alex thought again about that 'we' when he got home. For a long time the idea of Justin's being half of another couple had been so painful to him that he shut it out with a heavy black drop, like the curtain that comes down in the interval with 'For thine especial safety' written on it. Things had slowly improved, although the moment of turning back the duvet retained its charge of inadmissible misery; he took to sleeping diagonally, so as to occupy both sides of the bed. That first weekend in Dorset had made him almost hate his own loyal, retrospective nature. But since the night at Château so much had changed, change itself became beautiful to him, and he looked at Justin's new life with casual fondness and scepticism.

Even so, the 'we' had lightly winded him. He changed out of his suit into shorts and a T-shirt, put on the washing-machine, which he thought Danny could well have done earlier, opened a bottle of Sauvignon and went to sit in the garden. The palette-pricking gooseberry of the wine was a phenomenon, and he commented on it in an undertone, in a knowing day-dream that Danny was also there. And that, he supposed, was the point: how much Danny wasn't there, and how far he was from the legitimate use of a 'we' himself. Danny needed air and distraction. Alex groaned with wonder at the thought of a week with him in the country, but he hardly dared put the plan to him.

This evening Danny was seeing his friend Bob, a handsome Jamaican who had shocked Alex at the party with his assertion that at thirty-one he had never been in love. Alex had cross-questioned him in a coke-fuelled harangue and clutched at his arm until Bob clearly thought he'd fallen in love with him. 'We young ones don't fall in love,' he said, with a large emotionless

153

smile. 'Oh yes we do,' said Alex gamely. Bob's auntie was an air stewardess, and often swallowed fifty or sixty small packets of cocaine before a flight back from Kingston. Danny was supposed to come home with something tonight, and Alex was so excited by the idea, and by the matter-of-fact criminality to which Danny had introduced him, that he persuaded himself it wouldn't happen.

Of course it was difficult for young people – really young ones. Nobody could quite explain it, but it seemed to be impossible for Danny to have a proper job. Robin didn't help him much – there was surprisingly little family money. Alex thought Danny's whole upbringing had been so dispersed, back and forth between schools and colleges in England and America, that it had somehow affected his powers of concentration; or maybe it was an early diet of Class A drugs that was responsible. There was something almost self-mortifying in the jobs he did take on; and he had left two of those since Alex had met him, and was moodily disinclined to explain why. The phone was ringing and Alex hurried inside.

'Darling, it's your erstwhile lover,' said Justin.

'Um . . . who would that be?' said Alex vaguely.

'Very funny, darling. Now look, have you heard from Robin?'

'Yes.'

'And are you going to go down to Hinton Gumboil and mow the lawn?'

'I don't know yet. Is mowing the lawn part of it?'

'It's the essential part, darling. I'm amazed he didn't mention it. There will be a list on the draining board – hedging and ditching, topping and tailing, mopping and mowing . . .'

Alex laughed tolerantly. 'I don't mind all that.'

'Because as you'll have gathered we're going to be away for a couple of weeks, and frankly without my *incessant* attention the garden will become a mess.'

'Yes of course. I can see that. You'll be in Clapham, will you?'

'Well, he will. I'm in the Musgrove.'

'How do you mean?'

Justin paused. 'Ah. He didn't tell you.'

154

'We only spoke for a moment.'

'We're having a trial separation, darling.'

'Good god . . . Are you all right?'

'Things have been hopeless lately, as you can't have failed to notice.' There was a large swallowing noise – not emotion, Alex realised, but gin. 'Frankly, I think it's over. But I've agreed to have a further think. So I'm doing it in the Musgrove, which is marvellous. He doesn't know where I am, by the way. I'm just having a pre-dinner drink.'

'Where is the Musgrove?'

'Don't you know it? It's just next to Harrods. I'm the youngest person here by about forty years. It's where old lady dons stay. They all wear brown felt hats in the dining-room. I think a lot of them are lesbians. I mean real lesbians – you know, female ones.'

'Well, I don't know what to say.' Alex was surprised to find his scepticism so quickly vindicated, and surprised at how he felt for his old friend, when it should have been Robin he identified with. Justin was clearly quite drunk; he pictured him in this funny hotel – the elderly side of his character. He thought he must want company.

Justin said, 'I'll probably buy a house.'

'Right . . .'

'They've finally sold Daddy's place, so I'm swilling in money. There's no rush, of course. I'll have a look round while I'm here.'

Alex couldn't imagine him doing anything so practical. The mention of Justin's father lit a fuse, which he tried to stamp out, to the muffled explosion of a year ago, the awful week of his death and the funeral. 'Where were you thinking of?'

'What's Hammersmith like these days?'

Alex said, 'I think you need somewhere more central', rather quickly and frigidly.

'Anyway, we'll see.' And Justin passed suavely to another question. 'So how are things with Miss Daisy?'

'Fine.' Alex found that despite the openness about Robin there was something impolite and even treacherous in discussing his own new affair with his ex.

'Mmm?'

155

'It's fine. I hope he'll like the Dorset idea.'

'I should warn you that we're hideously unpopular down there.'

'Since the party?'

'They weren't mad about us before, but they loathe us now. There were formal complaints. PC Bertram Burglar came round and gave us a wigging.'

'Did he darling?' Alex was sorry to have missed that. 'It was only noise, wasn't it?'

'It was homosexual noise. That's what they don't like.'

'We were very tidy.' Alex remembered the time, about 4 a.m., the sky already paling, when they had all started clearing up obsessively; apparently it was an effect of the cocaine. Glasses were gathered and washed, bottles collected; disco-queens darted round with dusters and damp cloths, furniture was swiftly and exactly rearranged; he had found Danny in the lavatory, putting all the back-numbers of the *Architectural Review* into chronological order.

Justin said, 'They don't really know you, so you should escape the worst of the contumely.'

'I certainly hope so,' said Alex, tickled, lightly haunted, to hear that word again, which Justin had learned in an audition piece and kept on using with a variety of meanings.

'Mrs Dodgett is still with us, of course, and the Halls. The Halls are virtually outcasts too, but they only play Gregorian chant.' And following a clear process of suggestion Justin paused to refill his glass - Alex heard the clink of the ice and the joggling noise as it rose in the fizz of the tonic. 'So you're in love, are you?'

'Yes, I think so. I mean, I am. He does seem pretty keen.'

'Don't keep too tight a rein on him,' Justin said impatiently, as if this was something he'd meant to get off his chest a year or more ago.

'No, darling.'

'Did Robin say anything about it?'

'He apologised again for what he'd said before.'

Justin seemed satisfied by that. 'It came as a bit of a shock to us,' he said, in his parental mode. Then, 'Is it an open marriage?'

'Certainly not. No, we're living together. You know I'm incapable of an open marriage. He has every opportunity, but I'm sure he wouldn't mess around.'

'He's fully settled in at Brassica Road, then.'

Alex was a little exasperated by this. 'Well, he has his own place, but mostly he's here.'

'I'm just trying to picture it, darling. I'm rather jealous.'

'You don't need to picture it, it's nothing to do with you. Jealous of whom?'

But Justin laughed tremendously at that.

Afterwards Alex saw that he should be flattered by this vicarious interest. He had a quite pleasant sense of himself going up as Justin went down, and of being recharged in Justin's eyes by his success with Danny. But then he saw that if Justin left Robin he would be on the loose again, and he felt a feebly possessive instinct realerted. He also thought wistfully how nice it would be, on top of all his other perfections, his sulky beauty and manic energy, those breathtaking sprints and tranced lulls, if Danny made him laugh like Justin did.

They didn't travel down together. Danny, who was free to do so, went down the day before on the train, and had arranged to be met at Crewkerne by Terry; Alex wasn't sure if he was paying him. He went disconsolately to a straight dinner-party in Wandsworth, in the house of contemporaries who seemed to him already middle-aged; he felt he had dropped a decade. He wanted to tell them about his new impromptu life, so remote from these pleasant predictable evenings, and he noted their nostalgia and worry when the talk touched on what their teenage children did, but he kept it to himself. He always took the young people's side, which was droll for someone who worked in pensions. His last dinner-party had been a take-away at Danny's friend Carlton's, where they sat on the floor and listened to techno. Techno was like house, but 'harder', as Danny said, and seemed to have no words or tunes in it; you could only have it on very loud. It wasn't the perfect *Tafel-musik*, but Alex had loved crouching there and bawling his head off.

157

Danny rang early next morning, as excited as a child. 'Hurry, hurry, hurry!' he said. 'It's fantastic down here. I've been up since six. It's a fantastic day!'

'I'm just on my way, darling.'

'Good. I can't wait to see you.'

'I'm longing to see you.' Alex laughed. 'I do adore you, Danny.'

'Oh I love you so much,' said Danny, and rang off as if too elated to say anything else. Alex gazed at the phone with tears running down his cheeks and an aching erection.

He hardly noticed the three hours of the journey, they were eaten up by his thoughts and feelings. It was a hazy morning which clarified into stunning heat, and he roared along with the roof down in a private vortex of wind and sunlight. He sensed there were comparisons to be made between this journey to Dorset and the earlier two, but he left them luxuriously unexamined. The points on the route, turn-offs, sudden views, an ugly garage, cropped up with the stumbling fluency of something almost learnt, expected as soon as seen. When he came to the junction where an old white finger-post made the first reference to Litton Gambril his heart raced with proprietary emotion. He had to remind himself that the villagers were all against him; though when he drove past the church and the cottage gardens with their pink rose arches and the early lunchtime groups outside the Crooked Billet, he knew the place was nothing more than indifferent to him.

The gate was open and he ran the car in on to the bricks. Any moment he would have his first sight of Danny, perhaps leaping up through the garden to meet him – he jerked his bag out of the boot with a smothered smile as if already being watched. But there was no sign of him yet, there would be a tiny delay, which seemed worse, now Alex was here, than all the solitary hours before. Danny's faded pink tank-top was hanging from the back of a deck-chair, a casual flag of occupancy.

The front door was locked, and Alex went round to the back; he heard Danny's voice before he saw him and the knowledge that he wasn't alone was like the small black cloud that briefly cheats a sunlover. He scowled to think some terrible bore had called in, to complain perhaps; or even that Danny had asked someone else to stay – he was startled at how his mind ran to that unlikely possibility. But it was only Mrs Badgett. She had her back to Alex, but Danny saw him and lost the thread of the talk as he looked past her and started smiling. 'You remember Alex . . .'

'Hello Mrs Badgett.' For the moment he just nodded amiably at Danny, as if he knew all about him but hadn't yet been introduced.

'Ah, there he is! I was just saying to Danny how you couldn't keep away.'

'Not possibly,' said Alex rather archly.

'Now, have you brought any champers this time, that's what we want to know.' Alex merely grinned at this. 'Ah, you boys had a good time, anyway.'

'I wish everyone was as nice as you,' Danny said, scuffing his bare feet on the grass. It seemed all he had on was a tatty old pair of shorts. Alex saw that he still wasn't wearing the gold chain, another tiny cloud, but it burnt up and vanished in the glow of his gaze. He was astounded that Danny, who was a ravishing idea of his, could actually be standing in front of him, the perfect and only embodiment of himself, reconstituted in every detail, remembered and unremembered – after a moment he had to look away. Mrs Badgett's presence added a hallucinatory element of suspense.

'I'll tell you something,' she was saying: 'they're a lot of stuffy old buggers in this village. When did they last go out dancing, I wonder? They've got no idea of how to have fun, most of them.' And she swung her hips as if she wouldn't mind having a bit of a dance right now. Alex tried to refocus his attention on her. He thought that the green-fingered motherly side of her character coexisted with something gypsyish that you saw in Terry too. Perhaps that explained their connection with the caravan business. Terry had told him something about Mr Badgett at the party, but he couldn't recover the facts from his blurred memory of the whole odd episode, during which he had got the impression that Terry was offering him sex for money. He'd been somewhat offended by that, on top of his trifling jealousy of Terry as a former bedmate of Danny's.

159

Danny said, 'Are you going to the disco up at Broad Down?', not quite seriously.

'I might well,' she said. 'I might well. I'm not sure I'm exactly in tune with the music these days. If I can get Terry to put on some of the old slower songs, I wonder if he's got them though.'

Alex thought the conversation was never going to end. He stepped back to pick up his bag from the lawn, and gave Danny a staring, hungry smile over her shoulder. They only had four days here together, they couldn't waste time like this.

'Mind you, when I was your age,' she said, half-turning to take in Alex as well, which proved how much younger he'd become, 'we went into Weymouth for the rock 'n' roll dances every week. I'll tell you who was a great dancer, was Rita Bunce. You know Rita, don't you, up at Tytherbury. Of course she's a fair bit older than me, she married a Yankee airman over here in the war. There was a whole lot of them stationed up at Henstridge . . .'

'I'm just going to take my stuff in,' Alex said.

He went through the kitchen, where a wasp was tapping and fretting against the window-pane, and into the sitting-room. Everything had been tidied away, and there was a fusty stillness inside the house which added to the mood of sexual expectation. He felt as if he had broken in – he couldn't explain the dreamlike sense of truancy; he supposed it was something to do with Robin's not being here, with his butchly assertive way of knowing how to do everything, as though each loaf baked and log chopped implied a scorn of you for not having baked or chopped it yourself. And then Alex did remember his earliest visit, seeing Justin naked and amazing in the kitchen as the bread rose, before he even knew that Danny existed; his testing the nature of his feelings, despair and perseverance in a dubious alloy.

Danny was laughing and shouting 'Alex!' from the kitchen. Alex said nothing, but stood where he was, almost helpless with the certainty of happiness. Danny strode in and ran at him with a comic growl, jumping up on him with his arms round his neck and his legs round his waist and smiling so much that it was difficult to kiss.

*

160

They slept in Robin's – and Justin's – bed; and again Alex had a sense of transgression, which faded when he was in it, with Danny in his arms, but came back to trouble and please him when he woke in the early light with one arm numb from Danny's weight, and the beams, the bedside table and all the furniture of that other relationship steadily materialising out of the dark. The nearly noiseless tick of Justin's little clock, and its visible quivering escapement, lent an eerie continuity. Then he slept again, and woke and slept, always with the reassurance that Danny slept more heavily while he himself was fitfully vigilant and protective. Afterwards he thought of the cottage on these days as a place of sleep, and the garden too as a sleepy hollow, in its dull high-summer greens now the blossom was over, with wood-doves in the trees and the stream dwindling and trickling in the heat as if half-asleep itself. Despite all his alertness to Danny's presence, and his honeymoon sense of luck, he kept waking up and squinting at the time and finding how much sleep had got the better of him.

Danny seemed to share his awareness of the absent couple. To him they were usually a fairly comic proposition, though now there was a note of puzzlement and concern about his father. He would ask Alex idle questions about them as they lay on the grass with the papers or soaped each other in a lukewarm summer bath. 'Do you think Justin and Dad will get together again?', 'I wonder what Justin's doing tonight.' Alex was no more likely to know the answers than he was, and Danny laughed in his disquieting private way, as if at a strain of romantic folly to which he was himself immune. He seemed intermittently aware of Alex's shyness on the subject.

In the bathroom on the first night, getting ready for bed, he said, 'You don't know what it's like having a gay dad.' Alex thought of Murray Nichols, his own father, distantly benign, industrious, hidden in his work, and tried to imagine him seducing one of the junior partners: he couldn't even get the hand on to the knee. He said,

'I suppose it's a further twist on not being able to imagine your parents having sex.'

But Danny said, 'I can imagine him and Justin only too well.'

161

'Yes, so can I,' said Alex, and changed the subject abruptly. 'Aren't you wearing your chain any more, darling?'

Danny started to clean his teeth, and made a garbled noise with the brush in his mouth. 'Whore Darn Laid Learn!' he explained.

'I didn't quite make out . . .'

He stooped and spat and found Alex's eye in the mirror. 'I said, Sorry darling, I left it in London.'

'That's okay – you don't have to wear it all the time . . . You don't have to wear it at all.'

But he was treating the matter seriously. 'No, I want to. Actually I took it round to George to get it valued. I thought it ought to be insured. I meant to pick it up before I left.'

'Oh . . . It's not that precious,' said Alex.

'It is to me,' said Danny, with sentimental promptness.

Alex pushed in at the basin, the light adhesiveness of skin pressed against skin. 'You didn't say you'd been to George's.'

Danny was baring his teeth and peering in the mirror. 'Yeah.'

Alex thought he'd almost rather hear that the chain had been lost. His instinct had been against George from the start. The fact that Danny never talked about his friendship with him, even when asked directly, was odd, since he gossiped graphically about everyone else he knew. Alex was certain he'd invented the valuation business just as a pretext for seeing George. 'How is old George?' he said, as if he weren't afraid of him.

'Mm? Fine . . .'

'Well, give him my best,' Alex said, undecided what degree of irony to go for.

Danny was slipping him an old-fashioned look in the mirror, and when Alex said 'What . . .?' he shouted with laughter and then kissed him on the cheek. Alex hoped for a second that the whole thing had been a tease; but Danny said,

'Since you obviously can't stand him!'

Well, it was good to have the truth broken out like that. Alex blushed and murmured in a pretend refutation, though Danny was already putting his arms round him – he tensed and relaxed as a purposeful hand slid under his waistband.

Every morning when Alex woke he thought of Danny; his

162

thoughts emerged from the watery interview or vanishing railway-carriage of dreams, stumbled on for a few forgetful instants, pale and directionless, and then fled towards Danny in a grateful glow of remembered purpose. It was love, and all the day would be coloured by it. Or perhaps love was the primary thing, on to which the events of the day were transiently projected – that was how it seemed afterwards, when his memory gave back rather little from these months. Alex could never picture Danny as a whole – he was an effect of light, a cocky way of walking, a smooth inner thigh, a lithe sweaty weight, a secretive chuckle, a mouth drawn back before orgasm as though he was about to be sick. Alex woke up, thought of Danny, and on these lucky days felt his breath on his neck, or the curve of his hip under his hand.

On the first morning at the cottage, Alex lay for a while exploring his mood. It seemed they had announced themselves as a couple after all, by coming away, it wasn't like one of them sleeping over at the other's place. He could say 'we' now, but felt a superstitious reluctance to do so after trying it out in an imaginary phone-call. And it was true that Danny's own riotous yacking sessions on the mobile, when friends rang from London, left Alex largely unmentioned, and foolishly unoccupied too, while the unheard jokes came thick and fast and the interrupted mood thinned out and disappeared ... He raised himself on an elbow and looked at Danny, sprawled on his front with his head turned away; then ran his fingertips very gently across his shoulders, over the bare nape of his neck where the chain might have wriggled under the touch, the deep blue ineradicable knot of the tattoo, and down the long smooth slide of the back to the smooth buttocks where the kicked-off single sheet of a summer night dipped between and hid the rest of him. One or two pale hairs showed and a smear of wiped gel. He didn't know if Danny was awake, and couldn't tell if his super-delicate caresses were giving pleasure to both of them or merely to himself.

In the cool of the evening they went for a walk up the hill. It felt unnatural to Alex to be in the country and not have a walk each day, but Danny said he thought that was only if you had a dog. They went up the back lane by Mrs Badgett's and out into the fields – the way he had gone with Justin on that first late afternoon. Danny wasn't protesting like Justin, but seemed even less certain what it was one did on a walk; he bounded about with a sudden access of energy after a day spent sunbathing and dozing while Alex mowed around him. At one point he climbed a tree and Alex waited in a prolonged paroxysm of boredom, saying, 'Jolly good, darling, come down now.' He held hectoring conversations with uncommitted-looking groups of sheep. When they got to the stream, more stone than water now, and hedged in with tall coarse grass, he stood on the plank bridge and did a little shuffling dance, grinning at Alex as if they could both hear the music. Alex explained how this was the same stream that ran down and round and past the cottage, and had a moment's recall of boys peeing into it, and finding the stars a poor approximation to clublight. He mocked Danny for his ignorance of country things – he couldn't tell wheat from barley or an oak from a beech.

Alex was looking out for the giant's sofa, where he had sat with Justin six weeks earlier, but its shallow declivity was covered up with thick green bracken, and they climbed on past it and left it, like any of those unspoken sadnesses or unguessed embarrassments that one partner keeps from the other for ever. Higher up there was a tiny local outcrop of flat grey stones, and Danny loped up on to it. Alex followed and they stood for a while with their arms round each other and a sense of unspecified achievement. Danny smelt of sun-oil and sweat, sweet and sharp. They sat down, and he stretched out with his head in Alex's lap and a happy sigh. It was as if he was leaving it to his older friend, with his particular knowledge of trees and probably harmless enthusiasm for crops, to appraise the landscape while he rested and chatted and purred under his hand.

The end of day was extraordinarily still. Even the great ragged bulk of a grey poplar was motionless, until a breeze too slight to feel moved a little patch of it in a glinting whisper. Its shadow slipped towards them across the hillside, and everywhere between the shadows the light grew tender and solicitous after the rigours of the day. Alex's fair skin felt tight and warm – he'd childishly tried to keep up with Danny, who tanned easily. 'You'll have to plaster me in aloe vera,' he said.

'I will, darling,' said Danny fruitily. 'I will.'

Alex looked down at him, the sun-pinked nose, the dip at the base of the throat, the lop-sided tenting-up of his shorts that any friendly physical contact seemed to bring about, the bare ankles scratched by grass stalks. It would have been unreasonable to expect more than this from life. He picked up Danny's hand and kissed it.

Danny said, 'Is Justin rich?'

Alex recognised that he and Danny didn't often follow the same line of thought, so that when they did there was something explosively funny or sexily mysterious about it, like the first double-take of love itself. This moment was a different kind of telepathy. It struck Alex for the first time that Danny might be jealous of Justin. He said, 'I was just thinking about that – in a way.'

'Really?'

'In a way. Yes, he is quite rich.'

'He doesn't show it. I mean, he doesn't have anything.'

'He says he's going to buy a house – though you'd better not tell Robin that. He's not mean exactly, but he does find it difficult to spend. Sometimes he gives himself a treat. He always goes in for the lottery, and occasionally wins the smaller amounts, you know, a few hundred quid.'

'Of course I never win anything,' Danny said.

'Then he came into a lot of money when his father died. I don't know if I told you. His father had a factory. He made a rather ridiculous object of common domestic use.'

'Oh . . .?'

'He sold out in the eighties some time, as Justin didn't seem to see his future in the die-cast business. The father was about sixty when Justin was born, it was quite unusual. He adored him and believed he was going to be a great actor, and never seemed to notice his lack of progress. There was a terrible bronze bust of Justin in their house, done when he was about twelve. He was very wounded when I laughed at it, it was

165

highly idealised, and very sulky – it was the ideal sulk, I suppose; though I can tell you it was nothing compared to the moods he got in later on.'

'Really?' said Danny encouragingly, like a child who wants to hear a particular bit of a story. And Alex hesitated at the thought of this one, because he had never told it and was afraid that merely telling it would fail to convey his meaning. He looked down at the village and the wooded hills rising beyond in the penetrating light, and thought of sitting almost here with Justin and taking in the view as if it were another unexpected part of the inheritance. Now he wondered if Justin would ever come back here, except to pick up his clothes and his clock. The horizontal sun shone right in among the trees and he saw a woman with a dog emerge from under them and skirt the field below as clearly as through binoculars, though she must have been half a mile away. In the field itself he saw how tractors had drawn curlicues in the silver-gold corn.

'We'd gone away,' he said. 'I suppose it was rather like the trial separation, except we were trying to be together. This was a bit over a year ago – last June.' Alex didn't know how much to say; he felt he might make himself unattractive to Danny by giving him a true picture of his earlier failure, and the futility he had only recently been rescued from. He went on quickly, 'We'd been having less and less sex – sometimes we went for weeks just lying side by side, or there'd be a quick hug and a "good-night". Sometimes the vibrations would wake me up and he'd be having a wank.'

'Dear oh dear . . .'

'I know, darling.' Alex thought he wouldn't believe him if he told him how long he had once gone without sex. 'He made me feel like a stranger in my own bed.' He could see this was also an alien concept to Danny, who rocked his head consolingly against Alex's hip. 'Anyway, I decided to take him to Paris on the train, and he said he didn't want to go, he was perfectly happy staying at home and going to the off-licence. But I got a package deal at the George V, and that did finally seem too good to turn down.'

'I hope you got a decent shag out of it,' said Danny, frowningly representing Alex's interests.

166

'Sure . . .' Alex swallowed again on the bitter lesson of that afternoon, Justin kissing him as though he'd been paid to do so, the sex only just possible. 'Anyway, it didn't last long. That night we got a call to say his father had had a stroke. Justin was out of the room for some reason, and I answered the phone, and had to tell him. He took it very badly.'

'Well, that's hardly surprising.'

'I mean he was furious with me: for taking him away at a time when his father might have died. He said he had been worried about it all along; though in fact his father's only symptom was being ninety-four or whatever he was.'

'What about the mother?'

'She'd died, from drink I think probably, when Justin was a schoolboy. I'm sure that increased his sense of guilty panic – he was the only one left. Actually guilt's a huge problem with him, but that's another story. I don't know if you've ever seen one of his tempers, but in my view they're always violent repudiations of guilt. So we rushed back on the first train, we were almost the only people on it, and then we got another train straight to Coventry, but when we reached the hospital his father was already dead.'

'Hmm.'

'And then after that it was just awful. I could understand what was happening, but if I tried to make him see that he was displacing everything on to me he thought I was attacking him. You couldn't help him. And then there was the funeral and something very strange seemed to happen to Justin as he walked round, it was a baking hot day, and he realised he was the owner of this large ugly house full of Maples furniture. I have an image of it, I can't really explain, I sort of dogged his footsteps, hoping I might be allowed to help him; but he was already taking possession, going from room to room totting things up in his head. We went out across the lawn to get away from the others, who were mostly retired old men from the works whom Justin simply couldn't cope with, and who obviously knew nothing about *us*. I said, "Are you all right, darling?" or something simple like that, and he just looked at me, it was quite chilling, and said, "You are unforgivable", and then turned and walked back to the house. I suppose he'd been

167

drinking all morning. Anyway we never . . . made love again. That was the end for us. He was probably already seeing your father.' Alex glanced down at Danny, who appeared to be working it out. 'Though actually I don't think that was the point. It was the money. At last he'd got it, and he couldn't bear the thought of sharing it.'

Danny said, 'Well, you said he was a taker, not a giver.' It was always interesting to see what he had remembered.

The light was changing more rapidly, and only the long green top of the far hillside now caught the sun. Through the stillness Alex heard the distant scrape of a dog's bark, and voices from the farm below, with its grass-grown ricks and empty sheep-pens, to show that there was life there after all. He loved this time of day, with its delicate atmosphere of reward, and this evening especially he was touched by a sense of pattern, or providence. He said, 'It's such a miracle we met.'

'It is, darling,' Danny agreed, with an upward cartoon gape of joy which stealthily declined into a yawn.

When they got in, Danny put on some dance-music – there wasn't any talk about it, and Alex, who'd actually been feeling a bit Vaughan Williamsish, suppressed his disappointment. He'd brought down a double CD of Barbirolli conducting the 'London' Symphony and the 'Pastoral' Symphony, though its aptness was to remain a purely private satisfaction. He spread out the Sunday papers on the sofa and sat at an angle reading them while Danny danced loosely around with a bottle of beer held out in front of him. He found he had a new impatience with newspapers, and only skimmed the first paragraph of most articles before his eye twitched to another piece; he especially disliked full-page reports from crisis zones, with their out-of-date assumption that he had nothing more pressing to do than read them. He sometimes looked at opera reviews, but the only stories he really liked were ones about drugs. Another teenager had died that week after taking ecstasy, and happily there were several articles about her, forking over the same old lies and opinions. Alex, having taken the drug once, and read a lot of other articles on it, felt he possessed the subject, and sighed indignantly over what he read, while his heart raced and his stomach tightened in recollection of the experience. He was shocked and rather thrilled to find he was angry at the girl for fucking up. And now the music reached him like a hypnotist's coded phrase, and set up a moaning hunger for some beautiful stimulant. He sat back and stared his hunger at Danny, who worked across the room towards him, like an over-animated stripper, until he had one foot up on the arm of the sofa and was inching his zip down and wheezing with stifled laughter; at which point the phone rang. They both stared at it peevishly, until Danny let Alex answer.

'Oh, is that the wrong number?'

'This is Bridport, um, 794 – '

'Darling!'

'Oh, Justin . . .'

'I thought I'd ring and find out how you're getting on. It sounds like a disco down there.'

'We're just listening to some music.'

'Things have certainly changed, darling. I mean, it's not exactly Frescobaldi, is it? Act Twelve, Leonora's delirium.'

Alex mugged regretfully at Danny over the receiver and watched him go off into the kitchen. 'Have you had dinner?'

'I wasn't all that hungry.' It was worrying, sober oneself, to hear the quick decay of his speech, the half-conscious pauses and runs. 'How are you getting on with Daniella Bosco-Campo?'

'Extremely well.'

'Did you know that was the Italian for Woodfart?'

'We were on the brink of having sex when you rang.'

'Let me see, where is it . . . Pettirosso Bosco-Campo is the father's name,' Justin went on.

'You've clearly signed on at a language laboratory since you got to town.'

Justin grew arch at the slap of a sarcasm. 'Let's just say I've been talking to an Italian with a very large vocabulary.'

Alex found he didn't want to know. 'Anyway, you're getting on all right. Have you spoken to Robin?'

'No, you don't speak, darling, if you're having a trial separation. You remain in your room, obviously much of the day is spent in meditation. It's a time for plumbing the depths, darling.' Justin paused, and Alex suddenly had the impression that he wasn't alone: an unrelated movement, a door tactfully closed, Justin perhaps unaware of these sounds, and the awkward collusion they demanded from Alex. 'I don't suppose he's rung you?'

'Not me. Danny called him this morning, I think it was, just to check up on him. Dan's quite anxious about the whole thing, actually.'

Alex thought Justin was absorbing this, with an unusual intuition as to how his actions affected other people, but after a moment all he said was, 'I must say, it's marvellous not being in the country.'

Alex said stoutly, 'Well, we think it's marvellous being in the country.'

Justin gave a dryish laugh. 'Ah yes. It's called Love in a Cottage, darling. Make the most of it, because it doesn't last long.' He pondered his own words, and then said again, 'Anyway, I just wanted to see how you were getting on.'

'Thank you. It's heaven,' said Alex. And as he rang off and stood there with the music pulsing past him through the empty room he thought that that was how it would resolve itself, the doubts and subtle disappointments would be forgotten, and it would be heaven after all.

He went towards the kitchen and on a sceptical impulse stopped by the little commode and tugged open the top drawer. For a moment he thought he'd done Justin an injustice (that was an old play on words). There was a large album there, which he didn't like to look in, and under it the Scrabble box, but already he had seen the edge of red paper and, loosely wrapped in it, the instantly discarded, never remembered book. He supposed that it would stay there for years after Justin had cleared out, and no one would know what it was.

Danny was sitting at the table meticulously rolling a joint. Alex leant against the cold Rayburn and half-watched him, with disguised interest and relief. He thought how his little sighs and delayed breaths of concentration were like his breathing in bed. 'We can just have this,' Danny said, 'and then we can drop an E.' He ran his tongue along the paper's edge. 'That music's really put me in the mood.'

With the whole of gratification suddenly in view, Alex decoyed negligently. 'I suppose you don't want something to eat.' He didn't know what it would be; he was a decent cook but felt unmanned by Robin's kitchen with its hung-up switches of herbs and magnetised Sabatier knives. One of the cupboards contained a jumbled armoury of disassembled mincers and other patent devices in pitted aluminium and chipped enamel such as you might find in the pantry of an elderly relative. Another held labelled bottles of home-made wine, some with their corks rising. 'It would be lovely to just find a meal,' Alex said, 'all steaming on a tray.'

Danny grinned and said, 'Have some of this instead.'

Five minutes later he said, 'Feeling mellow?' and Alex nodded and kissed his cheek. There was something mellow in agreeing to the smug old hippy word mellow; just as there was something thrilling in submitting his high feelings about ecstasy to the drug's autistic jargon, drug-fucked, monged, off yer face. They were lying on the sofa, and the CD, which was one long supple ride over a dozen linked tracks, had reached its cruising speed, and out beyond the dazzling rhythms a woman sang 'Oh-oh yeah!', the three notes shining and resonating as if called from a dome. It was just a sample, Danny said, the phrase came back identically perhaps a dozen times – the only words in the song. But Alex was instantly fixated on it, and closed his eyes to see it in its imagined height and depth. It sounded like a welcome and an absolute promise, the yes of sex and something bodiless and ideal beyond it – what it might be like to float over a threshold into total acceptance by another man. Danny's head was nodding gently to the rhythm against Alex's chest – 'Fucking great, this one,' he said.

'Mm,' Alex murmured, and then started smiling at the thought of the pill. He didn't know you could do it if you weren't in a club, with its religious sense of belonging. He said, 'When we take the pills, darling, which I hope will be soon, what are we going to do? Sort of dance up and down in here for four hours?' He didn't mind, but was afraid he would keep hitting his head on the ceiling.

171

Danny said, 'You'll see', and Alex understood that all this had been planned for him; or perhaps was an improvisation passed off as a plan. The music ended, and Danny bustled about preparing the tray of their alternative feast – water, gum, a couple of bottles of beer, garibaldi biscuits, a nameless videotape, and a deep-blue coffee-saucer holding the off-white tablets. Alex thought of the beta-blockers his mother placed in his father's dessert-spoon, to be sure he would remember them; and had a sharp contraction of guilt that he hadn't rung home this weekend – a routine had evolved of a call at sherry-time before Sunday lunch: it meant they didn't have to run in crossly from the garden, and the inflexible timing of lunch gave the conversation a natural term. Now it was too late – 10.30 was emergencies only, and he would have to ring tomorrow with some explanatory hint at what he so far hadn't mentioned to them, the new man in his life. Danny too was clearly briefly elsewhere. He said, 'Ricky Nice is playing at BDX tonight.'

They went upstairs, got undressed and dropped their tabs in the bedroom, which had the still warmth of an airing-cupboard even though the windows were open under the eaves. They lay in a loose embrace and watched the moths come in, clumsy ones that knocked about inside the lampshade and others, with long transparent wings, that gathered noiselessly on the ceiling, and made a random frieze along the tops of the walls. Alex liked this decorative invasion of nature, the drug came up, Danny massaged his swiftly sensitised shoulders and back, and he tingled with a sense of the closeness of trees and fields and animals trotting warily about.

It was very different from the first time, and afterwards he saw how clever Danny had been to make a direct comparison impossible and so defer any feeling of disillusion. Time accelerated, but was never lost; the thrills were more measured; he was clenched around Danny in a shivering hug without music and dancing to set his adoration alight. They watched a video compilation that Dave from the porn-shop had made, which Alex feared would be three hours of close-up sodomy, but turned out to be a magical sequence of cartoon shorts and nature films: they gasped at the throb of colours as flowers sped from seed to bloom, a storm of flamingos rose from a

172

lake, and the sun set over the Grand Canyon. Alex felt very hot, and drank a lot of water, but couldn't pee; he chewed and chewed, and gripped Danny with an impossible snail-like longing to touch all over at once. There was something invalidish about them, on the bed there, glowing and incapacitated.

He slept shallowly, with racing dreams of ceaselessly mutating forms, bright and artificial as toy jewellery. He felt they ought to be frightening, but for some reason they weren't. They were like the speeded-up orchids and ephemeral desert blooms, but alchemised into plastic. Some churring night-creature woke him up, an owl on its prey perhaps, and though he closed his eyes again he was still awake. The woman's bright voice kept calling out 'Oh-oh yeah!' from the threshold of total happiness, the phrase was stuck in his brain and began to mock him and turn to rubbish with repetition. He tried to counter it, each time it came, with what might have been its opposite, Chopin's A minor mazurka, with its mood of etherised regret, and after a while he found they had fused into an unlikely new genre; he almost woke Danny up to tell him about it, the house mazurka. Maybe Ricky Nice would do a remix of it. The flickering dance rhythm ran on for ever, like a night-train over points.

Already the darkness was turning grainy and dimly translucent where a glass of water stood; the wardrobe mirror answered with the greyest gleam to the first hint of dawn at the window. Soon the birds would start up. He thought back to his walk through the streets in London after Château, hand-in-hand with Danny, the astonishing crowds on the pavement at 5 a.m., buses surging up for unheard-of antiquarian destinations, Whipps Cross, Chingford Hatch, the blearily milling boys smelling of sweat and smoke, pupils huge and bewildered by daylight, fag-ends imbedded in chewing-gum stuck round the welts of their shoes – the rapturous novelty of it all. Absurd though it was, with the same beautiful young man snoring naked beside him, he longed to be back there again, looking out for the improbable taxi that would take them home together for the first time, in the magically protracted hour when he knew that his life had been given back to him.

173

13

Tony Bowerchalke said, 'I can't remember what I said.'

Robin smiled discreetly. 'You only said you'd had an idea.' Tony's message on his Clapham answering machine had shown a certain alarm at the machine itself, which he treated like a dictaphone, signing off with 'All best wishes, Tony Bowerchalke'.

'Well, I hope you'll like the idea.' They were standing on the gravel circle, where Tony had been waiting, perhaps all morning, for his arrival. 'That very smart car belongs to the people in flat one,' he said, nodding towards a soft-top silver BMW parked beside his own peppermint-coloured Nissan Cherry.

'They're in already . . .'

'They took it immediately. I don't know if I'm not asking enough. It's a young banker and his fiancée.'

'Are they all right?'

'They're perfectly charming,' Tony said, in a way that might have intimated some huge reservation; but he went on, 'It's very pleasant having other people in the house, I find. I think they'll stay.' He looked at Robin with an unsteady smile, and there was an impression of a half-memorised speech being glanced at and thrown away. 'So that was, and remains, my idea: more flats. Turn the whole house into flats. Actually, if I'm to stay here, I think it's the only way.'

Robin nodded slowly. It would certainly help to solve the unpleasant emptiness of the coming year; so far the only job he had was the commission for a neo-Georgian toilet-block in Lyme Regis. And the ongoing worry of the pyramid, of course. 'I'd be happy to do it,' he said, 'if you're sure.' Tony seemed to have nerved himself up for change, and Robin thought he might have reached his decision only by ignoring its implications. There was an uneasy cheerfulness about him.

They went into the low vaulted hall and Robin felt the semi-derelict gloom of the place grip him consolingly. It was work, at least, technical, and imaginative in its latter-day way; he had his sketchpad in his briefcase and his tape-measure clipped to his belt and a hidden but hungry sense of usefulness. After a week in London, where he had tinkered artificially with late decorative amendments to the Kew job, before rushing home to eternal half-pissed evenings by the silent phone, the call to Dorset was like a firm hint from a friend.

In the library, in the smell of crumbling leather and vague rawness of papery damp, Tony had put out the tooled black album containing the original plans of the house. Robin glanced at them again with his professional sense of familiarity, the eye's fluent movement among the old inked lines and wire-drawn annotations of every closet, corridor and stair. Victorian country-house plans still had their special appeal; they were like board-games mimicking the business of a social labyrinth that had once been serious enough. To the converter they were almost too rich in novel backstairs opportunities. He turned the pages, and felt his pleasure of a few moments before had been exaggerated and was abruptly wearing thin. The rapid twist was typical of his mood these days, when his thoughts were ragged and hard to control, and rushes of excitement could be stifled by a black chill.

He said, 'Why don't you show me over the whole house? There's a lot I've never seen.' He needed to find out if there was a contradiction between Tony's dogged love of the place and his new need to let it go. The emotions seemed to him obscurely parental.

They spent an hour or more going systematically from room to room, Tony saying again how the house had always been reviled, how in the thirties and forties it was the apex of bad taste, and yet how his mother had loved it, and how, seen in the right way, it was if not beautiful then at least remarkable and certainly unique, a rogue, in Robin's word, among the discreetly elegant seats of the county. Robin was glad that Tony had taken on the rogue idea; he couldn't deny that the house's

175

mixture of Tudor, hotel rococo and early French Gothic was astoundingly uncouth; but it showed too the bracing indifference to opinion of someone doing exactly what they wanted.

There was a sequence of large bedrooms, the south-facing ones already full of dusty heat. Robin paced around each room, to get the measure of it, and there was a touch of professional con too, a hint at more mysterious calculations. One bedroom adjoined a boudoir with a painted ceiling of flowers on trellises – it was Tony's mother's room, and still had her silver-backed hairbrushes and tassled perfume spray on the dressing-table. At the front of the house was a room that Tony called the Lake Room, apparently because his aunt, who was always given it, and who recorded her dreams, had said over breakfast one morning, 'I dreamt that there were two lakes in my room.' 'People were always pleasantly surprised to be told they were in the Lake Room,' said Tony, standing at the window and peering down at the waterless circle of the drive.

At the end of the main corridor was his own room, which he opened up with self-conscious briskness. With its high single bed, formica-topped table and Germolene-coloured satin eiderdown it had the air of an old school sanatorium. The square of carpet was laid over beige linoleum. On the table was a transistor radio and an oldish book about wartime espionage. A further passage led into a tall narrow space enshrining the polished teak bench and scalloped porcelain bowl of the 'Clifford', a majestic Victorian water-closet. Robin didn't like to examine the bedroom too closely. He knew little about Tony's intimate life, but the singleness of the room agitated him, as if he had suddenly come on evidence of something he would rather ignore. On the wall there were framed photographs of permed middle-aged women, some pre-war children, a bull-terrier, nailed up in the inartistic but serviceable way that was perhaps Tony's version of the family blindness. He thought of his own life, which seemed in retrospect to have been gripped and shaped by sexual love, the constant indispensable presence of another person, one after another, and overlapping – he thought of his awful behaviour in Simon's last days and couldn't suppress a certain shocked admiration for his own instinctual drive. Later Robin realised that this room had also

176

carried a hushed resonance of the Wiltshire nursing-home in which his mother, the 'redoubtable' Lady Astrid, had spent her last unreconciled year.

The top floor of the house could be reached by three different staircases, which Robin said would be convenient. Tony said, 'They take some getting used to. Let's go up this one. My aunt used to say that she came down this staircase but she would never go up it because she didn't know where it went.'

After a minute or two Robin, with his normally fine sense of orientation, said, 'I see what your aunt meant.' Up under the roofs there was a maze of odd-shaped stuffy rooms with tiny windows, linen-cupboards with skylights and ladders of empty shelves, unannounced changes of level. In several rooms chamber-pots or old tin basins had been placed on the threadbare carpets and bare iron bedsteads to catch dripping rainwater; though now they held only chalky stains. Tony flung open numerous cupboards, as if wanting to make a clean breast of the thing, though again it was only emptiness that he revealed. Robin felt very remote from the outer world. 'You don't often come up here,' he said.

'I did in my Sardines days,' Tony said, with one of his nervous schoolboyish gestures of straightening and neatening himself. 'Those low cupboards under the eaves were admirable hiding-places.' Robin could imagine him crawling into one and pulling the door shut. 'I go up to the Top Room, of course.'

'Oh yes, I want to see that.'

It appeared to be another closet with an ill-fitting door, but inside there was a narrow staircase, with fluffy dust at the side of the treads, and bright daylight up above. The Top Room was Tytherbury's attempt at a tower, a little lookout among the chimney-stacks, with its own small summer-house fireplace and rattling leaded casements on three sides. In the old days visitors had always wanted to see it, and those with connections were invited to scratch their names on a window-pane with a diamond. Florence Hardy, Hallam Tennyson, Muriel Trollope: an interesting if strictly secondary collection. There was also an R. Swinburne, which Tony said people wanted to believe was A. Swinburne having trouble with his stylus; and a Wm Shakspere, facetiously introduced by Tony's grandfather when he was a boy. 'It's ice-cold in winter,' Tony said, 'and as you can see baking hot in summer.' Robin looked at the south-facing sills, which were warped by sunlight and rotted by rain-water. Beyond the glass the view was compromised: the light-industrial chimney, the new barns and silos on the Home Farm, part of the vanished layout of the garden visible in dry weather as in an aerial photograph; not the sea, but the straggly pines above it, and the top of the pyramid. That particular structure was taking on a further symbolic burden, as the task that wouldn't go away, the problem that a younger man would already have solved, but which filled Robin with a paralysing sense of responsibility.

Tony asked him to stay to lunch, which they had in the kitchen. Robin knew that life here was already confined to a few of the smaller rooms, and that the occasional Campari he had had in the barely furnished drawing-room represented a special social effort. It was hard to praise the meal, of tinned tongue, with a tomato, a spring onion and a curl of lettuce; but Tony said, 'These spring onions are jolly good.'

Rita Bunce said, 'You're going to split the old place up, then.'

'Well, I've only just started thinking about it.'

Her smile was responsible, and so seemed to hint at her anxiety about Tony. 'We'll all be much better off,' she said, which they each appeared to think about and find true. 'No more housework. I don't know what I'll do all day.'

'Oh, I'll keep you busy,' said Tony, perhaps more rakishly than he intended.

It was very like the grind of Justin's old joke as he explained his plan to stay in a hotel: 'With no housework to do, I shall have some time to myself for a change.' Robin was lost at once in the gloom of that other story, which undercut the good fortune the three of them were quietly welcoming. Work, which was a salvation from empty misery, was shown up by it as the feeble consolation of the loser. The secret technical joy he had always got from buildings and the art of building shrivelled away, as if poisoned. He set down his knife and fork and asked for another glass of water.

'I hope you approved of young Terry's efforts in the flats,' Mrs Bunce said.

'He made a decent job of it,' said Robin. 'I was pleasantly surprised.'

'He's turned out a good lad, after some bad beginnings,' Mrs Bunce said. 'He's very clean.'

'He's a buster, isn't he,' said Tony.

'He'll be busy with the discos now, of course,' said Mrs Bunce.

'You ought to go over one night,' said Tony. 'Rita's a great dancer, you know.'

'Going back a bit!' Mrs Bunce said, while a blush surfaced through her cream and powder. Robin glanced at her with courteous interest, and she went on, 'No, that was the jitterbugging we used to do. They don't do that these days, or else I'm very much mistaken.'

'I'm afraid not. I'm not even quite sure what it is.'

'And I'm not going to show you!' Robin saw that she'd brought the faintest hint of sexual sparring into the conversation, even though she was turning him down. 'That's how I met my other half,' she said: 'Billy Bunce from Clifton, New Jersey. He could jitterbug them all into the ground. That was magic. Well, I've never seen anything to touch it since. The modern dancing, oh dear, you see it on the telly.'

'I know,' said Robin, with a widowed sense that he would never go dancing again, and that his style of Mick Jaggerish strutting and shaking had already gone to join the jitterbug in dance limbo, along with the twist and the charleston, the quadrille and the gavotte.

The mood clung to him as he drove on to Litton Gambril. He was miserably distracted by the idea of Justin's freedom in London, the complete freedom he had chosen from the botched experiment of life down here. Robin pictured him at the garish little newsagents in Clapham where he had first seen him, or among shoppers in Long Acre, and was horrified by the fact that mere chance had brought them together in those two places. For the first time, it struck him as absurd to expect loyalty from someone he had met in a toilet.

Normally when he arrived at the cottage he felt happily

179

divided, and opened the place up in a capable adult way while his eyes and thoughts ran round the house and garden like imaginary children, making contact with their favourite spots. But today, in the sunless heat, he could only think of how he missed Justin, and the house in its private hollow looked like an elaborate emblem of failure. He had to have someone always around. Nights spent by himself were more and more bewildering to him. It was clear that Dan and his friend had slept in the big bed, and there seemed something inexorable in that. The kitchen showed signs of the misplaced tidiness of guests, everything subtly wrong. It was like the endless summer weekends he had spent here when Justin was still living with Alex, but darkened now by a hint of dispossession.

He did what he could to counter the mood. He got into shorts and hurried round with a show of unchallenged physical energy. The lawn in this dry weather didn't need mowing again, and he saw that the dead-heading of the roses had been done exactly to his instructions. There was only a little perfectionist weeding to do. He carried the heavy black book of the Tytherbury plans to the work-hut, but the air there was stifling, and the book lay on the desk like a penance: he looked out at the long field and the hanging wood which were the constant counterparts to his working thoughts and wondered how he could ever make a drawing again. Everything was flavourless, or slightly bitter.

When it was cooler he went for a run round the fields. The wheat was coming on with its usual evenness of purpose, but it was a scruffy time of year, the path dry and cracked among dead cow-parsley and tall brown grass. A field of rape had been cut and left in its unEnglish chaos of gigantic tussocks. He didn't see anyone else in the half-hour he was out, and he had the feeling he was the only person who had put up a resistance to the heavy heat of the day. He pinched the sweat out of his eyes.

When he got in he had a long shower and examined himself in the mirror as he dried, with a sportsman's attention to particular muscles and a firmer acknowledgement than before that something in his bearing was changing, that the flow and swing of his body were becoming strange to him. Of course

180

you saw it in others at the gym, the little fold of skin at the armpit, gooseflesh at the throat, the flattening of the buttocks, the slump of the chest. A wiry young man had a perceptible stoop, a regular heart-breaker's smile took on a worried persistence. In some of them the marks of time were sexy – as Robin's own baldness obviously was. He thought of Justin, with his plump little underchin, his contained sleekness mysteriously yielding, the pattern of his hair-loss revealing itself, and found every detail rousing and real. Grow old along with me, the best is yet to be. He smiled sternly at his sun-browned handsomeness, and remembered the absurd remark Tony once dragged up about his father's being the handsomest man in Wessex. It was funny because it was both so pompous and so camp; which didn't mean that it wasn't also quite likely to be true. His father would have frowned at the phrase and thought there was something pansy about it; but in the privacy of his dressing-room he probably turned it over and admitted it was pretty near the mark.

It was oppressively still in the house, where every window was open, and when Robin stood at the back door he saw the sky to the west was full of purple-black promise; he leant against the door-frame with a bottle of cold beer pressed to his bare chest and waited for the first miraculous spits of rain on the path. There was a blink of lightning and he counted the seconds and worked out that the storm was breaking over Lyme and Charmouth; he pictured the dusty water running down the steep streets towards the sea. He felt his mood shifting, his cleanness pricking with fresh sweat, and the prospect of the long loveless summer evening already coloured by the storm with an enjoyable mood of crisis. The Wessex Woodfields rose to a crisis. It was the indeterminacy of recent weeks that disheartened him: he had been cheated of a crisis and left to wander in a private desert, which to everyone else still had the look of a richly cultivated landscape.

He hadn't come for nearly seven weeks, by far the longest abstinence in his thirty-five years of maturity. (He once said to Justin that he had probably first ejaculated on the day that he was born, but Justin seemed to detect some impropriety in the alignment.) He was surprised by the pattern of sensation –

181

the taunting sex-urge that built up after three or four days of being pushed away had quickly declined at the end of a week, and apart from the night of Dan's birthday, when it was abnormally provoked, it seemed to have gone into a monkish kind of aestivation. It was a mystery he had never even hoped to experience, he was proud of his sex-life and impatient of any sort of sex 'problem'; but now he found there was some symbolic magic to it, like the private discipline of a prisoner which gives him strength to wait for the moment of release.

He saw he would have to get drunk. He thought of ringing Mike Hall, but felt too delicate for the sarcasms and abuse of Mike's 'late' phase. He cracked up some ice and made himself a Justinian half-pint of gin and tonic. He considered smoking more of the famous hash, which must still be hidden in the work-shed, but then felt it would be futile to escape from loneliness into a state that only focused the longing for another person. It grew darker in the house and there were gratifying stamps of thunder, as if someone had dropped a safe upstairs. When the rain started, abrupt and vertical, Robin left the windows open and let the displacement of damp air flow in over his chest and shoulders. He pictured Justin coming to stand behind him in a rare unironical surrender to the thrash of the rain and the retina-printing lightning; though in fact Justin was nervy in storms and roamed around sulkily to disguise his slightly shaming anxiety. Robin took a mouthful of gin and tonic, and chewed it like a taster to make the chilled bubbles seethe across his palate.

He thought he would put on some music, and stood looking along the shelf with an indecision that threatened to let the misery in again. The little flickers of elated sensation, from the power of his body or the colour of the storm, expired upwards like the bubbles that plinked and whispered in the glass, and left him with a darker sense of solitude. His old vinyls, in bumped, coffee-ringed sleeves, were all here, the Beatles and the Stones, the Doors, the Incredible String Band. To look at them was to risk the tumble into a picturesque past of essay crises, car troubles, sleeping with girls. He peeped at the Kinks, in their crotch-gripping flares, and recalled rolling joints on *Revolver*. Robin had the small accidental CD collection of someone uninterested in music, who still made the occasional purchase and sometimes bought the wrong thing because he couldn't remember what it was that had been recommended. He hadn't even known that he owned Vaughan Williams's 'London' Symphony, and had certainly never listened to it. Anyway, he didn't want to think about London. There was something that must be Dan's, *Dance Forever*, that he thought he would just try, but after a minute of primitive repetition he guessed you had to be in the right mood for it. He tried some Mahler, which was loud in a different way, but it got on his nerves. In the end he settled for a Beethoven quartet, which he found he knew quite well, and hummed along to without apology. He got himself another gin, and coming back among the deep shadows of the sitting-room where only the oscillating displays of the stereo gave out any light, he imagined candles. The storm rumbled close again, in an exciting sabotage of the music; on the window-sill was an old silver candelabrum and he liked the thought of struggling flames against the backdrop of downpour. There were matches somewhere in the little commode, and he went through the top drawer impatiently. Underneath everything else was the box of Swans and for some reason a book, wrapped in torn, shiny paper. He pulled it out with a frown, couldn't think what it was, and left it on the top to look at later. He wondered if it was something Justin had planned to give him, and then saw that he was being absurdly sentimental.

The effect of the candles was romantic, and perhaps funerary, a wake or a vigil, he didn't know. The rain hissed, the quartet busied along, and when a voice emerged from the edge of the grudgingly retreating thunder Robin shivered and grunted and twisted round with the split-second certainty he was about to be attacked; and the immediate cover of showing he thought it was a joke. Terry Badgett was standing in the doorway to the kitchen, with an anorak hanging by its hood over his head for a dash through the rain. 'Sorry to make you jump,' he said.

Robin supposed Terry must have knocked, he knew he was getting a little deaf, and wondered if he should offer an explanation for listening to chamber music shirtless by candlelight.

183

Then he thought there might be some emergency to do with his mother. He said, 'Hello Terry?'

Terry looked at him for a second, so it seemed to Robin, with the amorous amazement of a figure from below-stairs. 'I just saw all your windows were open in the car,' he said.

'Oh my god . . .'

'I didn't like to touch it in case it's alarmed.'

'No. Thank you so much.'

Robin ran up barefoot through the dwindling rain and had to start the car to activate the windows. It must have been gustier than he realised – the odd Swedish tweed of the passenger seat was soaked, and the glove-box and radio were drizzled over by the blown wet. He gave it a wipe, and decided he would leave it till tomorrow; he locked the car and the rain stopped, then it came back in a dash, like the last bit thrown out of a bucket, then stopped again. Terry's Talbot Samba was parked at the gate. Above it the sky was toweringly dark where the storm moved eastwards, but beyond the cottage it had thinned into a brown-grey haze that half-obscured the fields like a coat of wood-varnish. Somewhere beyond that, discernible only in odd pressings and squeezings of light, the sun was setting. Robin took in the unusual effect, the sparkle on the dripping trees and hedges, and the astounding stink of the country after such heavy high-summer rain.

Terry was sitting on the sofa, leaning forward expectantly to learn the extent of the damage. He seemed disappointed not to have detected some more serious problem. 'Only I just saw it . . .' he said.

'You deserve a drink,' Robin said. 'If you have time.' He went through to the kitchen, and called back, so that Terry followed him, 'I was hearing good things about you today.'

'Oh yes . . .?'

'I was at Tytherbury this morning. Mr Bowerchalke seemed very pleased with the work.' Robin still had a sense of Terry's being on probation, after his trouble-making teens, and needing encouragement to keep him steady. In the resentful memory of the village he remained the youth who got the Bishop girl pregnant and let the water out of the Horensteins' swimming-pool. 'A beer okay for you?'

184

'Thanks very much.' Terry hung the anorak on a chair and looked round the kitchen with the ambitious interest of someone angling for promotion. He had had his hair cut, square at the back in the way of small-town barbers, and there was a new pale stripe above the sun-tanned neck. Robin noticed the salty blots where the sweat had dried in his black T-shirt.

'So what have you been doing today?'

Terry took the bottle. 'Oh, running around,' he said, with a distant smile. 'I'm getting a fair bit of work now.' Robin gestured them back into the sitting-room. 'I've just come over from Bride Mill.'

'You get on well with Roger and John,' Robin said, referring to the Mill's corduroyed co-hosts.

Terry smiled. 'Yeah, I have a good repartee with them.'

They sat at either end of the sofa, the candles glowing in Terry's dark eyes. Robin sprawled with his drink held loosely at crotch level. He wasn't sorry to have the company of someone fresh and handsome and remote from any intuition of his own gloom. Terry's face had lost the thickness of adolescence and the pained, untrusting expression of a boy who is always in the wrong. Robin liked the way he showed his curiosity, sometimes unguardedly, sometimes slyly. He believed he was a figure of some social fascination to Terry, and was pleased with his own relaxed manner with him. He said vainly, 'I'm sorry, I ought to put a shirt on.'

Terry took a quick sip from his shining brown bottle. 'Don't mind me,' he said; and his eyes lingered on Robin again for a moment. 'You by yourself tonight then?' – glancing away at the somehow ritualised room.

'I'm afraid so,' said Robin casually.

'Where's that Justin then?'

'He's still in London.'

'Oh yes? He made me laugh at that party.'

Robin smiled warily. 'He can be amusing. But we mustn't talk about him behind his back.' He was aware of his own desire, after a couple of drinks, to be critical of Justin, but alert to any mistaken intimacy on Terry's part.

'It'll be good to see him again,' Terry said indulgently, but also as though he had in mind a particular date. 'Where is it we're all supposed to be going, Italy is it or something?'

'Sicily, wasn't it, for some reason?' said Robin, with forced hilarity of recall.

'That's right, Sicily. To celebrate his so-called new-found wealth. At one point I worked out he was taking about twenty of us.' Robin said nothing, and already half-regretted having let Terry in, like a boy with a rod, to angle in the sullen pond of his misfortunes. 'Of course he's probably just taking you, isn't he?' Terry added quietly.

Robin thought Justin would never spend anything on him, and began to understand that there was some deeper connection between the money from the house coming through and Justin's deciding to move on, as if the cottage had been merely a convenience. Which, after all, as Justin often plonkingly joked, was what a cottage was. The quartet ended, rather oddly, and he got up to eject the CD; it was only as he pressed it back into the case that he saw it had five movements. 'Mm,' he said. 'But you don't know Justin' – a phrase which brought the whole year of luxurious sexual privacy in a shocking rush before his mind's eye.

'I don't know him like you do,' said Terry, in a very diplomatic tone.

Robin looked along the CD shelf – there they were again, Van Morrison, Abba, some Mozart, Vaughan Williams's 'London' Symphony, of course. He had one arm raised against the shelf above, the biceps squared up and veined. He was surprised by his need to be admired by the boy. And the effect was so quick, almost too easy.

'You're looking good,' Terry said.

'Ooh, I've looked better.'

'You been to that new gym in Bridport?'

'Um . . . no, not yet. Any cop?'

'Oh yeah. They got all the machines. One of the instructors is a mate of mine. I was trying to get Dan to go. I told him I could get him in free.'

'No, he's not into that sort of thing,' Robin said, and seemed to be claiming some slightly embarrassing exemption on his behalf.

186

'No. He's got a nice little body, though,' Terry said, with a shy insistence that he did have some private connection with this decadent household of Londoners. Robin said to himself, in his bare-chested sceptical way, that he couldn't get worked up about this kid who slept with his son; but when he thought back to that small-hours encounter in the bathroom, Terry muddle-haired and still boyishly stiff after sex, he had a stifled shudder of longing, as if someone had breathed in his ear, and wondered bleakly whether there was much point to all his romantic good behaviour.

'Let's not bother with music,' he said, and sat down again. It was getting cool, with the windows open, and he really would have to put a shirt on soon. He said, 'Did you see Dan when he was down?'

Terry said, 'My mum said he was down with Alex', which wasn't quite an answer. Robin wondered how tender his feelings for Danny were, and saw that despite various things that had happened he didn't really think of Terry as being homosexual. But perhaps Terry had similar doubts about him.

If so, his next move didn't show it. 'You look cold,' he said, with a wide, tense smile, sliding, half-crawling along the sofa to chafe Robin's upper arm. He leaned across him to stand the beer-bottle on the carpet, and then slid his other hand between his legs. There was an absolute lack of transition that might have been explained by either ignorance or genius. 'Let's go upstairs,' he said.

Robin pulled back his head with a soft snort of surprise; then looked away from the boy and back at his waiting face in a small enactment of his dilemma. If he did, it would be his first betrayal of Justin, though what was more uncomfortable was the hinted betrayal, the furtive shadowing of Dan. He smiled at the unusual delicacy of the situation. 'You know I'm a quarter of a century older than you, don't you?' It was very strange to be making such a protest.

Terry took his hand from Robin's thigh, and sat back a little. 'If you don't want to,' he said.

'Well, yeah, I want to,' said Robin, though he thought it was a good question; he blushed for the first time in years at his own hesitation. 'I'm just thinking of . . . other people.'

'They won't know, will they,' Terry said. 'Anyway, I've had my eye on you for some time.'

'Really . . .'

Terry breathed in Robin's face: 'Only ever since you came down here, when you got this place.'

There was something remotely threatening about him. Robin had the picture for a moment of one of those teenage gangsters with a couple of kids in different households and a forty-year-old woman he sees in the afternoons. He wasn't going to say how he remembered Terry from that time. Simon was always complaining lustfully about the little hunk in the back lane, who sat on the wall to watch the workmen and had a dick like a trapped animal in his pocket. Robin kissed Terry on the nose, out of courtesy, or as a token of the omitted seduction. Or perhaps he thought the last seven years had been the seduction, the haphazard, unrecognised approach. 'Come on then,' he said; and heard other unspoken words that might have followed: 'It's late', 'It's past your bed-time.'

After it was fully dark the wind got up quite quickly, and Robin lay with his back to the lamp listening to the stirring in the trees. It was a hissing and pattering like a clever dry sound-effect for rain. Terry was curled in against him, talking desultorily and pretending not to doze. Robin thought of the day, at varying times from spring to spring, when you were first aware of the wind in the leaves, not the empty moan of winter but a new impression of vast, almost substanceless resistance. It was hard to hear it in town, where the spirit of the place was often muted. It was one of the reasons he wanted to sleep beside trees and fields.

He had been wise to hesitate about Terry, though perhaps not foolish to give in. In bed Terry was lively but self-regarding, as if he wanted to show this older man that he knew how to do it – he was quick and vain; beautiful, but he didn't touch Robin in any but the most mechanical sense. He was a merely cursory kisser, whereas Robin always wanted to snog heavily, especially with strangers. Terry seemed to find that too intimate or too compromising. He was very proud of his broad-backed dick, which reared off at an angle as if long since tugged askew by the obsessive attentions of his right hand. He had an idiotic patter about it, but Robin shut him up in the simplest way he knew; even so, occasional noises emerged, like the conscientious rejoinders of a dentist's patient. He seemed somehow displeased by the dense but fountaining volume of Robin's ejaculation; and Robin himself observed it as a phenomenon of nature, with an almost total absence of sensation. It wasn't the ending he had hoped for through his spooky weeks of continence.

Even so, afterwards, drifting sleepwards, he was glad to have Terry with him. His hands rubbed across the skin and joints and smooth transitions of a body that hadn't yet dreamt of the changes Robin had studied earlier in the mirror. It was interesting – like an eerily privileged visit to his younger self, or to some aspect of it. But he wouldn't want to make the journey often. How could all the ageing lovers of boys bear it, the distance growing longer and lonelier year by year? Robin liked the particulars of Terry, the very hairy calves and the smooth thighs, the marks of sweaty chafing between his legs, the small scar on the wrong side for the appendix, the damp talcky knots of his armpits. Had he really fancied Robin when he was fifteen? They got the roof on the house in time to have his fortieth birthday party between its unplastered walls, with builders' caged lamps on long flexes clipped to the beams, and a tilting JCB backed up outside in the rutted mudslide of the garden. He cooked long skewers of sea-food in the open fireplace. He had been unsure about forty, but then in the new house, with Simon, he saw that forty was only a beginning. Of course he thought Simon would be here with him for the rest of his life, by which he meant his own life.

It wasn't clear whether Terry was staying. He seemed to have quite settled in. Robin thought it must be strange for him to find himself in this room, when he had recently spent the night in Dan's bed, a couple of doors along. Now he was sleeping, his jaw had dropped, he was a mouth breather. Robin curled round and turned off the lamp, and it was only that small domestic action that startled him with the image of Justin, or rather with its opposite, the sudden teeming darkness in which Justin disappeared each night, as they turned and settled in each other's arms. The great loves in his life – and here he was

189

with a pointless trick, and all the vague social disadvantage that would follow.

Terry swallowed and mumbled 'All right?' as Robin hugged him.

'Mmm.' He wondered if Justin was alone at this moment, if he was really in a hotel; he half-admired the stony way he had stuck to his resolution, and not rung home – like other addictive personalities he had a mystical respect for the total ban, as the only alternative to chaos. Still, the effect was severe. Robin listened to the wind, and thought of that other day, at the far end of summer, when a little shift occurred in the weather, that might have been nothing, a morning's chill after weeks of glittering heat, but was in fact the airy chink through which the autumn came pouring, with its vivid forgotten lights and ache of inexact memory and surprising sense of relief.

'I ought to be off,' Terry said flatly. 'I haven't had my dinner.' Robin pulled him closer, with a sentimental growl.

He must have slept, maybe only for a few seconds, and when he woke it was to a subtly confused apprehension of where he was. Terry stretched and sighed and seemed to kiss his arm, but in the darkness Robin drifted on the unexamined certainty that he was with someone else. He murmured a half-awake phrase, blunt but solicitous, with the routine humour and dry wistfulness of some established intimacy. It happened sometimes in moments of giggly sweetness, when you found you were treating one friend as if he were another older and better one – a sudden access through a similar gesture or simply through the likeness of friendships. Quite often, Robin called Justin Simon, and was forced to apologise. In the dark, as breathing slowed and the hands lost the sense of where they lay, it seemed one lover could become another, like the smoothly metamorphosing figures in dreams. In Robin's dream a stranger was shouting; he woke up and it took him several frightened seconds to work out that Terry was asking him for thirty pounds.

14

'No, you're right, sir. This room would need a bit of work.'

'If seven maids, with seven mops . . .' Justin trailed away.

'Sorry sir?'

'Nothing.'

'It does enjoy a south-westerly view.'

'If it enjoys *that* view,' said Justin, standing back from the window, 'then it must be a masochist.'

Charles the estate agent gave an embarrassed chuckle. 'Point taken, Justin,' he said. 'Point taken.'

Justin wished he would decide what to call him, and stick to it. Charles was a tall, not unhandsome man in his late twenties, with the high colour and camel-like gait of a certain kind of public schoolboy. It was boiling hot, and he was in shirt-sleeve order; he had a bright joky tie which Justin imagined was a gift from a girlfriend who didn't want him to turn into a fuddy-duddy. He kept smoothing it down as if he would like to smooth it away. 'I've got another one to show you,' he said. They went downstairs and got into Charles's white Rover – or 'Rover car' as he called it. As before, there was a bit of trouble starting. 'You run up quite a mileage in my job,' Charles said.

It was inexpressibly strange to be back in this neighbour-hood, though the shock came not from what had changed but from what was exactly unaltered. There was that corner house with crazy 'stonework' stuck over the brick, there were those peculiar children playing outside the dry-cleaners, there was the strikingly named Garbo's off-licence, which had done so much to enhance the glamour of drinking alone; they were actually going to pass the end of Cressida Road, and he craned round to get a glimpse of Alex's house, half-way along. 'It's a pleasant area, this,' said Charles. By and large, Justin thought he preferred the cockney Derek, from the other agency. The trouble with boys like Charles was the recurrent hint they gave off that they, and certainly their parents, lived in somewhere far grander than the properties they were trying to sell. Hence the note of pity, the wavering forms of address, and the ironic attachment to the euphemisms of the trade. 'This next house has been the subject of interior design,' Charles said.

The woman of the house had stayed in to be available to them, and sat on the sofa with her legs crossed, drinking milky coffee and doing the *Daily Mail* crossword. When they had been upstairs for a while, she came up to see what was happening and showed them how the loft ladder worked. Justin saw that as a vendor she had come to believe the estate agents' literature, and would be offended by almost anything he said about the house. He was itching to leave the place for ever, but found himself in a spasm of parodic politeness asking further questions about the central heating and just having another quick look at the little bedroom. As the front door closed behind them he realised he had been rather a success.

'So what did you think of that one?' Charles asked when they were back in the car.

Justin made a face of retching grief, and Charles laughed and said, as the car finally started, 'You ought to have been an actor.' He looked around and went on cheerfully, 'Well, that's about it for now. Can I drop you somewhere? Or have you got the rest of the day off?'

'I need to get back to Knightsbridge,' Justin said, with a frown at his watch.

The days in London passed wonderfully quickly. If he wasn't doing something, then he was luxuriously planning to do it. The estate agents' bumf came in multiple envelopes each morning, and he looked through it in a trance of horrified amusement. Once he chose to view a place solely for the blinding vulgarity of its décor. He felt cheated when they only gave a photo of the view from the house. He needed to find somewhere, and had an image of the light and space in which he would live, but nowhere that he looked at had the right circulation, as Robin called it, the right flow of space and, what was it, disposition of offices. Justin's new era, in which

192

he starred as a virtually teenage heir who was also in some mysterious way retired from life, would depend on the discreet presence of staff. He was more and more fascinated by having people do things for money.

For the first few days he had been very good. He had only seen Gianni, whose number he had kept from way back, and who had provided all those amusing translations of people's names into Italian. He was fine, but suffered from the common syndrome of having grown in memory. On the following Monday Justin went to see Mr Hutchinson, his father's stock-broker, and left his Marylebone office feeling almost giddy with financial security. The detail of what Hutchinson said evaporated within seconds, but a sustaining sense of power remained. He went, from need, into the Gents at Oxford Circus, where the same skinny black guy he had sucked off years ago was standing in exactly the same place and gave him the same furtive glare; but Justin thought not. He strolled on into Soho in the late morning sunshine, entranced by the animation around him, the boys dashing about, the cyclists like acrobats. How anyone could prefer the country, with its cows and sheep, both literal and figurative, was beyond him. He went into a gay bar that had just opened for the day and wasn't yet playing any ghastly dance-music, and had a beer and a chat with the barman and left with all the free gay papers under his arm.

Back at the Musgrove he spread them out on the bed and lay there like a child with his heels in the air and his chin in his hands. The personal services pages seemed to have grown in number and frankness in the year since he had last used them, and a lot of the advertisers now had full nude photos, though sometimes with the face smudged. Others had a picture of their face only, which he preferred. Better still were the purely verbal ones. He liked maximum suggestion combined with surprise, like an optimal blind date. If they hit it off he might see them again, but the real point was the arrival of an absolute stranger. Justin was a gorgeous young man of thirty-five, of course, so the strangers themselves were usually relieved and excited. Sometimes they asked why he didn't just go to a bar and pick up.

193

Perhaps there were too many rent-boys now. Justin had to get a pen to mark the possibilities. He thought there should be some stricter calibration of the superlatives of 'well-endowed'. No one admitted to being less than VWE, many were VVWE or Massively VWE, which surely wasn't right, it should be V Massively WE. He ringed Mark (the d he put in 'buldging' was unaccountably arousing), as well as stunning Carlo, Italian hunk, biggest in town, and German Karlheinz, who offered watersports ('let me quentsch your thirst'). He saw that black Gary, aka Denzel, was still running the same ad ('You're in for a big surprise'), and wondered what had happened to him on the night of Danny's party; it had been a big surprise all right to see him there in the kitchen, and Robin's jealousy had been almost uncanny. He'd have liked to see him again. His eye fell on the nondescript one-liner, 'Phil. Central. In/Out', whom he suspected was probably the best of all.

Mark, as big as a building, wasn't answering, but Carlo came on at once, rather snappily. He was busy now, but he could be there at seven o'clock; Justin made it clear he wasn't after a mere half-hour, and Carlo spoke with sulky eagerness of large vague sums of money, to which Justin agreed without listening.

'Okay, so where is, please?'

'It's the Musgrove Hotel.'

'Oh. I never been to that one before.'

'No, I don't imagine there would be much call for you here,' Justin said, picturing his boundingly virile arrival in the chintzy front hall. 'Incidentally, Carlo, how big are you?'

'Yes, is twenty-five.'

'Goodness . . .'

'That's in centimetri, of course, I mean to say.'

'Ah yes.'

'That the circonference . . . No, only jokin!'

'Ha-ha.' Justin sometimes felt he should wear a tape-measure clipped to his belt, as Robin did when he was on a job. 'Well, see you this evening then.'

Which left him with a whole hot summer afternoon of waiting. He didn't know what to do. He went down for a late lunch in the antique quiet of the Musgrove's dining-room, and then sat with coffee and the *Daily Telegraph* in the lounge. People clearly mistook him for the nephew or grandson of a guest at the hotel. And part of his pleasure in the place was the reminiscence of holidays spent with his father in establishments chosen for their digestible cooking and ban on children; hotels where the lounge was empty by 9 p.m., though grumbles of conversation and bursts of high-volume TV could be heard from the rooms as he set out again for a stroll along the front to the improbably listed back bar of another hotel. From his armchair he could see through the lobby to the brilliant sunlight in the street. The stout old doorman, in maroon morning dress, was talking to some workmen outside, and stepped back to greet an elderly couple, guests who obviously knew him well. The rough tick-tick of a waiting taxi could be heard, against the fainter roar and distant squeals of traffic in the Brompton Road, a block away. The routines of London were so beautiful, calming and exciting at once, like being in love. In the words of certain masseurs, stimulating *and* relaxing. He thought of poor old Robin, over in Clapham, and Alex high up in his office in Whitehall, glancing out at the day through greying net curtains, and was gently aroused and lazily amused by their love and lust for him. He saw them standing side by side, with their very different penises sticking up in bewildered supplication as he swept past. They had been stopping-stations, hitching-posts in that embarrassing early part of life before one has quite enough money or knows what one is meant to do. Then there was a moment of change, of clarification. Money made everything clear.

He walked up the road to the seldom crowded designer basement of Harvey Nichols and sorted negligently through the rails of the better houses; here and there a young assistant would break off from an exacting afternoon of club gossip and shirt-refolding to solicit his custom. He tried on a couple of suits, loose summer linens, but they made him look fat and hot, like an old-fashioned sex-tourist. 'It's not right,' he said, with a note of more general protest. The prices too were rather tawdry. He got a taxi to Issey Miyake, where he was welcomed with ritualised surprise, like an arrival at a remote Zen temple. In the forty minutes he was there no other customer came in,

195

but when he left with a suit and a shirt he had spent a fraction over £3,000, and he hailed another cab in a mood that was best summed up by one of his earliest word-muddles: he was in a state of beautitude.

Back at the hotel a more urgent excitement set in. He couldn't help wondering what Carlo was going to look like, and the thought of having him here entirely at his disposal for hours on end made him prickle with pleasure. He wondered what he was doing now: working out, perhaps; or, more probably, simply working. An afternoon appointment with a dandruffed married man. Justin liked the idea of Carlo as a sex-machine, but hoped that he wouldn't already be tired out at 7 p.m. Carlo was a strong name, though, like a fortified version of *caro*, which was the Italian for expensive. Of course the English for Carlo was Charles, which was the name of his estate-agent friend. That was a coincidence. Maybe Charles too was Massively VWE. It was hard to tell with those expansive pin-stripes. How would he put it? – 'enjoys a substantial erection' . . . well, who didn't? And perhaps there had been something a bit sexy, after all, about chugging round with Charles from house to house. Carlo, though, would be more than a bit sexy. But then you had to remember that Carlo almost certainly wasn't his real name. There was still an hour and a half to go. Justin was so worked up that he wondered about getting another rent-boy round, to fill in the time.

In the last minutes of the approach he rather lost interest – it was only sex, and would probably be a disappointment. The phone rang at five to seven, and the pleasant Scots girl, who made Justin think of bare knees in a cold wind, said, 'There's a Mr? . . . a Mr Carlo, to see you.' Justin was already in the towelling bath-robe that the hotel provided, powdered and sprayed in coquettish deference to his visitor, who might not share Mr Robin's taste for b.o. He arranged himself in a chair, but then had to get up to open the door.

As Carlo came in, the couple in the next room were going down to an early dinner, and Justin heard the words 'youth hostel' pass between them in a jolly but disconcerted tone. There was superficially something outward-bound about Carlo, in his homosexual boots and socks; the padded straps of his knapsack set off the curves of his chest and shoulders like a harness, and his black shorts, though baggy in cut, still caught and stretched around his thighs and buttocks as he moved. He was the urban parody of a hiker that you saw in any gay bar. He was by no means as tall as expected, but he was swelteringly good-looking; he had the mask-like orangey tan that comes from using the wrong 'no sun' lotion. He shook Justin's hand and looked round the room with an appreciative, comparing eye as he shrugged off his knapsack. Justin knew he'd made another good choice. The boy was like a package holiday on legs.

The next few moments had their usual fascination – the hand-over of the money, the little dent this made in the scenario of the romantic visit, and the immediate boost to it again after Carlo had counted the fold of notes; the hesitation as to what was wanted – a pretend love-scene or sex without preamble or some charged personal variant. Justin loosened his bath-robe to reveal the natural tan that was his reward for so much country tedium, and Carlo came up and started kissing him in the automatically imploring way of a shorter person. There was something pretty passionate about his warm snufflings, Justin thought, as he reached down to grasp the heavy stirring in the boy's pants. But then Carlo stood back for a moment with a silly apologetic expression. 'Only one second,' he said. 'I need to use your toilet.'

Justin gazed at him forgivingly. 'Darling,' he said, 'I am my toilet.'

He couldn't explain what happened a couple of days later. He went out with Charles again in the morning and looked at a smallish house off the Fulham Road that had been totally renovated. He didn't expect to like it, he found the mere mention of Fulham depressing, and perhaps he only went because of his dotty new fixation on Charles, the secret stud. Charles picked him up outside the hotel, and his new pitch was a superstitious reluctance to talk about the house at all, as though anything he said might threaten the beautiful outside chance of Justin's falling in love with it. 'I'll be very interested indeed to know what you think', was all he said. He had the unlasting aura of a person one has surprisingly and happily had sex with in a dream; but he appeared not to notice Justin's quizzical glances. There was an old signet-ring on his right hand, but his wedding-finger was reassuringly vacant.

Outside, the house was sameish white stucco, with a bald front garden where a cement-mixer had stood; but inside it had been given a coldly avant-garde make-over, and had lost all reference to the consolations of an ordinary home. The two men marched moodily over the creaking expanses of blond flooring, and Charles gave clumsy demonstrations of various concealed fixtures: Justin thought this must be his first visit to the property, and suspected that he had a significant hangover; he watched him take off his jacket and lay it on the graphite-coloured kitchen worktop, and took in the hinted bearing of chest and buttocks with revisionist indulgence and fascination. Then there was the trill of a mobile, and Charles wandered off trying to get a good reception. 'Yes, I'm there now,' he was saying; and other laconic, shielded remarks, as if he couldn't speak freely. Justin was alone for a moment in the kitchen, and quickly felt in the horizontal breast-pocket for Charles's wallet – it came out with a tug, a fat old buttoned billfold, bulging with credit card slips and petrol vouchers. Behind the little glassine window inside was a snapshot of an extraordinarily beautiful black girl.

Well, that was all he needed to know. He moved to put the wallet back just as Charles, with an irritable turn of speed, was coming through from the front door. 'Sorry, Pete, this bloody phone's still playing up,' he said. 'I'll ring you later.' There was nothing Justin could do, and he started forward, saying hectically, 'So this room doubles as a dining-room', as he crammed the thing into his own pocket.

The rest of the inspection was purely histrionic. Justin ranged about and asked questions as though from a transparently remembered script, but all he could think of was the wallet and getting rid of it. Charles seemed relieved by his sudden liveliness, and perhaps thought he had had an undeserved success. At each stage of the following business, Charles picking up his jacket, their leaving the house, getting into the car, the ten-minute drive, and Justin's getting out of the car, various ruses seemed briefly possible but then had already lost their moment. A straightforward explanation would have been humiliating. At one point he had the thing – so much not the thing of Charles's that he wanted – in his hand and was about to slip or throw it into the back of the car, but his nerve failed him.

After being dropped he went into the hotel for a moment, and then emerged again with a certain unavoidable shiftiness, and ambled along the street. He couldn't hand the wallet in, because he couldn't be associated with it in any way. He couldn't leave it somewhere, because another person might use the credit cards and cause Charles even more nuisance. He felt too guilty to look inside the wallet himself. This was among the more ridiculous things he had done, but was not to be classed with odd bits of trouble he'd had at school with taking other boys' things. The thought that his momentary caprice was about to become a horrid little crisis for someone else required swift and frowning censorship. A huge garbage-truck was progressing down Beauchamp Place, with overalled men in fluorescent waistcoats lobbing sacks and boxes into its moaning and crackling tailgate. Justin stood and watched it pass, and as the men ran forward he stepped out to cross the road and tossed the wallet into the rearing jaws of the machine.

He decided to miss lunch, and got a taxi into Soho. He went to a bar where he had sometimes met up with Alex after work in the earlier, more outgoing phase of their affair; but it too had been the subject of interior design, and its new surfaces of polished steel and industrial rubber forbade nostalgia. He ordered a nutritious bloody Mary. He felt that he wasn't drifting but adrift. He didn't know what to do about the houses. He would have to see Charles again, to offset suspicions, but the idea of looking over another property was already vaguely sickening to him. He imagined ringing the office and being told that Charles would no longer be looking after him. And then he could simply abandon the search, it would be a sweet release; he could buy a brown felt hat and see out his days in the considerate hush of the Musgrove Hotel. He had a recurrent

199

delusion, which seemed to him authentically criminal, that he could still smell the high-summer stink of the garbage-truck, beer-slops and rotten apples and cod-liver oil.

By mid-afternoon he had been round three bars, accompanied on the last leg by a talkative young man called Ivor, who had met him and Robin at a party last Christmas. Justin had only a filtered recollection of that earlier occasion – of being shown off by Robin, of being very beautiful and amusing, and, perhaps, of Ivor being one of those he had impressed. 'I often repeat that joke of yours,' Ivor said.

'Oh . . .' said Justin.

'When I said what a pillar of strength you were to Robin, and he said, "Oh, more than that", and you said, "What, an arcade?"' Justin chuckled bashfully, and thought it was quite funny, or would have been when he said it. Ivor seemed to be mesmerised by him, his chatter was partly nervous, and when Justin started speaking he sat with his lips apart, as if to memorise what he said. He was a nice enough looking chap, with short black hair and sporty club gear that he must have thought suitable for daytime wear. The opportunity never quite arose for Justin to tell him he had left Robin, and he sheltered behind Ivor's understandable ignorance, and found it comfortable, and then uncomfortable. 'I'd love to have you two round for a meal,' Ivor said, 'while you're both in town. Or perhaps you'd like to come and see my new show.'

'Sure . . .' said Justin, turning to signal to the barman.

'You don't remember what I do, do you?' said Ivor, clearly thrilled by his own insignificance.

Justin didn't like to say that, strictly speaking, he couldn't remember Ivor at all. He said, 'We'll only be here for a couple more days.' And then, 'Do you want another drink?'

The bar they were in was small and sparingly lit, with walls of mirror to allay the sense of being in a trap. It was clearly a haunt of Ivor's, and they were soon joined by a loose group of his friends. Justin bought drinks for them all, with a strained heartiness that wasn't his natural style. One of the boys said to him quietly, 'Are you okay?' He was a thickset rugger blond, whom Justin had immediately hoped to impress – it was confusing to be shown this wary solicitude. He had had what, four bloody Marys and then a couple of summery screwdrivers. He wasn't that far gone. But maybe his gaze at the boy, who was still soberly shy and reasonable, had been unwittingly heavy. He said, 'I'm fine', and the boy shrugged and lifted his bottle and murmured, 'Cheers.'

Later, he was buying a drink for another man, and told him he was looking for a house, three or four bedrooms, in west or south-west London, but north of the river. He may have rather bragged about his requirements. The man said, 'Well, let me know when you find one. I suppose you won't need a lodger?'

Justin said, 'I might have a sort of paying sex-guest.'

This didn't seem to be what the man had in mind, but he laughed, and said, 'Anyway, you must have a boyfriend.'

'Yes, I must,' said Justin.

Ivor, who tended to audit and sample anyone else's conversations with Justin, said excitably, 'He's got a bloody gorgeous boyfriend. Haven't you? He's this gorgeous architect.' He took a sip from his salt-rimmed glass, and added, 'They're made for each other', with a note of extravagant regret.

Justin looked in the mirror on the facing wall. The bar was reflected in it, and their group of seven or eight, and his eye tracked across it to find himself. The skin of his face felt tight, with the dry tingle of afternoon drunkenness, the hint of giddiness and dissociation . . . He knew he should leave, but winced at the thought of the bright sunlight outside, and saw the wince in the mirror as an ugly little convulsion in the indefinably alien stiffness and slackness of his face. Everyone else seemed to be all right, he saw that the man who might be his lodger had noticed him looking at himself, and was smiling ironically at him. The bar was really terribly small. He took in, with delayed displeasure, that the cool quiet jazz of earlier had mutated, as the afternoon ran over some invisible threshold, into louder dance-music, with its threatening chemical eagerness. Ivor was saying something else to him, more unguarded as he got drunker himself. Justin turned and stared deliberately at the polished surface of the bar. His breathing was rapid and shallow.

As soon as he was out in the street he felt better, and he

201

walked a block or two unseeingly in short charges and pauses. Whenever he thought back to the bar the panic returned, with a sudden wrong beat of the heart; but the effect diminished a little each time. It might have been all right, but he avoided looking in shop-windows or car-windows. He went into Soho Square, which he thought would be free of reflections, and sat firmly on the grass, in the middle of the lawn, under the airy canopy of the planes. One of the gay boys near by came and asked him for a light, but he just shook his head. After a while he got up quickly and went to a phone-box. He jabbed at the numbers and listened to the ringing tone without a clue what he was going to say. He felt it was out of his control, and that whatever he said would come to him in the moment that he said it. He had a vague image of the Clapham flat, the sex-box as he used to call it, and Robin darting to the phone. A preoccupied and not quite recognisable voice said, 'Alex Nichols.' Justin winced, and for a paranoid half-second thought that Alex was there with Robin; then he started to wonder how he had dialled that number, by some flustered instinct – it was well over a year since he'd rung Alex at work. 'Alex Nichols,' the voice said again, wearily. Justin stood there panting, like a pervert, and heard Alex hang up. Then, more deliberately, as if trying to see where he had gone wrong the first time, Justin keyed in the sex-box number. Within a second he heard the muffled clatter of the ansafone, and Robin's voice, unlifelike, businesslike, making the impossible announcement that he had gone away.

By the time he reached Crewkerne it was dark, and he saw the last taxi pull out from the station yard as he emerged with his bags. There was a slight chill and a sharp grassy smell in the air. He went to the phone-box to call a cab, and then stood under the lamp at the station door. The ticket-office was closed, and the lit platforms and waiting-rooms were unmanned, in the modern way. Occasionally a car that wasn't his cab came slowly past, and then accelerated away. The edge of a small country town at 10.30 at night, with rear lights disappearing: it was a definition of loneliness.

He noticed that the driver didn't take credit cards, and decided not to tell him he had no cash. He sat in the back, with his overnight bag clutched on his knee, and watched the car's headlights sweep corner after corner of the high-hedged lanes. The driver took them fast, and several times raised a squeal. He probably wanted to finish for the night, this was far out of his way – Justin was indifferent to him but glad of the mood of emergency. He swung from side to side, gripped by the muddled emotions of coming home and going into exile. He had made a mistake, but he didn't know which it was.

When the car stopped at the gate he did a cursory mime of dismay over his wallet. 'It's all right, I live here,' he said; but the driver held on to his luggage. He hurried down through the dark garden, hoping more than ever that Robin would be in. A light was visible through the apple-trees – it was like a house at the end of the world, and he had a sense that he had left it thirty years ago, rather than ten hapless days.

Some punctilio, or maybe a taste for drama, made him ring the bell, though his keys were in his pocket. He heard the springy thump of Robin's footsteps, and knew he would be barefoot, and pictured his puzzlement at a late-night visit. The door was plucked open, and there he was, shockingly himself, utterly lifelike. Justin saw his sigh of surprise, and then the doubting but unstoppable smile. 'Have you got twelve quid, darling?' he said. 'I've got to pay the taxi.'

Robin came up to carry his bags, and Justin thanked him quietly, as for an expected but still agreeable tribute. In the kitchen they had a quick hug, but sat apart across the table. Justin had the beginnings of a dry headache. When he looked up he saw that Robin was crying.

He always rather froze in the presence of other people's distress. He had only once seen Robin cry before, not long after they'd met, when he had told him about Simon – and it was true that on that occasion he had found it terribly sexy. Now he said, 'So when did you come back?'

Robin pulled a hand across his face and cleared his throat. 'Um . . . about three days ago. I couldn't stand not hearing from you – knowing you were somewhere near by.' Justin read his desire to ask a dozen questions, some of them important. 'Are you going to tell me where you were?'

'It doesn't matter.'

Robin sniffed and stood up. 'Drink?'

'Yep. Scotch.'

He got glasses and a half-empty bottle. 'Did you have fun?'

'Yes, for a bit. I needed time. You mustn't forget I'm a city girl, darling, at heart. I grew up in Solihull.' He took the glass that Robin slid towards him, and peered into it absently. 'Anyway, then I decided it was time to get back to dear old Luton Gasbag.' He smiled briefly and then drank, but with no show of celebration. He was anxious to prevent avowals from being made. 'Did you get up to any mischief in my absence?'

Robin hesitated for a moment, as though trying to make up something silly, and said, 'I slept with Terry Badgett.'

'Huh . . . I see.' Justin scraped back his chair. 'That's a bit pathetic, isn't it?'

'Totally pathetic. I was lonely, he jumped me. It was a waste of time. And money.'

'You don't mean you paid him for sex?'

'The sex was hopeless, and then he woke me up and asked me to pay for it. He obviously sees himself as some kind of hustler.'

Justin tried to show he was above such things, but he felt bitterly wounded; and baffled by Robin's motives in telling him. 'I'm not sure I needed to know that,' he said.

'Well, you asked. I've never had secrets from you, and I'm not starting now. I thought you'd left me, for fuck sake. I haven't taken a vow of chastity.'

'Maybe I have left you,' Justin said. He felt his anger waking up, with its exhilarating potential to take him far from home, and he slammed the hatch down on its head and bolted it shut. 'Anyway, I hope he didn't stay the night.'

'No,' said Robin impatiently. 'He was only here about an hour. It was nothing.'

An hour, thought Justin. An hour of betrayal. He said, 'I don't want all the village knowing about it'; and then started laughing, and carried on laughing for longer than was pleasant.

When they were in bed he curled up in Robin's arms and

felt his hard cock pushing apologetically against the back of his thighs – he thought it was more like Alex's shy lust than Robin's usual masterful advance. He said, 'Do you mind if we don't tonight. I have, genuinely, got a headache.' He shifted away, but reached back to grip his powerful hand.

In the morning Robin lay in much longer than usual, and kept rolling on to Justin with pretend-sleepy humphs and gropes. But Justin could outsleep anyone. Eventually Robin swung his legs out of bed and went to the bathroom, leaving the door open. Justin listened for the boyish noisiness of his peeing, always straight into the water, and the flush pulled just before he finished. A minute later he heard rattling in the kitchen beneath. He lay there waiting for the Terry thing to break loose again; but nothing very much happened, and he wondered if perhaps he didn't care. He intuited some motive of revenge in the whole business, which made it amusing in a way, and he saw that it was something he could always bring up. He pushed back the covers, and turned round on the bottom sheet like a dog in its basket. It didn't take him long to find half a dozen bent black hairs, which he picked up fastidiously and took between thumb and forefinger down to the kitchen. Robin was laying the breakfast, and Justin set them down with a conscientious frown on his side-plate. 'How much did you have to pay for these?' he said.

Robin's face was instantly shadowed. 'I said, I didn't know you were coming.' He turned away with a shake of the head, as if he could never do anything right.

It was extraordinary to have such power over someone to whom you longed only to submit. There they both were, half naked in the kitchen, the back door open, the noise of birdsong fading under the gathering roar of the kettle. Justin said, 'Shall we do housewife surprised over breakfast by meter-reader? Or are these the Lucy Rie plates?'

Robin said, 'Mike Hall rang and asked us to go round. They're having the new man from "Ambages". I imagine he wants some moral support.'

'I'm not sure I can give that,' said Justin. 'What's his name?'

He was very cheered by the thought of a social evening, with old people.

Robin went to the phone, where he'd written it down. 'His name's Adrian Ringrose.'

Justin raised an eyebrow. 'He sounds like the ballet critic of a provincial newspaper.'

'That's what he may well have been. I think he's retired down here.'

'He'll be awfully glad he's met us,' said Justin, with a companionable yawn, and a sense of the significance of the first person plural. 'Still, there's lots of time before then.'

'Masses,' Robin agreed, and raised his eyebrows optimistically. He had taken the day off work, to be with Justin, which was both comforting and oppressive. He came back across the room to sit beside him on the sofa, and put a hand on his thigh.

Justin said, 'Shall we have a game of Scrabble, darling?' in a special broody tone.

Robin seemed to ponder for a moment if this was code for something even more enjoyable, and then modified his caress into an encouraging rub. 'Sure, if you really want to.'

'I do, darling.'

'Okay.' Robin jumped up to get things ready, with a slightly exaggerated air of keenness and self-denial, like a hospital visitor. Their two previous games of Scrabble had been reduced to absurdity or even aborted by Justin's childish resentment of the rules. It was especially risky if they played one of the Woodfield variants, where the rules had been devised by Robin himself. 'What shall we play?'

'I don't mind, darling. You decide.' Justin was charmed by his own cosiness and pliancy, and couldn't have said how ironic he was being, or where it would all lead. 'Something a bit different?' He knew that Robin and his mother had played obsessively in her last years, and that Lady Astrid had made and memorised a list of all the two-letter words in the language.

'Okay.' Robin offered him the letter bag. 'Let's have nine letters, then; and seventy-five extra if you put them all down.'

'Fine.' Justin smiled mysteriously, picked out an A, and added, 'Oh, and no two-letter words.'

Robin drew breath to complain, but then thought better of it.

Justin held his letters away from him and scanned them fondly for a couple of minutes. 'Do you know what my first word is going to be, darling?' he said.

'I don't.'

'Well it begins with a G, and it ends with a Y, and the middle letter's an A.'

Robin pursed his lips in the briefest pretence of amusement, and was already entering his score on the sheet when Justin put down GRAVY. 'Ah. Very good, twenty-four,' he said, before doing a quick reshuffle of his rack and then laying out across the board, with calm ruthlessness, the word EXASPERATE. 'Um . . . let me see . . . sixty, and the bonus . . . one hundred and thirty-five.'

'Marvellous,' said Justin, arranging his new letters and sending his mind off on a wilfully naughty excursion through his sexual activities of the past ten days. Gianni, and Carlo; and then Mark, who had bulged rather less than promised. No, Carlo was definitely the best. When he focused again on his rack he could only see a hedge of consonants, like a Welsh village. He thought how absurd it was to be doing this for fun, by choice; when surely the point about getting a little bit older and having money was that you never had to do anything that you didn't want to. He put down GENTS, as a flat joke, and also, in their case, a romantic one, and scored a suicidal eight – he felt Robin's disapproval of the wasted resource of the s. 'Shall we have a drink, darling?' he suggested.

While Robin was out of the room Justin hopped up and looked at his rack, on which TEMPORISE was waiting to be deployed. He saw that if Robin laid it across the s of GENTS he would get a quadruple word score plus the bonus; which after a moment's mental arithmetic would doubtless come out at several thousand points. He was back studying his letters, and accepted his gin and tonic abstractedly, only looking up when Robin had set down his tiles. The word he had made was PROEMS; which came to a timid twenty-six. 'Rather a good word, I think,' Robin said.

For Justin the game was over at that moment. If they were both going to play deliberately badly, even though from quite

207

different motives, then what was the point of continuing? He shouldn't have looked at Robin's letters, perhaps; and he remembered that though knowledge was power it could also involve a good deal of disappointment. Still, he couldn't admit to having peeped, which might be considered a kind of cheating. He took about five minutes to make his next word. 'Sorry . . .' he said at one point.

'It doesn't matter,' said Robin, suppressing his gaping impatience as if playing with a child.

Justin was thinking about going out later, and the wonderfully unorthodox guide to village life he would be able to give to the newcomer. All he knew about him came from Margery Hall's vague remark that he was a bachelor and rather musical, from which he had built up a convivial portrait of a boozy old opera queen who would of course find him very attractive and amusing. Then he did something most annoying, and put down half his word before hastily taking it up again. He said, 'I think it would be nice to just sort of put down words.'

Robin frowned equably. 'Isn't that what we're doing?'

'I mean, wherever we liked.'

'Oh I see,' said Robin. 'Well, that might make an interesting variant. I think it's probably best if you engage with your opponent's words . . .'

Justin took a drink, and then quickly put down PIRRENT. 'Eleven, darling.'

'What on earth is that supposed to be?'

Justin blinked offendedly over his sabotage. 'It's PIRRENT,' he said.

'Why don't you have PRINTER?'

'Oh I far prefer this.'

'Yes, darling,' said Robin, clearly thinking he was being mocked, but remembering to indulge Justin, like someone senile or mad. 'But what does it mean?'

'Oh . . .' – Justin kept shaking his head as he searched for the definition. 'It means . . . sort of *vainglorious*.'

There was a long pause before Robin said, 'I'm afraid I'll have to challenge that.'

Justin twisted sideways to pick up his drink, and the jerk of his knee fetched the Scrabble board off the low table, and

scattered the letters across the floor. 'You know how superstitious I am,' he said. 'I'm sure that must be a sign.'

15

Danny went down to Dorset for a few days to put some distance between himself and Alex; though the reason he gave was that he wanted to check up on his father and Justin. He knew Alex couldn't object to this kind-hearted plan, and he tried to persuade himself that Alex too might feel ready to cool it. He brought his big notebook with him as usual, and his more secret plan was to try to write a play about some of the people he knew on the club scene, Heinrich and Lars and a few others, with talk of an enigmatic older man, which would be his homage to George, as well as a kind of revenge on him. He didn't envisage any technical obstacles to writing something stageable and sensationally topical; he spent one morning planning the guest-list for the first-night party, and going over certain points in the interviews he would give.

At the end of the week Alex came down to join him. Danny half-hoped that Robin might make a fuss about this, but his father treated Alex these days with amiable indifference, perhaps out of respect to Danny's boyfriend, perhaps because he guessed he wouldn't be his boyfriend much longer. He arrived soon after ten on Saturday morning, which like so many of his actions made you calculate the exact degree of inconvenience and eagerness that lay behind it; he'd have got up at six at the latest. He stood about expectantly in the kitchen as the others ate a halting, hung-over breakfast. He had some photographs of their long weekend with him, and showed them round dotingly, like an excited voyeur of his own happiness. Justin was rather pointedly studying the Equity prices in *The Times*; Robin served up more and more fried food. Danny's impression was that the two of them were having a lot of sex and a lot of rows, which was probably better than having neither, as had been the case before. Robin did what he could to shield him responsibly from both things, and made him wonder if he could dodge those two things himself this weekend.

It was a breezy blue day, and Danny thought they should get out of the house. 'Shall we go down to the beach?' he said, with a tug on Alex's shirt-sleeve, and an awkward sense of a withheld endearment. He stuffed some towels and a book he was reading into his knapsack, but left his notebook behind, as he didn't want Alex getting interested in his play, or indeed in some of the other things it contained. They went up to the car, and Danny leapt into the passenger seat without opening the door. The car was fun, after all, and freedom. He switched on the CD player, which whirred and checked itself and jumped to the middle of some slammingly hard house that Alex must have been listening to *en route*. Really he wondered at times what he'd turned this nice Donizetti-fancying civil servant into. As they drove up the lane, Mr Harland-Ball was standing in his gateway, and Danny called out, 'We're queer!' in a helpful tone.

Alex changed into top on the Bridport road and let his hand drift from the gear-stick on to Danny's thigh. And it was true that Danny was tinglingly randy after a night of red wine and Irish whiskey, and had been feeling a touch redundant, alone in the house with a busy couple – it required a certain tactful blindness, and deafness. He sprawled back for a moment, so that Alex could feel his cock, but then said, 'Actually, you'd better concentrate on the road.'

Alex said, 'It's strange having the other two in the house again, after we had it all to ourselves.'

Danny paused and said, 'It is their home.'

'I know, darling. That's not quite what I meant.'

'You mustn't be so possessive,' Danny said, and smacked Alex's knee to make a little joke of it; when he glanced at his face a moment later he saw his blush, and knew he was silently absorbing and refuting the charge. Danny turned off the music, which was a bit strong for eleven in the morning, and started fiddling with the radio. Alex said,

'Did I tell you I saw Dave the other day?'

'Dave who?'

211

'Your friend who works in the porno shop.'

'Oh, right.' Danny found his favourite dance-music station, but it kept warping into a programme of hilarious advertisements in French. 'You really need to get a better sound system,' he said, not for the first time.

'What is his surname, anyway?'

'Whose?'

'Dave's . . .'

'I don't know,' said Danny. 'I'm not that intimate with him.'

It was already busy at the beach, and they had to park some way from the refreshment cabins and the edge of the shingle. Danny's eyes moved mischievously around behind the unreadable black discs of his shades. He noted Terry's Lovemobile drawn up at the side of the Hope and Anchor, by some special arrangement he had with the landlord; and there were some nice big teenagers and a few sexy young dads mixed in with the trashier holiday-makers. Danny glanced at Alex to see if he had noticed them, but he seemed absorbed in the practicalities of the expedition. He walked a few yards ahead, past the Fo'c'sle Fish Bar and the Kiss Me Hardy gift kiosk, which had lost the last letter of its name. And even that detail seemed to raise the sexual pitch of the day.

The top of the beach was a low ramp of shingle, but further down there were patches and stripes of coarse grey sand. To the right the deep channel of the river opened out between its timbered walls. Alex didn't know about the death of a local boy there, who had dived on to a pleasure-boat and broken his neck; Danny had read the story in the *West Dorset Herald* and preferred not to look at the shrivelled flowers and blotched messages that were still heaped on the quayside. He trailed on towards the further end of the beach, where the cliffs reared up again, and there weren't so many little kids. He wanted to sit down near some lads he could get into conversation with. Alex came along, upset and inquisitive about the death, and why Danny hadn't waited for him. 'I think we should go here, darling,' he called, indicating the last free patch of sand; and Danny mopingly complied and turned back.

He had two contradictory feelings. He wished Alex wouldn't call him darling all the time in public; and on the other hand

212

he was so conditioned to a world in which everyone was gay that he found it hard to bear in mind, down here, a hundred miles from London, that almost everyone wasn't. He raked the beach with a cruisy steadiness, a mysteriously knowledgeable smile, as if he had only to decide. Alex settled the bags and towels like an obstacle to escapades which, Danny briefly admitted, were never likely to happen. But there again, rationally, statistically, magnetically, there was a real chance that he might have picked up.

They sat down and he turned his attention to the sea, which Alex was reacting to in a forced, appreciative tone. There was a dazzle, even through sunglasses, on the small, noisy breakers, and the frothy film of water that slid back down the beach. A short way out there was an almost hidden rock over which a bright hood of foam reared and fell from time to time. After summers on the long surfing beaches north of San Diego, with their stilted lifeguard stations and neck-ricking parades of god like men, Danny found the English seaside tackily spartan. Even on a hot day like this, there was a rough little breeze that hummed and buzzed over the nearby stones. He kept his T-shirt on and lay back looking at the sky; where there was nothing to see, except the highest faint plumes of cirrus. Alex said he thought there was something specially ethereal about the clouds, they were so high that it was hard to think of them as related to the earth, they were like vapour-trails of a war in heaven, or something. Danny, who had spent an instructive weekend with a Scotsman from the Met Office, said more scientifically that they were seven or eight miles up, and at that altitude would be composed entirely of ice-crystals.

When he sat up again he saw that Alex was looking at him, and said, 'What . . .?'

'Nothing, darling. Have you heard from George about the chain, by the way?'

Danny sounded cross. 'No, I haven't. I haven't seen George, or heard a squeak out of him for weeks.' It was only as he said the sentence that he decided who he was being cross with. 'I think he's dropped me, the bastard.' He frowned very hard to stifle a grin. It was fun to have this entirely fictional pretext to talk about George. Alex looked both pleased and troubled.

213

'I hope you'll get it back soon.'

Danny nodded and looked out to sea. 'You never told me where you got it,' he said, with half-hearted wiliness.

'I can tell you if you like. It was left to me by my grandmother.'

'Really . . .?'

'I think she thought I could give it to my wife.'

Danny guffawed anxiously. The next stage of his plan had been to confess that George had lost the chain or sold it out of a misunderstanding. He wished he could just say that it had been stolen – and quite possibly swallowed – by a satyromaniac Brazilian dwarf. But it was never easy to be brutal to Alex. In fact the need to treat him delicately, to protect him, as you protect your parents with small lies and omissions, was a strong part of Danny's love for him. It was a kind of respect, and the lies themselves were coloured by solicitude. At times, the success of his deceits gave him a dizzy feeling of competence, at sustaining a double life; and that in turn made him proud of his affair with Alex, as an achievement, unlike the straightforward world of his miscellaneous fucks, with its perishable feelings and minimal commitments. But the grandmother's jewellery, the wayward convictions that must have led Alex to make that gift . . . It was like a creepy bit of private magic, a secret engagement ring. Danny said, 'I had thought of asking George down this weekend. I think you two should get to know each other better.'

Alex said, 'You had, had you?' and Danny laughed. It was so easy to trigger Alex's jealousy, and funny that he didn't realise that George was virtually the one person in his world that Danny could never have. The prohibition made the memories of him cruelly arousing, and he hunched forward to hide his erection.

Alex made quite a performance of changing into his swimming-trunks under a towel, like a straight person who has grown suspicious of the atmosphere in a locker-room. 'Just get changed,' Danny said. 'Nobody cares.'

'Thanks very much,' said Alex. 'I notice you're not getting ready.'

214

'I've got my shorts on under my jeans,' Danny said. 'Besides, you wouldn't catch me going in there.'

'The young of today have no fibre,' said Alex, pulling his shirt over his head, and standing for a moment, square-shouldered and head back, to make a joke out of his self-consciousness. Danny glanced up at his tall flat body, and remembered how he had found it fascinating and elegant, in its lanky way, after all the superfluous muscle he was used to being gripped by. And Alex was surprisingly strong, even if the ghost of an old back injury warned him away from some of the more demanding sex holds. Beside Danny he looked eerily pale, though if you'd taken his trunks off you would have seen the thin priming of tan on the rest of him. 'Well, I'm going in,' Alex said, and stepped forward, still in mock-heroic fashion, knowing he would be watched all the way to the water. 'And I don't want you talking to those rough boys,' he said, with a repressive nod at a group about twenty yards behind them.

When he was in quite deep and his head rising and dropping on the swell with a sleeked, stoic, solitary look, Danny gave him a wave, and thought maybe he was more like a child than a parent. Once you got him happy and absorbed in some activity you would be free to take up your own compromised interests again. Alex waved back, with a gasping grin, and seemed encouraged to strike out on a further lap. Now and then Danny saw the upward flicker of his elbows.

There was a rattle of shingle and Danny turned casually to see a couple of the rough boys hobbling down from their encampment of lilos and six-packs. One of them was blond and brawny, the other wiry and slight, with a dark pony-tail and Gothic tattoos: he had a boogy-board under his arm. Both of them wore long baggy shorts, as Danny liked to himself, though he knew they did it from a laddish fear of revealing themselves. He gave a tutting nod of greeting, and the dark boy said, 'All right?', which in a deep Dorset accent had a niceness, even a kind of chivalry, that it wouldn't have had in London.

'All right?' said Danny. And then, 'That your board?' The bright skeleton-key of thoughtless phrases that unlocked each new contact, the quick-witted focusing of tone: he kept telling

215

Alex there was no one you couldn't talk to, if you wanted to, it didn't matter what you said; but Alex was always worrying about the content.

It turned out they were Carl (blond) and Les, local lads. Carl was blushingly revealed as engaged, but Les was on the rebound and desperate to score. 'I know what you mean,' said Danny, and colluded with hesitant half-phrases in their appraisal of the nearby girls. Les was hardly his type but he had an unexpectedly sweet smile. He said,

'This sea's crap.'

Danny said, 'You need north Cornwall, don't you, for the surf?' He tactfully withheld his Californian credentials, which he thought might crush the boys; he couldn't imagine boogy-boarding in these stocky northern breakers if you'd done it out there, and could remember the jolting zoom of the ride in across a field of foam a hundred yards wide.

Carl said, 'It's usually better than this', with a mixture of local pride and vague provincial discontent. 'Where are you from then?'

'London, yeah . . .' said Danny, looking down and brushing sand from the towel he was sitting on. 'My dad lives down here – well, Litton Gambril.'

'Ah, nice,' said Les; but didn't ask anything more.

Carl said, 'I don't know about that one, Les. I reckon she'd do for you' – his eyes following a biggish teenage girl in her timid but heavy-footed approach to the water. Danny snig-gered, but apparently the suggestion was serious: the two of them wandered a few paces away, and he read the skull-crowned Motorhead tattoo on Les's left shoulder as he squinted seawards. Really, hetero life was so archaic and mad – Danny let out a quiet chuckle of relief at his own good fortune. And maybe Les too had his doubts:

'No. She'd squash me,' he said. 'She'd squeeze all the life out of me, that one.'

Then up from the sea came Alex, so that they seemed to be staring at him: he clearly wondered what was happening.

'Here comes your dad, then,' said Carl. 'Well, we'd better get in that sea if we're ever going to.' And off they trod, as butchly as possible, but stooping and jabbing out their arms

216

as they went over pebbly bits. Danny noted a kind of social cringe in their avoidance of Alex. He watched him approach, breathing roughly, tilting his head sideways to shake water from his ears, and of course he felt the romance of it, his lover coming up from the waves, in the flush and shiver of his exertion, leaning out of the noon sky to pluck up his towel. And then it passed.

At lunch-time they trekked along to the Hope and Anchor, asking Carl and Les's other friends to keep an eye on their things; though Alex was fretful about the arrangement. In the restaurant section at the back Danny spotted Terry, looking very handsome, in a blue-and-white striped sweat-shirt, like a minor sixties film-star, being treated to a huge lobster lunch by a man with glasses and a linen jacket, who might have been an Oxford don. It was amazing how well he did down here, with a little help presumably from Roger and John at the Mill. He looked up and winked at Danny over his patron's shoulder.

After a couple of pints of strong lager Danny felt much more cheerful, and for a while was full of randomly focused energy. Alex only drank Appletise, because he was driving, or didn't want to get a headache. He watched with a tense half-smile when Danny drifted away from him to gossip with strangers, feed crisps to their children, and briefly take part in a game of darts. It was a compulsion of Danny's, he wasn't being deliberately neglectful, in fact he introduced Alex to a good-looking man he had just introduced himself to, but Alex was so stiff, and the conversation died as soon as he left them together. When they were outside again Alex started talking in a hopeless farcical way about someone who worked in his office. Danny scanned the parking-lot and then the beach as they walked along, and said 'Yeah' with adequate regularity. An athletic-looking blond couple were walking ahead of them, both presumably in swimsuits, but they were covered by long T-shirts, so that they seemed from behind to be wearing nothing but the T-shirts. The man had beautiful muscular legs, with a glimmer of down on the back of the calves; the back of his head was square and Germanic, cropped short up to a thick topknot, which was stiffly untidy where salt-water had dried in it. The woman laughed and put her arm round his waist, his hem-line rose a fraction and showed the edge of his tight blue trunks. Danny was imagining licking the back of his neck as he fucked him. 'Well I thought it was funny anyway,' said Alex.

Danny looked at him poker-faced, and then laughed, and said, 'It is funny, darling. Very funny.' He wondered how long it was since the Germans had had sex, and how much longer the woman could possibly defer having it again. He dropped a little behind Alex, as he sometimes did, in the caressing grip of his own thoughts, and also with a sad but liberating recognition of something quite obvious: they had nothing in common. Their paths in life had joined for a moment, Danny had done a good deal for him, one way and another he'd got him sorted, and now it was natural and right that he should send him gently on his way. The process was so logical that he thought Alex himself, after the first upset of it, would be bound to see that it was right.

Back at their spot, Danny said, 'Okay, time for a kip, I think', and lay out flat on his towel. Alex hopped about between him and the sun, getting undressed all over again. He said,

'Aren't you taking anything off?'

'Oh all right,' said Danny, sitting up and twisting off his canvas shoes, one against the other. 'You don't want to get skin cancer.' Actually it was very hot, but he enjoyed the tease of keeping his jeans and T-shirt on. Alex was always looking at him, time and again he would be gazing at him when he woke up, as if he couldn't believe his luck. 'Anyway, you've seen it all before,' he said.

'Hm,' said Alex, clearly thinking that was rather beneath him. And Danny saw that being so much younger he must resist the temptation to be childish. He decided to read, and got out the bizarre book he had found in the lav at the cottage. If you started it at the front it was called *Memoirs of an Old Man of Thirty*; but you could turn it round and start from the back, where the text, which otherwise appeared upside-down, was called *Loves of a Young Man of Eighty*. It seemed to be a dodgy piece of 1890s smut; the Young Man of Eighty referred to his dick as his yard, which Danny took a while to get the hang of. He couldn't see why people kept wanting to look at his yard. Alex said, 'What are you reading?' and when he held up the book he seemed oddly put out by it. 'Are you enjoying it?' he asked.

'Yeah, I guess.'

And then rather anxiously, 'Do you find it sexy?'

Danny made a moue of uncertainty. 'I suppose you could just about wring a wank out of it, if you were desperate.'

Alex inspected the book prudishly and winced at the overlapping wine-rings on the white vellum binding. 'It's been half torn out of its covers,' he said, and threw it down again on the towel. 'But what does it matter? It's only a rare book. Perhaps you'd put some stuff on my back.'

'Sure.' Danny knelt and squirted out a curl of aloe cream between Alex's shoulder-blades and rubbed it in briskly all the way down towards the black edge of his Speedos. He thought how uncertain sex-magic was. It struck, and there was a tingle in the air around a man, and when you touched him it flowed round you too. Some people kept it for you for years, and when you saw them there was the same dependable shock, the shiver of rightness, the cool burn deep between the legs, the gentle thump on the chest, the private surrender of a smile. And with others it faded, like a torch left on, or with the quick disillusion that followed a hit of coke. A couple of months ago he adored Alex's back, he had mauled it and scratched his heels across it, amazed by Alex's fierceness on top of him; and he had arched over it too, in the lovely dismissive lust of a fuck from behind, getting crueller and crazier to the tune of Alex's shouts. Yet oddly, here on the beach, he could think of those things without a twitch. Presumably the light swipes and probings of his fingers were giving Alex pleasure, but to him this was a sportsmanlike task. He gave him a couple of slaps and said, 'You're done.'

Then he lay down again and slept and half-slept, in a tumult of bright dreams that shrank away when a child shrieked or the pebbles clattered, but then crowded back at once with their unlikely predicaments and jabber of new arrivals. He was aware of Alex talking and had the sense of himself as a joke, lying there while they talked about him and said 'I don't think he's really asleep'. He smiled to show that he wasn't, and after

219

a necessary moment's calculation said, 'Hello Terry', without opening his eyes. 'Come and join us.'

Terry had evidently said goodbye to his lunch companion and had time on his hands before going up to Broad Down to sort out the disco. Danny made a space for him, and Alex moved too, without much enthusiasm, and said, 'You do things over at Bride Mill, don't you Terry?'

'I have been known to,' said Terry.

'And what's it like? I gather it's on the expensive side.'

'Gor, the prices there. It's very nice, mind, it's beautiful.'

'I thought I might take Danny for lunch tomorrow.'

'Well, very nice,' said Terry. 'It's, you know, it's posh. It's mainly for people of the older persuasion.'

'You don't have to do that,' said Danny quietly; though what sounded like a flattered demurral masked a moment of decision for him. He couldn't go to the Mill with Alex. He couldn't sit with him in the oak-beamed dining-room, and chatter at him over the fresh-cut roses and the leather-bound folio of the wine-list, and smirk with him about the chorus-line of cow-licked young waiters as if nothing was wrong that couldn't be made right by a little fine living. He could feel the quality of anxiety in Alex's extravagance, and foresee the claustrophobic cou-pledom of Sunday lunch under John and Roger's velvety patronage. So whatever was going to happen would have to happen before then. He found he had a deadline, and that meant he had a few words to prepare.

Terry said, 'I got that Billy Nice, is it, CD.'

'Oh, Ricky Nice,' said Alex, before Danny could say anything.

'Yeah. It's great when you've had a few.'

'A few what . . .?' said Alex.

'You want to hear him live,' Danny said, and pushed at Terry's knee impatiently. 'You've got to come and see me in London, man. I'll take you down to BDX.' He hadn't planned the first person singular, but it was true to his mood and his instantaneous vision of Terry naked and face down in his Notting Hill room.

'Yeah, we'll show you a good time,' Alex said.

After a minute, Danny said, 'Gosh, I'd like an ice cream, or a cold drink.'

'Yeah,' said Terry, with a slow nod and a look of ready but undirected cunning.

Alex said, 'I am a bit dry . . .'

'Perhaps,' said Danny, 'darling, you might be a complete hero and go and get us something. I don't think I could face walking all the way back. What do you want, Terry, a Coke? I think I'll have an ice lolly. Oh please . . .' and he made a feeble gesture of supplication and fell backwards on to the towel.

Alex pulled on his shoes, and began his long tramp over the shingle, holding his money in his hand. When he was thirty yards away Danny and Terry both got undressed, with the absent-minded rapidity of something often rehearsed. Under his jeans Terry had on a pair of very tight yellow swimming-trunks, cut square across the thigh, with a gold medallion like a belt-buckle sewn on the wide waistband; either they were camp sixties retro or had remained in stock since that time in one of the slower-moving Bridport outfitters. Danny was in his usual boyish shorts, stone-coloured but semi-transparent when wet. He passed Terry the sun-block and got him to massage it into his back as he lay with his chin on his fist, and his stiffening dick pressing into the sand. Terry himself was a wonderful colour – the patchy burns from different outside jobs had fused by now into a steady Greek or Spanish brown. When he'd finished he stretched out beside Danny, on Alex's towel, and said, 'I suppose this is as far as it goes.'

'Um . . . I'm not sure about that,' Danny said. He had a funny little sense of responsibility.

'You two not getting on so well any more?' said Terry, in his blundcringly intuitive fashion. Danny looked up to where Alex could still be seen moving away, his long strides hampered by the slipping pebbles. 'I reckon he's still tipping his hat at you, anyway,' Terry said.

'He's a really sweet guy,' Danny said. 'I love him very much. But, you know how it is. I used to jump on him, now he jumps on me.'

'Well then. You're not in love with him.'

221

Danny wondered if Terry knew what he was talking about. 'I've only been in love once,' he said; and decided in a second not to elaborate. He'd seen George chatting up Terry at the party, and had been careful not to find out what happened – it was one shake of the sex-dice he didn't want to contemplate. He said, 'You know me, Terry. I'm not ready to settle down. I have to keep things from him all the time. We're just not meant to be together.'

'Still a chance for me then,' said Terry, touchingly enough. Danny looked him over, his eyes coming back to play between his legs, where a stealthy upheaval had already taken place.

'There will always be a place for you in my, um . . .' he said, and reached out to snap at the elastic of his trunks. He wondered if there was some futuristic way they could have sex here, in the middle of the beach, without anyone knowing. Then he said, 'Or do you mean a chance with Alex?'

Terry pondered it. 'I'd say he's quite nice-looking. And I dare say he's quite well endorsed.'

'Okay. Sure – none of that's a problem.' Danny remembered the days of his rapid initiation into the scene, and how anyone who had split up said 'The sex was never that great'; so that he wondered after a while why anyone had a partner, and after a while more whether any couples actually had sex – at least with each other. And now he found the same words at the front of his mind, as an easy alternative to the more peculiar truth.

'How come you two got together?' said Terry. 'I wouldn't have thought he was your type.'

'I don't have a type, darling,' said Danny, whose utopian policy was to have everyone once. 'I thought you knew, he used to go out with Justin.'

Terry wasn't expecting that. 'Well I wouldn't have thought he was his type either.'

'Oh, you know,' said Danny: 'shy top and bossy bottom, it happens all the time', and watched Terry absorb this crude but worldly insight.

'Right,' he said. 'So how did Justin get off with your dad?'

Justin himself was quite free with the story of the Clapham Common Gents, but a kind of family pride, or maybe just snobbery, dissuaded Danny from passing it on to Terry. 'Oh, they met in London someplace.' In fact his laughter when Justin first told him had covered a few lost seconds of incredulity and shock.

'I suppose if I was Justin, I'd probably prefer ... Mr Woodfield, rather than Alex,' said Terry, enjoying the new mood of frankness. 'I always thought he was a bit of all right, your dad.'

'Hey, no you don't! Hands off my old man!' said Danny, as if speaking in subtitles; and noticed the now uncontrolled mutiny in Terry's trunks. 'Justin's fair enough ...'

Terry blushed and turned on to his front. 'And so's Simon,' he said, 'I suppose', with an effect of hurriedly covering one piece of mischief with another.

Danny worked it out behind the black sheen of his shades. He wasn't totally easy with knowing about Justin's indiscretions; they troubled him because they were bad jokes against his father, who had always seemed immune to attack and powered by a scandalous personal authority. 'You'd better tell me,' Danny said.

Terry sensed his reserve and said, 'Nah, it doesn't matter.'

'Go on,' said Danny, 'if it doesn't matter' – thinking of that Jewish funeral, and his father's freaky stoicism, like indifference, as if his homosexual loss could not be mixed with the family's grief and embarrassment.

'It was years ago,' said Terry, laying his head on his arms and giving Danny a charming porny smile. 'He used to catch hold of me and, well ... interfere with me.'

'Really,' said Danny, and smiled back, because it sounded such a simple and idyllic thing to have done.

'He used to say, "Is that a ferret in your pocket, Terry, or are you just pleased to see me?"'

Danny tried to analyse his mood, it was distilled randiness laced with anxiety, which made the randiness even stronger. He saw Alex coming down towards them at a stumbling trot, the orange melt from an ice lolly dripping through his hands and blown on to his long pale legs by the breeze. He said very quietly, in a straight-faced parody of Terry, 'I'd like to interfere

223

with you an' all', and then wondered if there was some equally effective spell for making your dick go down.

Alex's bad mood wasn't helped by the stifled giggling of the boys. He nudged his way on to a corner of towel and sat sucking primly at the angled straw of a fruit-juice carton. 'I hadn't realised it was National Snogging Day,' he said, and scowled over his shoulder. 'Every couple I passed were glued together at the larynx.'

'Must be the weather,' said Terry.

Danny was twisting his lolly round to catch the drips and mumble up the slushy fragments that slid off the stick at the lightest bite. He knew Alex was watching him and tensely day-dreaming about the kisses he still thought they were going to share.

'The thing about Ada Ringroad,' said Justin, 'is that Mike can't stand him, but Marge is being stubbornly nice to him. She asks him round almost daily, the old fag-hag. Last time we were there, Mike called him a deviant of the worst kind.'

'How did he take that?' asked Alex.

'Well he was pissed, and we all laughed like lunatics, and he seemed to get the idea.'

Danny had just come down from a shower, and was buttoning his shirt and holding his own gaze in the sitting-room mirror, with a sense of readying himself for a testing première. 'What does he do?' he said. He saw Justin come up behind him and felt him too as he slid a hand around him with a kind of sexiness that was somehow made possible by Alex's presence, as if nothing could come of it.

'I believe he used to be a schoolmaster, darling.' Justin peered into the mirror. 'One can see him being pretty eager with the slipper. He wears a bow-tie, which is a well-known sign of penile inadequacy.'

'I wasn't actually thinking of him as a sexual partner,' said Danny, gently freeing himself.

'He has those schoolmaster shoes, like vulcanised Cornish pasties.'

Robin came into the room and slipped an arm round Justin

in his turn. Justin glanced at his trousers and said, 'That's better', and Danny knew he must have asked him to change. A little power-shift had happened as the price of the new togetherness: his father had been lightly pussy-whipped, or botty-whipped perhaps was the word, and once again the two of them were hugging and groping each other. He wondered for a second, in a spirit of fairness, if some new contract could save his affair with Alex; but saw how unalike the situations were. He didn't need Alex.

Justin said, 'I should warn you he's very keen on the church; he plays the organ, and as you know Mike has a blood feud with the church. Adrian's already very thick with the Bishops. I mean the people called Bishop,' he explained to Alex.

Danny said, 'You seem a bit obsessed with this chappie.'

Justin turned back to the mirror with a pout. 'In village life, darling, one seizes on what interest one can.'

'Yeah, right,' said Danny.

Alex got up and crossed the room to put a hand on Danny's shoulder – it was a friendly gesture that had gone stiff with premeditation: it looked as if he was trying to restrain him.

The four of them set out through the village, sometimes like a gang across the road, then pairing up in different ways when a car came through, or a bouncing unharnessed tractor. Danny noticed the self-consciousness of the others. He thought of himself as a free person threatened by the muddled commitments of this group of older men. When his mobile rang, he answered it with a yell, and dawdled obliquely across the road, for privacy.

It took a moment to work out that it was Heinrich the barman, his boyfriend for a good ten days in the spring, who was clearly some way off his face and was talking without his usual courteous preambles and connections. 'So, I want you to come across,' he said.

'I can't come across, darling. I'm in Dorset.'

After a while Heinrich said, 'Oh my god!', as though he was the last to hear of something outrageous. 'You know I am thinking about you quite intensely.'

'Are you by yourself?'

'Yes, I have taken an ecstasy by mistake, because I have a

225

headache, so as you can imagine I am feeling very great indeed, but I have no one with me. And still I have a headache. Quite soon I will go to work.'

'Are you working at the Drop tonight?'

'Yes, of course.'

'I wish I was there!' said Danny, with a childish groan of frustration. He pictured Heinrich's hairy legs and big friendly backside.

'Maybe we can have sex by the phone,' Heinrich suggested.

'Yeah, I can't, darling,' said Danny, pushing his other hand into his pocket. 'We're just going out to drinks. We're in the street' – he could do it as a dare, but he knew he would laugh too much.

'So who are you with just now?'

Danny looked at them across the road, in a moment's alienated vision of them as another set of people who had nothing in common, Robin with his sportsman's stroll and Alex anxiously slowing his angled stride and Justin, who had small feet, somehow hurrying between them. 'Oh, with my dad, and some friends.' He raised his voice and smiled at them, to confirm their suspicion he was talking about them.

'Of course you will say this is because I am drug-fucked,' said Heinrich, showing a German sense of extenuation none the less, 'but you know what I think about you. You know to me, well, you are the best.'

Danny saw his friend again, with exact sexual recall, in the mirrored brilliance and blackness of London bars and clubs, and felt an aggravated regret for the night they would not be sharing there, the habitual regret of the pleasure-lover, but shaded with a darker discontent by the sense of something needlessly thrown aside, out of fear perhaps, though the reasons were mysterious, he had slipped away from Heinrich in an amiable absence of will, like a dreaming passenger on a slowly departing train. He said, 'I'll ring you as soon as I get back', and ended the call.

'Who was that, darling?' said Alex.

'Yes, who *was* it?' said Justin. 'They've got you quite pink.'

Robin smiled at him encouragingly, confident it was some other lover seizing his chance; and Danny sensed that his father's acceptance of him, which was so much clearer than two months ago, was easier if he was uncommitted.

As they approached the Halls', the church clock struck six, and Justin said, 'Listen to that! The collective whoosh of tonic-water from every middle-class home in the land'; but after only a few seconds of this imaginary susurration they heard instead the charmless preparatory tolling of the bells being raised.

'I'm afraid we're in for some campanology,' Alex said.

'That will make Mike hopping mad,' said Justin.

In the lane beyond the church there was 'Lostwithiel', formerly the rectory, then the frivolously pretty 'Ambages', which Justin said would turn anyone queer who lived in it, and then Mike and Margery's apparently nameless house, which he proposed should be called 'Gordon's'. 'Lostwithiel', which looked semi-derelict, was the home of the senile but beautifully spoken Miss Lawrence, who wandered in the village and forgot where she lived. She had been burgled over and over, and though nothing had been proved, Terry Badgett was still thought to have been involved. Her old untended damson-tree dropped small copious fruit across the path; where it fizzed with wasps, and people messed their shoes with it, and it gave off a sharp stale smell.

They had to wait a minute at the Halls' front door. Danny noticed how the area round the Yale lock was scoured by innumerable rough attempts at getting the key into it. When Margery opened, she said in her melancholy way, 'Sorry, they're watching the cricket.' Justin jumped at her and hugged her, in the style that he called 'bringing the West End to the West Country'; Robin greeted her with the usual bungled chivalry of a second kiss. Danny watched Alex shake her hand, and thought how exasperatingly formal he was.

In the sitting-room Mike Hall and Adrian Ringrose were standing watching the television, as if they knew it should be switched off and were abetting each other in deferring the moment. Margery introduced Alex and Danny over the commentary on a dubious dismissal; then Mike snapped the telly off. 'Crawley and Knight are doing well,' he said.

Alex said to Adrian, 'Are you interested in cricket?' and he replied, in a mild but precise tone,

227

'No, not at all.'

Danny sat down in a high-backed armchair with Alex beside him but hidden from view by the wings of the chair; he didn't want to cuddle up to him or to be catching his eye all the time. Already, in the hall, Alex's hand had rested on his shoulder again, as if for guidance around the obstacles of the evening, and then trailed down secretively to touch his bum. He had wriggled away, but felt the presence of his rebuff, like a bruise in the air behind him. He was saying his words in his head, repeatedly and with exaggerated confidence. He wanted the business done with fast-moving dignity, and to his own credit. It was important not to miscue it, or be hurried into it on a wave of irritation. 'I love you very much, but you know I can't go on seeing you.' It steadied, and became reasonable, and at the same time, like anything repeated, began to sound like nonsense. Robin was saying, 'Yes, Dan is my son. And Alex is, well, originally a great friend of Justin's . . .'

'I see,' said Adrian, with a delayed flicker as he stored this information, though without, presumably, the hint that Danny heard, of the family closing ranks. 'I hadn't thought of you as old enough to have a grown-up son,' he went on, in a drily fruity way.

'You're very kind,' said Robin, tumbling into a low armchair. 'Oddly enough, if you lose your hair before fifty, people tend to think you're younger.'

'It's the hormones,' Justin explained, like the owner, or perhaps the trainer, of a thoroughbred.

Adrian himself had crinkly old-fashioned hair, very dark for a man in his sixties. Danny's lazily accurate sensors failed to detect in him whatever it was that might make them friends – a capacity for abandon, perhaps. He gave him a preoccupied smile and looked round the room, waiting to be amused. If his sensors picked up sex, Danny could talk a functional kind of drivel, but in a situation like this he felt it was weak or dishonest to show an interest you didn't feel. Maybe it was just the tension of tonight, but he wondered for a sober half-minute what the fuck he was doing in this dreary room, with its worn floral carpet and crocheted cushion-covers and the various bits of short-tempered wiring that Mike had rigged up. His father

228

said you had to get drunk here to numb the aesthetic nerve. The few pictures of Highland cattle and Spanish dancers – though, as Justin pointed out, never the two together – showed a kind of hostility to art.

Mike had gone out to get some ice, and came back in a stinging shimmer of eau de cologne, perhaps having sniffed himself in the kitchen. Danny remembered the fragrance from earlier occasions, and pictured him shaking it all over, like vinegar on to chips; last time the drinks themselves had been faintly scented from where Mike had handled the ice.

They were all taking their first two sips as the church bells broke loose in a plunging peal. Margery set down her drink as if it cost a thousand pounds and went to close the windows. 'This *is* a disadvantage of village life,' she said to Adrian.

Mike said, 'They're bloody bastards.'

Adrian gave a deprecating smile and said, 'Oh, it's a fine sound if it's well done.'

'They come from Salisbury,' said Mike, 'or Southampton, deliberately to ring the bells. Now we shall have to *shout* all evening.'

Clearly Margery thought this would be nothing new. 'I suppose it is rather a fine sound,' she said.

Danny could tell he was going to get drunk. He seemed instantly to have swallowed half of his tall Scotch and ginger ale. He thought of Heinrich again, and the striking fact of his having rung this evening, before going off to the all-night scrum of the Drop, where doubtless at some point a wide-eyed Spanish boy or French boy would lure him out to the corridor at the back. There was Heinrich himself, who was taking on new definition as a neglected suitor, and there was the world where Heinrich earned his living, where hundreds of men were forever catching his eye and poking money at him, and Danny felt jealous of both. 'Of course I love you, Alex. But we're not meant to be together. You know as well as I do. We have nothing in common.' He swayed his head to the bells, which seemed for the moment to be improvising on Madonna's 'Bedtime Story' and its recurrent good idea, 'Let's get unconscious, honey'.

229

Adrian said, 'I don't need to tell you that Litton Gambril has the oldest peal of eight bells in the county.'

'Is that right,' said Mike, none too pleased to be lectured on the matter by someone who'd only been in the county five minutes.

Margery smiled graciously. 'Do you peal yourself?' she asked, with a tiny throat-clearing to bridge her doubt about the verb.

Adrian's long fingers smoothed and balanced his bow-tie. 'I used to ring. I rang for Cambridge. But I fear a tendonitis made me something of a liability in the chamber later on.'

'Well I *ran* for Cambridge,' said Mike, in one of his mordant asides. 'No bloody g.'

'I think tonight we may hear a full grandsire major.'

The noise was muffled in the room, but still all-pervasive, and Danny found himself listening to the dense sonic aura of the overtones, which seemed like some acoustic perception you might have in the trance of an E; though the hypnotic thing was the evolving eight-note phrase, which imposed itself on the conversation, and broke up your thoughts.

Adrian, who had rapidly reverted to schoolmaster mode, was explaining some niceties of change-ringing to Justin. 'So the conductor, as he's known, calls out "bob" at the lead ends to produce a new row, from which further changes can then be rung.'

'What, "Bob" . . .?' – Margery tried it distantly, as though recalling someone she had once been fond of. She looked into her drink. 'I suppose there must be *dozens* of changes.'

Adrian simpered for a second or two. 'Well, with eight bells the number of possible changes would be factorial eight.'

'That's eight times seven times six times . . .' Robin said.

There was a pause for thought. Justin said, 'So if they rang the full grandmother's footsteps it would be over four million changes . . .!'

'Fucking hell . . .' muttered Mike, and emptied his glass.

'No, no,' said Adrian, with a bright nervous giggle. 'But it would be well over forty thousand, obviously.'

'Well, they'd better not do well over forty thousand tonight,' Mike said, getting up and standing over Adrian while he gulped down the rest of his drink.

Alex was very quiet, and Danny wondered if he knew what was coming. He probably did, he was very sensitive; and he'd been through this kind of thing before. Danny looked casually at Justin, whom he found alien in many ways, and saw that they were about to share the shabby distinction of having thrown Alex over. He knew from his break-up with George what the pain might be like. And he noticed that having been through it himself he felt somehow authorised, and even empowered, to inflict it on someone else. It was the hard currency of human business. Slightly giddy from his own philosophy, he reached up to take his second cold drink.

Adrian said, 'I do think we're so lucky in having this marvellous castle in the village.' He had the surprised talkativeness of a buttoned-up person abruptly filled with alcohol.

'I hadn't realised just how lucky we were,' murmured Margery.

'There's not much *to* the castle, is there?' said Justin doubtfully.

'My darling Justin has never actually seen the castle,' said Robin, with a funny gloving of his gibe. 'But he's only lived here a year.'

'No, ten months, actually, sweetie, and three days,' Justin said. 'Anyway, I never thought it wise to go down Ruins Lane.'

Adrian, who was disconcerted by jokes, said, 'I found poor Miss Lawrence wandering up there yesterday. She had no idea where she was going.'

'There you are,' said Justin.

'She needs taking care of,' said Mike, with a certain softening of tone. 'What are the so-called fucking social services doing?'

'She's as mad as a house,' said Justin. 'Did I tell you I saw her talking to a beetle?'

Danny smirked, and drew a finger through the wet on his glass. Mike said to him, 'You're very quiet tonight, young feller-me-lad.'

'He's always quiet,' said Margery. 'It's nice.'

Justin said, 'It's the country air that tires him out. He's not used to all this oxygen, are you darling. He normally goes round in a cloud of LSD, don't you darling.'

'I don't think you smoke LSD,' said Adrian.

231

'No, you don't,' said Alex.

'I'm sure Danny doesn't, anyway,' said Margery.

Adrian said, with the casualness of the shockable, 'Do you see anything of all this drugs business up in London?'

Danny felt it would be absurd to lie. 'Oh yeah,' he said warmly. He could be nice to them, he guessed, but he hated the silly compromises that were forced on you when you entered the remote moral atmosphere of closety old bores. As he didn't say anything else, Adrian nodded and coloured and said,

'You do . . . yes . . .' (Yes, thought Danny, in a spasm of frustration and worry, and I can get in free to any club in London, and get off my face for days on end, and have anyone there I want.) 'Yes. I saw a lot of it in South America, of course. There was cocaine everywhere, which I believe cost almost nothing. I must say, I was never tempted to try it.'

'Really . . .?' said Alex, who was leaning forward to catch Danny's eye.

'I didn't know you'd been in South America,' said Mike, irritated by this claim on his curiosity. 'Whereabouts?'

'Oh, very much so. I was with the British Council in Caracas, and then in Lima for four years. This was in the late fifties, after Cambridge.'

'After your ringing years.'

'Yes . . .'

'They used to say they were all flower-arrangers in the British Council,' said Mike.

Adrian looked down for a moment, to give this remark time to clear, and went on, 'I've got some very lovely folk-art that I brought back, some of which you'll see when you come to "Ambages". I have a beautiful Peruvian hanging in my bedroom.'

The words themselves hung in the air, lightly and evenly stressed, against the background clamour of the bells, and it was Margery who started to laugh first, an almost noiseless polite snuffle, and then a cackle came from Justin, Danny heard the chug-chug of Alex's laugh, and then he got it himself, through the glaze of his preoccupation, and started to giggle breathlessly, with an edge of hysterical relief, before Mike gave

232

out his rarely heard whimper. It was never quite clear whether Adrian had seen the joke. The amusement was too general for him to go against it, and he sat smiling bashfully, looking sideways at the floor.

After a while, Margery struggled to make a long face, and said, 'Adrian, I'm so sorry', with the insincere regret that follows a burst of instinct.

Embarrassed, and obliged to show willing, Adrian said, 'Well, Danny, perhaps you should go to South America. People sniff cocaine in Lima like you and I drink sherry.'

Danny nodded with another after-tremor of laughter. 'Yeah, that might be good.' He looked away. 'Actually, I'm going back to the States next month. I think that's more the sort of place for me.'

When he looked up again, Justin was making a 'Get her!' face, and Robin said with a tender frown, 'It's the first I've heard of it.' Alex, of course, he couldn't see – only the convulsion of his legs uncrossing and crossing the other way. 'You're going to your mother's?' Robin mastered the situation.

'Yeah, I think so,' said Danny. 'She says she can always get me a job out there again.'

'And where is that?' said Adrian.

'San Diego . . .'

'No, I don't imagine I'll ever fly again,' said Mike, loudly and slowly, as though that were the really interesting aspect of the matter. Danny saw Justin looking gently in Alex's direction – to the others, of course, this sudden birthing of a plan was neither here nor there.

He said, surprised by his own note of involuntary bitterness, 'Well, there's not much to keep me in this country.' When you had an audience you could say things easily that were almost impossible to bring out one-to-one, even in bed. Though perhaps it was also easy to say too much.

Mike said, 'I suppose we could hang each bell-ringer from his individual rope.'

'I'm quite getting used to it,' said Margery. 'I think we'll all rather miss it when it stops.' Then, seeing Alex had got up and was going towards the door, she said, 'It's across the hall and turn left.' He blinked and went out.

233

The conversation ambled on, given sly prods and perverse turns by Justin, who seemed to feel responsible for the success of the occasion, in a way that he never did at home. Mike was wincing at the wall, too caught up in the smoulder of his outrage to make his usual polemical sallies. Danny had the childish sensation of being ignored and unvalued after his clumsy moment in the spotlight. He couldn't think about how cruel he had just been to Alex, and when he tried to run through his resignation speech again it had a horrible echoless deadness to it, like something said in a recording studio. He looked along the faces of the others, wondering what they were talking about. His father's expression was specially husbandly and benign. Then Danny found Justin was staring privately at him, and he knew he was right when he twitched his head towards the door. 'I must just go too,' Danny said under his breath as he slipped out.

The lavatory door was shut, and he waited for a minute outside, suddenly fidgety for a pee himself. Then he thought, well he's still my boyfriend, and tapped and went in. But Alex wasn't there; and in the white emptiness of the stuffy little room Danny knew the crisis had closed in on him. As he peed he looked sideways into the mirror, and saw how terribly beautiful he was: the image itself was reflected again off some hard vain surface deep in his eye, and he thought, with easy pity, how little Alex would want to lose him. On the narrow shelf above the basin was a thinning hairbrush, and a comb, and a square bottle of cologne: he pulled out the stopper to confirm it was the one they had been breathing all evening, and turned down his mouth in the mirror when he saw it was called 'Bien-Etre'.

Alex was sitting on the back-door step, looking down the sloping, untidy garden. Danny came through the kitchen and sat beside him, but without touching him. Alex said, 'Oh Dan' – it was very rare for him to call him by name.

'I'm sorry,' Danny said. He thought perhaps by some miracle Alex had understood everything.

'I really do think you might have told me about this US thing.'

'Yeah . . .'

'You terrify me at times.' Alex reached for his hand, and he let him hold it, but without any return of pressure. 'I mean, what happens to us? I can come and see you, of course. I look forward to that. But it's hardly very convenient.'

'Well . . .'

'Or perhaps you're not really going,' Alex went on, in a tetchily forgiving tone. 'But if you are it would have been nice not to have heard it announced in the middle of a drinks-party.'

They had never had a row, merely separate hurts and irritations which they seduced each other out of. Danny saw that he hadn't done this right, and it made him sulkily aggressive. 'I may not go,' he said, and withdrew his hand.

'I mean, I'm your boyfriend. That lanky bloke whose arms are round you when you wake up, and who then goes off to make your breakfast: that's me.'

'Yeah, I wondered who it was,' said Danny. 'Look, it doesn't really matter whether I'm here or in San Diego, I can't go on seeing you, Alex.'

Alex had already drawn the breath that should have carried his next remark, but he halted and let it out in a tragic sigh.

Danny stood up and strolled back across the kitchen and drew a glass of water. The whisky was giving him a slight headache; rather like poor Heinrich . . . 'I'm very sorry,' he said.

When he glanced round, Alex was sitting in the same place, but tipped sideways against the door-frame, as though he had been thrown there by a blast. The pose was somehow histrionic and got on Danny's nerves. He saw him roll his head, once, quickly, to see where he was, and Danny had the feeling that he himself had become the embodiment of something dreaded, that could hardly be looked at.

Back in the sitting-room he was told to help himself to another drink. He knew he had been sobered by the adrenalin of the past five minutes, and unexpectedly humiliated by Alex snapping at him to leave him alone. The others all seemed pathetically drunk and old. Adrian was asking about ladies-that-did, and various village names were rummaged for, each followed by a horrifying cautionary anecdote.

235

'We've never had any fucking charwoman,' said Mike; which nobody pretended to be surprised by.

Justin said, 'You can always have nude housework done, of course.'

Adrian pursed his lips, but would clearly have liked to know more.

Mike said, in a marvelling monotone, 'You lot talk so much fucking tripe.'

'I'm not against nude housework,' said Margery, 'but I think I'd have to go out while it was being done.'

'Where's the silent Scotsman?' said Mike. 'Polishing his nails?'

Danny studied their five faces again; they all had a foolish look of temporary confidence, which he forgot he must often have had himself, in extremer forms too. Even Mike, who got furious on drink, seemed to have entered into a richer and more involving relation with himself. 'Alex is just getting a bit of air,' Danny said; at which Mike nodded and drummed his fingers on his knee. Both he and Margery had renounced ciga-rettes, and the peculiar ashtrays mounted on stirruped thongs had gone from the arms of the sofa; but still the magnolia paintwork was dimly varnished with smoke and gave the room an atmosphere of terminated pleasures. Perhaps the others didn't care, or were too sozzled to notice the room filling with shadows; but Danny never lost his sense of the speed of time. When he thought of Alex's epic hesitations – the years without sex, the unaccountable solitariness – it brought him close to a panic of impatience.

He saw that Justin was peering at him again, with a hint of a smile – he couldn't work out the ironies in it, it seemed encouraging and disappointed at the same time, as well as secretively sexual, as if they already had an agreement to meet up later. He knew he had just done something serious, and needed assurance that he had been right. Then the bells came tumbling down the scale and stopped.

The overtones swam there for a moment, and after that the ear was haunted by the bells and heard them fadingly con-tinuing. The silence was astonishing, being ordinary existence thrown into relief by the hour or more of incessant sound, unwavering in rhythm and volume. And then it wasn't silence. Mike got up and pushed the windows open, and there was a bird twittering, a car whining as it reversed, the dry runs of an old-fashioned mower, like a child's rattle. Alex was somewhere outside, in the wilderness of the garden. Danny had been sent in, but he guessed he would have to go back out to him.

Mike sped across the room with the brawler's roll he had when drunk. 'Right!' he said, switching on the old blue-leather Philips gramophone, which he had confidently attached to an even older-looking valve amplifier and big, BDX-size, speakers.

'I think they've cut it rather short,' said Adrian, unwisely.

'Don't get me wrong, Ringrose,' said Mike over his shoulder. 'But your bell-ringing pals are fucking cunts.'

'Oh dear,' said Margery.

'I'm afraid so,' said Mike, exhilarated to have reached this stage of the evening already.

'I'm just going to check on Alex,' Danny said.

He was in the kitchen when he heard the music start, and then it came out very clearly through the windows when he stepped into the garden. It was Mike's retaliation against the bells, a crackly old record of Gregorian chant, turned up offensively loud, though the music itself remained more than unflappable: the spare and echoing rise and fall of men's voices, the ritual Latin. Danny stood for a moment by the two deck-chairs on the rough circle of lawn, and thought of calling to Alex, like someone getting a child in for a meal or bed. But he saw that the tone would be wrong: he was annoyed with Alex for still being here, and then a second later he was a little frightened at his responsibility. He stooped past the woody buddleia and down a path under apple-trees. There was a shed, and a fruit-cage covered in convolvulus, and one weedy but cultivated patch of kitchen-garden. After that the lot tapered, and there was only wild grass thigh-deep, and a big old tree at the bottom where the fences met. He saw Alex perched on the fence, with his back against the tree-trunk, looking unapproachably lonely. You could still see the curving track he had made through the grass, and Danny, out of some barely conscious symbolic scruple, made a separate wading path towards him. The grass was dry, and bleaching from the mid-

August heat, and where Danny's hands trailed into it they found it dusty and sometimes sticky with secretions like bubbled spit; underfoot there was a crackling, and he realised he was treading on tiny grey snails – and there were dozens of them clinging like seed-cases on the thicker stalks. By the time he came to stand at Alex's shoulder, his baggy black jeans were streaked and powdered from the field. He thought Alex might be crying, and that he'd been sent away so as not to witness that, but when he peered at him sidelong there was no sign of it. 'I've come to see how you are,' he said.

After a while Alex said, 'It's like fucking murder in the cathedral.'

'The music, you mean,' said Danny, with a snigger.

Then Alex went on, very tensely, as if afraid of anything Danny might say, 'You remember we walked up there not long ago.' He swept his hand up quickly, to hide its shaking.

Danny detected some sentimental reproach. 'Yes, of course, it was a beautiful evening,' he said; though he did find it striking that Alex should mention it, because that evening up on the hill had been the silent turning-point for him, with Alex talking about his failure with Justin, and a sense of failure coming off him, like someone you would be unwise to set up business with. Danny said, pretty confident that it wouldn't be put to the test, 'You know we'll always be friends.'

Alex half-turned but still didn't look directly at him. 'Is it George?' he said.

Danny chuckled sourly. 'George wouldn't let me anywhere near him.'

'It's not Terry, for god's sake?'

'Alex, it's not anyone!' He wanted to touch him consolingly, but also to push him off the fence, where he was nodding forward and hugging himself delicately, as if every liaison of Danny's were a broken rib or an unhealed cut.

'I'm sorry,' Alex said, 'I can't take in anything you're saying. You seem to be talking gibberish. We're two people wildly in love with each other, and you're saying you can't see me any more.'

'Well, I've changed, darling, people change. I'm sorry.' He glanced back over the full two months of their affair, and remembered getting dressed in front of Alex on the first evening he came round, and thinking he'd never seen anyone so well-mannered and so sex-starved. It had been at a strange moment in his own little number with cynical black Bob, and he could see now that there had been something defiant and capricious, perhaps, about taking up with Alex.

'I haven't changed at all,' said Alex. 'Apart from coming to love you more and more.'

'You know, we don't have anything in common,' said Danny, and had to acknowledge that it didn't sound that great.

Alex shook his head. 'I thought the affair itself was what we had in common,' he said.

'Yeah, well . . .' Danny stuck to his idea that there was nothing to talk about. He frowned and blinked away the muddled imagery of their nights together, the happiness and sweat; and he knew there was a dappled prospect of things he could have learned from Alex, if he'd given him time and attention. But for the moment, and so perhaps for ever, he needed the story to be bare and shadowless. They'd gone out and got off their faces, and Alex had had his mind opened to dance-music. And now they were ending up in music, something altogether more monastic – even if distantly interspersed with Mike shouting 'Cunt!' out of the window. Danny decided quickly and analytically that Alex, in spite of his wounded bafflement, accepted what had happened. There was no immediate suggestion of working out problems, or a trial separation. He couldn't put it into words, but he saw something fatalistic in Alex rush forward to acknowledge the disaster. 'Come on,' said Danny.

As they toiled out of the long grass, he gestured courteously to Alex to go ahead of him, and followed a few paces behind him up the rather notional path. The chanting grew grander as they approached the house, and he knew there would be some solemn moments ahead; but he quite admired the way he'd brought it off. It was the first big break-up he had been responsible for, and with an older man there was of course that further question of respect. He stopped to brush and slap at the mess on his trousers.

239

16

'Fabulous finials!'

'I know!' Alex stepped backwards through the long damp grass to look up at the top stages of the tower: the hooded niches, the little pinnacles like stalagmites that grew from the ledges of the buttresses, the taller pinnacles, three to each corner and one to each side, that crowned the whole thing. The effect was extravagant, and like many strictly superfluous things it was what he most remembered. Not that he'd ever looked at it properly in the Danny period. Danny wasn't big on finials, and they had hurried on by.

He turned and watched Nick wandering among the grave-stones, stooping and scratching off moss with that pleasant thoroughness he had, the suggestion that even if something wasn't worth doing, it was worth doing properly. Nick was the first person Alex had slept with who was older than himself, and though at their age it hardly made a difference, there was something, well, restful about it, and solidly grounded, after the jolting berths and squealing point-changes of nights with Danny. The pattern had been broken, since Nick wasn't a taker, and shared Alex's own determination to give; his amused absorption in every aspect of Alex's life, as if Alex's story were the one thing to master and see the beauty of, had felt almost invasive after Danny's fidgety indifference.

'I know there's an interesting wall-painting,' he said, coming back and poking his arm through Alex's to steer him into the porch. The gesture, like many of Nick's, seemed to compress time: they were romantic undergraduates from some Oxonian golden age but also a nice old county couple who hadn't lost their appetite for life. The leap of the latch echoed into the interior, and reminded Alex, who felt warily suggestible today, of the characteristic clatter of the latches in Robin's cottage;

though beyond that there were fainter echoes, of church-visiting on childhood holidays, and of going in to play in the pulpit while his mother did the flowers. It was a sunny October day, and the church, which was unwarmed, was full of light. Nick strode about appreciatively, while Alex, who always believed in reading the instructions, studied the information bat.

The fragment of wall-painting was in the north aisle, and showed Tobias with the Angel Raphael. It was executed in various shades of brown, which merged with the discolouration of the plaster and the rough blots where the plaster had been patched, one of which rendered the angel enigmatically jawless. But the fat little boy could be seen, in his brown jerkin, and holding up his brown fish. Alex said, 'It says here it was painted with a brush made from a squirrel's tail.'

'It's hard not to suspect an *element* of conjecture in that,' Nick said.

The angel guiding Tobias had flowing curly hair and a belted tunic; he was about eight feet tall, and strode forwards on a thickly outlined right leg with a very elegant foot – heel raised and long toes taking their purchase on the ground, which was implied by a dandelion-like tuft. It made Alex think of his last day with Danny, on the beach, and the memory was surprising even though this little trip to Dorset was all memory – ever since London he'd been waking himself up from the troubled trance of the past. At the end of that afternoon, he had walked with Danny along the sea's edge, the sand was firm but sodden with water, and at each step a shiver of silvery light seemed to flash from under their feet. Alex pointed out the effect, in the lyrical but cringing tone that was forced on him by Danny's coldness, and Danny had merely cleared his throat, with an unamusable downward curl of his big mouth.

Nick hugged him from behind, and they went out of the church. He was being vigorously kind this weekend, and any tension he felt about meeting Justin and Robin, and pottering round the landscape of Alex's previous affair, was disguised as excitement and a hunger for ancient monuments. 'And now the castle!' he said, as they came into the road.

'There's not much *to* the castle,' murmured Alex, who was

241

covering his tension less well, and was ready for a drink. 'The Crooked Billet is a marvellously unspoilt old pub.'

'Art before alcohol, dear,' said Nick. He was a person who expressed large clear feelings and wants of all kinds and then showed a special charm in tuning and surrendering them to other people's moods – or at least to Alex's. 'Of course, if you'd really rather not . . . I know this must be strange for you. You must tell me everything you're thinking' – a phrase which to Alex always had the effect of a sudden inhibition.

'No, let's go to the castle.'

They got back into Nick's car and drove out of the village and along Ruins Lane, which had the stony dryness of summer still, though the chestnuts were already dropping their leaves and there were scarlet shocks of haws in the hedges. One other car was in the car-park – it had a caged rear section for a dog, and the forlorn admonishment about puppies being for life in the window. Nick led the way over a stile, and into the lumpy field where the ruins stood, or crouched. There was one picturesque bit, a towering fragment of the hall, with the airy grid of a bay window high above, and the barred-off opening of a narrow spiral staircase. Next to it was the kitchen, where Alex stooped under the lintel of the fireplace and peered up the chimney to the pale blue chink of sky.

Alex knew he would have loved it here as a boy, with his taste for lonely places; it was somehow akin to a hollow, roughly habitable oak in the woods at school, and to his dusty, torch-lit 'house' in the cupboard under the stairs, with the ceiling that stepped down like a trap on the already long-legged child. 'I've been playing hide and seek,' he used to say; and his mother said, 'It can't be hide and seek if no one's coming to look for you, darling. It's just hide.'

He walked off to the edge of the site, where some newly sawn pine-logs were stacked and giving off their fresh vomit smell as the sun warmed them. He watched Nick bustling about the stony knolls, reading the old Ministry of Works signs that said 'Storerooms' or 'Chapel'. There was an element of conjecture there too, no doubt. He thought how Danny had lived his youth, and followed his appetites, and slept with such a variety of men that you couldn't see any common thread beyond the blind desire to know the world through sex. The thought made Alex sag with envy and loss, even though he had Nick, and though sex, of course, was not the only way to know the world. He wondered what Danny had meant when he said he loved him, or adored him, and whether meaning something had even entered into it. He clearly had no idea of the psychic shock, to someone like himself, of falling in love. Danny would be a great lover, that would be his career, though he knew next to nothing about love, just as some great musicians knew nothing about music, beyond their gift for making it.

In general he was very happy now. There was something sweet and justified about reliving the solitary excitements of his past in the company of someone as handsome and generous as Nick. Mornings of ruins and evenings of *L'elisir d'amore*. It must just be the fact of being here again in Litton Gambril that rekindled his sense of surreal and arbitrary injustice. Today, like every day of the past fourteen months, was a part of the life he had thought he would be sharing with Danny, and he was spending it without him, and to that extent he was spending it alone.

The Sicily tickets had come the morning after his return to London. They were to have been a beautiful surprise for Danny, and lay on Alex's kitchen table, beside the brochure of the Excelsior Palace Hotel, Taormina, with the unforgivable ignorance of mail sent to the newly dead. Coming back into the room, preparing to go to work but still expecting to hear himself phone in sick, he saw the tickets again and started crying quite violently, pushing them around the table with a stiff, unaccepting arm. Later, he put everything back in the envelope, and went into the office.

In the evening he rang Hugh and cried some more through the inadequate medium of the telephone. Hugh said, 'I'm so sorry, darling', with real tenderness, as well as an irrepressible note of vindication.

'These have been the worst three days of my life,' said Alex,

243

sincerely, and believing, in his retentive way, that you could compare one pain with another that was only remembered.

'Tell me again how old he was,' said Hugh.

'He was twenty-three. I mean, he still is.'

'Yes,' said Hugh. 'They don't want the same things as us, you know.'

Alex was so struck by the wisdom of this remark that he instinctively rejected it. 'We were madly in love,' he said.

He went round to see Hugh the following evening and they got drunk in his flat before going out for some pasta. As they left the building they had to make their way through a small crowd of theosophists whose grateful expressions he attributed broadly to the effects of a seance. The restaurant was as always half-empty and too brightly lit, as though to draw attention to its meagre popularity. The hand-coloured photographs of Etna and Palermo Cathedral conspired in the gruesome excess of irony which bristles around any crisis.

Alex had favoured and then suppressed the idea several times, but at the end of the meal, loose on Corvo and a couple of grappas, and full of gratitude to his oldest friend, he said, 'How would you like to come to Sicily with me next month for a couple of weeks, staying only at the best hotels?' As he said it he found he already regretted it – Hugh would get on his nerves and be a perpetual disappointment as he sat in Danny's place, Alex would be ashamed of him in his tweed jacket and compromised by him in the Casanova pub and the Perroquet disco . . .

Hugh was looking down in the sudden flush of delicate feeling, and Alex was moved to see how touched he was, and instantly forgot his regrets – of course it would be better to visit the temples at Agrigento in the appreciative company of someone who sweated classical learning than in a state of sexual distraction with Danny, and anxiety at every moment that he might be getting bored. Not, of course, that he could go with Danny: that was why they were having this conversation, it was the still new fact, and it leapt up like a hot liquid burp in his throat, and brought tears to his eyes.

'It would be marvellous,' Hugh was saying. 'But I really don't think I can.'

'Oh, come on,' said Alex. 'You can't stay in boring old Bloomsbury for ever. It would be fun. Think what a great team we were in Greece, all those years ago.' Though this wasn't quite how he'd thought of it at the time.

'The thing is, I'm going to be away then myself, actually. This didn't seem the right moment to tell you, but I'm going off, with a friend, to, er, to Nigeria for three weeks.' Hugh looked shaken to be making this announcement, but couldn't help smiling. 'I'm already having the jabs.'

'Good god!' said Alex, in a tone of cheery alarm. 'And who is this person?'

'Oh . . . he's called Frederick.'

'I see. I assume he's Nigerian, is he?'

'What . . .? Yes, he is.'

'And how old . . .?'

'Um . . . he'll be thirty-six next month – well, whilst we're in Lagos, as it happens.'

'I won't ask you how you met him': at which Hugh looked a little crestfallen, for all his air of thrilled reluctance as the facts came out. He piled and smoothed the sugar in the bowl into a tiny Etna of his own.

'I'll tell you anyway. I picked him up in Russell Square.'

Alex sat back and nodded at the revealed logic of this *fait accompli*. He knew what question Hugh wanted him to ask next, and he brought it out with airy courtesy: 'What's his dick like, by the way?' Hugh's glow of tactfully suppressed pleasure deepened to a triumphant blush.

Alex wasn't sure, over the following weeks, what he felt about Hugh's unprecedented affair. He was moving through the obscurely delineated phases of grief, and his reactions to matters outside himself were unpredictably null or intense. In the first few days the slightest pressure made him weep, and he nearly got in a fight with someone he swore at from the car. After that came a phase when he longed to weep, but couldn't, which seemed perversely like yet another failure. He went round, just for a drink, to meet the boyfriend. Frederick was slender and a little shy, and had a deeply melancholy look even when he was laughing. He enquired, with disconcerting politeness, about the well-being of all Alex's relatives. As the

245

drinks went down, he grew more and more physical with Hugh, and Alex too came in for brief knee-strokings and lingering smiles. When Hugh went out of the room, Frederick said, 'Hugh told me your boyfriend left you.' Alex merely nodded, and Frederick took his hand and said, 'Well, I'm more than sure you going to find another one', with a long glance that was not only flirtatious but had an embarrassing prophetic certainty. Soon afterwards Alex kissed and hugged them both, and left. He was naturally delighted by his friend's happiness. Those were the words he used to himself as he tried to eliminate the small residual feeling of envy and betrayal.

He had very little contact with Danny, beyond a few impossible phone-calls, one of them an absurdist vignette of blocked communication because of the bad reception on Danny's mobile. 'I said: This has been the worst week of my life,' Alex barked, three or four times, till he sounded more furious than miserable. Danny left a message on his machine to tell him when he was going to California, and Alex groaned at the way that silly idea had been allowed to harden into a life-changing fact. He was sure he would never see him again; and then bleakly soothed by the knowledge that he couldn't bear to see him anyway. He wrote him a long letter, which he worked on and recast in his head and on paper for days and days, so as to make it reasonable; he dropped it into a pillar-box in Whitehall after work and was immediately terrified that he might reply.

Justin rang several times and asked a lot of questions; he was tender but fairly probing – it seemed almost as though he had found a way to observe the effects of his own break-up with Alex, but from a later, guiltless angle; or perhaps there was an element of atonement. Alex himself, sighing and switching about in his bed, was typically alert to the pattern. This second failure was a shocking reinforcement of the first. And yet he had to admit that there was something ambiguously easier about it too: he already knew the lesson, he knew the bereft amazement of finding that you had unwittingly had your last fuck, your last passionate kiss, your last taxi-ride hand-in-hand in the gloom; and he knew too that on both occasions there had been signals, like the seen but noiseless drum-strokes of a tympanist checking his tuning.

One Sunday in late October he made the long journey right across London to have lunch in Hampstead with a kind colleague from work; and coming out a bit drunk into the street decided he would go up on to the Heath and see if he bumped into anyone. It was a bright blue day, and though by now the warm sunshine was going from the streets, it was still dazzling when he emerged on to the westward slopes of the hill. He wasn't exactly sure where to go, but he saw a sympathetic-looking man with short grey hair and a darker goatee turn purposefully down a path ahead of him, and followed on at a casual pace, but with a quickening sense that something important was being allowed to happen. He looked about keenly. The chestnuts were already bare, but the oaks were thick with gold and withered green, and a half-denuded poplar stood in a reflecting pool of its own fallen leaves. It was that time of day he loved, when the lowering sun struck right in among the trees and made every branch burn.

He came down into a more shadowy area of woodland, with patchy tall undergrowth and vague paths crackly with beech-mast. There were a number of men mooching about in the bushes. He couldn't see the man he had followed, though he kept a certain presence in Alex's mind, as a guide who had silently appeared and disappeared. Now he had to fend for himself, and he was useless at cruising, even in somewhere as unchoosy and anonymous as this. He walked on, had a look at his watch, wondered if he should just go home after all, and then within a few seconds he had stumbled into a large and still relatively leafy bush with a dark, thickset man, and was kneeling in the sex-litter and soft loam with the stranger's stiffening cock in his mouth. The man chewed gum and looked around, apparently indifferent to the exquisite thing that was being done for him. Occasionally he said 'Yeah', like someone on the phone. Then he pulled his hips back quickly, and nudged out a little load over Alex's cheek and nose.

As sex it was about the least gratifying Alex could remember; the man was hardly his type, and had clearly had no interest in reciprocating the favour; also his trousers would now have

247

to go to the dry-cleaner's. Yet the episode struck him as significant. He strode back up through the woods, casually observed by the same waiting men, and down again through the steep narrow streets to the station, with the fascinated feeling that he'd acted out of character. The street-lamps were starting to glow through the odd neutral light after sunset, and the faces of people he passed took on a kind of romance – he couldn't say why. On reflection he thought you couldn't really act out of character, and he went in under the arch and down in the lift with the sense that he had just paid a visit to a remote suburb of himself. Through the following days he sometimes remembered the taste of the stranger, the roughness of seam rivets and stitching in his thick denims, the heavy atmosphere of permission in the wood. In bed, the event took on a beauty it had lacked at the time, and Alex thought he'd quite like to see the man again.

In December there were parties in the early evening, and he would often find himself, about nine o'clock, speedy and unselfcritical with drink, stepping back out into the clinging chill of the night, and ready for the new kinds of fun he had learnt from Danny. He saw he had started to recoup the Danny disaster in an obscurely private way. He had an appetite for drugs again, but no clear idea how to get some. He knew it would be a bad idea to ask his secretary. He'd heard that the murmuring boys you walked past in clubs would happily sell you paracetamol or household cleansers, and he knew they could tell that he was a patsy. He hadn't kept in touch with Danny's friends, but he still had Jamaican Bob's number, and one night when he got home he gave him a ring.

'. . . yeah I know, that's his problem,' Bob was saying as he answered. 'Hello.'

'Oh, is that Bob?'

'Yep.'

'It's Alex here – Alex Nichols.' There was the sound of several people discussing something, a television on. Alex heard the tension in his own voice, and when he looked up at the mirror he saw his fawningly needy expression.

'You'll have to help me,' said Bob.

'Danny's friend . . .?' And that turned out to be a hard phrase.

'Oh yeah, I remember. You're the one who falls in love.'

'That's me.' Alex chuckled obligingly. He had a feeling you mustn't mention drugs by name. 'Bob, you know your auntie . . .?'

'I'm sorry my friend, I can't help you,' said Bob. 'Bad timing, yeah?'

'Oh . . .' Alex wasn't sure if that just meant he should ring back later, or if it was code for some major fuck-up in the international traffic.

'I just got a card from Dan, as a matter of fact. You heard from him lately?'

'Not for a bit,' said Alex.

The next day after work he thought he might try Dave at the porno shop again; he was always reliving the sublime hour, or half-hour, he had spent in a shirtless embrace with him and Lars back in June, and he couldn't believe that that wasn't a very special memory for Dave as well. When he got there he studied the menu of the next-door Chinese restaurant for a minute, then darted aside through the horrible bead curtain. It had never occurred to him that the patterns of employment among porn-peddlers might be somewhat erratic, and that Dave might not be there. But that was the case. A cheerful Irishman in late middle age was warming himself at a fuming Calor-gas stove beside the counter. 'Yes my friend,' he said.

'Oh . . . er . . .' Alex turned away and looked quickly up and down at one or two cellophane-wrapped magazine covers, like someone with bifocals at an art gallery. Three men in leather harnesses and haircuts of circa 1970 were grouped around the tethered body of a fourth. A glowing young blond smiled back as he sprawled over a pool's edge, buttocks spread – he was a bit like Justin, except of course that Justin couldn't swim. Alex realised he couldn't face enquiring after Dave, he felt disadvantaged enough being here at all, amid the alien porn. It would surely be culpably obvious why he needed Dave. He bought an optimistic pack of rubbers and hurried out.

He had just turned along Old Compton Street when he heard his name shouted. This only ever happened when some popular

249

person called Alex was by chance within a few yards of him, but he looked across the slow-moving traffic, and there, hand up like a referee, and choosing his moment to dart between the taxis, was Lars himself. He gave Alex a kiss and asked him what he was doing. Alex said 'Nothing', with a kind of smiling passivity – it was distinctly magical that he had appeared at this moment, sparkly-eyed and breathing a pale cloud into the night. His blue puffer-jacket showed a Norwegian respect for winter, but it was open to display his muscular chest and stomach in a tight white T-shirt. Alex loved having been claimed by him on the busy street.

They went into a bar that he and Justin had used in the early days of their affair, though it had been fiercely refitted since then as a high-tech cruising tank. Fast dance-music was playing, it wasn't great for conversation, but Alex felt the tingle of arrival again. He grinned at Lars, and started to wonder if there was any reason they shouldn't have sex; then saw that he was running ahead of himself. When he was cheerful, as he had been once or twice in recent weeks, there was something manic and fixated in the emotion.

'So,' said Lars, clinking his beer-bottle against Alex's, 'it's good to see you.'

'You too.'

'Been busy?'

Alex blinked. It was a common formula that he thought must have some criminal meaning. He was never either busy or not busy. 'Oh, you know,' he said. All he wanted Lars to be clear about was that he'd spent the past twelve weeks in heart-break. That was his story, and he'd had frustrating evenings with people who'd failed to grasp it. Sometimes he was childish enough to act miserable, to get attention. Sometimes he said, 'I'm just so miserable', and people thought he'd said, 'I am, as always, fine', or if they did understand they began to talk spaciously about some minor success they'd had.

'Well of course I heard about you and Danny,' Lars said, not flippantly, but with a suggestion that it was all a long time ago. 'I guess Danny's just not ready to settle down. If he ever will be.' Of course that was the trite official line. Alex was pretty sure Lars had had a fling with Danny, after all everyone had;

but he wasn't yet ready himself for that fondly sceptical tone. In fact now that they were talking about it he couldn't quite think what to say. Lars said, 'Sure, he's a fun guy, but he's not exactly Mr Reliable. Anyway I hope you're not wishing now that you'd never met him.'

'If I hadn't, I wouldn't be with you tonight,' said Alex, in the bar's blue compensatory gleam.

Lars had something amusingly on his mind. 'Do you know, I think that is the only family I have met where the father is even hotter than the son.'

'Oh . . .' said Alex. 'I know some people do, um . . .' It was beyond him at times to grasp what they'd done to him. First the father smashed him up and then the son. They were terrifying to the outsider, like the Doones of Exmoor or something. 'What is it they've got? The Woodfield . . .' – Alex pouted and shook his head.

'The Woodfield wotsit,' Lars said.

'That's right.'

'Oh boy. Sometime, I will tell you a little story. But not now.' And he smiled like Danny used to, like all these boys on the scene did as a glimpse came back to them from their huge cross-indexed files of sexual anecdote; then he straightened up. 'So, have you been out?' he said.

'No,' said Alex; and with a rather sly pathos: 'I haven't had anyone to go out with.'

Lars didn't rise to this immediately. 'That was Château, am I right, where I saw you and Danny?'

'Absolutely!' said Alex. He thought if he took his time Lars might suggest they went there again. A week ago he had found himself driving past it, the shutters down and padlocked, the neon logo grey and indecipherable in the dank late morning. It was a narrow façade, like a little old warehouse, with a mouth and two blacked-out eyes; the ordinary commuter could never have guessed what dreams unfurled behind it.

'Well it's not so good at the moment.'

'Oh?'

'As you may know, they got raided. Last time half the queens are standing there just with a beer or whatever. Not so great for techno dancing.'

'I should think not,' said Alex, who felt he had been personally insulted; and then went on craftily, 'Anyway, you can get the stuff somewhere else, obviously.'

Lars glanced round and then shrugged his jacket back to show more of himself. Maybe it was just Alex's habit of idealising anyone he found attractive, maybe Lars wasn't Mr Super-Reliable himself, but for the moment the boy seemed to have it all. He said, 'Sure, we don't have to go there. And don't worry, darling, I can get you anything you want.'

Nick went back to the car for the bottle he'd insisted on bringing, and Alex waited by the gate, looking down at the cottage through the yellowing trees. Now that they were here the reasons for the visit escaped him. He didn't like Robin, and he knew he was going to fuss over Nick and Justin to make sure that they saw the best in each other. It irked him that Justin had stayed with Robin after the promising disaffection of last year. At Christmas they had sent out a specially printed card, with a picture of the cottage on the front, under snow; it took Alex a minute to work out that they had signed each other's names. And here the cottage still was, with them inside it, under that smothering lid of thatch. From above you saw thin smoke fading above the chimney, and vivid pink roses. Alex thought of arriving here and seeing Danny's pink tank-top hanging from a deck-chair, like a mark of casual possession. He thought of Danny in uniform at the Royal Academy, and Danny's account of his admirers pressing their numbers on him, like dollar-bills in a stripper's G-string. He thought of Robin, barging in to find them naked and dozy after sex, saying, 'Christ, Dan, you can't be serious.'

It was Robin who let them in, wearing a short apron over his jeans, and a patch over his left eye. Alex murmured concern about the patch, though he was privately very pleased by it, and felt it balanced out his own social disadvantage as a double Woodfield casualty. Robin said it looked worse than it was, and excused himself to get on with the lunch. Justin was in the sitting-room reading the paper, and plucked off a pair of frameless spectacles as they came in. 'I saw that,' said Alex, giving him a big moaning hug, and grinning at the shock of how much he loved him.

'Don't, darling, it's like Moorfields in here,' said Justin. He looked affectionately at Nick and said, 'Hello, darling', as if they were old friends agreeing to forget a tiff. For once Alex saw that a formal introduction was unnecessary. He stepped back with a feeling he shouldn't intrude on a tender episode, one that was novel to him, and unexpectedly rich – the meeting of two of his lovers, with its momentary sequence of hidden appraisal and denial.

The room was subtly altered, and more cluttered. Other little pictures of a very different taste – Regency silhouettes and framed caricatures – filled in the gaps between the family portraits and Robin's creepy watercolours of the cottage. Several highly varnished pieces of furniture – a magazine-rack, a china-cabinet, a nest of scallop-edged side-tables – had been thrust into an unlikely marriage with the resident arts and crafts. Alex realised that these were things saved from Justin's father's house. He strolled towards the book-shelves, saw something else, and after a moment's consideration let out a shriek. On the deep window-sill, turned sideways to catch the best of the sun but glaring back into the room in a consummate sulk, was the polished bronze head of Justin, aged twelve, that Alex had always found so amusing. 'I see you've salvaged "The Spirit of Puberty", darling,' he said.

Justin came across, his features perhaps unconsciously jelled into an adult version of the same expression. Alex watched him decide he could take the joke at last. 'You mean the Litton Gambril Ganymede. Yes, darling. Though the insurance, as you may imagine, is a frightful drain.' Nick stood around behind them, in a leisurely uncertainty about the pitch of irony.

They went into the kitchen for drinks, and Nick drew out Robin – who kept twitching his head round to find things – by asking him about the castle and other local landmarks. Apparently Robin had been building some more flats in that hideous house they'd all been dragged off to see on Alex's first visit, but the nice old boy who owned the place had died, and the plans had all come to nothing. Robin spoke about all his wasted work as though that were the real tragedy of the thing.

253

Justin was clearly bored to the limits of endurance by the subject, and tugged Alex gently through the back door into the garden.

'I'm sorry about Captain Blood, darling,' he said, when they were more or less out of earshot.

'I hope it's nothing serious,' said Alex.

'No, I don't think so. He burst a blood vessel, and it's all gone rather horrid.'

'Does that mean he's lost his sight?'

'Oh he can *see*,' said Justin. 'But it looks so frightful for everyone else. I had to get him to cover it up.'

Alex wasn't sure who was being protected by this. 'How did it happen?'

'In bed, darling. Apparently it's caused by sneezing, or vomiting, or, um ... Of course now I don't dare suggest sex, in case it happens to the other one. He'd have to wear a blindfold!'

Alex took a swig from his bloody Mary. They were standing at the low wall between the lawn and the long grass, where he had found Justin sunbathing on that day last summer, which was also the day he had first set eyes on Danny. He felt very confident with Nick, but still he wanted Justin's approval, or at least some palpably jealous withholding of it. 'It's good to be back here,' he offered blandly, staring out towards the stream and the rise of the hill beyond, and feeling again the mood of sexual jostling and sarcasm that went so oddly with the pastoral unconsciousness of the place.

'You should see it in winter,' said Justin. 'There's nothing but those sort of dead brown plants.'

'Docks, you mean.'

'Mm.' Justin looked into his glass and shook the vivid last half-inch. 'Well, you've found yourself a real man this time, darling.'

'I think so,' said Alex, though Justin's implicit self-disparagement took the zest out of the thing.

'You didn't tell me much about him.'

Alex said, 'It seemed rather bad manners.'

Justin said, 'You say you met him in a club', with a wary,

judicial tone that almost masked his envy of the world of meetings.

'Yes.'

'So you just go to clubs now, do you?'

Alex smiled; and of course it was sweet to be teased on the subject. 'I went out with that boy Lars, Danny's friend, you remember.'

'Oh yes. I think General Dayan's rather keen on him.'

'That's because he's a retread of you, dear. In a way. He's what you'd be like if you were twelve years younger, came from Oslo, and lived in a gym.'

Justin seemed to find that satisfactory. 'Well, I'm impressed that you threw him over for someone twice his age.'

'Nick's only forty-one,' Alex said. And of course it hadn't been quite like that, he hadn't been sure if something was happening with Lars or not, and it was only when Lars said that if Alex didn't move in on Nick, he would, that Alex began to understand what was possible – or, as it seemed through the empathetic lens of the drug, inevitable. 'He was terribly friendly,' Alex went on. 'You know, it could have been the friendliness of a lunatic or a bore, but in fact he's only a little bit of either.' He saw he was keen not to wound Justin by praising Nick's real merits.

Justin said, 'Well, you're used to lunatics, darling. Have you heard from Miss D., by the way?'

'I had a card about . . . ooh, nine months ago. How about you?'

'He was here for a few days in the summer, with a shattering Spanish boyfriend. They seemed happy,' said Justin, who was perhaps less careful of Alex's feelings, though he gave the impression of speaking from outside some conspiracy of happiness.

After lunch Nick said he wanted to see the cliffs, and Robin said he knew the best place to go. Justin refused to take part in the outing if Robin drove, and told Nick with uncomfortable candour about the time when they had all nearly been thrown to their deaths. Alex was drinking pretty intently, since for once he wasn't driving; so it was agreed that Nick would take them. Robin sat up front with him to give directions.

255

When they turned into the narrow lane at the end of the village, Nick said, 'Going up!' and powered ahead, just as Robin had done; it was some boyish physical thing that Alex had never had. He sprawled back and touched the button to let in a rush of air. The banks were high on either side, and the hedges above were festooned with the soft swarming stars of traveller's joy, already turning grey and mothy. One or two brown fans of chestnut leaves dropped across the bonnet. As before, there was no one coming the other way.

Robin got out when they reached the gate, and Alex thought how enjoyable it would be to leave him there, and watch him running up to meet them, pretending he took it as a joke. Nick drove through and waited for him, watching in the mirror, till he came back and opened his door and said, 'I'll run the last mile. Just keep going towards that gap.' So they bumped on without him across the steep incline, the grassy tussocks hissing along the bottom of the car. Alex looked aside and saw the whole panorama inland come steadily clear, the line of ascent from the valley bottoms, the silage-heaps weighted with old tyres, little fields overgrown with alder, up past sheltered farms under hanging woods and low bald pastures, and on to the open hilltops, the windwalks and long ridged heights.

They came into the wide dip between the two swelling caps of cliff, and Justin said, 'This is quite far enough, darling, thank you.' Nick stopped, and they climbed out and walked the last hundred yards. The air freshened towards them, and though the long grass was fading and scruffy the wind seemed to buff it and put a shine on it as it laid it flat.

Justin stopped a prudent distance from the crumbly edge, and Nick and Alex, who had gone on romantically further, came back, with the humorous good conscience of a successful couple, and took hold of him in a slightly awkward embrace, Justin clutching at the pocket of Alex's denim jacket. Then Robin's panting could be heard through the bluster of the wind and above the distant crash of the waves. He came up beside them, roaming round with hands on hips to get his breath back, and then decided to join them, and dropped an arm round Nick's shoulder, at the end of the line. For a minute or two they watched the inky zones of the sea-bed, as the small cloud-shadows sailed across them; then as the sun dropped westward, the surface of the sea turned quickly grey, and they saw the curling silver roads of the currents over it.